KU-060-993

To Jay Worrall, Jr.,
and Carolyn Worrall

FOREWORD

By 1798 THE FIVE-YEAR-OLD WAR BETWEEN KING GEORGE III's United Kingdom of England and Scotland and the revolutionary Republic of France had reached a stalemate. The 1797 victory of the British over the Spanish fleet off Cape St. Vincent had forestalled for the time being any direct invasion of England. France continued a string of military victories on the continent, most notably those led by the twenty-eight-year-old Napoleon Bonaparte, whose armies had been responsible for successes across northern Italy and had forced the withdrawal of Austria's Hapsburg Empire from the conflict. Looking for other ways to strike at London, the ambitious general conceived of a seaborne invasion of Egypt as a stepping-stone to attack her rich possessions in India. Troops and ships soon began to assemble in Toulon and Genoa and other French-controlled Mediterranean ports.

For their part, the British virtually abandoned the Mediterranean following the Battle of Cape St. Vincent, in order to concentrate on the blockade of the Spanish fleet at Cádiz. In April the government directed the admiral commanding the Mediterranean Fleet, Sir John Jervis (recently awarded a peerage as the first earl of St. Vincent for his victory), to dispatch a small squadron under the newly promoted rear admiral Horatio Nelson into the inland sea to demonstrate British power and bolster Austrian resolve. This force consisted of three seventy-four-gun ships of the line, three frigates, and a brig. It is reported that a party of

American tourists traveling across Italy and the South of France arrived in Cádiz, where they managed to inform St. Vincent of French preparations. Nelson's orders were consequently revised to include a close investigation of the naval base at Toulon.

On May 19 a severe three-day storm beset the squadron, damaging Nelson's flagship and scattering his frigates. In his anxiety to determine whether the French were still in the port, Nelson returned to Toulon as soon as his seventy-fours could be repaired. He discovered the port empty, the French fleet departed for a destination unknown, and immediately set off in pursuit.

The frigates, not knowing where Nelson had gone, assumed the mission was over and returned to Gibraltar—all but one. Her commander, Captain Charles Edgemont of His Majesty's twenty-eight-gun frigate *Louisa*, continued doggedly in search of his admiral. In so doing, he may have altered the course of history.

A NOTE ON MEASUREMENTS
AND VALUES

Money

IT IS NOT POSSIBLE TO DIRECTLY EQUATE THE PURCHASING power of currency between the late eighteenth and early twenty-first centuries. It has been suggested, however, that the value of an English pound in 1790 might be multiplied by a factor of seventy or eighty to give an approximate year 2000 equivalent. From pounds to American dollars, the ratio might be 1:100 or 110. English pounds were divided into shillings, pennies, and farthings: 20 shillings to a pound; 12 pennies to a shilling; 4 farthings to a penny. A full loaf of bread cost about 4 pence.

Distance

Units of measurement for distance at sea were not always standardized. The author has used:

   1 league = 3 nautical miles = 5.6 kilometers
   1 nautical mile = 6076 feet (1.15 statute miles) = 1.9 kilometers
   1 cable length = about 200 yards (⅟₃₀ of a league) = 185 meters
   1 fathom = 6 feet (⅟₉₀₀ of a league) = 1.8 meters

Time

Time on British naval ships was measured in watches and bells. The day officially began at noon and was divided into seven watches, five of four hours each and two of two hours:

Afternoon:	noon to 4 P.M.	Middle:	midnight to 4 A.M.
1st Dog	4 P.M. to 6 P.M.	Morning:	4 A.M. to 8 A.M.
2nd Dog:	6 P.M. to 8 P.M.	Forenoon:	8 A.M. to noon
first:	8 P.M. to midnight		

The ship's bell was rung in cumulative half-hourly intervals during each watch. Thus, three bells in the afternoon watch is 1:30 P.M., and four bells in the middle watch is 2:00 A.M.

ANY APPROACHING ENEMY

PROLOGUE

April 1, 1798
All Fools' Day
Cádiz, Spain

MR. ADOLPHUS JONES OF PRINCETON, NEW JERSEY, STOOD in a poorly lit, high-ceilinged room and half bowed toward the rather flamboyantly attired Spanish harbor functionary behind the desk in front of him. His objective was to induce the man to perform the somewhat unusual task of escorting him and his two female companions to one of the hostile British warships blockading the port. Mr. Jones considered himself an excellent judge of character. Looking at the brilliant official in his vermilion jacket frogged in yellow, he didn't think convincing the man would be all that difficult.

Jones was a rugged man in his late thirties with unruly brown hair. For this occasion he had dressed expensively but carelessly in an only-just-out-of-fashion suit. He stood slightly stooped, and spoke with an exaggerated lisp, as he imagined a scholar might do.

"Excellency, if I may introduce my wife, Mrs. Jones, and my niece, Miss Constance van Delft of New York City." Mrs. Jones, a formidable-looking woman, chose not to acknowledge the Spaniard, now risen from his chair and bowing toward her. She had been given to understand that he was the second assistant to someone in the port administrator's office, and she wanted him to know she was displeased that no one more highly placed would see them. Constance, on the other hand, curtsied deeply and gave a sparkling smile. She was handsome and dark-haired, with worldly eyes and an outgoing manner that suggested a certain accessibility often reputed to young American women traveling on the continent.

"And may I assistance you how?" the Spaniard asked in almost passable English. His eyes darted from Mr. Jones to Mrs. Jones and fixed on the niece, whose hands were now clasped in front of her bosom as if in supplication.

"Our situation is most pressing," Mr. Jones responded, forcing a tremor of desperation into his voice. "I am a doctor of classical antiquities at Princeton College in the United States. It is a highly prestigious position, sir. I consult often with President Adams himself. My wife, our ward, and I have been traveling these past months across the South of Europe, studying the monuments of the ancient Roman Empire. In Toulon we received word that Mrs. Jones's mother has fallen ill and is likely in her last months. Since then we have inquired at every port along the way in an attempt to arrange passage home. At each place we were told that Cádiz was our only hope. I must find sea passage to America immediately. It is possible that relations between our two countries will be influenced by this."

The Spaniard's face fell. "A thousand—no, a million pardons, but I cannot assistance to you. Not even as a favor to your *presidente*," he said with genuine remorse. "There are no such ship in all the port of Cádiz. As you have seen, the British have the harbor under constant blockade. No ship may entrance or departure."

Mr. Jones, of course, was well aware of the blockade, and that there were no suitable ships available in the port.

"Oh, Most Excellency," Constance implored, leaning forward and breathing deeply in case he had missed any of her more obvious attributes, "we are desperate. I'm sure a man of your abilities can help us. We have traveled all the way from Italy, across all of France and Spain in the worst coaches and over the most terrible roads. My entire person is abused. You are our last hope. Please, please, can't you do something to help us? I would be *most* grateful."

The Spaniard looked truly downcast, Jones thought, and it was apparent that Connie's phrase "most grateful" and the image conjured up by her "entire person" was not lost on him.

"This is a waste of time, Adolphus," Mrs. Jones interjected. "This little man clearly has no interest in our dilemma. We must look elsewhere."

"There is no elsewhere, my dear," Mr. Jones responded with a renewed quaver in his tone, patting his wife's arm consolingly. "Cádiz was our only chance." Turning toward the port official, he begged, "As citizens of the United States, we are neutrals. As an academic, I am no threat to anyone. The British might be persuaded to allow us to pass unimpeded. There must be some neutral vessel from Denmark, or Sweden, or the Two Sicilies in the harbor that could take us on board." Lowering his voice, he confided, "I am a man of some means and would be willing to pay twice the normal tariff. You would find me more than generous for any assistance you could provide. I don't even care where such a craft is bound so long as we can find another ship to take us home from there."

"Alas, Señor Jones," said the man, "if there were such a craft, I would take you myself to her on this instantly. But the English do not allow even the craft of, how do you say, unbelligerents to entrance or departure. I am prostrate with regrets."

A silence descended on the room, as there seemed to be nothing left to say. Mr. Jones turned back consolingly to Mrs. Jones, in whose eyes tears had begun to well. "It will be all right, my dear," he said just loudly enough for the official to hear. "I will spare no expense. We will find a way; there has to be a way." His voice held out little hope.

"Oh!" Constance exclaimed brightly. "I have an idea."

"What?" Mr. Jones asked without enthusiasm.

"The British themselves! We saw the British warships just outside the harbor. The little ones, what did you call them?"

"Frigates," Mr. Jones answered, disinterested. "Their frigates are stationed inshore on close blockade. They might let us pass, but I doubt they would agree to assist us. We're Americans, still rebels to them. There is little love lost between our countries."

"But we could ask, couldn't we, Adolphus," Mrs. Jones said, dabbing at her eyes with a handkerchief. "We must at least try."

"Well, my dear, I don't think—" Mr. Jones began.

"We must ask," Constance insisted excitedly. "They might be willing if we asked them." Turning to the Spanish official, she said, "They would help us, wouldn't they? Oh, if only we could speak to them." In her enthusiasm, she hurried behind the desk and grasped the Spaniard's arm, pressing it against her chest. "You'd help us to at least ask them, wouldn't you?" she said, looking into his eyes. "You seem so . . . capable."

"Constance," Mrs. Jones reproved sternly. "This is highly improper. After all, Spain is at war with England. I am sure he can do no such thing. It would take great personal courage for a Spanish official to approach an enemy ship of war under these circumstances. And he would have to take leave of his duties to accompany us. I am sure he hasn't the slightest interest, even if he had the fortitude to do so."

The Spaniard drew himself up and, despite Constance clinging tightly to his arm, managed a small bow. "Señor, it would be my very honor to assistance you. I can easily commandeer a small craft to take you to inquire of the British under a flag of truce. You have only to say what day would be convenient."

Constance released her grip but kept adoring eyes on him. "I saw one of those little warships just outside the harbor only this morning. I'm sure it's still there. Couldn't we go immediately? It is only to ask if they will help us. We would be back well before supper. We could invite Your Excellency to dine at our hotel this evening, as a token of our gratitude. Don't you think so, Uncle?"

Mr. Jones looked downcast. "I am obliged to call on some scholarly associates in the town this evening. Perhaps our friend would be content with your company and that of Mrs. Jones."

"You know I am exhausted from our travels, Adolphus. I had planned to retire early," said Mrs. Jones. "I may not stay for the entire meal, but if Constance is willing to carry the burden of entertaining our guest, I don't see why not."

"Oh, I'd love to," Constance asserted, turning toward the man, glowing with conspiratorial promise. "We will have to hurry, señor, if we are to return in time."

———

"AHOY, WHAT BOAT?" came the challenge from the deck of the British frigate, her hull painted dark gray, cruising slowly under weathered topsails about two miles from the entrance to Cádiz Bay, just beyond the range of the batteries protecting the harbor.

Adolphus Jones studied the warship with an experienced eye. She was French-built, without a doubt, small even as frigates went, about 125 feet along her gundeck, and rated at twenty-eight guns, almost certainly twelve-pounders. He saw a number of added carronades on her forecastle and quarterdeck. In all, he thought, she looked professionally commanded and bluntly purposeful. "I wish to speak with your captain on urgent business," he shouted back through cupped hands. His voice sounded out loud and firm, any trace of sibilance vanished.

A ship's officer, a lieutenant by his uniform, appeared at the railing and took a moment to survey the Spanish vessel. Mr. Jones noted with satisfaction that a number of marines in their red coats and black hats had appeared along the rail with their muskets at the ready. There should be no problem, he thought; the British could easily see that the undecked, lateen-rigged tartan was unarmed and contained only him, two women, one Spanish official, and a crew of four. The warship neatly laid her foretopsail against the mast and came to a stop in the water.

"You may come alongside," the lieutenant shouted down. "What's your business?"

Under the lee of the frigate, Mr. Jones could speak much more easily. "I have confidential information for your captain of a most urgent nature, sir." The Spanish official looked alarmed at this exchange, but Mr. Jones ignored him.

"Come aboard," the lieutenant answered. "Just you."

Mr. Jones quickly grabbed the sideropes and climbed the battens that served as the ladderway up the ship's side. On deck he was soon confronted by the ship's captain, a lean, tallish man with dark hair and a single gold-fringed epaulette perched on his right shoulder, denoting that he was of less than three years' seniority. Mr. Jones's impression was that he seemed young, not much past his middle twenties, to have achieved his captaincy. Still, he had an open countenance, intelligent eyes, and an air of quiet authority.

"I am Charles Edgemont, sir," the captain said. "How may I be of service?"

"Bring the two women in the boat on board this minute," Jones said directly. "You'd best send a few armed men down, it's possible the Spaniards will object. Then—"

"May I know your name, sir?" Captain Edgemont interrupted. "And your business?"

"Jones, Adolphus Jones, sir. It is sufficient for you to know that I am under most secret Admiralty orders and can report only to your commanding officer. That would be Admiral Jervis, I believe."

"Lord St. Vincent, as he's known now," the captain said, then, turning to the lieutenant standing nearby: "Winchester, have a whip rove from the yardarm and lower a chair for the women in the boat. You may send a few of the marines down to keep order."

"Aye-aye, sir," the lieutenant answered smartly.

"I take it," Edgemont said, "that you would like us to transport you to His Lordship's flagship."

"I must insist on it the moment my companions are on board," Jones answered. "The intelligence I convey is pressing."

As they waited for the chair to be lowered, curiosity showed by degrees on the young captain's face. As the older of the two women was hoisted onto the deck, he said, "If it is not impertinent, sir, may I ask the nature of this intelligence?"

Jones watched as the chair lowered again. A marine private assisted Constance into it, for which he received a gracious smile. As she was being lifted upward, she gave the bewildered Spanish official a regretful look. "I am sorry, señor. Perhaps another time."

Satisfied, Jones turned back to the British captain. "I suppose you'll learn soon enough anyway," he said. "The French are assembling a powerful fleet in Toulon, and a very large number of troop transports all along the coast, large enough to carry an army of fifty thousand or more. It's possible that their destination is Ireland, or even England itself. There, is that urgent enough for you?"

The moment Constance touched the deck and the last of the marines had debarked from the tartan, Jones watched as Captain Edgemont turned to his lieutenant. "All plain sail she'll carry. Have Eliot lay a course direct to fetch *Victory*."

Constance, Jones noticed, eyed the captain with a measure of interest. "You have my undying gratitude for assisting us, sir," she said warmly.

"It is my pleasure, ma'am," Edgemont replied. His eyes flickered briefly but appreciatively over her, then he looked back to Jones as his attention returned to the earlier subject. "To effect a landing in the British Isles—you're sure?" he said. "Toulon in the Mediterranean seems an unlikely port from which to launch such an invasion. I should have thought Brest, or even Ferrol, in Spain, to be more suitable."

Mr. Jones drew himself upright and spoke with some heat. "I have not yet been able to uncover their destination, sir. But I will tell you in the strongest terms that this expeditionary force is intended to do serious damage to British interests. It must be found and destroyed, sir. It must be found and destroyed utterly."

ONE

May 19, 1798
South of Cape Sicie, Gulf of Lion
The Mediterranean

"EMERALD IS SIGNALING AGAIN, SIR," LIEUTENANT JACOB Talmage reported with a heavy emphasis on the word "again." Talmage was the newly appointed first lieutenant to His Majesty's frigate *Louisa,* and at thirty-five was almost ten years older than her captain. "Sir, it's the second time. It says—"

"I know what it says, Mr. Talmage," Charles Edgemont interrupted. He stood by the weather rail of his quarterdeck with a long glass held up to one eye, the other screwed shut. He didn't need the telescope to read *Emerald*'s signal flags, as she was only a mile and a half to the north. It was the surface of the sea beyond the larger British frigate that held his attention. "Captain Pigott wants us to add more sail," he said to prove that he'd seen the signal. He lowered the glass and turned toward the lieutenant. "He thinks we're lagging behind."

"Shall I give the orders, sir?" Talmage asked.

"Not yet, if you please. However, you may hoist the acknowledge." He glanced again at *Emerald* and her signal flags, numbers three-seven-four, *Increase sail in conformity to weather.* Pigott was flying all his plain sail from courses to royals and a full set of jibs. *Louisa* carried only topsails and topgallants in addition to her jib and mizzen. The wind was moderate enough for more canvas; the sky was a low dull gray, somewhat darker to the north. He'd checked the barometer in his cabin a quarter hour before and found it falling. The sea had a brisk chop, stirred by a gusting breeze, with just a hint of underlying swells, but its surface seemed uneven in the distance, unsettled. Add to that his ankle ached, a reminder of an earlier injury that didn't usually bother him. Something was wrong, but he couldn't put his finger on it. The air seemed . . . hollow.

A sharp bang echoed across the water. "Sir, she's fired a gun," Talmage said, clearly perturbed at Charles's inaction. The single cannon firing from *Emerald* was to emphasize the order to increase sail and to show Pigott's displeasure.

"All right," Charles said, irritated at Pigott for his impatience, irritated at Talmage for hectoring him, and irritated at himself for not being able to make up his mind. "Send the men into the rigging."

"Thank you, sir," Talmage said with both relief and exasperation in his voice.

"Just send them onto the yards, Mr. Talmage. That should please Pigott for the moment. Don't have them bend on any additional canvas just yet."

"But sir, you have been ordered—"

"I know my duty, both to Pigott and the king, thank you," Charles snapped, his patience wearing. "See to it, please." To forestall any further debate, he turned away to survey the rest of the small squadron spread out over the sea. They were seven ships in all, under the command of Horatio Nelson. The squadron constituted the first naval force the Admiralty had ordered into the Mediterranean in almost two years. Three were two-decker, seventy-four-gun ships of the line: *Orion*, *Alexander*, and Nelson's own flagship, *Vanguard*. These were hull down well to the south, and Charles could just see their masts in the distance.

Captain John Pigott of *Emerald*, a thirty-six-gun, eighteen-pounder frigate, was the senior captain among the three frigates present and thus in command when they were detached. The others were the handsome thirty-two-gun twelve-pounder *Terpsichore*, commanded by Captain Edward Bedford, and Charles's *Louisa*, the smallest, rated at twenty-eight guns. Charles was the least senior captain of the three. He found Bedford both competent and friendly. Pigott, however, with eighteen years' seniority, struck him as rigid, unimaginative, autocratic, and altogether too ready to send up signal flags, punctuated by guns, on the most trivial of matters.

The seventh ship in Nelson's squadron was the brig sloop *Pylades,* with her two square-rigged masts and fourteen six-pounder cannon, under Commander Daniel Bevan. Charles and Bevan had served together and been close friends for most of their naval careers. Bevan, a Welshman and formerly the first lieutenant on *Louisa,* had also been promoted as a result of the encounter with the Spanish frigate *Santa Brigida.* Ironically, Bevan's promotion was seen by the Admiralty as a compliment to Charles, and while he was pleased for his friend's advancement, he secretly would have been even more pleased if Bevan had been left where he was. Charles was not altogether comfortable with Talmage.

He had been told that the squadron's purpose was to show the British flag in the Mediterranean after so long an absence. He knew that their mission also had to do with the information that the American party had brought with them from Cádiz. Cape Sicie, the principal landfall for the port of Toulon, lay just over the horizon. He assumed that they would look into the port the following morning. That is, if the weather cooperated.

"The hands are aloft, as you requested," Talmage reported. At least the lieutenant was making an attempt to be accommodating, Charles thought. "And are awaiting your orders, sir," the lieutenant added, which spoiled the whole thing.

Charles raised the glass again to study the horizon to the north. The sky had grown noticeably darker, and the surface of the sea in the distance seemed to have turned a pale gray, almost white. He felt an uncomfortable knot growing in the pit of his stomach. As he lowered the glass, the breeze faltered, and then a fresh gust passed over the ship from out of the north, causing a momentary slatting of the sails.

"The wind's backing, sir," said Samuel Eliot, standing by the binnacle with his nose high, as if smelling the air.

"What do you think?" Charles asked.

"I don't like it. This region is prone to rapid anemological changes." Eliot, a solidly rotund man with apple cheeks mostly covered by impressive muttonchops, served as *Louisa*'s sailing master. Partly deaf and well into his fifties, he seemed to have an unerring sense of the ways of the sea and a no-nonsense, practical manner that Charles respected deeply. That Eliot might be concerned was enough.

"Mr. Talmage, get the topgallants off her and strike their masts to the deck. I want all of the canvas off except the fore and mainmast topsails."

"But, sir," Talmage protested, "you can't—"

"I can," Charles replied in a tone to end the discussion. "See to it now, if you please.

"Mr. Winchester!" he bellowed toward a lean figure standing erect in the waist of the ship. Stephen Winchester, at twenty, was younger than either Charles or Talmage, and had served as *Louisa*'s second lieutenant since Charles took command. With Bevan promoted, he had asked to have Winchester raised to first, but Admiral St. Vincent had refused and appointed the presumably more experienced Talmage instead. Winchester was also, by some small coincidence, newly married to Charles's sister, Eleanor, which may have had some influence on his preference.

"Yes, sir?" Winchester called back, starting up the aft ladderway toward the quarterdeck.

"Clear the decks. See that the guns are double-breeched, if you will, and that the ship's boats are secure."

"Aye-aye, sir," Winchester replied.

"Mr. Beechum," Charles called to the gangly signals midshipman standing across the deck by the lee rail.

"Sir?" the boy answered smartly as he approached.

"You may signal *Emerald*: 'Submit, storm approaching north-by-northwest.' Do you know the flags?"

"Yes, sir," Beechum answered with a small smile, "but I'll just use the signals book to double-check." Charles had been encouraging Beechum to memorize the signals book entire, something he had been required to do as a young midshipman. He'd found it painful.

"Very good, see to it quickly, if you please."

Charles turned, glass in hand, to look over the weather rail again. He didn't bother to raise the telescope. The horizon to the north and northwest had become an ugly thick gray that reached from the sea surface high into the cloud cover above. He thought he could see the muted flash of lightning within, but no sound reached him. The sea beyond *Emerald* was a surging froth of white kicked up by a rapidly approaching squall line. He noted with momentary satisfaction that Pigott had finally sent his topmen aloft to reduce sail, although his signals to do the opposite remained on her halyards.

With frightening speed, the line enveloped the distant frigate. The ship heeled violently, almost onto her beam ends, as a brute force of wind slammed into her. Charles tried to calculate how long *Louisa* had before the storm caught her and decided it would be only a matter of moments at best. He stole a quick glance at *Terpsichore,* several cable lengths ahead, and at Bevan's brig, *Pylades,* a similar distance off the starboard bow. Both ships were hurriedly shortening canvas, *Pylades* already turning to present her bow to the onrushing gale.

"How long until the topgallant masts are on deck?" Charles yelled to Talmage across the strengthening wind.

"Only a minute, sir," the lieutenant called back. "There's some difficulty with the mizzen."

"Belay that; it'll have to do as it is," Charles shouted, an increasing note of urgency in his voice. "Get the men down out of the rigging."

"Aye-aye," Talmage answered, then he called the new orders through his trumpet into the tops.

"Mr. Eliot"—Charles turned back to the sailing master—"we will take the first of it bow-on. As soon as she's settled, we'll lie to and ride it out as best we can."

"Yes, sir. I think that's wise," Eliot replied, his voice almost lost in a sudden gust across the quarterdeck.

Charles watched wide-eyed as the line of the storm advanced toward him. The gale crashed across *Louisa's* decks with a pounding force of windblown spray, followed immediately by twin bolts of lightning and a deafening explosion of thunder. The bow began to swing to starboard at once. Before Charles could think, she was almost broadside on and heeling steeply under its relentless pressure.

"Brace the yards around and hold her! Hold her!" He screamed to be heard while he clutched desperately at the windward rail to keep from sliding down the sloping deck. Whether Eliot or the two men struggling with the ship's wheel heard him or not he couldn't tell, but the vessel slowed her turn and began to claw back into the wind. She had just begun to right herself when a white-topped swell crested against the starboard quarter, sending an avalanche of green water across the waist and quarterdeck. The railing wrenched itself from his grip as the mass cascaded over him. He lost his footing and felt himself being swept across the deck to come up with a breathtaking jolt against the opposite rail between two tethered nine-pounder cannon.

Torrents of rain and scud, blown sideways on the wind, pelted against Charles as he tried to cough up the seawater that seemed to have filled his lungs. He noticed that his hat was gone. He struggled to stand, clutching the rail for support. The driving rain was too thick for him to see to the tops of the masts or much beyond the waist of the ship. The two quartermasters were still at the helm, although where Eliot had gone, he couldn't tell. A blinding stroke of lightning broke almost directly overhead, flashing down like the talons of some unearthly demon.

Winchester appeared on the aft ladderway, his uniform sodden. "Are you all right, sir?" he yelled through cupped hands.

Charles nodded rather than attempting a vocal response, fruitlessly trying to wipe the water away from his eyes. "The ship," he managed, "did anything carry away?"

"I don't think so," Winchester answered. "All our masts are standing. We took on a fair quantity of water through the gratings. Not more than the pumps can handle."

"Did the topmen make it down in time?"

"Most of 'em were still in the shrouds when it hit," the lieutenant answered. "They were probably safer there than on deck. I don't know yet if we lost anyone."

Eliot reappeared in an oilskin hat and coat, which, except for his eyes, covered him down to the toes of his boots.

"How are we riding?" Charles shouted.

"Too much canvas for'ard, sir." Eliot's voice was muffled by the sou'wester. "She wants to gripe something fierce." Talmage appeared on the ladderway.

"We will reef directly," Charles shouted. "See to it, if you please, Mr. Talmage, to the last reef points."

Talmage turned away and called out, "All hands to reef sails; waisters to the braces."

"Stephen." Charles spoke in a more normal tone to his second, bending close in order to be heard. "Did you see *Pylades* before the storm struck? Do you know how she fared?" A small ship like Bevan's brig easily could have been swamped in the first surge of heavy sea.

"I saw her for just a moment before the weather closed," Winchester answered carefully. "I don't know. She'd gotten at least some of her sails in. I can't say about afterward."

"Thank you," Charles said. "Daniel's a good seaman. He'll have made out all right." He knew he was expressing more hope than certainty.

Charles watched as the topmen swarmed up the gangway and back into the shrouds. Some had donned oilskin jackets. He smiled inwardly at the way they jumped to the ratlines and hurried up toward the wildly swaying topsail yards with a certain fearlessness, even enthusiasm. Charles knew that he wouldn't relish climbing to those heights to work his way along the uncertain footropes to the end of a spar under these conditions—well, under any conditions, but especially not in a rising wind, driving rain, and plunging seas—to fight with the stiff, billowing canvas that could rip off fingernails or break fingers. One careless misstep or a sudden unanticipated shift in the wind could mean sudden death if one were lucky and fell directly onto the deck, or, if he missed, a lingering drowning in conditions that absolutely prohibited any chance of rescue.

Good topmen were both rare and exceedingly valuable, the cream of any ship's crew. They tended to be young, broad-shouldered, cocky, and courageous to a fault, all qualities required for the tasks they performed. As a result, they also tended to present more minor disciplinary problems than their proportion among the crew would suggest. Charles had long since decided that this was fair trade and cut them some leeway, although he'd gotten an argument from his new first lieutenant every time he did.

"Down the helm," Charles yelled through cupped hands at the quartermaster as soon as he saw that at least one of the outermost topmen had nearly reached his position at the end of the spar.

"Ease the clews," he heard Winchester call to the hands on the lines.

"Haul the reef cringle." As *Louisa* came up into the wind, the sails shivered, then flogged, losing their tension. "Haul the buntlines"—this to force the canvas to spill its wind. The men balanced on the yardarms furiously fisted in the head of the sail to tie off the reef points.

"Haul the clew lines and belay," Winchester shouted, to retighten the foot of the sail and secure the lines.

"Up helm and catch her," Charles called to the quartermaster, signaling by making circles in the air in case he couldn't be heard. The bow quickly fell off the wind; the shortened sails volleyed loudly and began to draw. *Louisa* lay over under the renewed pressure and resumed her struggle to hold her place against the howling wind and surging sea.

Charles cautiously left his relatively secure perch by the lee rail and climbed the deck toward Eliot and the ship's wheel, bent almost double against the pressure of the elements. He could feel the ship riding somewhat easier under the reduced pressure of sail, but still pounding through each oncoming crest.

"What do you think, Mr. Eliot?" he asked, shouting each word separately to be certain he was understood.

"Aye," the master's disembodied voice intoned. Eliot, in his glistening rain gear, stood in the center of the deck with one hand resting casually on the binnacle. "She'll do for the present, and we've plenty of sea room. But the wind's only just starting, unless I miss my mark. It'll be worse before it gets better." Almost as he spoke, a stronger gust shrieked through the shrouds, raising their timbre to a higher pitch.

Out of the corner of his eye, Charles noticed his elderly steward, Timothy Attwater, struggling up the ladderway and clutching a bundle that Charles took to be his own wet-weather covering. He became conscious that he was soaked to his skin from the rain and spray and the dunking he had taken.

Charles spoke loudly: "I am going below, Mr. Eliot."

"What?" Eliot shouted back, bending closer and with a hand cocked beside the hat where his ear should be.

"I'm going below," Charles yelled into the cupped hand. "Call—if—change—sail."

"Aye," the master said, and turned his attention to the men at the wheel.

Charles took a last look at the newly reefed topsails and saw that they were already taut to the point of straining under the force of the wind. *They'll do for now,* he thought.

"I've brought yer boat cloak, sir," Attwater shouted from close beside him as he shook out the heavy tarpaulin garment. The wind instantly caught the cloth, standing it out sideways, then effortlessly snatched it from his grasp and sent it sailing out over the sea like a misshapen bird. There was such surprise and then disappointment on his steward's face that Charles laughed. "Come, we shall go below," he said.

Once in the relative calm of his cabin, Charles gratefully allowed Attwater to help pull off his dripping uniform. He toweled himself dry and put on fresh clothing all the while holding on to a bulkhead to balance himself against the wild movements of the ship. Then he took down his chart for the Mediterranean below Toulon, unrolled it on the dining table, and began to study their position relative to the nearest bodies of land.

A loud knock came at the cabin door. "Yes," Charles shouted.

A marine sentry stuck his head through the doorway. "Begging your pardon, zur. You're wanted topside."

"Thank you, I'll be there directly." He quickly pulled on an old sou'wester, covering himself as much as he could.

Abovedecks, he saw that the sky was more like night than day, with low, roiling clouds racing toward the southeast. The rain lashed at them in curtains. White-topped swells heaved masses of windblown scud across the decks at regular intervals. He found Eliot and four of his men by the wheel, in addition to Lieutenant Talmage and a miserable-looking Midshipman Beechum, all covered in their bulky wet-weather gear. A glance upward told him that the double-reefed fore and main topsails were straining dangerously, and their yards bowed. Talmage crossed from the weather rail as Charles appeared.

"Wind's increasing. I thought it best we reduce sail, sir," Talmage shouted above the gale.

"I should have thought it best to do it before now," Charles replied crisply. He cast a glance at Eliot and received an irritated shrug in response. He guessed that there had been a disagreement between the two men, and wished that his lieutenant would have just followed the sailing master's advice.

"Didn't want to disturb you before it was necessary," Talmage explained.

"Better sooner than too late," Charles answered. "Call the hands."

While Talmage turned to call the orders through his speaking trumpet, Charles made his way up the deck toward Eliot. "What do you think?" he shouted next to the master's ear.

"The wind keeps picking up. We should have taken the topsails off this quarter hour past. Something's bound to carry away."

"Yes," Charles said. "We'll heave to and put her under a storm jib and the maintop staysail.

"Mr. Beechum!" he yelled, gesturing at the young midshipman.

"Yes, sir?" Beechum said as he arrived skidding down the deck.

"Get below and inquire as to the cook's plans for supper. Ask him how much prepared food he has on hand and how long it will last." The galley fires would have been extinguished as soon as the storm hit, for fear of the embers spilling out, so dinner would have to consist of cold boiled beef and whatever else the cook had the foresight to have on hand.

"Aye-aye, sir," the boy said, and turned to leave.

"Beechum," Charles called him back.

"Yes, sir?"

"Has anyone seen anything of the rest of the squadron?"

"We saw one, sir," Beechum answered. "About one bell ago, maybe two miles awindward during a clearing in the squall. Can't be sure, but Eliot thinks it was *Emerald*. Looked like she'd lost her foremast. Don't know where she is now, though."

"And *Pylades*?" Charles asked carefully.

"No, sir, not a thing. Not since it began to blow."

"Thank you," Charles said. "Now, report back to me what the cook says."

Charles stayed at his place by the lee rail for several hours, through the first dog watch and into the second. While it was light enough to see them, he anxiously watched the few sails the ship carried, and studied the relentless procession of ever growing waves, blown white at their crests, passing angrily under *Louisa*'s bow quarter. He felt the heave and tremble of his ship's frame through the deck as she fought the elements. Beechum relieved one worry by reporting that the cook had enough prepared beef and pork on hand to last "two, maybe two and a half days if we go easy." Charles sent back an order that the portions be cut to three in four.

He could feel through his shoes the rattle of the chain pumps as the hundreds of gallons of water that had seeped in through the hatches, decks, and hull were laboriously forced up out of the bilge and back into the sea. Mostly, he tried to guess where the wind and current were taking them. How much leeway was *Louisa* making? With the weather off the starboard bow, she was pointed more or less westerly, but her actual course could be anything from true south to south-by-east. He knew that the island of Sardinia was the biggest worry. Cape Falcone, the northern tip of the island, lay under 150 miles to the southeast when the storm had hit; Cape Sperone, near the southern extremity, bore perhaps 225 miles south-by-southeast. He could do the sums in his head. If they were making three knots leeway, it might take between two and three days to come up with the mountainous shores of Sardinia immediately under his lee. A storm such as this could easily last three days. In any event, he told himself, it hardly mattered, except to make their course as southerly as possible in hopes of missing the island entirely. The coast of Africa was at least another 150 miles farther to the south. Few storms lasted that long.

He also wondered about Admiral Nelson and the remainder of the squadron. The relatively small frigates and Bevan's tiny brig would be scattered widely and blown to who knew where, should they survive at all. The three seventy-fours had been more tightly grouped when the wind hit them. With their greater size and weight, they would be able to ride out the weather more easily and might even be able to stay within sight of one another. Whatever their situation, it would be days, weeks possibly, before all of them would be able to reassemble and continue with their mission.

At the second bell in the second dog watch, Attwater appeared out of the fading daylight to urge him to come below for his supper. "It ain't right for you to not have nothing in you," he insisted. "Wouldn't young

Mrs. Edgemont not be 'appy if she knew." Charles relented and went below. As his steward helped him out of his bulky covering and set him at the table, his mind turned irresistibly toward "young Mrs. Edgemont." Penny, her face, expressions, laughter, her tenderness were never far from his mind or heart. They had been married these four months now. It seemed only yesterday that they had celebrated their wedding day at his home in Cheshire. That had been the one day they were together as man and wife before he was ordered back to sea.

While Attwater placed a plate of cold boiled pork, cold pease porridge, ship's biscuit, cheese, and a tankard of porter beer in front of him, he reasoned, as he had a hundred times, that Penny would be well cared for in the large house on his estates. His elder brother, John, had agreed to oversee Charles's properties. There were several letters back and forth, of course. Two had arrived together shortly before the squadron had left Cádiz three weeks before. From what he could tell in between her expressions of affection and the news of his sister Ellie's (and Winchester's) impending expectancy, she was in good health and occupying her time looking after the welfare of their tenants. There had been no mention that she herself might be in a family way, and Charles had felt it too indelicate to ask directly.

He pushed his food around with a fork, nibbled at a few pieces of the pork, sipped at his beer, and decided that he'd had enough. Before Attwater could return, Charles donned his oilskins and crept out of the cabin to go back on deck. The sky had turned pitch dark. The force of the wind and the heaving ship made mounting the ladderway to the quarterdeck an arduous struggle, requiring him to hold on to the railing with both hands. The wind came in powerful gusts that he judged to be stronger than when he had gone below. He could feel *Louisa* labor as she took each crest, filling the air with spray. He saw Eliot standing by the wheel, lit by the dim glow of a single storm lantern on the binnacle, and crossed to speak with him.

"I was about to call for you," the master shouted.

Charles nodded. The unearthly shrieking of the wind through the shrouds made any attempt at normal conversation impossible.

Eliot cupped his hands around Charles's ear. "The breeze is freshening. Should take in jib."

That would leave the foremast staysail as the only scrap of canvas flying. Charles thought of asking Eliot if it was sufficient, but decided the sailing master had probably already thought of that. Communicating the question would be too difficult anyway. "See to it, if you please," he shouted back.

Charles continued across the deck to the lee railing, where Winchester stood watch. Another midshipman—Sykes, he thought it was—sat in a bundle of sou'wester on the deck beneath the railing, huddled against the wind and wet. Charles nodded by way of greeting to his brother-in-law, who silently touched his hat in return, and settled against the railing to brace himself. The ship's stern swooped upward, then fell precipitously as it proceeded rhythmically from wave crest to trough.

He tried to warp his mind to the endless calculations of course, windage, currents, drift, and the eventual perils of the Sardinian coast but realized that it was all supposition leading nowhere very definite. It would be a miracle if their actual progress were in any direction other than backward and sideways. He didn't even know where they were, except in the broadest terms: some distance south of Toulon and presumably still to the west of Sardinia; hopefully well to the west of the island.

A rendezvous off the coast of France was specified in his orders, to be used if the squadron was dispersed. The seventy-fours would probably arrive first, since they would have been the least affected by the storm. There was also the possibility that the French fleet in Toulon would use the favorable northerly wind to up their anchors and set off for whatever purpose they had in mind. Admiral Nelson would know this, and Charles suspected that he would be in a state of high agitation while he waited for the smaller ships to rejoin him one by one before he could look into the port.

When Winchester went below, he was replaced by Talmage, who took up his station by the weather rail, a respectable distance away. Charles stayed where he was, too tired to climb the inclined deck. There was nothing the first lieutenant could tell him that he didn't already know. Alone, huddled in his rain gear with his back turned to the wind, he found his mind turning back to Penny. What would she think if she knew that *Louisa* was struggling for her life against surging seas and a howling gale, possibly to be driven against a rocky, reef-strewn lee shore?

Actually, she probably wouldn't be as troubled by his current situation as she had been after learning of the *Louisa*'s battles with the *Santa Brigida*. Even then, she hadn't been concerned solely for his safety. One of her peculiarities was that she was of a Quaker family and held strong pacifist views. She had told him several times that she did not approve of his profession and had initially refused to marry him because of it. Charles sighed. That would work itself out in time, he told himself. She would adjust. Wives always adjusted to their husbands' ways. He knew it to be true, everyone said so.

His attention shifted as a master's mate paused by the binnacle, clutched it for support, then bent and turned the half-hour glass. Charles saw that the man pulled the lanyard to ring the ship's bell eight times. The ringing sound, if there was one, was instantly carried away on the wind. Eight bells, it must be the beginning of the middle watch: midnight. Charles realized that his limbs were cold and stiff from the long hours on deck, and he was almost stupid with fatigue. The wind may have abated a trifle; at least the song through the stays seemed a fraction of an octave lower.

His joints complained as he pushed himself off the railing and made his way toward Eliot at his place beside the helm. Too tired to attempt communication, Charles took up a slate used for navigational computations and chalked on it:

AM GOING BELOW.
CALL IF WEATHER CHANGE.

The master read it and nodded in acknowledgment. Charles shuffled across the deck and down the ladderway to his cabin. Careful not to wake his steward, he sloughed his oilskins and his uniform coat, slipped off his shoes, and climbed into his bed otherwise fully clothed. By ten minutes after twelve, he was fast asleep.

At one o'clock he sat bolt upright. He could hear that the wind had risen to an eerie high-pitched whistle, and he could actually feel the vibration of the rigging through the deck. *Louisa* plunged raggedly and seemed to stagger each time the bow dropped before rising again. More seriously, something had come badly adrift, its banging sending rhythmic jolts the length of the ship. Attwater pushed his way through the curtain to the sleeping cabin with a small lantern. Charles was already frantically searching in the darkness for his shoes.

"You're wanted on deck. The weather's up," Attwater announced.

On the ladderway to the quarterdeck, an insane wind grabbed at his flapping overcoat, filling it like a sail. He clutched tightly at the rail to keep from being blown overboard. He pulled his coat together with his fists and struggled onto the deck. Talmage came across to him immediately. "Mizzen topmast . . . carried away," he yelled, and gestured upward. Charles could see the mass of loose halyards and stays snapping in the wind, the topmast section entangled below, swinging with the roll of the ship and hammering furiously against the still-standing lower mast. *Why hasn't Talmage dealt with it before now?*

Angry but unable to express it, he yelled, "Cut—it—loose—over—side!"

Louisa was being pounded mercilessly by the sea, burying her bow with each oncoming wave. She could not withstand this kind of punishment long. Eliot stood at his usual place by the wheel, and Charles started toward him. A vicious gust swept the ship, laying her over nearly on her beam ends. Charles clutched at the binnacle to keep from sliding down the sharply canted deck. For a moment he hung from the box with no purchase for his feet. He found Eliot's sturdy form beside him, his hand clutching the back of Charles's coat, the way a mother cat picks up a kitten by the scruff of its neck, and pulling him to his feet.

Charles took a speaking trumpet from its place in the binnacle, put the horn directly over the master's ear, and shouted into the mouthpiece, "We will bear away and run before the wind."

Eliot nodded vigorously.

Charles knew too well that turning the ship from lying to, with the bow taking the wind and waves head-on, and swinging to present her stern to the elements presented two significant perils. First, as she fell off with the wind, her vulnerable side would be exposed to the seas, where she would be in danger of being rolled over or swamped, either an ordeal from which she might not recover. Further, once she was around, she would immediately require sufficient speed to prevent the onrushing waves from sweeping over her from behind and driving her under, stern first. He saw that Winchester had arrived on deck and beckoned him to approach. Using the speaking trumpet as he had with Eliot, he found that he could speak almost normally. "We will wear ship and put her before the wind," he said. "The instant she is around, set the main topsail, close-reefed, then haul down the staysail."

"Aye-aye," Winchester shouted and started forward.

Charles could neither see the seas nor gauge when to begin the turn except through the deck as *Louisa*'s bow began to rise. There was no point in waiting. "Hard aport!" he screamed at Eliot, too far away to hear; he windmilled his arm to signal his intent. He watched closely as the helm came over. Immediately, the ship's head began to fall off, the turn accelerating as the wind caught the fore staysail sideways and pushed her around like a weather vane. The force came broadside on, heeling the ship more sharply. *Pray God we aren't swamped.* They were in the trough between the waves, the next racing down on them. *Louisa* was turning, still turning, the wind beginning to come around to the stern quarter.

"Ease the helm," he shouted at Eliot, "midships!" Knowing that his words could not be heard, he signaled with his arms. He squinted forward into the dark and made out the men on the mainmast yard sheeting home the reefed topsail. Turning aft, he could see the black menace of the next wave irresistibly rising. Charles held his breath. He thought he could feel the pull of the topsail as it began to fill. The wave closed on them, still closer, until it seemed to loom overhead and must crash down on them. He clutched reflexively at the railing. *Louisa*'s stern began to rise with the swell. A quantity of water burst over the taffrail, but in no great force.

Charles let out an explosive burst of breath. He breathed in again. She had gained enough way to mitigate the blow, and the crisis had passed; at least *this* crisis had passed. They were now running directly before the wind and still gathering speed, so that she slid back down into the trough, seemed to pause there, and then began to rise onto the back of the wave ahead. She would be safe for the moment, so long as they kept up just enough way over the sea to allow the rudder to bite and keep her from yawing. A glance at the compass told him that they were now steering directly south-by-east, with a following sea at what must be a prodigious speed, straight toward the unwelcome coast of Sardinia.

The howling scream from the wind became marginally less, as they were sailing with it on their backs rather than clawing into its teeth. Charles crossed the deck to the sailing master and shouted, "Put her head south-by-west." Allowing for leeway, he calculated that this should put their true course at something close to due south, which would mean that if they hadn't run aboard Sardinia already, they probably never would.

Charles's legs ached from the constant struggle against the force of the wind, and from keeping his balance on the heaving deck. He leaned against the binnacle to rest for a moment and noticed Winchester and a number of the foremast topmen descending the shrouds. It must have been a fearsome ordeal with the wind threatening to tear them from the wildly gyrating yardarm, but the task had to be done, and their timely execution of it might have made the difference between safety and sinking. He pushed himself upright and started toward the ladderway to the waist of the ship. He met up with Winchester, returning at the break of the aftercastle, where they were sheltered a little from the wind.

"That was nicely done, Stephen," he said.

Winchester nodded, looking worn. "Thank you," he said. "The men deserve the credit. I tried yelling out the orders, but no one could hear anything up there."

"You have my thanks all the same," Charles insisted. "I will mention your name in my report."

Winchester's face cracked into a small smile. "You mention my name in every report. The Admiralty will become suspicious."

"I'm doing my best," Charles asserted. "The father of my nephews and nieces should be an admiral, at least. You need to pick up the pace if you want to get their lordships' attention."

"I'll get to it presently," Winchester answered. Then, as if to change the subject, he asked, "Are you going to turn in?"

"No, I thought I'd go below and speak to your topmen."

"Why?" Winchester asked.

"I owe them my thanks for what they've done. We all do."

Winchester raised his eyebrows. "I'm sure they'll be grateful," he observed doubtfully.

Charles continued across the waist, down through the main hatchway, and into the bowels of the ship. The wind ceased as soon as his head dropped below the level of the deck, a welcome change. This was the ship's heart, he reflected as he made his way forward, where the crew lived, slept, and ate. The space was damp, scarcely ventilated, and dimly lit. He could make out dozens of hammocks, one almost touching another, suspended from the deck beams and swaying in unison with the ship's movement. The powerful smell of unwashed bodies met his nostrils, competing with other, more noxious odors from the bilge farther below. The sounds of waves washing past *Louisa*'s hull and the groaning of her timbers reverberated loudly. He heard muted laughter and conversation coming from a more brightly lighted area near the bow.

Charles proceeded carefully, stooping as he walked to avoid hitting his head on the low ceiling beams. He soon found a group of men, about a score in number, sitting on the deck or on wooden crates. One had broken out a pack of cards and was preparing to deal them. Others sat in twos and threes, talking or lighting their pipes. Two lanterns swung from the ceiling above.

"God's bones, it's the cap'ain," one of the men in the card game exclaimed and leaped to his feet. The man with the cards tried to scoop up the lot and hide them in his pocket while he rose to his knees, dropping seven or eight. Undecided whether to collect the errant cards or stand, he remained frozen where he was. Everyone else stood immediately.

"As you were, please," Charles said. "Where's Saunders, the captain of the foretop?" The men remained rigid, as erect as the deck beams would allow. Even the card dealer elected to rise to his feet.

"Here, zur," a short, burly man Charles recognized as Bobby Saunders said, stepping forward apprehensively and knuckling his forehead. It wasn't often that a ship's captain arrived unannounced belowdecks, and when he did, it was usually for something unpleasant.

"Please be at your ease," Charles repeated. "This is a friendly call, not an official one. I just wanted to tell you, all of you . . . to express my appreciation of your efforts in the rigging just now."

This was met with uncertain stares all around. Charles thought he should say something more, so he added, "I am grateful and I want to show it. I intend to send a bottle of tolerable French claret around to each of your mess tables at supper in place of your usual spirits."

There were murmurs at this and glances exchanged. Still, none dared speak.

"Dickie Johnson," Charles called to a man who stood looking downcast at the edge of the group. "I understand that you have had your drink stopped for a week by Lieutenant Winchester for indiscipline." Actually, Dickie had overslept his watch two days before, after having been observed drinking both his own and a messmate's rations of spirits the night before.

"Yessur," the man said shyly.

"I will make an exception for this one meal, Dickie, but you must serve out the remainder of your punishment after."

"Yes, sur, thank you, sur."

Charles looked around at the men and felt unreasonably pleased. He knew all their names and could remember when most of them had first come aboard in Portsmouth: a raw crew, many inexperienced and untrained. A few had been released directly from gaol into the navy as so-called sheriff's quotamen. They had grown into capable seamen as he watched. "We're not out of danger yet, so look lively," he said to bring his visit to a close. "And don't expect a bottle of wine every time you climb the shrouds."

There were some smiles at this, but Charles knew that his presence was awkward for them. "Well, then," he said, "if you will pardon me, I'll return to my duties on deck."

"Zur," Saunders interjected.

"Yes?"

"Zur, if it ain't too forrard"—the man glanced meaningfully at several of his mates—"some of us were wonderin' if you've heard from Mizzus Edgemont and how she might be farin'."

Charles was surprised at the question, then remembered that most of these men—most of his crew, in fact—had been present at the wedding. "She is doing very well, from what she writes," he answered. "She mentions you men in her letters and often inquires after your well-being."

This line of conversation seemed to put them more at ease; there were significant glances and whisperings all around.

"Well, zur, thank you, zur," Saunders said.."If you would please write that we asked after her."

"I will be sure to," Charles answered.

"She's uncommon fine, sir," another seaman named Connley said boldly. "She spoke with some of us at the wedding party, she did, and asked us personal to take special care that no harm comes to ye."

This was new information to Charles, but it was very like Penny to have done so. "I will be sure to pass on that so far you have all done excellent jobs." An outburst of laughter filled the space, followed by a loud "Shut all yer fucking gobs, you sons of whores. We're trying to sleep here," from one of the hammocks.

"Sorry," Charles called back. To the men before him, he said in a softer voice, "Thank you all again for your efforts. If you will excuse me, I must return to my duties."

He made his way back between the hammocks and onto the deck, reminding himself to tell Attwater to deliver three bottles of his diminishing supply of claret to the men's messes. Attwater, he suspected, was not going to like it.

Charles returned to the quarterdeck and stayed there as the dawn broke, revealing racing clouds that looked to be almost touching the mainmast truck but were probably a fair deal higher. The seas were tall gray ridges, angry white across their tops, stretching as far as the eye could see. *Louisa* rode almost disdainfully, as if aware that these elements had done their best to destroy her and failed. She rose gracefully to the top of each line of waves, accelerated as the full force of the wind found her, flicked her stern sideways just enough to be noticeable as she crested, then slid ladylike and triumphant down into the trough. The wind still blew fierce and steady, but with the daunted determination, Charles thought, of a fighter who knew in his gut that the match had been decided against him. He considered briefly whether there could be some separate god for the seas, a Neptune or Poseidon that contested for seamen's fates. At that moment he could well believe it.

As soon as it was light enough, he took a sighting of the ship's wake with a pocket compass and decided that she was making more or less due south, perhaps a point westerly. He sent a lookout into the tops with a glass, but no other sails were seen on the empty, ill-tempered sea.

The overcast precluded any noon sighting to determine their position. The ship's bell rang for the afternoon watch to mark the official beginning of a new day, and the hands were fed another cold meal of beef, cheese, biscuit, and blackstrap. Talmage replaced Winchester as deck officer. Charles went below to his cabin to eat most of the indifferent food his steward put before him and drained his porter. Afterward he returned wearily to his accustomed place on the weather railing of the quarterdeck.

The long afternoon passed slowly. Conditions were too difficult to attempt replacing the mizzen topmast, too constant to call for a change in sail. At the approach of the first dog watch, he sent Midshipman Sykes to tell Attwater to deliver the claret to the mainmast topmen's mess in hopes of avoiding discussing the matter with his steward directly. Attwater appeared on the quarterdeck ten minutes later, grim-faced and clutching the three bottles tightly to his breast.

"But, sir," he pleaded loudly, "there ain't no more than half a case left in the larder. We'll 'ave to drink the port."

" 'We'?" Charles said, raising his eyebrows. He had long known that the steward helped himself freely to his wine supply, but had left the matter unremarked on.

"Didn't I mean 'you,' sir, I did," Attwater replied without a trace of hesitation. "I only sample to ensure that it ain't gone sour."

"Then I can do with the port," Charles answered happily. "See to it, if you please. And be pleasant about it."

Attwater twisted his face as if to complain further, apparently thought better of it, and turned reluctantly away, muttering under his breath.

The watch changed, Eliot assuming the responsibilities of deck officer. Toward dusk a narrow streak of clear blue appeared on the horizon to the northeast. Charles pushed himself off the quarterdeck railing, spoke briefly with the sailing master, and went below to his cabin to eat, drink as much of the claret as Attwater would allow, and find his bed. He lay for a time, too tired for sleep, thinking of Penny and her influence, even here in the middle of the sea, through her words to his crew, and how taken they were with her. His last thoughts as he drifted toward oblivion were remembrances of the warmth of her breath on his neck as they lay together, the softness of her breast . . .

He awoke slowly the next morning, stupefied with sleep, to the sound of many feet on the deck above, the rasp of a saw, and the pounding of hammers. The movements of the ship had eased greatly, he noted, and he guessed that someone had taken the opportunity to jury-rig the mizzenmast topgallant section. There being no pressing reason why he should be on deck, he lay beneath his covers and dozed fitfully for a time until he heard his steward padding about in the outer cabin.

"Attwater," he yelled.

The gray-haired head showed itself through the curtained doorway. "Yes, sir?"

"What o'clock is it?"

"Nigh on the forenoon watch," Attwater answered. "Which you don't need not to stay abed a bit longer."

It took Charles a moment to dissect the meaning of this last sentence, then he said, "Run along and see if the galley fire is lit. I would be pleased for a mug of coffee."

He appeared on deck a half hour later, feeling rested and refreshed, to a bright blue sky with much diminished seas, and a moderate gusting breeze that had shifted during the night from north-by-west to mostly westerly. Winchester was supervising the carpenter, boatswain, and their mates in hoisting a suitably modified spare mainmast yard onto the mizzen top to replace the lost mast section.

At noon all of the ship's officers and midshipmen clustered on the quarterdeck with their quadrants and sextants to take the noon sighting, from which they could readily calculate their latitude, which would tell at least how far south the storm had blown them. After sightings and scribbled calculations on their chalkboards, all agreed that they were more or less at thirty-eight degrees and twenty minutes north, except for Sykes, who found them magically in the Baltic, off Sweden.

"Does that make any sense to you, Mr. Sykes?" Charles said, taking the boy's slate and inspecting it.

"No, sir," Sykes answered agreeably.

"Look, you've added these numbers here when you should have divided."

"Ah, I see," Sykes intoned, clearly not seeing at all.

Charles sighed. "You will please call on Mr. Eliot when he is free and have him explain the calculations to you again."

"Yes, sir," Sykes answered. As soon as he thought his captain had focused his attention elsewhere, he grimaced.

Charles let it pass and turned his mind to fixing their location. Exactly where along the 38th Parallel they were was a matter of conjecture, but by dead reckoning, he thought probably about seventy-five miles southwest of Cape Sperone on the tip of Sardinia. The storm had driven them fully three hundred miles south-by-southeast from their starting point.

"We will increase sail directly the yard is crossed on the mizzen," Charles said to Eliot. "Set a course for ten leagues due south of Cape L'Aigle, if you please."

"That's our rendezvous?" Eliot asked.

"In the event the squadron has been dispersed, yes," Charles answered.

AFTER SEVEN DAYS, *Louisa* approached the appointed spot on the sea off the coast of France, midway between Marseille and Toulon, as specified in his orders. A brilliant midmorning sky shimmered over sparkling blue waters.

"Deck there," a call came down from the lookout in the foremast crosstrees. "Sail dead ahead."

"How many do you see?" Charles yelled back up.

"Just the one, sir. She's a brig. I think she's *Pylades,* sir."

TWO

"AND A GOOD DAY TO YOU, CAPTAIN BEVAN," CHARLES SAID as he climbed through the entryway onto *Pylades*'s deck. "Anything interesting while I was away?"

"Ah, the esteemed Captain Edgemont," Daniel Bevan answered. A large smile showed on his face as he extended his hand. "We worried about you in the blow. Didn't think you were used to seas much rougher than what you generally get in a bathtub. Not that you've ever found much use for a bathtub."

"Nonsense," Charles said as he shook the offered hand. "It was like a walk in the garden."

"Come below, Charlie, and we'll discuss it," Bevan said with a gesture toward the hatchway that led below to his cabin. "Mind, we're not as well supplied as the palatial *Louisa*." He made a pointed show of studying the relation of the sun to the nearest yardarm and added, "Would you prefer port or sherry?"

Charles took a moment to look around him. From his gig, he'd noted a freshly replaced foretopmast section and a hastily jury-rigged fore-bowsprit. From his vantage on deck, he saw that *Pylades*'s longboat was missing from its normal stowage place between the masts and that there was a splint scabbed onto the spanker's sprung lower yard. The gig was in its place, though. There were hands in the foremast crosstrees and on the bowsprit, apparently preparing for more permanent repairs. "How did you fare?" he asked seriously as they walked toward the ladderway.

"Touch and go," Bevan answered. "I saw you start to strike your top-gallant masts and couldn't think what you were up to with Pigott's flurry of signals and cannon fire to the contrary. When I finally did catch on, it was all we could do to turn and put her into the wind. We lost the upper part of the foremast almost immediately. Took part of the bowsprit with it."

Bending under the deck beams—even lower than those on *Louisa*—they made their way through the aft bulkhead into the cramped space that served as Bevan's cabin. Charles promptly dropped himself into the nearest chair so he could straighten his neck. "Must have been interesting with no headsails," he continued.

"There were moments, Charlie, that I feared it was all going to carry away," Bevan said earnestly. He crossed the cabin and opened a cupboard, removing a wine bottle and two glasses. Returning, he sat down across the table from Charles and pushed a glass across. "We set a drogue anchor to keep her bow to the wind and prayed like the damned until the storm blew itself out." Bevan uncorked the bottle and poured out two glasses. "And how's life aboard *Louisa*," he asked, "now that the best first lieutenant in His Majesty's Navy has moved on?"

Charles answered evasively, "About as good as could be expected, I suppose."

Bevan eyed him. "Not all sweetness and harmony?"

"It's not that. It's just . . . Well, things aren't running as smoothly as I would have hoped."

"Talmage?" Bevan guessed.

As Bevan knew, Charles had not requested Jacob Talmage as his first lieutenant. St. Vincent had named him. He was from a well-connected family with a long and distinguished military history, at the time serving as flag lieutenant on *Victory*. Charles wondered why he hadn't been promoted long before. Presumably, the admiral felt his protégé needed a little seasoning and a chance to distinguish himself before being advanced.

"Yes, well," he began, reluctant to speak ill of another officer but glad of the opportunity to share his doubts. "He tries hard enough. It must be awkward taking orders from a considerably younger captain. No matter how I look at it, though, he's no seaman. Just before the storm struck, there was some problem with the mizzen topgallant mast, and he didn't know what to do about it. That ended with the topmast eventually carrying away. On the second day, he had an argument with Eliot about reducing sail. An argument in which he was entirely in the wrong." He sighed. "I expect it will improve in due course." To change the subject, he said, "How do you find life among the high and mighty as commander of *Pylades*?"

Bevan made a sour face. "My God, it's all paperwork. From your example, I thought all I had to do was sit on my duff, ask my lieutenant what to do, and take all the credit. But no, there are reports to write and accounts to keep and people asking things like how much cheese there is in the larder. An uncountable number of things. Then the odd storm comes and scares the hell out of you."

Charles laughed.

"It's enough to drive a parson to drink," Bevan retorted, refilling his glass and reaching for Charles's.

"Or a priest, as Penny would say," Charles offered.

"Ah, the much admired Mrs. Edgemont," Bevan said, raising his glass for a toast. "Got a bun in her bakery yet?"

"If you mean with child, I don't think so. She hasn't said anything in her letters."

The conversation continued. When Charles had finished his drink, he pushed away his glass and stood. "I should return. God knows what they'll get up to if I'm too long away."

The two men made their way up to the brig's deck, where the boat crew waited, the gig tethered alongside. "You're the senior officer," Bevan said while the crew descended into the boat. "What are our orders?"

"We wait for Nelson and the rest of the squadron," Charles answered. "I'd expected them to be here ahead of us. It shouldn't be much longer."

CHARLES CAME ON deck the next morning to be greeted by clear skies under bright sunshine, and a breeze that made fine ripples on the deep blue water that sparkled like thousands of diamonds to the horizon. He opted to use *Louisa*'s second day at the rendezvous to exercise the men at the guns. It would be good for them to go through some honest physical effort after the days of cramped idleness below during the storm. Practice with the cannon normally emphasized one or more of the elements of accuracy, speed, or safety. On this day he was interested in how quickly the brutes could be fired from one shot to the next. He could not actually fire the guns while at the rendezvous for fear of the noise giving away their presence to a passing enemy, but he could have the men run them in and out, simulating firing, cleaning, and reloading.

Louisa carried twenty-four freshly painted black twelve-pounder cannon on her gundeck, twelve to a side, and four long nines on the quarterdeck, which accounted for her rating of twenty-eight guns. She also had eight brutally powerful short-range thirty-two-pound carronades divided between the quarterdeck and forecastle, which were considered supplementary. It was the main armament of twelve-pounders that Charles selected for a competition. Each gun was nominally manned by a crew of five, with specific roles as gun captain, loader, and sponger, all but the gun captain heaving on the relieving tackle to haul the two-ton cannon out against the side for firing. In actual practice, only one side of the ship was usually engaged at a time, and two crews would combine to serve a single gun.

"These are the rules for the first contest," Charles said loudly from his place near the mainmast to the men grouped around their cannon on the starboard side of the deck. Almost all of the warrants and standing officers stood on the quarterdeck, where they had a good view. Many of the seamen and marines crowded along the port side to witness the event. "You will run the guns in and out five times, quick as you can. We're not going to fire off any powder, but each action that you would normally take—worming, sponging, loading with powder, shot, and wad, priming, and sparking—must be clearly performed. Lieutenant Talmage, Lieutenant Winchester, and Sergeant Cooley of the marines will be watching to see that every step is executed properly." He paused to look at the assembled men watching him expectantly. They had all practiced at the guns many times before and knew how it went.

"We will begin with three guns competing against each other," he explained, glancing at some notes he had written. "First will be guns two, ten, and eighteen—I'm sorry." Charles remembered that he had allowed the crews to paint names for their weapons in discreet lettering on the sides of the carriages. He'd had to countermand only one of the names chosen: *Bend Over, Frenchie,* which he thought inappropriate. He smiled. "The crews for *Smasher, Instant Death,* and *Hellfire* will compete first. The gun that goes fastest through the motions five times will advance to the second round. Is everyone ready?" He saw the men assigned to the selected guns poised expectantly at their stations. The three gun captains raised their hands.

"All right, open your gunports, out tompkins. When the boatswain blows his whistle, you may begin." Charles checked his watch, then nodded to Keswick, the boatswain, who raised his call and puffed his cheeks: *Tweeeeet!*

Instantly, the men on the receiving tackles heaved, and the three guns, squealing on their trucks, rolled forward until they bumped against the bulwark almost as one. Two of the three gun captains made a show of sighting along the barrels before stepping back and jerking the lanyards, which would have caused the flintlocks to spark the priming powder, had there been any. *Smasher's* captain merely yanked his firing mechanism the second his gun was run out and thus was fractionally ahead of the others. Since there was no recoil, the men leaped to the ropes to drag the guns inboard.

Charles watched closely as the cannon were run in and out, in and out, their crews heaving and grunting while those not engaged yelled out encouragement for their particular favorites. *Smasher* had taken an early lead, but slowly, turn by turn, *Instant Death* closed the gap. In the end it was *Instant Death* that bumped against the ship's side for the fifth time, half a gun barrel ahead of the others. The delighted crew thrust their fists into the air and jumped up and down in victory. Charles looked at his watch and noted the time: five minutes and fifteen seconds, near enough. That would be one minute three seconds per firing, he calculated. Of course, there had been no recoil, and the guns had to be withdrawn manually, which added some time. But then there had been no actual cartridge, shot, or wad, and only the slightest nod at aiming. The net might be just over a minute per evolution under normal conditions. That was good, for some good enough, but not spectacular.

Charles stepped forward and held up his hand for silence. "*Instant*

Death will move on to the second round," he announced loudly. "Now, the crews of *Black Bess, Dorothy,* and *Rose Marie*—ah, the three sisters— will please man their guns." There was laughter among the onlookers and much excited chatter. "Be ready! Steady!" he shouted out, glanced again at his watch, and signaled to Keswick.

In and out the guns ran, the trucks screeching in protest. The gun crews, mostly barefoot on the dampened and sanded deck, and many stripped to the waist, heaved with purpose. Not even a gesture was made to aim or transit the weapons this time, only a grim determination to pull them out, pull them in, simulate cleaning and loading, and pull them outboard again. "Heave, you buggers, heave," one captain kept shouting. "Home, heave, clear!" *Dorothy,* with the most loquacious captain, won by a clear margin, five minutes and five seconds, by Charles's watch. Better.

As the morning warmed, all of the gun crews competed shirtless, some tying their kerchiefs around their heads to keep the sweat out of their eyes. The third set of guns competed, then the fourth. The fastest times were within seconds of five and a quarter minutes for each group. *Thunderbolt* and *Naughty Nancy* were added to the list of winners.

"Each of the crewmen who have made it this far," Charles said, "will receive an extra half-ration of spirits with this evening's supper. The victors in the next round will receive an extra half-ration both tonight and the night after. The crew of the champion gun will get a golden guinea from my own pocket. That's two shillings a man." He held the coin up above his head. There were good-natured cheers and a generally enthusiastic atmosphere, while the four remaining gun crews huddled around their captains to plot strategy with grim seriousness.

Instant Death surprisingly defeated *Dorothy,* with a time of five minutes flat, while *Thunderbolt* lost by a hairsbreadth to *Naughty Nancy* in five minutes and two seconds, members of both crews gasping for breath after they finished. Charles gave the winning crews a few moments to drink some water and collect themselves before the final. When he thought they were sufficiently recovered, he had the marine drummer tap out a long roll.

"Are you ready?" he called out. The men nodded, and the captains responded, "Yes, sir," and "Aye, we are, sur."

"Remember, a guinea to the winner." Two of the men on the receiving tackles spit on their hands and rubbed them together; others shuffled their bare feet on the deck for better traction. "Steady." He signaled to the boatswain. *Tw-e-e-e-e-e-t!*

The men fell furiously on the relieving tackle of both guns, yanking them back where the wormers, spongers, loaders, and rammers worked as fast as they could at the muzzles. Back and forth, in and out ran the guns. The noise from the onlookers increased, cheering and clapping, urging the men on. The two guns moved in perfect unison as if they were somehow connected. *Instant Death* and *Naughty Nancy* lunged into the open gunports up to their carriages and withdrew two times, three times.

On the fourth repetition, Charles thought *Instant Death* had gained an infinitesimal advantage. The guns were jerked backward, the wormers, spongers, and all did their work, and all twenty men fell on the tackles as one, even the gun captains grabbing at the lines and lending their weight.

Thunk-k. *Naughty Nancy* and *Instant Death* slammed hard against the bulkhead. "Clear," both captains shouted in unison. The lanyards jerked and the flintlocks sparked.

A silence filled the gundeck, broken only by the ragged gasping of the exhausted men lying or sitting on the deck by their guns. The cannon themselves rested hard against the side of the ship, quiet and unmoving. Charles looked at it a second time to be sure: four minutes and forty-five seconds. That would be—what?—fifty-seven seconds per firing. That was more than satisfactory.

"Well," Charles said, addressing the gun crews, "two winners, I hadn't counted on this." He made a small display of patting his pockets and even turned one out as if to show that he hadn't any more money. This brought some laughter from the crew. "Ah, here it is," he said, producing a second coin from an inside jacket pocket. He called *Naughty Nancy* and *Instant Death*'s captains forward and gave them each their coin. It would be up to the purser to change them into coins of smaller denominations.

"There is one more thing before you are dismissed," Charles said, turning serious and addressing the entire assembled crew. "Gunnery is why we exist. From time to time we may be called upon to engage enemy ships larger than ourselves and with more powerful armaments. To succeed, we must service the guns faster and with more effect than our opponents. This is our business. If you men attend to your instruction and give your full effort in practice, *Louisa* will be the most proficient twenty-eight-gun frigate in His Majesty's Navy, and a menace to any Frenchman unlucky enough to come within range." He paused for a long moment to lend weight to his words. Then he smiled and raised his arms. "A cheer for the winning guns!"

When the noise died down, he turned toward the lieutenants. "You may dismiss the hands, Stephen," he said. "Mr. Talmage, if you would be so kind as to indulge me, I would appreciate a word with you in my cabin."

"Yes, sir," Talmage answered, and the two men went below.

"How do we do it better?" Charles asked as he hung his hat and sword on their pegs along the bulkhead. He removed his coat and flung it on the settee under the stern windows. Talmage sat ramrod straight at Charles's table, his jacket neatly buttoned and his hat placed precisely on the tabletop by his elbow.

"Sir?" Talmage asked. "Do what better?"

Charles dropped heavily into a chair across from his lieutenant and glanced at the clock on the wall above his desk. It was a little after eleven in the morning. "Tea or coffee?" he asked.

"Tea would be fine."

"Attwater," Charles called out. "One tea for Lieutenant Talmage and a coffee for myself, please."

"Aye-aye," said a voice from his sleeping cabin. Charles guessed that his steward had been taking a nap.

"The gunnery," Charles said, turning back to Talmage. "You watched today's exercise. Ten men each on twelve-pounder guns, and most of them took near a minute between firings, and that without the slightest wink at actually aiming them."

Talmage looked puzzled. "Is that bad? I thought a broadside a minute was acceptable."

"Acceptable? Well, yes, it's acceptable, I suppose," Charles said. "But they won't be firing their guns once a minute in actual combat, not with any accuracy. We can do better. I've heard *Marion Castle* kept up a sustained fire of three broadsides in just over two and a half minutes at the Battle of the Saints. That is the rate of gunwork I'm looking for. If *Marion Castle* could do it, so can we."

"If I recall, sir," Talmage said rather primly, "*Marion Castle* carries thirty-two-pounders on her lower deck, and they have larger gun crews. *And*," he emphasized, "she was an experienced ship and had been at sea for several years with the same crew. Captain Wilkerson was also known to be something of a fanatic about gunnery. It wasn't like she was a normal ship."

This was not what Charles had wanted to hear. There was something about Talmage's manner that pricked at him. He was a good first lieutenant in most respects: an excellent administrator and a gentleman to his toes. He was said to be an exceptional swordsman. But there was a certain distance, an unrelenting formality, an assumption of superiority toward subordinate officers that made Charles uncomfortable. There was the time when an ordinary seaman had tripped and fallen heavily against Talmage's leg. The lieutenant had demanded the man be flogged. Charles refused and had had to smooth ruffled feathers.

Winchester, he knew from experience, would pick up a line and haul with the rest of the men. He could not imagine Talmage doing any such thing, even if his life depended on it. And there was a certain lack of imagination when it came to things like experimenting with gunnery evolutions. There was all that and also Talmage's want of seamanship. Charles thought the man would probably become one of those captains who loved a smart and perfectly run ship but would never willingly take her into danger.

Attwater padded back from the galley with a cup of tea and a mug of coffee on a tray. "If there weren't nothing more, sir?" he offered.

Charles looked at Talmage, who sat motionless, then thanked and dismissed his steward. As he carefully sipped the hot liquid, he thought of Daniel Bevan. Bevan and he thought alike, he decided. They had much the same backgrounds and had worked closely as lieutenants on the old *Argonaut* for a half-dozen years. What they didn't know, they picked at until they figured it out. But when Talmage was confronted with a problem he hadn't been prepared for by his tenure as flag lieutenant to Admiral St. Vincent—how to improve the rate of fire for the guns, for example—he was at a loss.

"I do not want *Louisa* to be a 'normal' ship, Mr. Talmage," Charles said. "I want her to be as effective in battle as she can possibly be."

"Of course, sir," Talmage said, bending forward and obviously attempting to be accommodating. "We could practice the men at the guns more often. Daily, even."

Charles knew this was not the answer he was looking for. He had already instituted a regular schedule for gunnery practice, three times a week, and sensed that more frequent repetitions would not help. He wanted a fresh approach. Something like a study of how the guns were worked, what individual tasks were involved, in what order. Was there a better way to do it? He'd had ten men on each gun. Was that better than eight? Or twelve? Or six? With the numbers and the way the tasks were distributed, did some of the men get in one another's way? Sometimes they did, he knew. Charles thought it worth examining. Clearly, Talmage was not the man to do it.

"That's not what I'm looking for," Charles said without thinking. "I'll have Winchester look into it."

Talmage's eyes narrowed fractionally, and his mouth tightened. "Sir," he began in a tone that signaled a long-pent-up protest, then he fell silent. Charles thought for a moment that he might have too directly called into question the lieutenant's abilities and would have to make amends. Before he could speak, he heard the lookout in the tops call down to the deck: "Sail ho, south-by-southeast, maybe twelve miles."

"We will continue this discussion at another time," Charles said, pushing the issue to the back of his mind. He rose and took up his coat. "We'd better go topside. That may be the rest of the squadron."

It was *Terpsichore,* recognized almost immediately by the lookout. Within an hour, the tiny white dots of her topgallants were visible from the deck. Slowly, more of the distant masts revealed themselves to include topsails and then courses. Charles scanned the sea with his glass but saw no sign of any other ships. A call to the tops confirmed that it was *Terpsichore* and only *Terpsichore* bearing down on them. As it would be at least an hour before Bedford's frigate came within hailing range, he called Winchester over to discuss his plan for an examination of the gun work. He noticed Talmage standing alone by the opposite rail, eyeing them sullenly. *It will pass,* he thought.

Terpsichore glided majestically across the shimmering sea in the late afternoon under a full set of sails, to make the best advantage of the light winds. Before she began to take in her canvas and heave to on *Louisa*'s weather side, the signal *Captains report on board* soared up her halyards. Charles's gig had already been made ready. "You have the ship, Mr. Talmage," he said formally to his unsmiling first lieutenant and descended over the side.

Charles's and Bevan's boats reached *Terpsichore* almost together. By centuries of naval tradition, Charles was given preference, Bevan doffing his hat and smiling broadly while his boat's crew backed their oars. Charles grabbed at the ropehold for the side ladder and hurried up over the tumblehome.

Captain Edward Bedford stood by the entryport to greet the two captains as they emerged onto the deck. Charles touched his hat and shook the offered hand. Bedford was a broad-shouldered man in his early forties, with thick black eyebrows and a weather-beaten face. Charles had heard somewhere that Bedford had worked his way up the ladder of naval command after beginning his career before the mast. This was a rare enough accomplishment in George III's navy and unheard-of in the army. Any man who could do it had Charles's automatic respect.

"How'd ye fare in the blow?" Bedford asked straightaway. Charles had already noticed while he was being pulled across that *Terpsichore* showed little if any damage from the storm.

"Lost our mizzen topmast," Charles answered. "Nothing serious. We had our moments, though."

"Aye, she was a fucking determined little tempest," Bedford responded, turning toward Bevan as he climbed through the entryport. "Ah, Captain Bevan, welcome aboard. I do love a Welshman. Born to be hanged, I say. And how did tiny *Pylades* survive the gale?"

"We're still afloat," Bevan answered. "Although only God knows why."

"Good seamanship is why," Bedford said seriously. "There was little enough time to prepare. I watched as that first rush damn near rolled ye over."

"Thank you, sir," Bevan answered.

Bedford turned back to Charles and chuckled. "It were a rare treat to see *Emerald* signaling for you to increase sail and firing off her guns while you were doing the opposite." He laughed heartily. "Pigott probably wet his breeches. And then the fucking wind comes up from behind and lays him right over on his beam ends. What a nasty surprise that must have been!" Bedford laughed so hard that tears came to his eyes.

"I did attempt to warn him," Charles said, vainly trying to suppress a chortle.

Bedford wiped at his eyes. "Pigott is nay the kind of man who pays much attention to signals from those under him," he said happily. "He starts with a lofty notion of his own importance and soars upward from there." Leaning forward with a conspiratorial wink, he added, "The Right Honorable John Pigott is an old sow's arse, the spot right between the hams and just south of the tail."

Charles couldn't help laughing but was shocked by such blunt speech about a superior officer. As he secretly agreed, he said nothing. Bevan discreetly cleared his throat.

"Ah, ye're probably wondering why I called ye on board," Bedford said, turning businesslike. "Two reasons: The first is to ascertain the state of yer ships." He looked meaningfully at Bevan.

"Our repairs are nearly complete," Bevan answered. "We're fit for whatever is required."

"Captain Edgemont?"

"*Louisa* is ready for duty, sir."

"Good, good. And the second is to request both of yer presence at dinner," Bedford said warmly. "I've already informed the cook, so ye daren't refuse, and I have a large quantity of an excellent Madeira which I can't possibly get through myself."

"Before we go below," Charles asked, "have you any orders?"

Bedford rubbed his chin. "We wait for Nelson and the others for a decent time, of course. Assuming he decides to show up at all."

"How do you mean?"

"Unless I miss my guess, Nelson may have already attended the rendezvous and moved on," Bedford said carefully. "If I know him, I'd say he may well have gone to Toulon without waiting, to see if the Frogs have used the time to sneak away. Still, we've orders to wait here. I'll give him three days, and if no one appears, we'll try there."

THE WEATHER CONTINUED fresh and springlike over the sea, empty but for Bevan's brig, *Louisa,* and *Terpsichore* rocking easily on the gentle swell. All three ships took noon sightings, and all three discovered to no one's surprise that they had drifted somewhat south of the specified waiting place. Bedford promptly ordered them all to beat into the breeze and make up the deficit.

The following afternoon Charles and Winchester assembled two gun crews in the waist and walked them repeatedly through their evolutions at the guns. Charles could find no obvious problems. He did discover that eight men were about as effective as ten, twelve was too many, and six resulted in a noticeably slower rate of fire. After a time, he left Winchester to work on the problem while he went to receive the boatswain's and purser's daily reports. Eliot, he noted, had the watch. He saw no sign of Talmage, who normally would have been on deck. As soon as he was free, he decided to go below to the officers' wardroom and speak to Talmage before the situation between the two of them became strained. He found the lieutenant seated alone at the wardroom table with a partly full bottle of wine in front of him.

"May I sit?" Charles asked.

Talmage looked up and then pushed his chair back as if to stand.

"Sit, sit," Charles said, gesturing with his hands. "This is not an official call." He pulled out a chair and lowered himself into it.

"Sir," Talmage began, slurring the word.

Charles lifted his hand. "I must apologize about our conversation yesterday. I'm afraid that I may have left the impression that I do not appreciate your services. I assure you that this is not so."

"Sir," Talmage repeated, rubbing a hand across his face. With an effort, he said, "I am only trying to do my tudy."

"I can well imagine how you feel," Charles said, after taking a moment to untangle "tudy." "Coming from *Victory,* with all the bustle and confusion there, you probably find this something of a challenge. *Louisa* is a very small ship in comparison, with different kinds of problems." Despite a certain blankness in his lieutenant's expression, Charles felt that he was making progress. He went on, "You know, it's only a little over a year ago that I was a lieutenant myself. I have a certain way of doing things that may not suit everyone. I'm sure that we will both adjust in time."

Talmage nodded somewhat dully. "I only want do to my tudy," he repeated. Then, apparently thinking he might have left something out, he added, "efficiently," and another word that might have been, "unhappy," although in what context, Charles could not imagine.

Charles glanced at the bottle. "Is this all you've had to drink?" He held the bottle up to the light and saw that it was about three parts in four empty. That wasn't so bad.

Talmage bent down to reach under his chair and came up with a second bottle, and then a third, both devoid of liquid. "Sead doldiers," he explained without emotion.

"I see," Charles said. "You've certainly done yeoman's work here. Can you stand?" He signaled to a wardroom servant, and the two men helped the lieutenant into his cabin, out of his uniform jacket and shoes, and onto his cot. "I expect you on deck tomorrow morning as usual," he said, but realized that in all probability, none of his words had made much of an impression. "Fetch a bucket and put it beside the bed," he said to the servant in an effort to be helpful. "I expect he'll soon be returning most of the wine, and his dinner, too."

The following dawn came golden bright under scattered white-bellied clouds and over the same placid blue seas. Talmage arrived on deck with the forenoon watch, red-eyed, pale, and tight-lipped. Charles greeted him with an observation about the beauty of the day and received a grunt in reply. A second gesture to open normal communications received a similar acknowledgment. Charles found this annoying but decided that his lieutenant probably needed a little time to recover his sea legs, as it were. He let it go and spent the remainder of the watch with Winchester, exercising the men at the guns, trying various combinations of wormers, spongers, loaders, and rammers. Reluctantly, he came to the conclusion that there were only so many ways to serve a cannon and that trying to overrefine it probably did more harm than good. He did discover, almost by accident, that if a fiddler were playing "Rule Britannia," the crews would get into a kind of rhythm, and the faster the fiddler played, the quicker the guns went in and out. He tried "Hearts of Oak" with similar results, but the effects of both were marginal, and he didn't see how it would serve in the chaotic din of battle in any case. In the afternoon he had the crew practice in the rigging and on the falls for a change of pace. Significantly, no new sails were sighted on the horizon—no sign of Nelson, the other seventy-fours, or Pigott. Since it seemed unlikely that all of the larger ships would have vanished in the storm, he thought Bedford's theory that they had gone on to Toulon increasingly likely.

That evening, after his supper, he decided that it was past time for him to write to his wife. The two letters he had received from her at Gibraltar were as yet unanswered in the flurry of last-minute preparations to leave the port. He retrieved the envelopes from his desk, removed their contents, and carefully smoothed the papers out on his table. For a long moment he looked at her neat, precise handwriting. He could hear her voice in his mind and almost see her face before him, her soft, fawn-colored hair, her expressions and smiles and laughter. His heart ached as he picked up the first, which he had read many times before. It began:

> 17th Day, first Month
> Tattenall

My Dearest Husband,
   It is less than one week since thou left for the sea and how I miss thee already.

There was a lengthy paragraph in this vein that he read and reread, then read carefully once more. She went on that the weather had turned very cold, with much snow, and the land was a beautiful white as far as the eye could see. *How about that,* Charles thought.

> I have conversed with thy brother, John Edgemont, about purchasing a quantity of fodder, as some of thy crofters' chattel can obtain little succor in the deep cover.

That was considerate, if somewhat extravagant. It was like her to be concerned about the welfare of others. His brother would probably reluctantly approve, moderating the expense as much as possible. It would cost him, but little harm would result so long as his tenants didn't come to expect it every winter.

Toward the end of the letter, she mentioned, apparently as an afterthought,

> I have found no schooling for the children of thy crofters. From my inquiries, many lack even an elementary knowledge of their letters or sums. I am troubled about their advancement.

What advancement? Charles wondered. They were the offspring of the tenants on his estates and would replace their elders in time. That was their advancement, as it had been for countless generations and would be for generations to come. He decided not to worry unduly about it. His brother would see to it that she was restrained in her adventures and did nothing so extravagant as to build a schoolhouse or hire a tutor.

The final paragraph returned to her affection for him and how she wished he were near, even referring to waking beside him and feeling his warmth. Charles read this over repeatedly. He sat staring at the words for some minutes. She had signed it:

> Thy loving and affectionate
> Penny

It almost made Charles's heart break.

The second letter was a little more difficult to fully fathom. Dated "14th Day, Second Month" (but without referring anywhere to Saint Valentine), it began with the familiar endearments and expressions of tenderness. He read these carefully. She went on about her plans for a school and the hiring of a schoolmistress to see to the crofters' children's betterment. Charles guessed that she had not yet spoken to his brother. He felt badly that she would be disappointed. She had evidently had discussions with her parents (her father owned a large water mill near Gatesheath), because she wrote of the need for a new mill located near his estates, to more conveniently attend the requirements of his tenants and the Tattenall community, and to ensure that all received fair profit for their produce.

Charles shook his head in amazement. He didn't know exactly, but he thought that constructing a mill would surely cost in excess of a thousand pounds and was well beyond anyone's serious consideration. He didn't know where the local farmers had their grist milled, and he wasn't worried about it. He chuckled out loud as he envisioned his brother's astonishment at any such suggestion.

There was a part of the letter just before the end that he didn't fully comprehend. Penny alluded to some papers, saying that she would "converse on this with him" when she next visited. He guessed that "visited" was another of her quaint Quaker expressions—like "labor with" for argue, or "First Month" for "January"—that referred to her letters and that at worst she planned to write, enlisting his aid in her negotiations with his brother. That would present no difficulties, he decided. *Louisa* would not expect to receive any mail so long as she was deep in the Mediterranean, and even if they did, it would be months before he could be expected to respond. He was sure that the issue would have blown over by then.

The letter ended with slightly abbreviated expressions of her tenderness and affection. He uncorked his ink bottle, laid out a clean sheet of paper, nibbled at the end of his quill, and that night penned four paragraphs on how much he missed her.

CHARLES WOKE WITH a sense of anticipation on the morning of their third day, the last day, according to Bedford's thinking, that they were to remain waiting at the rendezvous. As it did every morning when they were at sea, dawn broke with the cannon run out and the men at their battle quarters, on the chance that an enemy ship might have stumbled into their midst during the night. The horizons were clear, however, and the guns were immediately housed and secured. *Louisa* began her daily routine.

Charles washed and, as he had three days of stubble, allowed himself to be shaved by Attwater. After a quick breakfast, he called for his signals midshipman, Isaac Beechum, and sent him across in the gig to inquire of

Captain Bedford whether he still intended to take the three British ships to Toulon in search of Nelson, and if so, at what time. Beechum, eighteen, rail-thin, gangly, and in Charles's opinion the more promising of the two young gentlemen on board, returned a half hour later with the message that, pending unforeseen events, they would sail at noon.

Charles considered what he should do with the time. He thought he had no pressing business to attend to, when it occurred to him that he had not kept up with his entries in his captain's logbook. It was an irksome task, and one in which he frequently found himself in arrears. His was not even the ship's official log. That was the responsibility of the master, and Eliot, he knew, kept a meticulous daily record. Charles did what he always did—called for Eliot to bring his log and then sit in Charles's cabin while the captain copied the missing entries in his own hand. He discovered that his most recent entry (or the last time he had reproduced Eliot's recordings) had been a full week before the storm struck. Charles made his entries, promised himself to be more diligent in his log keeping, and passed the master's original back across the table.

"Thank you kindly, Mr. Eliot," he said sincerely.

"Humph." Eliot, who did not approve of this practice, took up his book and started for the door.

"Mr. Eliot," Charles said sternly, which caused the master to stop, turning to face him. "That would be 'Humph, *sir.*' I trust I won't have to remind you again," he said, then laughed out loud. Eliot himself burst out in guffaws, and the two were only just regaining control when they heard a call from the tops: "Deck there, sail fine on the starboard bow."

Charles snatched up his hat and was climbing the ladderway to the quarterdeck when he heard Winchester ask, "How many sail?"

"Just the one, sir," the lookout reported. "There's something strange."

Charles searched the horizon from the starboard rail but saw nothing. "What's strange?" he called up.

"It be hard to say, sir. She's ship-rigged. Looks as though she has no topmasts at all. She's sailing under her fore and main courses, not even a jib."

It took Charles a moment to digest this before it came to him: *Emerald.* He swore under his breath. He was not looking forward to a reunion with Pigott, not after ignoring his orders at the onset of the storm. He had a suspicion that having been in the right would earn him little gratitude. If only Bedford had decided to sail at dawn instead of waiting till noon, all of this could have been avoided.

Emerald's painfully abbreviated outline limped slowly over the horizon toward the rendezvous. Through his glass, Charles could see that not only had her topmasts been carried away, but her bowsprit was gone, and she carried a jury-rigged foremast. It appeared that all of her ship's boats had similarly disappeared. Awkwardly, *Emerald* hove to a cable's length from *Terpsichore* and ran her signal flags up to the mainsail yardarm: *Captains report on board. We would have to,* he considered as he descended to his gig. *Pigott has no way of coming to us.*

Charles ascended *Emerald*'s side steps after Bedford and before Bevan, as precedence demanded. Captain Pigott, a man with an unfortunately high forehead, a pinched nose, and close-set, watery blue eyes, was waiting as he gained the deck. "Ah, young Captain Edgemont," he said, with a heavy emphasis on "young."

"Yes, sir," Charles answered, smartly touching his hat.

"Before you even start, I'll have none of your excuses, damn your eyes," Pigott pronounced. "I'll not have any junior captains deciding which of my orders they choose to obey and which they don't. I am most displeased. I intend recommending to Admiral St. Vincent that you be hauled before a court-martial. What have you to say to that?"

"Sir—" Charles began, intending to be contrite.

"Captain Pigott," Bedford interrupted, "His Majesty's Navy is of little use at the bottom of the sea. Edgemont did try to warn ye of the approach of the weather."

Pigott glared at Bedford. "I'll have no excuses. No excuses. None."

Bevan took a step forward and touched his hat respectfully. "Begging your pardon, sir," he said, "but Captain Edgemont is a proven officer with a distinguished record. Jervis himself promoted him to captain." He hesitated, then added, "If there is to be an official inquiry, it will certainly include the nature of the orders he evaded and who issued them."

Pigott blinked at this. Turning once more to Charles, he said, "Well? What have you to say for yourself?"

Charles took a deep breath, well aware that he was very junior to Pigott and that an inquiry before St. Vincent might not go as well as Bevan thought it would. "I was doing my duty as I thought best for the safety of my ship and the good of the squadron, sir," he said directly. "I saw a danger that it seemed your lookouts had missed, and I acted accordingly. Of course, if you wish to request a court-martial, I shall willingly submit."

Captain Pigott looked around at the three junior officers and equivocated. "I don't mean to be harsh, young man," he said with deep condescension. "A stern warning may be all that is required, and I trust you will benefit by it. In this case, I'll put your behavior down to youthful indiscretion. But I warn you in the strongest terms not to let it happen again."

"Yes, sir," Charles answered, biting back any further thoughts.

"Now, then," Bedford announced loudly to change the subject. "Do ye know where Admiral Nelson and his three seventy-fours are?"

"I do not," Pigott answered tartly. "I had assumed them to be here."

"Nary a trace," Bedford said. "I expect they've gone on directly to Toulon to see if the Frenchies are out."

"Nonsense," Pigott replied. "I have always doubted that Nelson was a wise choice to command this squadron. He's far too impetuous, in my view. But even he wouldn't attempt so foolish a course. In all probability, he's returned to Gibraltar for repairs. A fierce storm it was; could have done any amount of damage." He glanced doubtfully over the rail at the other captains' relatively whole ships. "Or perhaps he's pulled into a cove somewhere to effect repairs and is yet on his way here."

"I think we should take a look up Toulon way," Bedford persisted.

Charles nodded tentatively in agreement, not wanting to provoke Pigott into hardening his position. In this he failed.

"And you would like to be the one to sail away on your own, wouldn't you, Edgemont?" Pigott said, shooting a glare at him. "No, I'll not divide my command. Our orders are as clear as day: to wait at this place in the event the squadron is dispersed. Well, the squadron is dispersed," he said triumphantly. "And we shall wait."

Charles felt his anger rising at Pigott's unvarnished arrogance and felt Bevan's hand on his arm, warning him to restrain his temper. "Fine," he said.

"For how long shall we wait, sir?" Bevan asked.

"For a decent interval," Pigott answered, then, realizing he needed to be more specific, added, "A week, I should think."

Charles groaned inwardly, careful not to display any emotion. "Thank you, sir," he managed. They were then dismissed, and on his way back down the side steps, he clearly heard Bedford below him mutter, "Fucking idiot," and felt himself in complete agreement.

THE WEEK PASSED with agonizing slowness as the hours and watches crawled one after the other. No sails were sighted on the horizon or anywhere else, except for a solitary xebec merchantman, which flags from *Emerald* promptly forbade anyone from pursuing. Charles and Bevan visited each other most nights, usually after dark so that Pigott would be less likely to notice the boats going back and forth. But it was at a meeting on *Terpsichore* that an actual strategy was plotted.

"Captain Pigott will certainly order us all back to Gibraltar in a few days," Bedford said at the outset. "This cannot be allowed to transpire. Pigott does not want us to have a look at Toulon, because *Emerald* is in such a sad state that she must return for repairs. If he goes back alone, it will reflect badly on him, as it should. By keeping us together, he thinks it will seem as if he stood in firm command and did all he could under difficult circumstances."

"How do we dissuade him?" Charles asked.

"Ah, Charlie," Bedford said with a wink, "in the last resort, ye must go off on yer own. Find some excuse to hang back; slip off in the night or some such. Ye have the highest standing among us with old Jervie, and it's possible ye'll get away with it."

Charles did not think much of this idea at all, not that he rejected it completely. "There must be a better alternative," he said soberly.

"Aye." Bedford nodded. "I suggest we try sweet reasonableness first."

Thus, at noon on the seventh day since Pigott had arrived at the rendezvous, Charles was prepared when the signal *Make sail, course south-by-west* rose on what served as *Emerald*'s masts.

"Mr. Beechum," Charles said to the midshipman standing beside him, "hoist the signal."

"Aye-aye, sir," Beechum responded, and raised the flags already laid out on the deck, *Request meeting of captains.* Charles noted with satisfaction the identical flags jerking upward on *Terpsichore* and *Pylades,* and immediately went down into his waiting gig.

Pigott scowled at the captains assembled in front of him. "What's the meaning of this?" he demanded.

"It's my doing," Bedford answered, "to prevent you from making a serious mistake."

Charles thought the senior captain was going to explode. His face turned bright red and his eyes widened. "I'll see you broken and put back before the mast for this, Bedford," he snarled.

"Just a moment," Charles said, stepping forward. "I think you should listen to what we have to say."

"You're in on this, too?" Pigott said in a voice intended to intimidate. "I should have thought you were in enough trouble already. This borders on mutiny, don't you agree, Commander Bevan?"

"No, sir, I do not," Bevan answered.

"We wish only to provide you with the benefit of our advice," Charles asserted, trying to sound conciliatory. "It is our duty to do so."

"It's only a suggestion, sir," Bevan offered. "For your consideration. We feel it wouldn't look good if Admiral St. Vincent doesn't agree with the course of action you've chosen, especially if he discovers that each of your subordinate officers tried to talk you out of it."

Pigott paused with an air of indulgent sarcasm. "All right, I'll listen," he said grudgingly, "but be quick about it."

"It is quite possible," Bedford said with a touch of anger in his voice, "that Nelson and the others have gone on to Toulon and are at this moment waiting for us there." He held up his hands to forestall Pigott's objection. "I didn't say it was likely or certain," he emphasized, "but possible."

"Of course it's possible," Pigott answered. "Anything's possible. But in my opinion—"

"Sir," Charles interjected, "it's not a question of whether they went here or they went there. The question that will be asked is what decisions you made and how many possible eventualities you took into account. For all we know, Nelson decided to take his seventy-fours to

Constantinople on a whim. But it is at least as likely that the squadron went to Toulon as that it returned to Gibraltar. The point is," he said significantly, "that you would be able to report to Lord St. Vincent that you have covered every probability."

Pigott's eyes shifted to the right and then to the left as he considered this. "All right," he said after a moment. "All right, I will admit to finding some merit in your argument. I will allow one of you to sail for Toulon. But if there are no ships of the squadron present, you must return direct to Gibraltar."

"I would be pleased to go," Bedford offered immediately.

Pigott looked at him with a certain satisfaction. "No," he said. "I'll send *Louisa,* she's expendable."

Charles shrugged off the implied insult. There was one additional thing he wanted, but he wasn't sure how to go about asking for it. He decided to try flattery. "Thank you, sir," he said. "I think you've made a wise decision. Naturally, I will require the services of Commander Bevan and his brig."

"Why is that?" Pigott asked suspiciously.

"I'm sure you've anticipated this, sir," Charles said in his most pleasant tone. "In the event any of the squadron are encountered, they will require someone to carry dispatches back to the fleet. *Pylades* is well suited for that kind of task."

Pigott reluctantly nodded his agreement, evidently not much caring what Bevan did. "But I warn you: There will be no excursions. You're to return straight to Gibraltar if there are no British warships present."

"Of course, sir," Charles answered agreeably. "We will return immediately in the event there is no indication of Nelson's whereabouts. You have my word."

Bedford waited in his gig while Charles and then Bevan climbed from *Emerald*'s side steps into their own craft. "Fucking idiot," he muttered to no one in particular. To Charles, he said, "Ye be the lucky one. Get under way before he changes his mind."

"The moment I set foot on my deck," Charles answered. "And thank you, sir."

Bedford touched his hat. "I wish you luck and Godspeed," he said, then nodded to his coxswain.

Daniel Bevan lingered for just a moment, looking curiously across at Charles. "Constantinople?" he asked.

"It's not impossible," Charles answered.

Charles climbed through *Louisa*'s entryport in a cheerful frame of mind. Winchester was at the side to meet him. "How did it go?" he asked.

"Better than anyone had any right to expect, Stephen," Charles answered. "Send the hands aloft. All plain sail; full-and-by. Course north-by-east."

"Toulon?" Winchester asked with a smile.

"Toulon," Charles answered with a larger one. "And better yet, signal to *Pylades,* if you please, *Keep station to leeward.* Daniel's coming with us."

"Bribery?" Winchester asked.

"Closer to blackmail," Charles answered.

THREE

"**D**ECK THERE. LAND HO, DIRECT FOR'ARD THE BOW." A thin mist clung to the water's surface like soft down in the early light. Charles collected his glass from the binnacle. He went down from the quarterdeck and walked forward along the waist. Near the bow of the ship, he mounted the starboard railing and started to climb the ratlines fastened across the foremast shrouds. Two thirds of the way up, he stopped, hooked his elbow through the ropes, and raised the telescope to his eye. In the distance, the dark speck of Cape Sicie, resting on the soft white carpet, danced in his lens. He lowered the glass and arched his head back to speak to the lookout in the tops, fifteen feet above. "How far would you say, Tom?"

Thomas Stutters's head appeared over the edge of the platform. "Good morrow to ye, Cap'in, sir," he said conversationally. "Hard to tell wif the fog. I'd say three, four leagues, near enough."

"Thank you," Charles said, "and a good morning to you, too." He swung around sideways on his perch until his eyes fell on *Pylades,* a seemingly ethereal craft ghosting over the sea-mist, two cable lengths away. After a moment a familiar figure in the brig's foremast shrouds came to his attention. "Hello, Daniel," he hollered across the gap and waved his arm. Daniel Bevan looked out and waved back. Satisfied, Charles glanced forward, saw that the distant heights of France had turned golden in the first rays of the sun, and descended to the deck.

The vapor quickly burned off with the rising warmth of the day. *Louisa* and *Pylades* glided under the ragged bluffs of the cape, far enough out not to invite any cannon fire from the batteries along the shore. The land fell away and then ran roughly eastward for another five miles to a second headland at Cape Cepet, which marked the entrance to the outer roads of the great naval port of Toulon, with its backdrop of rugged sandstone hills liberally speckled with the new greens of spring.

Charles had posted lookouts at all three mastheads and scanned the sea's surface himself with his eyes and his glass. He found no sign of Nelson or the other two British seventy-fours or, indeed, warships of any kind. *Louisa* sailed as close as he dared across the four-mile-wide mouth of the harbor, carefully skirting the squat forts with their rippling tricolor flags on either side of the entrance. A few ships lay anchored in the road, small merchantmen of different types and nationalities, but no warships or troopships or any activity remarkable enough to excite interest. When they had progressed far enough to see into the military harbor, he found it relatively empty. A number of craft lay moored to the quays, some with standing masts but few with their yards crossed.

Charles snapped his telescope closed with a sinking feeling. Two things were abundantly clear—Nelson was not at Toulon, and neither was the French fleet.

"Mr. Beechum!" he shouted.

"Yes, sir." The midshipman came running from the forecastle, breathing heavily.

"Send this signal to *Pylades: Captain report on board.*"

"Yes, sir."

Daniel Bevan arrived from over the side within the quarter hour. "What do you think?" Charles asked without preamble.

"There's no squadron, that's a fact," Bevan answered. "Maybe they did go to Gibraltar."

"There's no French, either," Charles observed.

"So?"

"Do you remember, back at Cádiz, months ago, I told you about this American and his two women?"

Bevan scratched his chin thoughtfully. "They said something about a big French fleet and lots of transports."

"At?" Charles prompted.

Bevan's eyes brightened. "Toulon. So you think the French are out in force, and Nelson's after them with his three seventy-fours?"

"It would be like him," Charles said.

"I don't think," Bevan observed, cocking an eyebrow, "that Pigott is going to like this one bit."

"Sod Pigott," Charles said seriously.

"I don't think that will help," Bevan answered. "Besides, we don't know where they've gone."

"No," Charles said. "I don't know where the French have gone, and I don't know what Nelson has done. But I do know whom to ask."

Bevan looked at him blankly. When Charles pointed toward a number of scattered fishing boats in the lee of the Giens Peninsula, he smiled.

"I speak a little French," Charles said confidently. "I'll buy some fish and see what I can learn. You return to *Pylades;* I'll let you know."

With Stephen Winchester at his side, Charles called down to a very frightened fisherman seated in his smack close up against *Louisa's* lee side: *"Misseur, av-e-vou le poi-son poor vent?"*

"Quoi?" the wiry man in a filthy woolen sweater, heavily patched trousers, and a weeks-old beard said, looking up at him with an uncomprehending and toothless grin.

Undeterred, Charles glanced again at his pocket French dictionary. *"Vent-a-vous le poi-son, see-vous-plait?"* he shouted in a much louder voice in order to be clear.

"Non comprend pas, Capitaine," the man responded with a truly expressive shrug.

Charles held out a gold sovereign by the tips of his fingers. *"Poi-son?"* he yelled.

This was understood. *"Oui, oui,"* the man said and, rummaging around in the bottom of his boat, came up with three large fish that he held out by their tails.

"Entrez, see-vous-plait," Charles said, gesturing broadly for the man to come aboard. He turned to Winchester. "Get Beechum, will you? He at least speaks Spanish. That should be of some help."

"Actually, Charlie, I speak French quite well," Winchester answered.

"Really?"

"Better than you."

The fisherman climbed nimbly over the side with his three fish and an odor that, in England, would have made him exempt from the press.

Charles smiled graciously. "Invite him down to my cabin," he said to Winchester. "We'll offer him some refreshment."

It took two hours for Charles to be rid of the fisherman and two weeks for his cabin to be free of the smell. For his golden coin—which probably could have bought the man's boat, his wife, and all his children, as well as his catch—Charles received three large sea perch and the knowledge that on the first day of the storm, all of the French warships—in number more than the fingers of two hands—and an inexpressibly large number of transports had slipped out of the harbor and sailed toward the east. Some weeks later—how many weeks the fisherman was vague about, but pretty comfortable it was a Sunday—three English warships, with two lines of gunports each, arrived from the south. They also bought fish, much fish, but regrettably, not the fisherman's fish. A few more days, and ten (two hands) additional English ships arrived from beyond Cape Sicie. All had two rows of guns. Then, "poof" (this came during the second bottle of wine and was accompanied by impressive hand gestures), the English departed, also to the east. To Genoa, it was said. This was only two, three days previous.

Charles thanked the man, gave him his coin and the remainder of the second bottle of wine, then guided him back to the entryport. With many a *"merci"* and *"bonne chance"* and *"vive les Anglais,"* he went over the side.

"We will pass within hailing distance of *Pylades,* if you please," Charles said to Winchester.

THE TWO BRITISH warships started immediately eastward, skirting the Hyeres Islands, and by nightfall they hove to well south and east of Cape Lardier, marking the seaward limit of the Bay of Cavalaire. Charles invited Bevan to supper by signal flag. "Yes, I know, sir," Beechum had said promptly when Charles approached him, "*Captain report on board.* I keep it ready."

While he was thinking of it, Charles asked Winchester as well and requested that he pass the invitation to Talmage. He was aware that he had not seen the first lieutenant on deck in the past several days.

"That would not be advisable," Winchester replied. "Mr. Talmage is indisposed."

"Is he ill?" Charles asked.

"No, not exactly."

Charles paused. "Has he been drinking?"

"It is not my place to say," Winchester answered carefully. "Mr. Talmage is an officer and a gentleman. It would be inappropriate for me to comment on his behavior or to speculate on the reasons for it."

"Thank you," Charles said, understanding exactly what Winchester had told him. Intended or not, Charles had called into question Talmage's abilities, and the lieutenant had taken it personally, perhaps even as an affront to his honor. Charles accepted that it was at least in part his responsibility. He had been careless in his speech and insufficiently considerate of Talmage's feelings. The man must have led a relatively sheltered existence on *Victory*. He was certainly ill prepared to be the first on a frigate. The whole thing was becoming irksome. Still, Charles thought, he should have been more careful. He had created an awkward situation, and he sensed that it was not going to be all that easy to repair. He looked back at Winchester. "You've been doing double duty on watch?"

"Eliot helps."

"All right," Charles said, "write me into the schedule. I'll stand one watch a day. We'll have to make some adjustments."

"That would be welcome," Winchester said.

"I'd still like your company at supper."

"Honored," Winchester answered. He paused. "You know, it's not your fault, Charlie. This has been coming since we left Gibraltar. Talmage knows he has shortcomings. He just doesn't want to face them."

AT DAWN THE next morning, *Louisa* and *Pylades* continued northeastward along the mountainous coast, *Louisa* sailing three or four miles from the shore and the smaller brig a similar distance farther out. In this way they stayed in easy contact and covered a reasonably broad swath of the sea. Charles looked into every midsize bay and harbor as they passed to assure himself that they held no captured or damaged British warships, in case that had been Nelson's fate. Saint-Tropez and Sainte-Maxime on the Bay of Saint-Tropez were empty except for fishing boats and a few small coastal traders. The same was true for Fréjus, which they reached by late afternoon. The harbor at Cannes contained a medium-sized Arab merchantman but no warships. Nightfall found them hove to several miles beyond the barren Saint-Honorat Island, with its ruined monastery. And so it went the next day, past Antibes and Nice and Monte Carlo, beyond the border of the French Republic and into the Ligurian Sea.

Charles spent the days mostly on deck, sporadically talking with Eliot and Winchester, watching the shoreline as it passed, and considering what he should or should not do about Talmage. That the lieutenant considered himself injured, there was no doubt. It was touchy when a man felt his honor slighted. That was why, on land, duels were fought; blood sometimes seemed the only remedy. Not terribly long ago, duels were common enough among sea officers as well, until the king expressly forbade the practice. Also forbidden was any junior officer calling out a senior, for reasons that were all too obvious—creating a vacancy for one's own advancement, for example. The Articles of War were inflexible on the subject, stipulating the penalty of death for the offender. For the present, Charles decided, it was probably best to do nothing. He had often heard it repeated, time heals all wounds, and he had plenty of time. Talmage would eventually come to see that no insult had been intended, and everything would be back to normal. And if not? Well, that wasn't so bad. First lieutenants went absent from their posts all the time. Usually, they were killed in battle or died of some disease. Charles knew of one case in which a first had so infuriated his captain that the man promptly shot his subordinate dead. Of course, the captain had been severely reprimanded.

THE PORT OF Genoa lay at the head of a long shallow sweep of coastline enclosing a gulf over a hundred miles across. The outer roads were open to the sea, while the port extended inland, the city spreading fan-like around the harbor into the surrounding low hills. Flags of the newly coined Ligurian Republic (minted in France) fluttered languidly over the forts guarding the harbor entrance.

About five miles to the west, Charles thought he saw something that might be the ribs of a wrecked man-of-war among some rocks under a low bluff. He directed Eliot to steer inshore and have a closer look. *Pylades* sailed on under a bright midafternoon sun with a steady southwesterly breeze. Satisfied that the ship's bones were neither recent nor substantial enough to be one of Nelson's seventy-fours, Charles ordered that *Louisa* stand back out and resume her former course.

Charles watched as *Pylades,* now almost a mile ahead, slipped across the calm sea, scattering a few coastal traders and fishing smacks as she went. The waters of the bay were a deep blue, the deepest Charles had ever seen. He could see no ships of any consequence in the roadstead; Bevan would signal if there was anything of interest. So Charles was surprised when *Pylades's* yards abruptly braced around, and her bow turned to put the wind on her quarter. He was just beginning to wonder at this when a shout came down from the masthead: "Deck there. Somefing's comin' out o' the 'arbor."

Charles snatched up his glass from the binnacle and steadied it on the harbor entrance. At first he saw nothing; it occurred to him that the wind was nearly foul for anyone attempting to exit its narrow mouth. He transited the lens in one direction, then the other, and then he saw them. They were two, no, three—no, four craft of a type he had seen only once before. He knew immediately what they were—long, narrow, and elaborately ornamented boats, each with a single mast but no sail unfurled. He swallowed hard. They were galleys, an ancient type of warship that had once ruled the Mediterranean but now had almost ceased to exist. He watched, fascinated, as the banks of oars flashed in the sunlight and then fell as one to churn the surface frothy white. The distant *boom—boom— boom* of drums marking the rowers' time reached him over the water.

The galleys picked up speed quickly, too quickly for Charles's liking. They skimmed across the surface, their gilded prows already curling a substantial wave. The four craft neatly divided into two pairs, diverging to starboard and port, and settled their courses to circle around *Pylades* and attack her from the bow and stern. With his glass, Charles could easily see twin twenty-four-pounder cannon on the bow of each galley, their crews heaving on the tackle to run them forward. The banks of oars rose like wings, then levered forward, then down. *Boom—boom—boom.* He knew that tiny *Pylades,* with her six-pounder broadside, had little chance alone in the light wind and calm sea. "Two points to larboard, if you please, Mr. Eliot," he said to the sailing master. "Mr. Keswick!"

"Aye, sir?" came a call from the waist of the ship.

"Drop the courses, if you will. And hurry about it."

"Aye-aye, sir," the boatswain yelled back, and Charles heard his shrill call to send the hands into the rigging to loose the large mainsails. The devil of it was that without Talmage, Charles had to rearrange his officers on the spot and do most of the duties the first would have assumed.

"Mr. Winchester," he said, the formality of his speech betraying his anxiety, "we will clear for action immediately. After that, if you would be so good as to take command of the gundeck."

"Aye-aye, sir."

"Mr. Beechum! Where the hell is Beechum?"

"Here, sir," a voice at the bottom of the ladderway answered.

"Good lad. You will place yourself on the forecastle and direct the carronades. Look to Lieutenant Winchester for your orders."

"Aye-aye, Captain, sir." The young man moved forward, loosening his dirk in its scabbard and testing that it was free. Charles felt that he could trust Beechum at the far extremity of the ship. The other midshipman, Michael Sykes, was a different story. Three years younger, he seemed to lack the focus of his older rival.

"Mr. Sykes," he called to the boy standing expectantly by the binnacle.

"Yes, sir."

"You will command the quarterdeck guns. You will attend directly to me for orders."

"Yes, sir," Sykes answered, smiling with pride. At least on the quarterdeck, Charles decided, he could keep an eye on him.

Charles turned back to study the progress of the galleys, now well out of the harbor. He stared at them in wonder: a scene from the long-bygone era of the great Greek and Roman navies. But the Greeks and Romans didn't have twenty-four-pounder cannon on gun platforms pointing forward. The farther pair were fast reaching a position where they might turn and fire into *Pylades*'s unprotected bow. The increasingly urgent meter of the drums echoed across the bay.

To Charles's surprise, he saw Talmage mount the ladderway to the quarterdeck, unsmiling and immaculate in his full dress uniform and sword. The nominal first lieutenant took a moment to survey the distant *Pylades* and the circling galleys, then approached.

"Your orders?" he said without saluting.

Charles was not pleased. He had already rearranged his officers to make up for the lieutenant's absence. Biting back the urge to dismiss Talmage's offer out of hand, he compromised. "You may replace Mr. Winchester on the gundeck. Send him aft and inform Mr. Beechum in the forecastle of your status."

Talmage's eyes narrowed. Without a response, he turned and descended to his appointed station. In effect, Charles had lowered Talmage's status to that of second and raised Winchester's to first. A circumstance that both Charles and Talmage understood perfectly.

Winchester arrived moments later, a quizzical look on his face. "Sir?"

"As of now, you are the acting first," Charles said. "Do you understand?"

"What about Talmage?"

"I don't give a damn what Mr. Talmage does right now," Charles said, his anger at the lieutenant's behavior coming to the surface. "Look, this is intolerable. I can't have him deciding to appear on deck one day and then disappearing the next, depending on how the mood takes him. It just won't answer."

"Yes, sir," Winchester said.

Charles forced Talmage out of his mind and returned his attention to Bevan's brig. His pulse quickened. *Pylades* suddenly turned, her sails ashiver before they were hauled and filled on a new track directly away from the harbor. This maneuver also brought her guns to bear on one pair of galleys, and a small cloud of gunsmoke erupted from her deck as she fired her tiny broadside at extreme range. Charles marked the waterspouts appearing about the Genoan warships, but saw no damage. As *Pylades* settled on her course, her sails braced up tight. The galleys turned on their keels to take up the slow-moving brig's wake and attack her undefended stern. Charles cast a quick glance at the second pair, now running parallel and on the opposite course to *Louisa*. In time they would come around and take up his own rear, he supposed. He decided to ignore them. *Boom—boom—boom—boom,* he heard clearly, menacing and insistent. The noise irritated him.

Still half a mile or more off, *Louisa* cleaved across the flat sea toward the gap between *Pylades* and the fast-closing enemy. Charles found his progress agonizingly slow. It was evident that he wouldn't be in a position to intercede before the Genovese came within easy range and opened fire. He gritted his teeth. There was little he could do except steer to shave *Pylades*'s stern as closely as possible and hope that she had not been disabled before he arrived.

"One point to starboard, please, Mr. Eliot," he ordered, trying to anticipate the point where *Pylades* would be when he came upon them.

"Yes, sir. One point to starboard," Eliot answered.

"Beat to quarters, Stephen," Charles said without removing his eyes from Bevan's ship and the rapidly closing galleys. *Boom—boom— boom—boom,* the quickening beat of the nearing galleys rang in his ears. Then came the *rat-at-at-at-at* of *Louisa*'s marine drummer as his crew ran to their guns and action stations. Above this came four sharp explosions as the galleys opened fire.

Charles noted two tall waterspouts along *Pylades*'s side. At least one hit midships, he thought. The galleys were closing fast, too fast.

"Starboard a half-point," he barked at Eliot. "Shot on shot, larboard guns," he bellowed in a voice that could be heard the length of the ship. "Run them out."

It would be a near thing, he realized. *Louisa* was within a cable and a half of *Pylades,* but the galleys were closer. Charles noticed his fingers beating a tattoo on the railing in front of him, frowned, and balled them into a fist. He watched as the two galleys ran their guns forward, backed their oars, and fired at pistol range. *Pylades*'s poop deck erupted splinters, and her mizzenmast cracked at the deck, canted to port, and swung down toward the sea in a rending crash.

Having disabled one enemy, the two galleys might have thought to turn and confront the other, but they'd left it too late. *Louisa* slid almost silently across the water, the damaged *Pylades* on her starboard, her port side cannon ready. The two galleys hesitated as if undecided, then, with a shouted order, the drums started. The seas alongside churned to froth as one bank of oars backed, the other pulling. They spun nimbly. There was no hope in that direction, Charles thought. He was already too close.

"You may fire when ready, Stephen," he said.

Winchester moved to the forward rail of the quarterdeck. "Fire as you bear, if you please, Mr. Talmage," he called down. Charles watched as Talmage acknowledged with a stiff nod.

Seeing their plight as the frigate swept down on them, the commander of the oared craft evidently decided to turn back and face the enemy. In some confusion, the drums pounded and the oars reversed. The bows swung back, their guns almost reloaded.

Beechum's forward carronades spoke first with devastating effect into the first galley's gun crews, throwing one cannon off its carriage and back into the first benches of rowers. Then a long ripple of explosions as Louisa's broadside fired, gun by gun, while they passed. The frail bow of the near galley disintegrated under the onslaught, opening the front of the craft wide to the sea. Charles had no time to watch as she quickly settled beneath the waves.

"Hold your fire," he snapped at Midshipman Sykes. "We'll save it for the second." To Winchester, he said, "Have the foretopsail and topgallant laid to the mast, if you please." To Eliot: "Down the helm."

The second galley, fifty yards off Louisa's bow quarter, fired her twin cannon, one striking the side with a crash, the other screaming through the rigging. Her oars fell into some disorder as she started immediately to turn away. Louisa slowed, with her foresails backed, and began to swing to starboard. As soon as Charles was satisfied, he turned to Sykes. "Now," he said.

The quarterdeck carronades barked and the nine-pounders roared. Debris flew up from the galley, her oars flailed uselessly, and Charles saw at least one ball cleave through the packed mass of rowers, convicts probably, chained to their oars. That was enough, he thought, but before he could speak, Talmage's gundeck twelve-pounders, by now reloaded, exploded inward. The frail craft dissolved before his eyes, a terrible carnage among the rowers, and began to fill with water.

He was thinking about lowering a boat to pick up the survivors, if any, when two loud bangs came from behind. A section of taffrail burst into pieces, and he felt the ball passing from aft forward. Over his shoulder, he saw the second pair of galleys close under his stern, their gun crews already sponging out their weapons to reload.

"Oh, shit," he muttered, then, "Keep the helm down," he yelled urgently, more in desperation than hope. "Brace the foresails back around." Charles mentally kicked himself for forgetting the second pair of galleys. Now they had crept up from behind. He knew that *Louisa* was in a serious position. If they disabled her rudder . . . He watched the four twenty-four-pounder cannon being heaved forward, ready to fire.

An unexpected series of explosions rent the air, and he saw a section open on the rail of the port side galley. She immediately backed her starboard oars while those on the left pulled. Her cannon went off together after the start of the turn and went wide. For a moment Charles couldn't imagine what had panicked the galley, for panicked she was. She spun sideways as her oars beat the water, entangling with those of her partner, some snapping loudly. Confusion engulfed both craft as they struggled to extract themselves.

Searching the sea around him, he found *Pylades* off his stern quarter, under foremast alone, her six-pounders already running out for a second broadside. Her guns fired in a single outpouring, the shot crashing into the galleys, but they had managed to fend each other off and went limping back toward the harbor with all the speed they could muster.

Charles removed his hat and wiped at the sweat that had collected under its band. "Mr. Sykes," he said to the midshipman, "signal to *Pylades Course south-by-east,* if you please. Look in the book for the numbers." That would put the wind behind them, and it should be a course Bevan's brig could hold. "We will shorten sail directly," he said to Winchester. "Otherwise, Daniel will never be able to keep up."

Remembering Talmage in the waist, Charles looked down from the forward rail, thinking to congratulate him for his handling of the guns and perhaps begin a conciliatory conversation. He searched the gundeck in vain.

Just before dusk, and well out of sight of the land, he ordered *Louisa* to heave to. Promptly, he called away his gig and had himself pulled across to *Pylades.*

"Jesus, Charlie," Bevan said, greeting him at the rail with none of his customary humor, "that was a near thing."

"We managed, Daniel," Charles said seriously. "So long as we stick together, we'll always manage."

"No matter what," Bevan said. "I'm deeply obliged for what you did. I've never seen so welcome a sight as *Louisa* sliding across our stern. They would have sunk us otherwise."

"The sentiment is mutual," Charles answered. "I don't know what I was going to do about that second pair."

"Likely, not much," Bevan said with a grin.

Charles asked, "How badly damaged are you?"

Bevan considered. "Apart from the mast, not too bad. You wouldn't happen to have a suitable spar, would you? We can replace the mizzen yards, but we've nothing for a mast."

"The largest I've got is a mainmast yard. I suppose something can be made of that."

They took the next day to make repairs on both ships, *Louisa*'s boatswain and his mates helping with the rigging of *Pylades*'s sadly insufficient jury mizzen.

Charles took the time to consider his main problem: Where were Nelson and his possibly reinforced squadron? And where had the French fleet gone? He strongly suspected that the two questions were linked, and the solution lay with the French and their intentions. If the curious American party who had found him off Cádiz were correct, then the French fleet may have departed Toulon and sailed east to collect additional resources along the French coast and Genoa. Charles had heard that there was a large French army in northern Italy, under the command of a young and enterprising general. What was his name? It was on the tip of his tongue . . . Bonasection, Bonapiece, Bonasomething. Charles had certainly seen no sign of an active French military presence around Genoa, nor any of the transports or supply ships that should have been there to support them.

The American had suggested an invasion of Ireland or England. Charles doubted this. If the French had sailed to Genoa and then doubled back toward the entrance to the Mediterranean, he and Bevan surely would have seen something of them. It was possible, of course, that they had gone south around Corsica or even Sardinia before turning west, but it didn't seem likely unless they had some reason to call there.

And if the British Isles were not their destination, the Kingdom of the Two Sicilies, which occupied the southern part of the Italian peninsula and the island of Sicily, was a possibility. The kingdom was at least nominally neutral in the great war, an occasional ally of Austria, sometimes friendly to Britain, and always nervous about the French. This might be motive enough for Paris to contemplate an invasion. Less likely but still possible were other objectives farther east, such as Greece, Crete, and the Levant, but for what reason Charles couldn't imagine.

Just for a moment he remembered the American, Jones, saying that the French force presented a serious threat to English interests and must be destroyed. He had been adamant about it. What did that mean? It was all rather dubious. But if the American had thought it important, Nelson probably did, too.

To turn his thoughts toward firmer ground Charles decided it was nearing time to think about the replenishment of *Louisa*'s food, water, and firewood. There was no urgency, they still had supplies for a month or more on board. But fresh water would be a large improvement over their current supply, already two months in the cask. It had long since developed a distinct odor, and a flavor that only a seaman could endure. Fresh meat, fresh vegetables, some good Italian wine to restock the supply, all would be welcome.

Naples—along with Palermo, the capital of the double kingdom— lay an easy four days' sail to the south, weather permitting. From his written instructions, he knew there was a British consul in the city, a Sir William Hamilton. Perhaps Sir William could arrange for their resupply and even secure a proper mizzenmast for Bevan. If Admiral Nelson and his squadron had sailed south along the Italian coast, he surely would have paid a call on the city. He might be in the harbor at this very moment. The more Charles thought about it, the more he settled on Naples as a reasonable destination.

Having decided on a course of action, he spent much of the evening composing additional paragraphs for his growing letter to Penny. He counted and found that it was now some thirteen pages in length. On this occasion, he described in detail the galleys he'd seen at Genoa, their beauty and speed, and their ancient heritage. He did not mention that he'd sunk two of them.

Over the next five days, *Louisa* and *Pylades* crept southward at the crippled brig's pace, along the Tuscan shore, past the island of Elba and the ports of Civita Vecchia, Ostia, Anzio, and finally, rounding Cape Circeo into the Gulf of Gaeta, just to the north of Naples. Along the way, they saw numerous remnants of the once great Roman Empire, usually in the form of clusters of roofless and broken marble columns, like fingers reaching for the sky. Eliot, surprisingly, proved well versed in the history of the region and kept up a running commentary: This place was a temple to Venus, that one to Mars; here a battle against the Etruscans, there a resort famous for its hot spas and red wine. The small port of Ostia had once been the most important in the empire, due to its proximity to Rome, which lay just over the hills inland. It looked insignificant now. A little farther south, the small town of Anzio, on a point of land, had seen the birth of two of Rome's most notorious emperors, Caligula and Nero.

That Sunday morning, as he did on most Sundays, Charles conducted a thorough inspection of the ship. In the middle of the morning, the crew, washed, shaved, and in their best clothing, turned out in their divisions. Charles walked the straight lines of men, partly to see that they were clean, healthy, and sober, and partly to test himself on all their names. As a general rule, he would make a remark or exchange a pleasantry every seventh or eighth man: a light or stern comment about a past misdeed, or a question about health or some special responsibility. Afterward, he made a close examination of the guns, the galley, the lower decks, the officers' wardroom, and so on through the ship.

Usually, about a half hour before dinner, he would speak to them all from the quarterdeck. Occasionally, he read a few passages from the Bible. Sometimes he talked to them about their work, an improvement he wanted, or, if appropriate, *Louisa*'s orders from the admiral. Once each month, he was required to read the thirty-five Articles of War, specifying in explicit detail the offenses that officers and men would be punished for and the severity of the penalty. Death was the required penalty for transgressing eight of the Articles and optional for eleven more.

The following Tuesday, they rounded the mountainous Cape Circeo, a location Charles knew to be described in Homer's *Odyssey*, where the enchantress Circe turned men into swine. To prove the point, Eliot spent the remainder of the day answering to orders with "Oink-oink, sir," and bursting into laughter. That evening the two ships anchored to the south of the island of Ischia so they could run into Naples with the first light of the morrow. From their anchorage, Charles could just see into the outer harbor with his glass. He saw several aging frigates flying the white flag with the Kingdom of the Two Sicilies' coat of arms, but not a sign of any British seventy-fours. That night he added a few more endearments to the letter for his wife and folded the sheaf of papers into an envelope, thinking he could leave it with the British consul for forwarding to England.

With dawn, both ships pulled their bowers and coasted on an inshore breeze toward the bay. Two miles out, they were met by a pilot boat and in time dropped anchor again, three cables' length from shore in the inner roads. Charles washed and shaved and donned his full dress uniform and best (and only remaining) hat. After breakfast, he collected his letter and the rest of the ship's mail, then ordered his gig into the water to call upon Sir William Hamilton.

"'Tis a beautiful day, sir," Williams, the coxswain, said as Charles stepped into the stern sheets and sat down. It was indeed a brilliant and fresh morning, with a bright sun about a quarter of the way toward its zenith. Golden sparkles danced across the low chop.

"It'll be warm enough by noon," Charles responded absently. "But a fine day, yes." He nodded to Williams to shove off from the frigate.

"Out oars," the coxswain said to the eight men at the sweeps. "All together, pull." The gig started quickly across the harbor, relatively crowded with skiffs, wherries, lighters, and all manner of small boats plying between the merchantmen and the shore. The gig's oars dipped and pulled, dipped and pulled, Williams adjusting the tiller from time to time to maneuver around the other traffic. Charles fingered his bulky envelope and allowed himself to think about his wife. How long would it be before his letter reached her? What, he wondered, would she be doing now? It would be early in the morning in Cheshire. Had she risen and dressed, or was she still asleep, her fair hair spread across the pillow? The thoughts made him unhappy, and he attempted to focus on the activities in the harbor around him. He noticed a small skiff with a single pair of oars pulling across on a course opposite his own. He idly noted that the craft held a passenger in the stern, a woman, with an umbrella held up for shade against the sun. He wondered what a woman was doing in the middle of the harbor; the wife or mistress to some ship's captain, he guessed. As the distance closed, he saw that she was dressed oddly in a plain brown dress, buttoned to her chin, and a gray bonnet. His heart ached. It could be his own Penny, dressed like that. Of course, not in the middle of the Mediterranean. He looked more closely. On their present courses, the two would pass within a hundred yards of each other. He saw the woman turn her head in his direction, focusing, he was sure, on his gig. It couldn't be.

"Williams," he said quickly, then, not having come to any conscious conclusion, "steer to close on that wherry." He pointed. "That one there; the one with the woman in it."

"Aye-aye, sir."

Charles raised his hand to shield his eyes from the glare. She was gesturing to her oarsman and definitely pointing in his direction.

"My God," he said.

"Beg your pardon, sir?" Williams said.

The woman stood and waved, which immediately set her skiff rocking violently.

"Close on that boat," Charles said urgently. "Put your backs into it."

He heard an achingly familiar "Charlie! Charlie!" across the water.

Despite the danger, he stood and gestured frantically with his arms. "Sit down," he yelled. Everyone was trying to get her back into her seat. Her own taximan had dropped his oars and turned to pull her down.

"Back oars," Williams ordered, and the gig glided to a halt beside the wherry. Charles found himself staring at the brightly flushed face of his wife.

FOUR

"ART THOU PLEASED?" PENELOPE EDGEMONT SAID WITH AN apprehensive smile. "I have come for my visit with thee."

"Surely I am pleased," he said quickly. "Very pleased, but . . ." Words failed him. "Well . . . umm . . . yes, and surprised." Turning to the coxswain, he said, "Can we bring her across?"

"Of course, sir," Williams said, and reached for a boat hook to pull the skiff close to the gig's stern. "I'll hand her over." He stepped deftly into the water taxi and, on his knees, scooped her up under her shoulders and thighs and swung her outboard. Penny reached and put her arms around Charles's neck as he collected her and set her on the bench beside him. The proximity of her body cast him into further confusion. Her arms slipped from his neck and grasped his arm tightly.

She was a woman of nineteen years, with pale gray eyes under finely sketched eyebrows, a narrow nose, and a slightly pointed chin. Her dress was plain, with no collar or cuffs, and was fastened with hooks rather than the more fashionable buttons. Nor did she wear any ribbons or lace or jewelry of any kind. To Charles, she seemed a picture of beauty, at this moment a picture of beauty anxious about his reaction to her presence.

"I thank thee, Owen Williams," Penny said as the coxswain slipped back on board. Following Quaker custom, she addressed everyone by his or her given and family names and never used titles denoting any manner of rank or privilege.

"You remembered, missus," Williams said shyly, looking pleased, and knuckled his forehead to her.

Charles tossed the skiff's boatman a silver coin. The man bit the metal to test if it was real, grinned happily, and started back toward the shore. It took a moment for Charles to order his thoughts as the motionless gig rocked gently under the morning sun. All eyes on board watched him expectantly.

"We will return to the ship," he said.

"Aye-aye, sir," Williams answered. "Put some muscle into it, lads."

"There's no urgency."

"No, sir."

Turning to Penny, Charles said, "I didn't expect you. Not that your appearance isn't welcome."

"I know," she answered softly. "I wrote to thee in Gibraltar, but when I received no reply, I supposed that thou had not received it." Her eyes studied his face. "Truly, thou art not angered?"

"I am far from angry. Honestly." He cracked into a smile. "Amazed, possibly. Whatever will I do with you?"

Her eyes narrowed, her face pinkened, and she smiled back. "I have some business concerning thy estates," she answered primly. Then, dropping her voice and leaning close to his ear, "I have come to visit with thee for a time . . . as a wife should."

"Oh," Charles said. He detected a slight emphasis on the word "wife" and felt his face go red. "I received your letters just before we sailed," he said. "I hadn't time to answer them before." He reached under the stern sheets bench and came up with his envelope. "I was hoping to send it on this morning. Here."

"What boat?" Winchester's voice hailed them. It was a pro forma question, since the lieutenant knew perfectly well what boat it was. Then Charles heard, "Oh my God!"

"We have a guest, Stephen," Charles called back. "Rig a sling, if you please."

Winchester turned to give the order and then turned back. "Good morning to you, Mrs. Edgemont," he said, lifting his hat.

"Good morning to thee, Stephen Winchester," Penny shouted upward. "I bring thee joy from thy wife."

A whip was quickly rove to the yardarm, and a chair for her to sit in was lowered into the boat. As soon as Charles was satisfied that she was properly secured, he shouted, "Hoist away," and she soared upwards. Charles climbed up by the side ladder onto the deck. Penny stood next to Winchester, a happy smile on her face. Winchester was beaming so widely that Charles thought it must surely injure his cheeks. "What is it?" he asked.

"It's Ellie," Winchester managed. "She's delivered me a son."

Charles grinned. "Congratulations, Stephen. This is truly a day for welcome surprises. What name?"

Winchester, not yet having thought of this question, looked to Penny.

"Stephen Peter Winchester," she said. "Born on the second day, fifth month. That's thy May, I think. He is adorable, large, and loud and healthy." Peter had been Charles and Ellie's father's given name.

"This calls for a celebration," Charles said, taking Penny by the elbow. "Will you join us?" he said to Winchester.

"I have the watch, sir."

"Mr. Beechum," Charles called to the midshipman, standing at the front of a group of seamen, mostly topmen, across from them on the deck.

The boy approached quickly. "Yes, sir?" he said, touching his hat, then removing it,. "Your servant, Mrs. Edgemont."

"Thank thee, Isaac Beechum," Penny said. "I trust thou art well."

"Oh, yes, ma'am," Beechum said.

"You have the watch," Charles said.

"Aye-aye, sir," Beechum said, smiling. He had never been asked to stand as officer of the watch before.

Charles had turned to lead Penny and Winchester aft to his cabin when he took a second look at the seamen, watching them expectantly. Their number had grown. "Just a moment," he said, and led his wife across. The men who wore hats immediately removed them.

"I am so pleased to see all of thee again," Penny said warmly. Some of the men touched their foreheads, others bowed, while the majority simply smiled. "I want ye all to know that I rest comfortably knowing that my husband is in thy care."

Someone inside the group said, "God bless ye, miss," and there was a chorus of "aye," and "yea," and "God bless," and other expressions of affection. Charles waited for the noise to settle and said, "Thank you. For now I'm sure each of you has some other duty to attend to."

Charles led her into his cabin, past the marine sentry, who snapped extra smartly to attention and even removed his hat as Penny approached the entryway. "Thank you, Private Burrman," Charles said. "But the hat business isn't necessary."

He found Attwater standing in the middle of the cabin with a wide grin on his face. "Ain't this a pleasure, Mistress Penelope," he said happily. "Didn't I wonder when you wouldn't arrive."

"Wine, if you please," Charles said loudly, a little jealous of all the attention his wife was receiving. "Not only are we celebrating Penny's arrival, but Winchester here is a newly made sire."

"There ain't naught but the port, sir," Attwater said sourly.

"Wine?" Penny said, looking at the clock above Charles's desk. "It is only ten-thirty, and in the morning yet."

"Oh, we always drink wine, miss," Attwater said. "The water's terrible foul."

"We also have tea and coffee," Charles offered.

"I will be glad for a glass of port. A small one, please," she said to Attwater.

"Make it four glasses, Attwater," Charles said, as if his servant wouldn't have thought of including himself.

Attwater poured out the port, and Charles stood a toast to the happy father. "The first of many to come," he added. They drank.

"And may I return your sentiments," Winchester said, raising his glass a second time, whereupon Penny's face again turned pink. Attwater, whose thoughts were seldom far from his mouth, said, "Ye'll be needing a larger bed, if you takes my meaning, sir." At this Penny turned crimson.

"That will be all," Charles said to Attwater. "If you would speak to the carpenter about it, please."

Muttering something under his breath, the steward collected the bottle and empty glasses and departed the cabin.

"If you will pardon me," Winchester said, taking up his hat, "I will return to my duties."

Charles nodded and soon found himself alone with his wife. "Ahem." His voice had suddenly gone hoarse. "I must call on the British consul in Naples on business. I was on my way there when I found you."

Penny took his hand in hers and stood close beside him. "I was on my way to find thee," she said. "It was William Hamilton who pointed out the *Louisa* to me."

"Sir William, the consul?"

"Yes. The Hamiltons have been kind enough to share their home with Molly and me."

Charles found her closeness disconcerting. "Molly is here?"

"She has been the companion of my travels," Penny said faintly, her fingers toying with the buttons of his waistcoat.

Charles's hands rested on her hips, then slid around her waist. She softly folded herself against him. "Molly?" he whispered, pulling at the bow fastening her bonnet. He pushed it off and slid his fingers through her hair.

"Yes," she breathed, raising her face to his, her lips slightly parted.

Charles kissed the upturned lips, long and lingering. "I could call on Sir William in the afternoon," he barely managed. His hands wandered, slipping the hooks that secured her dress.

"This way, Chips," Attwater's voice boomed from outside the door. "What the cap'in needs is a new, bigger bed." Attwater and Davey Howell, the ship's carpenter, burst into the cabin.

Penny immediately pushed Charles back with a small shriek and turned away to refasten her clothing.

"Beg yer pardon, sir," Attwater said, not pausing in his progress across the room. "We won't be a minute."

"Good morning, Mr. Howell," Charles said, not able to think of anything else.

"I do apologize, sir," Howell said, removing his hat. "I thought you'd gone into the port. I'm told you require a fresh bed." Glancing at Penny, he said, "Oh, I see. I do apologize, missus."

Having repaired her dress, Penny turned back to face the room. "Good morning," she said, her face a medium red. She had not met the carpenter before. As one of *Louisa*'s standing officers, he had stayed with the ship while she was being repaired and had not attended their wedding.

"Mr. Howell, this is my wife, Mrs. Edgemont," Charles said.

"I am pleased to make your acquaintance, missus," Howell said awkwardly. "I can return later, sir."

"It's all right," Penny said, having regained her composure. "Thy captain and I were just going into Naples to call on the consul."

"I see, missus. We'll have you all fixed up by this afternoon."

A BRIGHT SUN shone high in the sky; the day was rapidly warming to the extent that Charles felt uncomfortable in his full-dress frock uniform coat. "What kind of man is William Hamilton?" he asked his wife, sitting next to him as the gig made its way across the harbor for the second time that morning.

Penny's face composed itself in concentration. "He is a fine person, elderly but fit. He has lived in Naples for many years. I think he speaks the language perfectly, and seems to know everything. He is a scholar with a particular interest in the workings of volcanoes." She pointed toward the towering mass of Mount Vesuvius across the bay, its hollow cone smoking malevolently in the clear sky. "He writes treatises about them. I think him a wise and gentle person."

"I see," Charles said, more interested in how well informed about naval matters Hamilton might be than his fascination with volcanoes.

"He is married," she continued seriously, "to a much younger woman. She must have been very beautiful once. She is connected with artists in some way. She is not so cultured as her husband." Charles gained the impression that Penny did not care for the woman. That was all right. If he didn't care about Hamilton's volcanoes, he certainly wasn't worried about who Lady Hamilton might be.

"Oh, she is originally from Cheshire, over by Great Neston on the peninsula," Penny added, as if this might be a mitigating factor. "She and Molly have become confidantes. I think they have similar histories. Her name is Emma."

Molly Bridges, Charles knew, had been a common prostitute from Portsmouth whom Penny had adopted as some kind of a rescue project. He began to think that Emma Hamilton might be a more interesting person than he had previously supposed.

"And she poses herself as a great admirer of Horatio Nelson," Penny concluded. The gig backed oars and then turned sharply to port in order to pass between two lighters plying out from the harbor. "Bloody idiots," Williams shouted.

"Mind your language," Charles said sharply, but a glance sideways told him that Penny did not seem particularly offended. If she had sailed all the way from England, he thought, she'd certainly heard worse.

"Admiral Nelson?" he said. "What does Hamilton's wife know of Nelson?"

Penny smiled as if remembering a humorous story. "Not three days past, your Horatio Nelson brought his—what do you call them—all his naval craft?"

"His fleet?"

"Yes." She nodded. "He came with all his fleet and waited outside the harbor. It was an impressive sight, if I do say so."

"Nelson's fleet came here? To Naples? You're sure?"

"Oh, no," Penny answered, sensing Charles's interest, "they stayed just outside. He sent two of his sailormen into the city to call on William Hamilton."

"His sailormen?" Getting the information he wanted from her, Charles decided, was a little like walking through a bog.

"Yes, two," she said. "I spoke with them. Let me see, Thomas Troubridge and Thomas Hardey. They were helpful to me and very polite. They carried me out in their boat to visit your Nelson."

Troubridge, Charles knew well, was the very senior captain of *Culloden* and assigned to the Mediterranean fleet. Commander Hardey, of the brig *Mutine*, also served at Admiral St. Vincent's pleasure. It seemed likely that they were part of the reinforcements he had sent to assist Nelson. "So you spoke with Admiral Nelson," Charles said, a sense of unreality drifting over him.

"Oh, yes. I asked if he knew of thy whereabouts and related that thou spoke fondly of him. Thou didst not tell me that he had but one arm."

"That only happened this past year," Charles said, "at Tenerife, I think." He looked at her directly. "Penny, did he say anything about me or the *Louisa*?"

She nodded significantly. "Yes, he did. I told him I was thy wife, of course, and he congratulated me warmly. He said that thou wert a fortunate man." She smiled at this.

"Yes, I am," Charles said. "Think closely, did he say anything about me and *Louisa,* about our duty?"

"He did, possibly," she answered doubtfully. "But I should not say."

"Tell me anyway."

"Exactly?"

"Word by word."

She blushed a pale pink. "He said, 'Where in damnation is he?' "

"I see," Charles said. "Did he say where he was going with his fleet?"

"No. Is it important?"

"I have been searching for him," Charles said flatly. "I would like to know where in . . . heavens . . . he is."

"I am sorry, I did not think to ask."

Charles smiled. "That's all right," he said. "Tell me, what is your opinion of our Horatio Nelson?"

She looked seriously ahead. "I can see why thou thinks him a great man. He is very gracious and of considerable charm."

Charles nodded in agreement.

"But in some ways he is like a child in his emotions. I believe him to be very lonely."

SIR WILLIAM HAMILTON received them in the library of his villa, a comfortable book-lined room with numerous curios and statuettes here and there, and an excellent view looking out on Mount Vesuvius. The diplomat was a slender man of medium height with a high forehead and a polished manner that quickly put Charles at ease.

"So you have discovered your husband at last," Hamilton said to Penny. To Charles, he half bowed. "Captain Edgemont, I am honored to make your acquaintance. Mrs. Edgemont has spoken of you at length, and of course, I have read of your exploits at the Battle of Cape St. Vincent. There was also an affair with a Spanish frigate, was there not?"

"Your servant, sir," Charles answered, bowing in his turn. "Thus far I have been fortunate in war."

"And in love, I should say," Hamilton added with a wink to Penny. "I have ordered tea, won't you please sit."

"William Hamilton," Penny said directly, "I will leave thee to speak in confidence with my husband. I must find Molly Bridges and see to the transfer of our luggage."

"Certainly, my dear," Hamilton said. When she had left the room, he turned to Charles. "I do love Quakers, don't you? Your wife and I have had the most delightful disagreements. There's no artifice with them; one always knows where one stands."

"Yes," Charles said, finding no argument there.

The tea arrived in an elaborate silver service and was poured out by a smartly liveried butler. "Now, how may I be of assistance to you?" Hamilton said, leaning back in his chair.

"There are three things, Sir William," Charles said. "The first is, would it be possible to provide for the resupply of my two ships? The brig *Pylades* is also in my company."

"That can be arranged. Admiral Nelson forwarded a similar request on behalf of the crown when he visited these three days past. It has been approved by the government of His Majesty, King Ferdinand. If you would prepare a listing of your requirements, I will see if it can be done tomorrow."

"Thank you, I have it here, sir." Charles removed a folded paper from his coat pocket and passed it across. "Secondly, *Pylades* has lost her mizzenmast in an action off Genoa and is sorely in need of a replacement. Do you think we might obtain suitable mast sections in the port?"

Hamilton frowned. "It may be possible. I shall have to make inquiries. You must understand that the situation is delicate and the court is extremely wary of offending the French, as well they should be. The double kingdom cannot be seen to be of too much assistance to the enemies of the republic. Still, Nelson's appearance with a powerful squadron may have bolstered their courage somewhat. I should know one way or the other by tomorrow."

"Any assistance you may render would be greatly appreciated."

"Rest assured I will do my utmost," Hamilton answered, "but I am not certain as to the outcome."

"My third point you may have anticipated," Charles said, moving to his central concern. "Do you know where I can rendezvous with Admiral Nelson's squadron?"

Hamilton smiled. "I understand that he is quite vexed about the absence of his frigates."

"But he was reinforced," Charles said.

"With seventy-fours, and I believe a fifty and a brig only. He has no frigates and, I am told, sorely feels their want." Sir William leaned forward and steepled his fingers. "I have only the slightest notion of Nelson's intentions. I don't believe that he knew them himself when he departed Naples. Let me tell you what I do know so that you may draw your own conclusions."

Charles nodded.

"The French, as you are no doubt aware, have swept the field in northern Italy. The Kingdom of the Two Sicilies is practically the only outpost on the peninsula that has not fallen under their sway. The commander of the Republic's Army of Italy is a very young Corsican, Brigadier Napoleone Buonaparte, a protégé of the powerful deputy Paul Barres in Paris."

The name Buonaparte sparked a chord in Charles's memory. Barres he had never heard of. "Yes?" he said, wondering what all of this had to do with Nelson's whereabouts.

"Point is," Hamilton said, perhaps sensing Charles's impatience, "Italy is now subdued, at least all of it that France has any interest in, and Austria is driven from the war. This young Corsican is said to be brilliant, ruthless, and, most important, highly ambitious. I have heard from several usually reliable sources that he has regrouped the Army of Italy; loaded them on transports in Toulon, Genoa, and other ports; and sailed with such French warships as were available for protection. The assembled flotilla includes fully thirteen ships of the line, including the hundred-and-twenty-four-gun *L'Orient,* a number of frigates, and some two hundred and eighty transports. The army on board is said to number in excess of fifty thousand men."

At last, Charles thought, he was coming to the point. This was obviously the expeditionary force that the American at Cádiz had been so exercised about. "What is their destination?" he asked.

"If I knew that, I would know everything," Hamilton answered. "It is the same question your admiral asked. It is the question everyone asks. I don't know their objective and can only speculate. I have heard that the fleet stopped to collect additional resources along the eastern coast of Corsica and has been seen sailing south to the east of Sardinia. I relayed all this to Nelson."

Charles thought this not very helpful information. From the southeastern tip of Sardinia, the French could have sailed anywhere. He opened his mouth to speak, but Hamilton raised his hand.

"I received an additional item of intelligence only this morning. Malta has fallen to the French on the twelfth of June, nine days ago. The island is certainly not their final objective. One doesn't need fifty thousand men to reduce the defenses there."

"And your speculation as to French intentions?"

"The obvious choices are Sicily itself, or the eastern Mediterranean: Crete, Egypt, or the Levant. If I were a betting man, I would put my gold on Egypt."

Charles thought this fanciful. "Why would anyone, the French especially, want to strike at Egypt?"

"Why indeed?" Hamilton said, raising his eyebrows. "Except to use it as a stepping-stone to deprive England of her most prestigious and lucrative possession: India. Without the riches of India, His Majesty would be hard-pressed to prosecute the war."

Charles chewed on this for a moment. "I see," he said doubtfully. "You think Nelson may have sailed for Alexandria?"

"Nelson sailed three days ago without knowledge of the capture of Malta. His course was southward, through the Strait of Messina. If he learns of Malta's fall, which he must, he may well come to the same conclusion."

"Thank you, sir," Charles said.

"Our business is concluded, then?" It was a statement as much as a question.

Charles nodded his assent.

"Good. Shall we rejoin the ladies?" Hamilton picked up a small silver bell from the table beside his chair and rang it once. The butler who had served their tea appeared from a side door. Sir William spoke to him in

Italian, of which the only words Charles caught were "Signora Hamilton." The butler nodded and departed as silently as he had entered. Sir William pushed himself up from his chair. "This way," he said.

Charles followed into a spacious drawing room tastefully furnished with chairs, tables, and divans along the walls. An empty gilt picture frame, fully six feet tall, leaned in one corner as if it were a prop. Near the center of the room sat Penny, Molly, and a not quite young but arrestingly attractive woman whom he took to be Lady Hamilton.

She had fine pale skin, rich auburn curls that fell about her shoulders and breasts, a perfectly oval face, and large, round, almost violet eyes. The fact that she wore such a low-cut dress and had such an ample bosom made it hard for him to pull his eyes away. The fact that Penny immediately rose and moved to stand beside him helped.

"This is my husband, Charles Edgemont," Penny said, introducing him. "And this is Emma Hamilton, who has been so kind as to shelter Molly and me since we arrived."

"Your servant, ma'am," Charles said, extending a leg and bowing deeply. "I am in your debt."

"Captain Edgemont," Mrs. Hamilton said in a softly modulated voice, "I am so pleased to meet you in person. Your adorable wife has told me much about you. How fortunate she is."

Charles could just hear the remnants of a rural Cheshire accent in her voice, heavily overlaid with the more genteel tones of London society. If she had been a kept woman, as Penny had implied, she had probably been highly sought after and extremely expensive. That she was married to a man as accomplished and highly placed as Sir William, although he was at least thirty years her senior, spoke of her ambitions and abilities. "You are much too kind, Lady Hamilton," he answered, conscious that his wife had taken his arm firmly in her own.

Mrs. Hamilton rose from her chair, and Charles noted that she was full-figured. "Voluptuous" was the word he wanted, like a Dutch painting he had once seen. She moved gracefully, with a kind of mesmerizing quality, and he could easily understand how she would turn any man's head. "I have heard," she said, her deep eyes focused fully upon him, "that you are the hero of the Battle of St. Vincent, the veritable savior of England. You must tell us about your exploits in arms."

Charles felt greatly flattered.

"We would be pleased at another time, I am sure," Penny said hurriedly. "My husband would not be so rude, but I know that he has responsibilities on board his craft that require his urgent attention."

"What responsibilities?" Charles asked.

Penny rolled her eyes in exasperation. "Surely thou hast not forgotten," she said, squeezing his arm.

"Oh, yes," he said. A vivid memory of himself and Penny in his cabin at the moment Attwater had burst in went through his mind. "I do have duties, urgent duties, that absolutely require my personal attention," he said seriously, almost gravely. "I am afraid that we must return as quickly as possible."

"I understand," Lady Hamilton said with a disappointed look. "Perhaps another time, then."

"Yes," Penny said. "Another time. I thank thee again for thy hospitality. Thou hast been most generous."

Sir William provided a carriage and matched grays to carry them to the waterfront. The women's trunks were secured to the back. Charles, Penny, and Molly Bridges stepped inside and seated themselves. The footman mounted, the driver cracked his whip, and they started off.

"Ain't I glad to be out of there," Molly said suddenly as the landau rattled along. It was the first time she had spoken.

"Why is that?" Charles asked.

"Didn't that old man not half chase me from room to room every chance he got."

"Really," he said with a grin. "Did he catch you?"

"No," Molly said primly. "I ain't in that line anymore."

Charles took a moment to appraise the young woman. Molly was barely recognizable as the optimistic and highly imaginative bumboat trollop who had visited *Louisa* with the other "wives and sweethearts" in Portsmouth harbor the year before. She was still the pretty, dark-haired woman with the freckled face and lively eyes that he remembered, but her expression had a serious, determined aspect he hadn't seen before. For some reason he could not fathom, Penny had taken sympathy on the girl and insisted he give her honest employment on his estate. Bevan, he thought, also held some affection for her, but Charles couldn't imagine them having a deeper relationship. She sat demurely facing him, dressed conservatively and rather attractively, he thought, in a plain gray dress that covered her from her neck down to her shoes. He wondered for a moment about his wife and the odd things that were important to her. Glancing sideways, he saw Penny sitting comfortably beside him, her arm linked in his, staring straight ahead. "A penny for your thoughts," he said.

A smile flashed across her face. "A Penny for my thoughts? I'd be paying with myself." She snuggled closer.

"Still," Charles persisted.

"I was thinking about Molly," she said, looking across at her companion, "and how far we've both come."

"Penny—Missus Edgemont," Molly said, "has been teaching me my sums." There was a touch of pride in her voice. "She helps with my letters also."

"She's teaching you to read?" Charles said.

"Well, yes. That, too, but she helps me with my letters to Daniel."

"Oh," Charles said. He'd had no inkling that Molly and Bevan were communicating.

The carriage halted on the strand where his boat was tied up, its crew lounging nearby. Hamilton's footman opened the door, and Charles, Penny, and Molly stepped down. The trunks were lashed in the gig's bow while Charles and his companions crowded the stern.

"Push off," Williams commanded.

Charles turned his mind to his "urgent duty." Arranging for it would be complicated.

"Stephen," he said the moment he gained *Louisa*'s deck, "do you have the watch?"

"Yes."

"I do not wish to be disturbed for the next hour or so for any but the most pressing of reasons. Can you see to that?"

"Of course." Winchester grinned, then, as Penny was being hoisted over the rail, he assumed a serious expression and said, "Aye-aye, sir."

"Good," Charles said, then yelled, "Mr. Beechum."

"Yes, sir?" the midshipman said, arriving at a run.

"You will go down into the gig and escort Miss Bridges over to *Pylades*. She is to deliver an invitation to Commander Bevan to dine on board this evening. You may leave her there if she pleases; Bevan will bring her back." That, Charles thought, should occupy Molly for a suitable amount of time.

"Yes, sir," Beechum answered, and started over the side.

"Come," Charles said to Penny, risen from the chair and smoothing out her dress. "If we're lucky, we can claim some time for ourselves. The luggage will find its way on board presently."

She looked at him speculatively, nodded, and followed toward his cabin.

"Attwater!" Charles called as soon as they were inside and the door behind them had closed.

"Sir," the steward answered, sticking his head out from Charles's sleeping cabin. "I was just making up your new cot."

"Is it all done?"

"Yes, sir. It's as good as new."

Charles wanted to say "It is new," but it would take too much time. "Mrs. Edgemont and I will be entertaining Lieutenant Winchester, Commander Bevan, and Miss Bridges at supper this evening. As soon as the gig returns, I want you to go into the town to purchase provisions, especially fresh meat and fresh vegetables, and anything else you think we might need. Feel free to take your time, and make a thorough job of it." He opened a drawer in his desk, took up his purse, and removed a number of coins. "Beechum has taken the gig to *Pylades*. He'll be back in the blink of an eye. You may wait on deck." Pressing the money into Attwater's palm, he practically pushed him out of the cabin.

Then Charles turned and leaned against the closed door. Penny, he saw, had removed her bonnet, and her hair fell in silken waves around her shoulders. His heart began to hammer in his breast. She watched him with a small smile on her lips and a glow in her eyes. "There," he said, "that should serve." He crossed and took her in his arms.

"Thou art certain?" she said softly, her finger pulling at his collar, her lips moistening the flesh on his neck.

"Just one minute," Charles said, abruptly releasing her. He opened the cabin door and addressed the marine sentry standing outside. "No one, I repeat, no one, is to pass through this door until I tell you otherwise," he said in his sternest voice. "Send them to Lieutenant Winchester."

"Yes, sir," the startled marine said, "but what if the harbor is attacked?"

"Oh, all right. If the harbor is attacked or if the ship is sinking. But that's it."

"Not for fire, sir, or mutiny, sir?"

Charles regretted that he was not at that moment armed. "For a fire, you may knock softly," he said, "but the mutineers will have to work it out for themselves." He firmly closed the door.

ATTWATER RETURNED IN the late afternoon, just at the beginning of the first dog watch. Charles had the pleasure of listening through the thin bulkhead as his steward argued loudly with the sentry about whether or not, and why or why not, he shouldn't be allowed in the cabin. Penny lay next to Charles, her flesh warm against his side. He didn't know if she was asleep or simply enjoying the comfort of the moment. With a sigh, he pushed himself up onto his elbow and kissed her forehead. Her eyes flickered open and she smiled.

"Only the wicked may lie abed in the afternoon," he said, sitting upright.

"I know," she answered, and pulled the sheet up over her shoulders.

Charles rose and pulled on his clothing piece by piece as he found it scattered in the corners of the small room. He went out through the main cabin and opened the door. "It's all right, Mr. Attwater may enter," he said to the sentry. "Everything is back to normal."

"Which I ain't never," Attwater began, clearly agitated. "Didn't I not spend near 'alf the day bitterly 'aggling with Eyetalianos which was trying to steal you blind?" he remonstrated. "And strike me dead if I don't spend the other 'alf fixing your cabin special for your missus. This is all the thanks I get? Being barred from my own domain? And I've still the ladies' chests to deal with, 'aven't I."

"Did you find any good wines?" Charles asked.

Attwater's expression brightened. "Oh, yes, sir," he answered. "Both reds and whites and pinks. Six cases. They're all good. Didn't I sample them."

"A man couldn't ask for a better steward," Charles said. "Now, Mrs.

Edgemont is lying down for a rest. If you would be so kind as to see that it's quiet, and keep well away from the sleeping cabin."

"Of course, sir," Attwater said with a knowing wink, "if you had only told me."

Charles pulled on his undress uniform coat and went on deck to find Winchester and make sure that the ship hadn't caught fire and there was no mutiny. "Anything happen while I was below?" he asked.

"All's well," Winchester answered, then nodded forward. Charles made out the form of Lieutenant Jacob Talmage standing stiffly on the larboard side of the forecastle, looking out over the harbor.

Charles said, "We are having a special supper tonight in my cabin. Daniel is coming, I was hoping you would grace us with your presence."

"Honored," Winchester said.

"Do you think I should invite Talmage?"

Winchester shook his head. "I would not advise it," he said. "I spoke with him this morning, and he asked me to relay a message. This is the first opportunity I've had."

"Yes?"

"He knows that we are trailing Nelson and asks that when we find him, if you would arrange his transfer to one of the other ships."

"He probably doesn't have the seniority to be first on one of the seventy-fours," Charles said.

"I don't think that matters anymore. I do think it would be for the best."

"Nelson might send someone in exchange who is senior to you. I'm more than content with you as my first."

"Thank you, but that prospect doesn't trouble me."

"All right," Charles said, "tell Mr. Talmage that I will be pleased to recommend him for transfer at the earliest suitable opportunity."

"Without prejudice?" Winchester asked.

"All right, without prejudice," Charles answered reluctantly.

DANIEL BEVAN AND Molly Bridges were rowed over from *Pylades* with the fading light of the day. Charles went to the side to greet his friend as he climbed aboard.

"Welcome," he said. "How has your day been?"

"I don't know, Charlie," Bevan answered. "It could be worse, I suppose."

Charles had expected a warmer response, especially as he had sent Molly over for what must have been a surprise visit. Bevan, he thought, looked grave. The two men stood silently as Molly was hoisted aboard. No one spoke as they started aft toward the quarterdeck. Charles noted that Molly seemed not to have a hair out of place. He assumed that their reunion had not been one of rapturous bliss.

Penny stood at the head of the ladderway to the quarterdeck and greeted Bevan warmly but sympathetically, barely glancing at Molly. She knew something, Charles decided. What?

The two couples drifted toward the starboard rail, where a large gold-red sun slowly dipped into the Tyrrhenian Sea, lighting the underside of the few clouds a radiant orange. Penny stood close beside Charles, her arm in his. Bevan and Molly also stood together, leaning against the rail, closely but not close enough to touch.

As the last of the sun slipped below the sea's surface and the scattered lights of Naples began to shimmer across the ink-blue water of the harbor, Charles suggested they go below and nodded to Winchester near the binnacle to follow.

Attwater had laid a full table in Charles's cabin, and several of the ship's boys were shuttling back and forth between the pantry and the sideboard and the table. The two women were helped into chairs, and the three men seated themselves. The tension between Bevan and Molly seemed to fill the low-ceilinged room.

"A toast," Charles said, raising a glass of Attwater's pink wine, "to unexpected gifts."

"That's enigmatic," Bevan said, but smiling for the first time.

"I refer," Charles said, "to the arrival of Penny and Molly, and Ellie's greater gift to Winchester."

"I am in full accord with the first," Bevan said. "What did Stephen receive?"

"Siredom," Charles answered. "A man's greatest achievement."

Bevan broke into a wide smile. "Congratulations, Stephen," he said. "What name?"

With at least some of the ice broken, the supper became more convivial. Charles cast occasional glances at Molly, who spoke infrequently. She attended to that which went on around her, occasionally smiling weakly, but ate little and did not touch her drink. She did not speak to Bevan at all, although she frequently glanced in his direction. Charles slowly settled on the speculation that Molly had insisted she had moved beyond her past and Bevan had found himself caught between affection for her and the understandable belief that people would always be who they had been. Charles himself was perplexed.

The courses came and went, the men's glasses were refilled, conversation lapsed and started with comfortable silences in between. Charles watched and contemplated.

"Thou art fallen silent," Penny said after a time, laying her hand over his.

"Content," Charles said, "and curious."

"About Molly?"

Charles nodded. "And Bevan," he said.

Penny put her mouth close to his ear. "Molly is at a turning place," she whispered.

As the last of the plates were cleared away, Penny announced that she and Molly had brought gifts from Cheshire. Charles stared as his wife nodded to Attwater. The steward brought forth a medium-sized box and placed it before Charles. Opening it, he found a dozen jars of preserved fruit jams, neatly labeled as apple, blackberry, quince, and cherry.

"I made them myself for my love," Penny said happily, "so that he will not forget me."

"I could never forget you," Charles said, and kissed her cheek. "And now especially not at breakfast."

A large envelope was brought out for Winchester, with three smaller envelopes inside. One was a letter from Ellie; the other two contained locks of hair—one rich and auburn, the other short, thin, and blond. Charles saw the normally reserved Winchester swallow hard as he rubbed the strands between his fingers.

Everyone seemed content and took a moment to examine the gifts. Charles noticed Molly nibbling anxiously at her lip.

"There is more," Penny said. "They are from Molly, by her own hand." She gestured to her companion to deliver the gifts herself. Molly rose reluctantly, avoiding everyone's eyes. She went over to her chest and came back with three neatly wrapped page-sized squares. The first she laid on the table in front of Stephen Winchester.

"What's this?" Winchester said as he carefully removed the wrapping and held in his hands an intricately executed pen-and-ink rendering of a woman holding an infant against her breast. Charles leaned across Penny to look more closely. "My God," he said. The woman was instantly recognizable as his sister Ellie, Winchester's wife, wearing an expression of quiet maternal affection. Charles thought it possibly the most touching thing he had ever seen.

"Thank you," Winchester said, his voice gone hoarse. "It's beautiful, truly beautiful."

With more confidence, Molly placed the second in front of Charles. He unpeeled the wrapping and looked on the face of his wife, from the shoulders up. She wore a particular smile, and her eyes seemed to look into his own. It took his breath away. "I don't know what to say," he said.

"Didn't Penny go on about having to sit all that time then," Molly said, a true smile on her face, the first Charles could remember since she'd come on board. The smile vanished as she fingered the third and final square. Hesitantly, she lay it on the table in front of Daniel Bevan. Then she sat and watched his face.

Bevan picked up the package by its edges as if it might bite him. He glanced for an instant at Molly, then carefully folded back the covering. The drawing was of Molly herself, seated in front of an easel, her pen raised. She wore a tasteful and modest dress and an expression of serenity and concentration. It was a perfect representation, Charles thought, of Molly as she had become, without the road she had trod to get there.

Bevan sat stone-faced, staring at the likeness. "I never knew," he said seriously. Looking up at her, he repeated, "I didn't know."

"Do you like it?" Molly asked in a voice barely above a whisper.

"Yes. Very much." A strained silence followed.

"Tell us, Molly," Charles said, breaking the quiet, "how you found this talent."

"Ain't I pleased to." Molly smiled, as if grateful for the interruption. "I never had a paper or a pen before, so I didn't know, either. But don't

Penny practice with me on my sums and such. One day I was distracted, like, and began to scribble on the back of an old page a likeness of herself with my pencil. Well, she took it, and looked at it careful, and said it weren't awful."

"I did not," Penny protested.

Molly laughed. "You as good as did," she said. "The next day, didn't you take me into Chester to buy some fresh paper and special pens and ink. She looks over everything I did."

"Tell them about the book," Penny said.

Molly looked almost shy again. "One day she comes to me with a book, a big book what she ordered from a shop. We read it together every day. There are examples for me to copy out and exercises to do, and she judges them."

"I confess myself amazed," Charles said. "I've never known anyone with such an ability." He looked back down at his picture of Penny, noting the details around the corners of her mouth and eyes, the fine line of her nose.

"And didn't she make me promise to do one of each of you before we go," Molly answered with a grin. "Won't you hate sitting still for it."

Charles heard the ship's bell on the deck above their heads ring. He counted the strokes up to seven. The clock by his desk, which was not especially accurate, read eleven-fifteen. Either way, it was rapidly crowding on midnight. "Stephen," he said, "if you would toast the king."

Soon the room cleared, Winchester to his own cabin, where he would sleep for four hours until he stood the morning watch. Penny and Molly disappeared into Charles's sleeping cabin, and Charles accompanied Bevan outside to see him off.

"I gather things are not going all that well," Charles said. He did not have to explain what he was referring to.

"Jesus, Charlie," Bevan said, clutching his drawing. "I don't know what to think. She's a changed woman. We talked and talked this afternoon. She has some notion about herself and won't budge from it. She's pretty clear on the subject."

"Women's motivations are frequently obscure," Charles observed. He could feel his friend's frustration.

After a silence, Bevan said, "I just want things to be the way they were."

"Do you?"

"I don't know, Charlie. Honest to God, I don't know."

"She's soft on you," Charles said, "although I can't imagine why. You'll have to make up your mind—meet her terms, or cut her adrift."

"I know." Just before he stepped through the entryport, Bevan said, "You see, it's not Molly. She's fine. It's me."

Charles reentered his cabin expecting to find Molly in Penny's arms sobbing her heart out. Instead, she sat dry-eyed and tight-lipped on the storage bench beneath the stern windows.

"How are you, Molly?" he asked carefully.

She looked up at him and suppressed a sniffle. "I'm all right, thank you, sir," she said. "Ain't I been through harder times."

Penny came out from the sleeping cabin wearing a robe over an ankle-length sleeping gown. "I've sent Attwater to his bed," she announced. "He was unhappy about it."

"He'll recover," Charles said.

"Where will Molly sleep?"

Charles pulled at the lobe of his ear. He hadn't thought of this. He racked his brain and could think of nowhere on the crowded little ship where a young single woman, or any woman, for that matter, could rest in peace and safety. If only Bevan would have been a little more flexible, all this could have been avoided.

"Hell's bells," he said as he collected his hat, exited the cabin, and made his way down to the dimly lit area belowdecks. He went aft to the wardroom and rapped loudly on the door to the purser's cabin. After a moment, and some unnecessarily foul language from the other side, the door swung open to a figure in a nightshirt and sleeping cap with a lit candle in its holder. "I need a hammock, Mr. Black, to hang in my cabin," Charles said.

Early the next morning, a note arrived from Sir William Hamilton, informing Charles that supplies for *Louisa* and *Pylades* had been arranged and would be delivered in the middle of the morning. The note emphasized the desirability of completing the reprovisioning as expeditiously as possible. Mast sections for *Pylades* would be available from King Ferdinand's naval dockyard in the evening after dark. Regrettably, the dockyard facilities would not be available to assist in the stepping of the masts. It was further directed that this activity be performed outside the territorial waters of the Kingdom of the Two Sicilies. It was evident that the nervous kingdom wanted any British warships to remove themselves at the soonest opportunity so as not to arouse the ire of the French.

Charles took his breakfast alone in his cabin, served by a disgruntled Timothy Attwater, who grumbled more or less without pause about the increasingly constricted and crowded space and the inconveniences it caused him. Molly awoke before Penny and, after making Charles promise to avert his eyes, climbed down from her hammock and stumbled in her nightdress into his sleeping cabin. Charles fled to the quarterdeck, where he sent Beechum across to inform Bevan of Sir William's message.

At two bells in the forenoon watch, a waterhoy came alongside and began the long arduous process of shifting the ship's water casks and refilling them. The task of restoring the lot in the hold fell under the careful eye of Eliot, who as master was responsible for *Louisa's* trim.

As the hoy cast off, a second lighter, containing livestock, took her place. Bellowing and squealing loudly, a quantity of bullocks, swine, and sheep were persuaded into slings and hoisted inboard. The half-dozen cattle were immediately dispatched by the assistant to the cook who doubled as the ship's butcher. The beef had to be cut into eight-pound chunks, salted, and stored in barrels that also went into the hold. The pigs and sheep were, for the time being, penned on the forecastle. Quantities of flour, lemons, raisins, fresh and dried vegetables, and fowl arrived in smaller vessels and were stored below, or in coops forward. Finally came a small mountain of firewood, to be similarly swayed across and tucked away.

Charles spent almost the entire day occupied with the loading and storage, and passing small gratuities to the Neapolitan lighters' commanders to speed the work along. He took a hurried dinner with his wife and Molly in the cabin at noon and spoke occasionally with Penny when she came onto the quarterdeck. On one occasion, she asked if it was normal for him to attend to so much of the work himself.

"Not usually," Charles replied. "We are short of officers just at the moment."

"I thought thou had two assistants," she said. "I see only Stephen Winchester."

"Lieutenant Talmage is indisposed," he said sourly. "I expect to barter him for someone else as soon as the opportunity presents itself."

"Indisposed how?" she asked with some concern. "Is he ill?"

Charles did not want to dwell on his difficulties with Talmage. "Not ill. Unhappy. In particular, he is unhappy with me." Then he changed the subject.

Molly, he noted, spent her time in one corner of the quarterdeck, well out of everyone's way, with a paper and pencil making small sketches of what was going on around her. In the evening, near dusk, he sent *Louisa*'s cutter to *Pylades* so that both ship's boats could go into the dockyard to tow back Bevan's mast sections.

Everything reasonably complete to his satisfaction, Charles convinced his wife to join him in an early supper and an early bed. A time later, he fell into the sleep of the worn but content.

FIVE

"THE STARBOARD BOWER'S VEERED OUT, SIR," MIDSHIP-man Beechum reported. *Louisa* had dropped anchor in the lee of Capri Island, two cable lengths away.

"Very good," Charles said, "let go the larboard bower." He watched as the heavy cable ran out through the hawsehole, and heard the splash as the port side bow anchor met the water's surface on its path to the seafloor, five fathoms below.

"Bower's down, sir."

"Play out the port cable," Charles said. "Heave in the starboard." Slowly, the ship warped back toward her starboard anchor as the men in the waist strained against the capstan bars. One started up a verse from "Nancy Dawson," and soon the others joined in:

> *O Nancy Dawson. Hio!*
> *Cheerily man;*
> *She's got a notion. Hio!*
> *Cheerily man;*
> *For our old boatswain. Hio!*

The shanty lent rhythm to the work and helped it along. The capstan went round and round, the dripping cable rubbing its way in through the hawsehole.

O Betsy Baker. Hio!
Cheerily man;
Lived in Long Acre. Hio!

With Penny possibly awake by now, and within easy hearing in his cabin, Charles sent Sykes to speak with the men about skipping some of the more colorful verses.

When he judged *Louisa* to have reached the midpoint between the two anchors, Charles ordered, "Avast heaving. Pawl the capstan, and belay." With the cable secured, they were moored firmly against the breeze and current in the shallow water.

"You may signal *Pylades* to come alongside," he said to Beechum.

The two ships had pulled their anchors from the bottom of Naples harbor at the first hint of light, then sailed the twenty-odd miles due south to their present location. Capri was a pretty little island when you looked at it, Charles thought, with its green hills surrounded by crystal-blue waters. He would have to point it out to Penny when she came on deck. Bevan's ship acknowledged *Louisa*'s signal. As Charles watched, her yards braced around, and she began to approach. Soon *Pylades* glided toward them, her bow angling along *Louisa*'s side. When the ships were beam to beam, twenty yards apart, she took in the last of her sails.

"Pass the cables across, fore and aft," Charles ordered. "Warp her in and lash her tight."

"Aye-aye, sir," Beechum responded, his face a mask of concentration as he called out the instructions. Winchester stood next to Charles, watching carefully how the midshipman carried out his responsibilities.

"Do you think he'll do, Stephen?" Charles asked in a low voice as Beechum went forward to see to the tasks he was supervising.

"He'll do," the lieutenant said with a frown. "He's as green as mold, but willing." Charles remembered provisionally promoting Winchester from midshipman to acting lieutenant at the Battle of Cape St. Vincent after all of the commission officers on board except Bevan and him had been killed. Later, he had been able to prevail upon Admiral Jervis to make the promotion permanent.

"I recall another midshipman on *Argonaut*," Charles said. "Barely knew a capstan from a cathead, but also willing." Winchester laughed.

Owing to Lieutenant Talmage's continuing absence on deck, Charles was considering formally appointing Beechum to Winchester's previous position as second lieutenant.

"Good morning, Captain Bevan," Charles said, turning to the familiar figure of his friend climbing over *Louisa*'s side direct from *Pylades*'s deck. "I'm surprised to see you up so early. It's usually not until the afternoon watch, isn't it?"

"Morning, Stephen. Good morning, Charlie. It's a good thing for you they don't make captains based on their fine looks," Bevan retorted. "Speaking of agreeable looks, how is Missus Edgemont?"

"Haven't seen Penny yet. I assume she's about, though."

"All secure fore and aft, sir. Good morning, Captain Bevan," Beechum said, returning to the quarterdeck.

Charles saw the three new mizzenmast sections laid out midships on *Pylades*'s deck. Davey Howell and the brig's carpenter, whose name Charles couldn't remember, were measuring it with their rules to see if any modifications might be necessary. He assumed the carpenters' mates from both ships were belowdecks, knocking out the wedges where the heel of the old mast rested on the kelston.

"Find Keswick and have him rig a threefold block and tackle from the mainmast yardarm," Charles said. "We'll draw the stump." He stood easily with Bevan and Winchester, watching as the work progressed, with little for him to do. The carpenters and boatswains and their mates lifted the remains of the old mast, hoisted the new lower section, and carefully lowered it down through the partners until its heel rested on the step, the wooden block to receive it, which was bolted to the keel.

Charles could hear the *thump-thump* as the shims and wedges holding the foot of the mast in place were banged tight with mallets. In time the tackle was withdrawn, and the boatswains shifted their attention to fashioning the standing rigging while the carpenters prepared the platform for the tops. By midmorning, the runner pendants with their thimble-spliced eyes had been sliced in the middle and then cut-spliced back together to form the collar, the whole wormed, parceled, liberally covered in pitch, and served in order to keep the water out and the rope yarn from rotting. They had already been fit over the masthead bolster, and the end of the girt line was being made fast around the pendants.

He saw Penny in a fresh gray dress and bonnet, coming toward them, threading carefully among the seamen passing back and forth, and daintily stepping over the cables and lines laid out for *Pylades*'s rigging.

"What art thou attempting?" she asked, arriving at the rail and looking down at the activity on the brig's deck.

"We're giving Bevan a new mast," Charles said happily. "He broke the old one."

She looked to Bevan. "How camest thou to do such a thing?"

Bevan, aware of Penny's views toward warfare, answered, "Carelessness on my part. We couldn't move fast enough."

She watched the bustle of activity, uncomprehending. "Wouldst thou please explain?" she asked. "What art they doing?"

Charles made an effort. "Well," he said, "right now they're preparing for the shrouds to be warped from the hounds of the mast to the channels on the sides of the ship. The deadeyes will be turned in with a left-handed thread seizing, properly whipped and capped. They'll be made taut by the throat seizings, and attached to the turnbuckles on the mizzen chains. The ratlines will be seized horizontally across the shrouds with clove hitches in between and eyes spliced at the ends. That will make the ladderway for the topmen to climb up and down the mast."

He stopped when he saw that she was more bewildered than when he had begun. After a moment she made a face. "Deadeyes, throat seizings, ratlines," she said. "What horrid names thou hast chosen for the parts of thy ship."

"I didn't name them," Charles said defensively.

After a time he led her away, leaving Bevan and Winchester to oversee the work. They found Molly on the quarterdeck, sitting on an empty keg with a flat wooden box on her lap, upon which she was making a sketch of Capri Island.

"What a beautiful place," Penny said, leaning against the railing and looking outward. "How I would love to visit one day when there is no war."

"Wouldn't you like to see, sir," Molly said, tilting the top of her case toward him.

Charles saw that she had not only created a credible likeness but had also managed to give the softly rounded hills, with the tiny fishing village nested in the cove below, a tone of serenity that he would not have observed on his own. "You have a true gift, Molly," he said.

"Thank you, sir. Ain't I done dozens."

"Molly has been practicing her sketches all the way from England," Penny said.

"May I see some of them?" Charles asked, genuinely interested.

Molly looked undecided, then undid the catches on her case. "Some ain't as fine as t'others," she said.

The lid of the box flipped open on its hinges. On top was a supply of clean white paper. This she lifted off, then handed Charles a sheaf of drawings. They were all recognizable scenes to him: sailors at work, heaving on lines or climbing the masts. There was one of several officers he didn't recognize standing and talking, another of four seamen around a barrelhead playing cards. Men at their mess, or on watch, and one of a crew serving a six-pounder cannon. Most were everyday scenes of people doing everyday work, and they showed something of the dignity of their labors. One he instantly recognized as the Rock at Gibraltar; they would have called there on their way to Naples. The next made him stop.

Staring up at him from the paper was the weathered face of his commander in chief, Admiral St. Vincent. He was shown from the breast up, hatless and in his undress uniform coat. Most surprising was that he wore a warm smile, almost to the point of humor, which crinkled the corners of his eyes.

"You met Jervis?" Charles said in astonishment. He could scarcely imagine the gruff, blunt, hard-riding admiral smiling, much less on the verge of laughter.

"Of course," Penny said, as if it were the most natural thing in the world.

"You actually met him?"

"When we were in Gibraltar. We traveled there in search of thee. I did not know that thou would be elsewhere," she explained. "I asked a seaman, by his name Collingwood, if he knew of thee. He allowed that he did and had his small boat take us out to a grand warship."

"The *Victory*?"

"That was the name of the craft, I think. It was very large."

"Was the seaman's name Cuthbert Collingwood, and did he have a lot of gold on his uniform?"

"He said his name was Captain Collingwood, of middle age. A very pleasing man. He related that he knew of thee."

"I see," Charles said.

"On this ship we were inquired as to our business. I stated that I was thy wife and that I wished to call on John Jervis, a name that I had heard from thee, and whom the seaman Collingwood said was thy superior in the navy."

"So you dropped in unannounced on Admiral the Earl of St. Vincent and paid him a call?" Charles said incredulously. "And he received you?"

"I told thee already," she said with a touch of impatience. "He received us quite promptly in his residence inside the craft. I must say, I was taken with him. He is kind and attentive, and a truly gentle man."

"Admiral St. Vincent?"

"John Jervis, yes. He allowed Molly to do her drawing. She will finish it in ink and pass it to him on our return."

"He almost remembered me," Molly interjected. "Didn't he almost."

"Oh, my," Charles said, nearly aghast, "did you—"

"No, sir, I never," she said primly. "I did try to board *Victory* once, and he saw me. Didn't it make him mad, back in the old days."

"He spoke highly of thee at dinner. He said thou wert brave and industrious," Penny said, possibly to change the subject.

"Dinner?" Charles said. He himself had never been invited to dine with the admiral.

"I told thee he was gracious. He insisted that we stay to dinner. We conversed on many subjects."

Charles had a sinking feeling. "Did you talk with him about . . . well, your feelings about the war?"

"Of course I did," she said. "It is my Christian duty to do so. I told him that all violence is against God's will. I made my testament strongly."

"Oh, good. And his response?"

"He agreed in a thoughtful and loving way."

"He did?"

"Yes. He said he also desired peace. Unfortunately, he saw no other way. I remonstrated with him, but he remained steadfast."

Charles could imagine this conversation—he had exchanged similar sentiments with her himself—but could barely imagine the admiral's not exploding in anger and clapping his wife in irons. On the other hand, Penny could be charming when she wanted to be, and say the most astonishing things in a completely disarming manner. "So he arranged transport for you and Molly to Naples?" Somehow he couldn't see old Jervie doing any such thing.

"Not exactly," Penny said with a small smile. "He maintained that it was far too dangerous for women traveling alone. In truth"—she had a thoughtful look—"he forbade our going any farther. He did offer us transport back to England."

"Then how—"

Penny waved her hand in a dismissive gesture. "I appreciated his concern for us," she said. "Molly and I went direct to the harbor and found a seaman of a smaller craft who was to call at Naples. He agreed to carry us for a price that evening."

"So you went to Naples," Charles said in some wonderment. "Why Naples?"

"No one knew where thou wert," she said. "There were no reports, but thou must have been somewhere."

Charles could not imagine the two women traveling blithely across the Mediterranean in the middle of a war on the merest supposition of where he might be. Yet she'd done it on the strength of her faith that it was what she was meant to do, and therefore it would all end agreeably.

Charles soon returned to his cabin to read the purser's report on the stores taken on at Naples. He countersigned the accounting, to show that he'd reviewed and approved it. The report from the surgeon, Matthew Lincoln, showed that there was one ordinary seaman in the sick berth with a broken bone in his foot (he'd been stepped on by one of the bullocks), and there was continued treatment for four others with hernias who had returned to light duty. Lincoln also reported that his surgical and apothecary's supplies were satisfactory. Of course, Charles already knew all these things, but he affixed his signature anyway. He was about to pick up the gunners' written report on the ship's armament when Attwater mercifully intervened. "Your dinner's ready," his steward announced.

"Bless you, Attwater," Charles said, pushing the papers back and closing his desk. "If you would pass the word for Mrs. Edgemont and Miss Bridges."

After his meal, he went on deck to stand the afternoon watch and allow Winchester to devote his attention to *Pylades*'s rapidly rising mast. The forestay and backstays had been run from the hounds down to the deck, and were moused and collared. The decked top was in its place on the upper part of the trestletrees, and the topmast section at that moment was being swayed up to be lowered through the mast cap. The topgallant mast would follow once the crosstrees and the topmast cap had been put in place. Charles judged that the tackle from *Louisa*'s mainmast yard would soon be withdrawn and the two ships could be unlashed in the morning. With both boats' crews working in shifts, sunup to sundown, the thing should be finished by the following evening.

The following morning saw the attention on *Pylades* shift to raising her yards and setting the running rigging. The lashings that bound the two ships were unwound, and the brig kedged off to drop her own bower a cable length away. Charles ordered *Louisa*'s starboard anchor payed out until the port side bower could be pulled and catted home, and the ship returned to her place, riding at a single anchor. This partly relieved his concern that they would be found in a compromised position by an enemy. He would be even more pleased when the work was completed and both ships were under way. It occurred to him, not for the first time, that their situation would be more worrisome with his wife and Molly on board.

Charles stood the forenoon watch and mostly spent the morning answering Penny's questions about progress on *Pylades,* and what this or that was for on *Louisa*. Molly attended to her sketches. She did not frequently go down into the waist, Charles noted, probably for fear that someone might remember her as one of the women of easy virtue who had come on board when *Louisa* last called at Portsmouth. Charles thought it unlikely, since she presented such a different mode of dress and seriousness of appearance. Further, he doubted that any of the then-alcohol-and-lust-fogged men would remember much of anything.

Penny brought up the subject of Charles's estates in Cheshire. "If thou art not occupied at present, I wish to discuss my proposals for thy lands," she said.

It had been Charles's hope to avoid this conversation entirely, or at least to put it off for as long as possible. He had decided it would be preferable to have his brother tell her she couldn't have her school or mill rather than having to do it himself. He managed to look regretful. "I am sorry," he said. "I would willingly do so, but since I am standing as officer of the watch, I cannot leave the quarterdeck. We'll have to discuss it another time."

"But thou art not doing anything," she said. "No one even speaks to thee."

"All the same," he answered, "the watch officer must be instantly available in the event there is an emergency. There's no hurry, we'll attend to it when I can give you my undivided attention."

As the morning wore on, Penny fell increasingly silent and seemed content to stand idly beside him at the rail. At about six bells, he noticed the lone figure of Lieutenant Talmage by the forecastle at the far end of the ship, watching the work on Bevan's brig. Charles frowned. The lieutenant's fit of pique had become more than an aggravation. He knew that he could go forward, confront Talmage, and make amends, but he was damned if he would. It had been Talmage's own inabilities and touchiness that had created the problem. Talmage could come and speak to him if he wanted to repair it. Charles was quite certain that he did not want the lieutenant back as his first.

"Is that thy absent assistant?" Penny asked, following his eyes.

"Lieutenant the Honorable Jacob Talmage," he said, "taking his leisure upon the deck."

Penny stared in Talmage's direction. "He seems very isolated," she said at length.

Charles did not answer but guessed what she was going to say next.

"Would it be agreeable if I spoke with him?"

He expelled his breath slowly. "I don't think it will help. It has become an affair of honor. He apprehends that I insulted him."

"Didst thou?"

"In a way, yes. But for cause."

"I will converse with him," she said.

Before he could decide whether he approved of this or not, she had gone down into the waist and was walking along the deck. What harm could it do? He watched as Penny moved between the cannon tethered against the bulwarks and the passing sailors who stopped to acknowledge her with a half-bow or a touch of the forehead. She responded to their greetings with a nod. He thought she looked frail, almost dainty, among the hulking weapons and rough men, two things that he knew her not to be. Even when she was aboard his own ship, he realized, he could look on her from a distance with an ache in his heart.

As she approached, Talmage turned and quickly removed his hat. Charles saw his mouth move but could not hear the words. Penny's bonnet bobbed as she stood with her hands clasped in front of her. Charles did not want to appear to be overly curious about the meeting, so he moved to the rail as if to observe the work on the brig, casting surreptitious glances in their direction. He noticed as the conversation progressed that Talmage increasingly did more of the talking, perhaps all of the talking, once gesturing with his fist. Charles had no sense that the lieutenant was threatening her, or he would have gone forward himself, but clearly, Talmage was venting his anger. Penny nodded regularly in response. After a time, Talmage's volubility seemed to slow, though one hand rested on the hilt of his sword. Charles watched as Penny spoke for a few moments, her hands moving in front of her. Then she turned and started back, a look of concern fixed on her face.

Charles met her at the head of the ladderway. "How did you get along?" he asked.

"Well enough," Penny answered, not meeting his eyes. "What thou said is true. He is angry with thee, and others."

"What did you talk about?"

"Some of it is in confidence," Penny said slowly, "but mostly about his disappointments. He feels that he has been treated unfairly."

"By me."

"By thee, but also by Stephen Winchester." A worried look came into her eyes. "I have heard that men sometimes fight with swords and pistols for these reasons."

"Yes, but not in the navy, at least not often. In any event, I would not give him the satisfaction," Charles said. "Why is he unhappy with Stephen?" As soon as he asked the question, he knew the answer.

"His reasons are not always direct," she said. "He is affronted that Stephen Winchester willingly replaced him. I think he knows that he cannot easily touch thee and has diverted his anger elsewhere. I fear that Stephen would rise to a challenge if Jacob Talmage tried him." She paused, in distress. "Stephen is my brother, in the law and in my heart. This must not occur."

"I won't permit it," Charles said, and put his hand on her arm. "I promise you, I will not permit any such thing to occur."

She looked up at him seriously. "And what would thou do were he to insult me?"

"Has he?" Charles said. He removed his hand and stood in front of her, his jaw fixed.

Penny took both his hands and held them in her own. "He has not, I assure you. But if he felt that such an artifice would succeed, he might employ it." She squeezed his hands firmly. "Thou must promise thou wouldst not rise."

Charles said nothing. He didn't know what he would do if Talmage tried to hurt her, even with words.

"Thou must promise," Penny insisted. "Thou must armor thy heart with resolve against this. I could not live with myself if my husband did violence because of me."

"All right," he said at last, although he found himself angered at the thought of it. The situation was intolerable. He sincerely hoped that they found Nelson and his squadron quickly. The sooner he was clear of Talmage, the better.

By late afternoon, the work on *Pylades* was rapidly nearing completion. The mast was up in all its sections, the yards crossed and the sails bent on. A few ship's boats continued to ply back and forth, but mostly to return *Louisa*'s crew and equipment.

Charles thought to invite Bevan on board for supper, but considering the awkward relationship between his friend and Molly, he decided it would be better to go over himself, if only to discuss what they were going to do next. Before he could act, he noticed *Pylades*'s cutter pulling across with Bevan in the stern sheets. Charles went down to the entry-port to meet him.

"All's well?" Charles said as Bevan climbed aboard.

"Good as she'll ever be, Charlie," Bevan answered. "I want to say my thanks for your help."

"You're ready to sail?"

"In an hour, to be safe."

Charles scratched his chin in contemplation. "I make it we're a full week behind Nelson's squadron," he said. "All I know is that he's sailed by way of Messina. We'll do the same and see what we can learn. If there's no news, we might look into Malta. We know the French are there; maybe Nelson is, too. Beyond that I don't know, but we'll think of something. Give me a signal when you're ready."

Bevan nodded, then hesitated. "Do you think I might have a word with Miss Bridges?"

"So it's Miss Bridges now, is it?" Charles said. "I believe you'll find her on the quarterdeck with her sketches. You know the way."

Charles stayed behind while Bevan went up onto the deck and knelt beside Molly's chair. He began talking in low tones. The girl kept her head bowed and her eyes averted. After a few moments, Bevan touched her hand and she nodded in response, looking up at him for the first time. Bevan then rose and started back toward the entryport and his boat.

"How did it go?" Charles asked, intensely curious.

Bevan started over the side toward the cutter. "Well enough," he answered, and descended.

Within the half hour, *Pylades*'s signal flags carried upward from her new mizzen halyards: She was prepared to make sail.

"We will weigh anchor, Stephen," Charles said. To Beechum, at his place by the flag locker: "Signal *Course south-by-southeast, take position to leeward,* if you please." He welcomed the regular movement of the deck beneath his feet as *Louisa* loosed her sails and glided over the easy seas, going large with a moderate westerly wind.

"THERE, LOOK AT that," Charles said, pointing over the bow quarter to the rugged lump of island on the horizon.

"What is it?" Penny asked, her hand raised to shield her eyes from the morning sun reflecting off the ripples of the sea. Since the evening before, after rounding Cape Passero on the southeastern tip of Sicily, *Louisa,* with *Pylades* following to leeward, had been beating on the larboard tack against a stiff westerly wind, making toward the southwest and the island in the distance.

"Malta," Charles said, "the home of the ancient Order of the Knights Hospitalers of Saint John of Jerusalem. They go all the way back to the Crusades."

"Is it that old?"

"The Order is," Charles said. "They were in Palestine or Syria or somewhere in the Levant at first, I think. They came here only two or three hundred years ago and built their capital at Valletta. I called there once, four years back, on the old *Argonaut.* It's fantastic, you'll see."

"How long will it be until we come to the harbor?"

"Maybe three hours. It's not so far, but the wind's foul."

Louisa and *Pylades* had passed through the Strait of Messina—between the fabled Rock of Scylla and the Whirlpool of Charybdis—early on the second morning, after *Pylades's* repairs. Pilots came aboard both ships to oversee the transit. From them Charles learned only that a large British squadron had made the passage a week before and sailed toward Syracuse or Cape Passero. Beyond that, no one knew. It was a large sea. Nor was there any word of the French fleet, although everyone had heard that Malta had fallen.

Penny and Molly had come on deck to wonder at the sight of Mount Etna, bathed in the early light and spewing smoke high into the sky. Molly, of course, made a sketch of it.

With Malta slowly growing larger in the distance, Charles ordered the hands to dinner and sat down with Molly and Penny in his cabin to eat. Afterward, he went on deck and sent Midshipman Sykes into the rigging to inquire of the lookout in the crosstrees whether he saw any sign of British warships off the island.

"Naught, sir," Sykes reported some minutes later. "He says he can see the outer roads and beyond, but no sign of the squadron. No Frenchies, either."

Charles swore under his breath. "Thank you," he said to Sykes.

Where the hell was Nelson? With the prevailing wind from the west, it was unlikely that the French and their huge convoy of unruly transports had sailed in that direction. There were no reports that Sicily itself had been invaded; he certainly would have heard. So it must be somewhere in the east: the Peloponnesos, the Sublime Porte, the Levant, Crete, Egypt, even the Crimea, to attack Russia. It was a lengthy and widely scattered list. As long as he was at Malta, however, it would be useful to look into Valletta, so he could report on the strength of the French naval forces there.

"Mr. Eliot," he said to the master, "we will stand on to have a gander into the harbor. Heave to about a mile and a half out."

"Aye-aye."

"Stephen, clear the ship for action, if you please."

"Yes, sir."

"Mr. Beechum."

"Aye, sir?"

"Signal to *Pylades, Keep station to starboard.*"

"Aye-aye, sir."

The green spot in the distance resolved into hills and headlands and bays, with the entrance to the several ports of Valletta clearly distinguishable. Penny and Molly soon arrived on the quarterdeck.

"Thy crew hast taken our chamber away," Penny said, clearly frustrated. "Even our bed is removed. There is nothing remaining."

"It will be put back just as it was," Charles said. "It's only a precaution."

"A precaution against what?"

"In case we are set upon," he said carefully. "We are a British warship in French waters. It's possible they will be offended."

"Art thou planning to shoot thy cannon at them?"

"No, no," Charles said reassuringly. "We are only going to look into the port."

"Then why should they take offense?"

Charles thought her concern touchingly naïve. But it reminded him that he needed to consider what he would do if an enemy did attack them. He had thought about it before, but with little urgency, as the threat seemed remote. He wasn't cruising in the normal way, looking for a fight or even prizes. His duty was to find Nelson; that was all. Having the women on board made it more complicated. It would be natural for him to be cautious. He would have to put his mind to it one day soon.

"Oh, they won't, in all likelihood," he said airily, as if to belay all doubts. "It's just a precaution." If a French warship did exit the harbor, they would see it in plenty of time to make their escape.

Louisa angled across the sea, closing on the port entrance. At about two miles, he could see the battlements on Point Saint Elmo, the seaward defenses for the city of Valletta. To the left lay the entrance to the Great Port, protected on the far side by a fort on Point Sollile. The land fell away from there for five or six miles to Cape Sega, where the coast angled sharply southward. To the right was the entrance to the other main harbor at Port Marsanmciet and its forts at Point Dragut and on Lazaret Island. Beyond stood a bluff headland sheltering Saint Julien Bay on the far side.

Louisa hove to across the wind, her courses taken in, and the mizzen topsail braced around and laid against the mast. She came to a rest a mile and a half from the Saint Elmo fort.

"Mr. Beechum," Charles said, "if you would be so kind as to climb to the tops with your glass and report to me what you see in the harbors."

"Yes, sir," Beechum said, touching his hat extra smartly in Penny's presence.

Charles took up his own telescope and led Penny to the rail. "Look there," he said, opening the long glass for her and helping to steady it. With his naked eye, he could clearly see the miles of towering stone battlements and the high-walled city behind. He saw that the three main forts all had the tricolor flag of the French Republic streaming from their towers.

"So many cannons," Penny said in wonderment, one eye screwed comically shut, with the lens pressed tight against the other. "Why do they require such grand defenses?"

"I think it was as a defense against the Turks, or someone," Charles said, unsure of his history. "They don't seem to have helped much against the French, though."

"Captain Edgemont, sir!" Beechum's voice came urgently down from the masthead. "There's a ship rounding the point awindward. She's French, sir."

Charles twisted around and immediately saw three masts, fully dressed in canvas, just behind the end of the point, and then the bowsprit showing clear. He judged it to be not over two miles distant.

"Mr. Eliot," he said, "put her before the wind, if you please. All plain sail. Set a course to round Cape Sega."

Eliot nodded and turned to instruct the quartermaster at the wheel.

"Stephen, beat to quarters."

Beechum arrived nearly breathless on the quarterdeck. "She's a frigate, sir. Thirty-six guns. I'm sure she's seen us."

"I'm sure she has, Mr. Beechum," Charles said. "Did you see anything of the harbor?"

"Yes, sir. Two corvettes, sixteen or eighteen guns, and a number of supply ships. Didn't have time to count."

"The corvettes, were they preparing to make sail?"

"Not that I noticed, sir," Beechum said doubtfully.

"Thank you, Mr. Beechum," Charles said. "If you would resume your duties with the forecastle guns."

"Yes, sir. Thank you, sir."

Beechum's last words were almost drowned out by the marine drummer who had hurried to his position on the forward part of the quarterdeck and loudly begun his roll.

The frigate's bow showed clear of the point almost to her midships, Charles noted, and she was turning in his direction, her masts coming into a line.

"Ain't Daniel's sails all blowed out," he heard Molly say. "Why is that?"

Louisa's sails had been braced around. Her head was just beginning to fall off to leeward. Charles looked for *Pylades* and found that she was already around, but spilling her wind to cover his stern. "I'll have none of that," he muttered under his breath. "Mr. Sykes," he called to the midshipman standing nearby.

"Sir?" Sykes answered.

"You will have to manage the signals," he said. "Run up *Set all possible sail* and *Maintain station*. Do you understand?"

"Yes, sir," the boy said. "To *Pylades,* sir?"

"*Pylades* is the only ship we can signal to, Mr. Sykes."

"Of course, sir," Sykes said, his face reddening, and disappeared.

Charles looked back at the French frigate with all plain sails set to her royals, not a mile and a half astern and closing rapidly. *Louisa* was almost around, her sails slatting and beginning to fill. Charles knew he'd been careless, badly careless. He should have positioned *Pylades* farther out so she could have seen anything approaching from the other side of the point. He'd put everybody's lives in danger.

He glanced at Penny, who still stood beside him. She met his eyes. "What art thou doing?" she said.

"We are running," Charles said. "We've overstayed our welcome and have to leave."

The courses were dropped and clewed down. They filled with loud snapping sounds. He felt the ship gain way under his feet. "Mr. Eliot, we will hoist the royals."

Charles looked again at Penny. Her eyes never left his face, her lips compressed into a bloodless line. She must be frightened near to death, he thought, with her pacifist views. "You must go below, my love," he said in a reassuring tone. "You'll be safe there."

She did not move. "Why art thou running away?" she asked.

Charles didn't understand the question or why she had asked it. His central concern was to get her in as protected a place as possible, and that would be below the waterline. "We are running because that is a French frigate of war. She has more guns than we do, and they are larger than ours. It would be very dangerous for us to do otherwise," he explained as patiently as he could. He repeated, "Please take Molly below to the orlop deck or into the hold. I will send for you when it is safe."

The high promontory of Cape Sega approached rapidly to starboard. The Frenchman had settled on a course slightly to the north of *Louisa*'s, rather than directly taking up her wake. Why? Penny still had not moved, and Molly stood anxiously beside her.

"Art thou fleeing from thy enemy because Molly and I are present?" Penny demanded. "Wouldst thou stand and fight otherwise?"

Charles had to think. He had once chosen to fight another frigate larger than even this Frenchman near the mouth of a Spanish harbor. Was he being overly cautious because Penny was on board? Of course he was, but there was more to it than that. His duty was to find and provide assistance to his admiral, not to engage enemy warships. Even if he were to defeat the frigate, *Louisa* might be badly damaged, even crippled. And he might not prevail. "No," he said, "in the circumstance, I would run, no matter."

The high cliffs of Cape Sega appeared nearly even with *Louisa*'s bow. The French frigate followed at just under a mile behind, still angling slightly to the north. Charles needed a moment to think about this.

"Truthfully?" Penny said. "I would—"

"DECK!" A call, almost a scream, came down from the lookout in the tops. "Straight on the bow; dead on!"

Charles stared forward over the forecastle. There, as big as life, stood a second frigate barely a cable's length ahead, just emerging from behind the cape.

"Up helm, up helm!" he yelled at Eliot.

Louisa, already making a fair turn of speed, turned nimbly as her rudder bit and her mizzen came over. It occurred to Charles that the French captain must have been as surprised as he was. He saw that they would cross the frigate's bow, just now beginning to turn, at almost point-blank range.

"Stephen," he yelled down into the gundeck, "to port; fire as you bear."

"Bear on what?" Winchester called back, his view of the frigate obscured by the forecastle. Then, as *Louisa* swung around, Charles heard "Oh, never mind."

The gunports thrust open, the deck rumbling as the guns ran out. The frigate's bowsprit hovered in the sky, slowly swinging to take up a parallel course to his own. Her port side bow quarter presented itself as *Louisa*'s broadside roared out in a deafening blast.

Charles heard Penny give a small cry beside him, but he kept his focus on the frigate. He saw the shot pound into the enemy bow and snap her bowsprit near its beak. To his disappointment, the remainder of her masts seemed secure. The frigate continued her turn, her own gunports flipping up, the black tubes of her cannon sliding out.

"Charles, Charles." He heard his wife and felt her pulling on his sleeve. It was more than he could deal with.

"Goddammit, Penny," he almost shouted at her, "get below. This is no place for a woman." He cast a glance at the frigate's side, fifty yards away, her guns all poking through. He was beside himself with fear for her in what would soon follow. Molly, at least, looked properly awed.

"No." She glared back at him. "I will not leave thy side in this time of peril."

The Frenchman fired, temporarily lost in a cloud of angry gray-black smoke. Solid shot slammed into the hull and screamed across the quarterdeck. Penny flinched but did not move. Charles fought to steady himself. He noticed Talmage approaching the quarterdeck.

"Penny," he pleaded as calmly as he could, "if you want to help me, you cannot stay here. Your presence is too much of a distraction. I can't think about what I am doing. Go below. I am sure the surgeon will be grateful for your assistance. Please." If she refused, he was determined to have her arrested and escorted into the hold.

Penny stood silent, indecision on her face.

"Molly," Charles said in desperation, "do something."

"Wouldn't it be better if we did as he wants," Molly said urgently.

Penny drew herself up straight, her face ashen white. "Come, Molly," she said icily, "the captain has ordered us downstairs." With all her dignity, she turned and started at a walk toward the ladderway. She had never called him "the captain" in that tone of voice before.

"I am available for duty," Talmage said.

Charles found the man's sudden appearance almost infuriating. He'd had enough extraneous diversions, and he didn't need any more.

"Fucking hell you are," he swore.

The carronades on the quarterdeck barked out their thirty-two-pound balls; he saw the twelve-pounders on the gundeck being heaved forward. The two ships had settled on parallel courses, not a pistol shot apart, the wind nearly dead astern. Charles quickly looked for *Pylades* and found her on his port side beam. The frigate they'd spotted first was cutting across the sea several cable lengths beyond, angling to close off his escape. One at a time, Charles decided.

Louisa's increasingly ragged broadside exploded outward, the reverberations felt through the deck. The smoke quickly blew clear, and he saw that at least one or two of the Frenchman's guns were dismounted, one gunport beaten into a ragged gap. Her masts still stood. He turned his attention back to Lieutenant Talmage, his anger marginally controlled. "I am pleased that you have finally decided to attend your duties," he said with not entirely intended sarcasm. "You may replace Mr. Winchester on the gundeck and send him aft."

Talmage stood stone-faced for a moment, then spoke: "My business with you is not completed." Then he left.

Louisa's and the French frigate's broadsides fired very nearly together. Charles observed additional damage to his opponent's hull and railing. Looking upward, he noted holes in a number of his sails and a fair amount of newly cut rigging. *They've decided on disabling our masts,* he thought. Another glance at the farther frigate, and he knew that he could not afford to remain engaged as he was for long.

As soon as Winchester arrived on the quarterdeck, Charles ordered the boatswain and his mates be sent aloft to attend the damaged cables immediately. One more broadside, he decided, and they will have to bear away. No matter what, he couldn't allow the farther frigate to reach across his bows.

As usual, the carronades with their loud bark spoke first, one well-placed shot striking the foremast near the deck. The maindeck guns and the long nine-pounders on the quarterdeck rammed out through the gunports and immediately exploded inward in clouds of smoke. Charles saw what he thought were two balls smash into the forechains near the bow and watched as the foremast lurched forward and swung down over her forecastle. It wasn't a decisive injury, but it was enough.

"Four points to port, if you please, Mr. Eliot," Charles ordered. As *Louisa* bore up, the frigate fired the half of her broadside that was not masked by the fallen topmast, though to little effect that he could see.

He shifted his attention to the remaining Frenchman slicing across the sea at an acute angle from the north. Charles judged that on their present courses, the two ships would come aboard each other a scant quarter mile ahead. He noticed that Bevan's brig had slipped behind to cross the Frenchman's wake and take up position athwart the already damaged frigate's bow. He smiled as puffs of cannon smoke ballooned from *Pylades*'s deck while she fired her six-pounder broadside into the Frenchman's stem.

"Double-hot the port side cannon," he said, turning to Winchester. "Run them out and aim for her gunports."

Winchester relayed the orders to Talmage in the waist while Charles watched the closing French frigate. Two cable lengths separated them as the ship opposite opened her gunports and ran out her armament. In an instant, she had clouded herself in smoke, orange tongues poking through in a single orderly line. Several of the shot struck the sea, throwing up huge spouts. Two, he thought, struck the hull somewhere. The remainder screamed across the deck with angry buzzing sounds. "Too early," Charles said to himself, "too soon."

"Wait," he said to Winchester. "Wait." The two ships came up beam to beam, less than fifty yards apart. He saw the first of her cannon, reloaded, being run back out.

"FIRE!" he yelled.

Louisa's port side cannon and carronades fired as one, leaping inward, the smoke curling across the decks.

Charles looked quickly for Bevan's brig, still firing into the bow of the first frigate. He decided there was no point in waiting or exchanging further broadsides with the Frenchman across from him.

"Down helm, Mr. Eliot," he ordered. "We will bear away directly."

"Down helm it is," Eliot repeated. "Course, sir?"

"South-by-east. We'll let him try a stern chase if he wants it. Mr. Sykes."

"Yes, sir?"

"Signal to *Pylades* to break off and assume station to windward."

"Aye-aye, sir."

"Stephen," Charles said, "secure the guns and put as many men to work in the rigging as necessary. We will run." He had not even looked to see what damage the Frenchman had suffered.

Louisa's turn took the enemy frigate unprepared, and it was several moments before her sails braced around to take up his wake. Charles ordered as much sail as he thought the state of her rigging could support, adding more as the repairs to stays, lines, and halyards were completed. She ran easily, with the wind fine on her starboard quarter. For a time the French frigate closed marginally to a quarter of a mile behind. Charles breathed easier as it became apparent that she carried no bow chasers.

The distance steadied as more canvas was added, and gradually, *Louisa* and *Pylades* began to draw away. The sun dipped low in the west; darkness tinted the eastern horizon. With the last of the light, the Frenchman wore around and began the long beat back to Malta.

"Mr. Sykes," Charles said, "if you would be so kind as to call on the cockpit and inform Mrs. Edgemont and Miss Bridges that their presence would be welcome on quarterdeck, with my compliments." He was not altogether looking forward to the reunion with his wife.

SIX

"IT WILL MEAN ADDED RESPONSIBILITY, MR. BEECHUM," Charles said. "You will have to stand a regular watch schedule."

"Yes, sir," Beechum answered.

"You do know that it is a temporary assignment? I haven't the authority to promote you on my own." Charles sat at the table in his cabin, the women having been banished to the deck above. Beechum sat opposite him.

"Yes, sir. I understand," Beechum answered, sitting stiffly on the edge of his chair, absurdly eager.

"If your performance is satisfactory, I will recommend to the admiral that the step be made permanent. It's possible, probable even, that he won't approve it without an examination. Still, it won't hurt to have it on your record."

"Yes, sir. Thank you, sir," Beechum said earnestly. "I want to say that I appreciate your confidence, sir."

"Lieutenant Winchester will inform you of your duties."

"Yes, sir," the young man said, rising and taking up his hat. With a second "Thank you, sir," he backed out of the cabin.

Charles sat for a moment longer, savoring his too rarely found privacy. Beechum would do well, he thought. If not, it wouldn't be for lack of effort. He looked around his cabin and grimaced. The flotsam of Penny and Molly's occupation was much in evidence. Penny's traveling luggage lay in his sleeping cabin, covered by a growing pile of petticoats and stockings and other ladies' garments. Molly's were stacked on the seat under the stern windows. A shawl lay folded over the back of a chair, a bonnet draped carelessly from his desk. There was a dainty pair of shoes jumbled in a corner where they had been kicked. Attwater insisted that such items remain where they were; he claimed the women fussed at him when they couldn't find their things.

Grudgingly, Charles pushed his chair back from the table and stood. Collecting his hat and sword from their pegs on the bulkhead, he exited the cabin, nodded to the sentry, and went out. Stephen Winchester touched his hat as Charles mounted the ladderway to the quarterdeck. "Have you talked to Beechum?"

"Just this moment," Winchester said.

"Stephen, you're the official first now," Charles said. "I've entered it in the book. Beechum is acting second. I've listed Talmage as a supernumerary."

Winchester nodded in acknowledgment but said nothing.

Charles proceeded across the deck to Penny, who stood waiting for him expectantly by the weather rail. When he arrived, she placed her arm in his. "Did everything go well with Isaac Beechum?"

"Quite well," Charles said. She'd been on board ten days now, and not for the first time, he wondered about her and her thoughts. She had not reacted the way he'd thought she would two days before, when they had gotten into the running fight. She hadn't protested the cannon fire, hadn't sought safety for herself when they were fired upon, hadn't insisted on anything except that she remain by his side. Most surprisingly, when *Louisa* was well out of harm's way and he had allowed her and Molly back on deck, she had not been outwardly angry. She had looked at him carefully to see if he was injured and felt his arms and chest in case he was secretly bandaged.

"Thou art fortunate," she'd said when satisfied. "There would have been no end to my displeasure if it were otherwise."

"Then I am twice charmed," he'd answered, "uninjured and beloved."

Charles looked out over the rail and scanned the surface of the sea. In the distance off the stern lay the receding dot of land that was Cape Passero, the last extremity of Sicily, soon to sink entirely below the horizon. *Louisa*'s course lay one point southerly of due east, with the wind steady from the west, and was making a fair turn of speed—near ten knots, by the last casting of the log, and without even her studding sails set. If he leaned out over the rail and looked forward, he could just see the edge of her bow wave curling out from the stem. *Pylades* surged alongside, two hundred yards to port. Bevan flew every scrap of canvas that she would carry and still struggled to keep up. *Pylades,* Charles had observed, was not a particularly fast sailer on any point of the wind. She could lie a half-point closer to it than *Louisa,* however, and make more headway with her canvas braced up tight. At present the wakes of the two ships lay in straight parallel lines westward as far as the eye could see. Their course would carry them in two or three days to the southern tip of the Peloponnesian peninsula and into the waters of the Ottoman Empire. But he wasn't looking for land, Turkish or otherwise. The lookouts in the tops had specific instructions to search the horizons for sails, in particular the westward-bearing sails of merchantmen or friendly ships of war that might reasonably carry news of Nelson's squadron were it farther east.

There was the other question that he frequently returned to. Was it such a good idea to be sailing the length and breadth of hostile waters with Penny and Molly on board? He knew that it exposed them to unnecessary danger and, at least partly as a consequence, made him more cautious. But it was not as simple as that. The dangers were such that he could avoid them if he chose . . . probably. And, the thought came to him, he didn't fully understand why she had come, or for what length of time she intended to stay. She'd said in Naples that she wished to visit "for a time." How long was a time? He often found the workings of women's minds difficult to follow. Penny's were sometimes unfathomable. Could he ask her? Not directly, he thought. He couldn't say "How long are you planning to stay?" or "When do you think you'll be leaving?" She might take that to mean that he didn't welcome her company. No, he would be more subtle.

"How are you enjoying your time on *Louisa*?" he asked when she came onto the deck. His tone was one of polite interest.

"Very well," she answered. "It's so beautiful. I am very happy to be with thee. Dost thou not agree?"

"Certainly," Charles said, smiling at her. "I'll be disconsolate when you have to leave."

"As will I," she answered, smiling back at him.

Charles realized that he was rather quickly reaching something of an impasse. He cleared his throat. "Yes, it's delightful having you and Molly on board . . . for this time," he continued hopefully.

She looked out over the sea and squeezed his arm but said nothing.

He steeled himself. "How long do you think you will be able to stay?"

Penny's eyes remained focused on some indefinite point on the horizon. "For a time," she said after a moment. "As long as necessary. Dost thou wish me gone?"

"No, no," he said quickly. "I am very pleased . . ." His mind turned a corner. "Necessary for what?"

She stepped apart from him and looked around to see if they might be overheard. "I thought thou knew. I came to be with thee . . . as thy wife . . . so that thou and I might conceive a child."

"Oh," Charles said, "I see." He paused for a long moment, then put his head close to hers and whispered, "How will you know?" He had some thought that it would be months before she became large enough in the belly to notice.

She took a deep breath and explained it to him in low tones. Charles felt as if he were being made privy to the mysteries of some obscure cult. The only thing he knew, or was sure that he wanted to know, when she finished was that there would be some indication within two weeks of their progress thus far.

"I must also converse with thee about thy lands in Tattenall before I depart," she said afterward.

"All in good time," Charles answered, then remembered that he had to speak with Eliot about their course.

EARLY IN THE afternoon watch, the lookout in the foremast tops shouted down that he'd seen two sail headed westward five leagues off to the southeast. Charles ordered *Louisa*'s course altered to intercept them and signaled *Pylades* to follow. In time, the pair of sail became visible from the deck and were determined to be a snow and a brigantine, both of which ran up the blue and gold flags of Sweden as soon as the English warships came into view.

"We will display the Union flag," he said to Sykes. "Hoist out my gig. I'll go across." As *Louisa* neared, the two merchantmen hove to. Charles climbed the snow's side, two marines following close behind.

"May I see your bill of lading, sir?" Charles asked the master of the *Bengtsfors,* out of Gothenburg. The profoundly blond man of middle height and age, with tangled hair down to his shoulders, reached inside his jacket. He produced the document showing a cargo of wheat and oil from Crete, bound for Denmark.

"Thank you, sir," Charles said, returning the papers. "You are a long way from home."

"Ja," the master said, rubbing at two-week-old stubble on his chin. "Three month, more."

"Tell me, have you seen any other English ships in these waters?"

"No." The man shook his head thoughtfully. "No English. Many French."

"Many French? When? Where?"

The Swedish master was momentarily diverted by something he saw aboard *Louisa.* "You hab vimmen?" he asked.

"Yes," Charles answered, "the government issues them to us for long voyages. When did you see the French fleet?"

The Swede rubbed his chin again. "Five day," he said. "Ver' large. By Cape Kiros. Sail east. What name you vimmen?"

"Miss Bridges and Mrs. Edgemont," Charles answered, seeing the two watching from the rail of his quarterdeck. "Do you want to say hello?" He walked with him to the side.

"Hallo, Miss Bridges! Hallo, Mrs. Edgemont!" the Swede's voice boomed across the water. The two women waved back. "You hab two vimmen," he said seriously. "You sell one?"

"I am sorry," Charles said. "The other belongs to the brig."

"*Captain report on board,* if you please, Mr. Sykes," Charles said as soon as his feet regained *Louisa*'s deck. "Signal it to *Pylades.*"

"Yes, sir," Sykes answered, touched his hat, and left.

On the quarterdeck, Charles found Penny and Molly. "You had better be nice to me. I had an offer to sell one of you to that gentleman."

"How much?" Molly asked, which brought a frown from Penny.

"We did not get that far into the negotiations. I've signaled for Daniel to come across. I thought I'd warn you."

"Oh, my. I won't be but a minute," she said, and fled.

"Seriously, he did not offer to purchase us?" Penny said.

"I think he figured that so long as I had two, he'd probably be doing me a favor."

"Surely thou didst not consider it?"

"He seemed a very nice sort of fellow."

Daniel Bevan came aboard on the leeward side. After tipping his hat to Penny, he said to Charles, "What have you learned?"

"Well, that women have actual monetary value, for one. Also that the French were seen south of Crete these five days past."

Bevan removed his hat and ran a hand through his hair. "What do you think it means?"

"The women or the French?"

"Let's start with the French," Bevan offered dryly.

"I don't know what their objective is, except that it's something in the eastern Mediterranean, Crete itself possibly, or Cyprus, Alexandretta, the Levant, who knows. The consul in Naples thinks Egypt, but I don't know if I agree. Crete seems a little far north for their course to be in that direction. However, I do think that where the French fleet has gone, Nelson will sooner or later follow."

"What makes you think so?"

"If we can obtain intelligence on their movements from local shipping, so can Nelson. In the event, it's all we have. We'll bend a little southerly along Crete and see what we can learn."

Charles looked to Bevan for confirmation but saw that his friend's attention had been diverted by the appearance of Molly across the deck. She stood almost shyly by the far rail in a fresh dress, with her head erect and her hands folded in front. His heart went out to her. She looked both vulnerable and determined. He had come to have a certain careful affection for Molly.

"If you will excuse me," Bevan said.

Charles caught his arm. "Daniel," he said seriously, "whatever you do, do the right thing by her. She's done nothing to injure you."

Bevan nodded wordlessly and crossed the deck with a determined step. Charles watched carefully while trying to look as if he weren't. Bevan talked in low tones; Molly mostly listened, nodding occasionally, her eyes never leaving his face.

"What do you think she'll do?" he said to Penny, still standing beside him.

"It is not for me to decide," she said thoughtfully. "I hope she will do what she believes to be correct."

"Poor Molly," said Charles.

"Poor Daniel Bevan," said Penny.

After a few moments, Bevan fell silent. Molly nodded her head, said something, then left him to cross toward Charles and Penny. "Don't Daniel want me to come visit with him for a time," she said. "He says I can have my own place to sleep. I want to give it a chance."

"You have only to come to the rail and wave," Charles said, "and I'll fetch you straightaway."

Molly smiled. "Thank you, sir. Don't I appreciate it. I can take care of myself."

While she went below with Penny to collect her pencils and paper and some clothing, Charles walked over to his friend. There didn't seem to be much to say, so the two men stood silently waiting until the women returned. As Molly was lowered over the side, Charles finally said, "Good luck." Bevan touched his hat and descended the side steps.

Charles and Penny stood watching Bevan's cutter pulling back to the brig. "Do you know what this means?" Charles said.

"What?"

"That we'll have the cabin to ourselves."

"Except for Timothy Attwater."

"Well, yes."

Penny went to the cabin while Charles proceeded to the quarterdeck to give the orders for their new course. On the way, he passed Talmage, whom he acknowledged with a curt nod. He hoped they found Nelson soon. Seeing Talmage reminded him that he had not yet spoken to Winchester about the prohibition of duels. Then he thought that as nothing had happened thus far, perhaps it would not be necessary.

"We will make the course south-by-southeast," he said to Eliot. "Set her to weather Cape Kiros." He noted Winchester's presence as officer of the watch, thought again to speak, but decided it would be awkward to belabor something that Winchester presumably already knew. He went below.

Charles settled himself at his desk while Penny straightened some of Molly's left-behind things and replaced them in her friend's chest. Attwater began to lay the table for supper. A loud knock came at the cabin door.

"Enter," Charles called, pushing back his chair.

The door thrust open and Beechum almost fell into the cabin, his expression a picture of anxiety. "Excuse me, sir, you should come on deck," he said hurriedly. "It's Lieutenant Winchester and Lieutenant Talmage, sir."

Charles rose and snatched up his sword and scabbard, hanging on the bulkhead. "Find Sergeant Cooley and tell him to bring a half dozen of his marines. Run, man." He strapped his sword around his waist and reached for the door.

"Where art thou going?" Penny asked, emerging from their sleeping cabin.

"I have not yet spoken with Stephen about duels," he said, and hurried out.

Climbing the ladderway to the quarterdeck several steps at a time, he saw Talmage and Winchester facing each other. Talmage had his sword loose, its point touching the deck, his hands resting on its hilt. Winchester stood two paces away, tense and determined, his hand on the hilt of his own sword, still on his belt.

"Mr. Talmage, scabbard your hanger," Charles ordered as he crossed the deck.

"Ah, our esteemed captain," Talmage answered. His sword did not move. "This is a matter of honor between Mr. Winchester and myself. I will thank you not to interfere."

"I will interfere, Mr. Talmage. I'll have no duels on my ship. Put away your blade." He saw that his wife had arrived at the top of the ladderway, her hands to her face in alarm. Charles wished it were the marines instead. "What honor? There is no insult," he said.

Talmage appraised him coldly. "This puppy has unfairly assumed my place. A disrespect that I find I cannot tolerate. It was dishonorable for him to have done it, and it would be dishonorable for me to allow it to stand." The end of his sword raised off the deck to hover menacingly in front of him. "I have been grievously treated, unfairly insulted, sir." The "sir" came out as a sneer.

"You will do nothing," Charles said. "I will not allow it." He rested his own hand meaningfully on his sword. He knew his anger to be rising; he didn't care.

"If you will give me the gratification, I will happily address you first. That is, if you have the stones for it."

Charles's hand tightened on the grip of his sword, then he felt Penny press close beside him, against the side on which his scabbard hung. "Thou must not," she said. "Thou knowest this to be wrong." He made to pull away, but she clung to his arm.

"Hiding behind a woman's skirts will not save you," Talmage said, his faced turned to a scowl. "Madam, I will oblige you to go below. This is an affair between men."

"I will not, Jacob Talmage," she said. "I will not abide this foolishness."

Charles stared, disbelieving, at his wife. The man was holding a naked blade and knew well how to use it. Then he realized that Talmage would never willingly harm her. The thought helped him to regain some composure.

Charles heard the tramp of the marines mounting the ladderway. Talmage barely glanced at them. "I must insist that you leave, madam," the lieutenant said again.

"I will not," Penny repeated, glaring at him.

"Believe me, you will never in your lifetime win this argument, Mr. Talmage," Charles said, coming to a decision. He succeeded in disengaging himself from his wife. Her presence might be helpful, he thought, and he resolved that there would be no swordplay. To start with, he needed to defuse the situation.

"Stephen," he said, "go below to your quarters."

"Sir," Winchester protested, "I am bound—"

Charles cut him off. "I am ordering you below. If you do not go willingly, I will have you arrested and held under guard."

"Sir," Winchester protested.

"Sergeant Cooley," Charles said, "detach two of your men to escort Lieutenant Winchester below."

"Yes, sir."

"That won't be necessary," Winchester said in a disgusted tone. He stared coldly at Talmage and departed.

Charles took a moment to collect his thoughts. He knew that the situation with Talmage had elevated to this level at least in part because of his own inattention. He should have confronted the lieutenant directly about his shortcomings far earlier. He had allowed the problem to grow and fester; it was his responsibility to cure it.

"Mr. Talmage," Charles said, "your difficulties lie with me. If anyone questioned your abilities, it was myself, no other. Mr. Winchester was only following orders. My orders."

Talmage fixed his eyes on Charles. The sword in his hand lowered but was not sheathed. "You have done more than question my abilities," he said bitterly. "You have disrated me without a hearing or recourse. That is an unpardonable affront, sir."

Charles knew that Talmage was not entirely wrong. From his point of view, he had been unfairly treated. Being found wanting by his captain, a much younger man, must have stung. Being replaced without explanation by the captain's own brother-in-law might be considered an unfair preference. It was unfortunate that Talmage had gone to the extremity of drawing his sword against a fellow officer. Charles would be well in his rights to have him arrested and held for a court-martial under any number of the Articles of War. In any event, there would have to be an inquiry when they found Nelson or returned to Gibraltar. Talmage's had been too public an act.

"Put away your sword, Mr. Talmage," Charles repeated. "I'll not give you that kind of satisfaction."

"Then you are a coward," the lieutenant said flatly.

Charles sighed. Talmage wasn't making this easy. "I hope I am no coward. If your complaint did not have some justice, I would have a greater inclination to meet you sword to sword."

Talmage hesitated. "You admit that you are in the wrong?"

Charles thought he detected a hint of doubt in Talmage's voice. "I admit," he said carefully, "that we are both gentlemen and king's officers.

I admit that I should have discussed your situation with you in a forth-right and timely manner. I now regret that I had not done so. However, I do not admit that I would have taken any other course of action."

"I find that intolerable," Talmage said with some belligerence, but the point of his sword rested once more on the deck.

Charles knew that he couldn't stand on the deck arguing with Tal-mage indefinitely. He glanced at the marines lined up behind the lieu-tenant. "I ask you for the last time to put away your sword, or by God I'll have you thrown in irons."

Penny unexpectedly stepped forward and approached Talmage. "May I have thy weapon, please?" she said softly, removing the object from his unresisting hand. She then delivered it to a surprised Cooley.

The air seemed to go out of Talmage. He stared at those around him as if realizing for the first time the fullness of what he had done.

Penny returned to Talmage's side and took his arm in hers. Looking at Charles, she said, "Shall we go below to thy cabin? It is a less public place there. I can offer you both hot chocolate."

"We don't have any chocolate," Charles said.

"I brought some from Cheshire," she said, avoiding his eyes. "Timo-thy Attwater knows how to prepare it."

Sergeant Cooley approached, still holding Talmage's sword. "Will you be requiring my services, sir? I can give you two of my boys, just in case."

Charles thought for a moment. "Thank you, Sergeant," he said, tak-ing the blade. "If you would station them outside the entrance to my cabin. I'll call if they're needed."

In his cabin, Penny sat Talmage at the table, then held out her hand to Charles to surrender the lieutenant's sword. When Charles gave it to her, she held out her other hand for his own.

"My, aren't we careful," Charles said with a laugh and unhooked the scabbard from his belt. She took the weapons and dropped them heavily on the bench beneath the stern windows as if they were serpents. Then she went to retrieve her secret supply of chocolate and to find Attwater to send him to the galley for hot water.

"Mr. Talmage," Charles said, appraising the man sitting across from him, "I regret that it has come to this."

"As do I," Talmage responded coldly.

Charles tapped his fingers on the tabletop while he struggled to decide what to do. Should he be harsh or lenient? What would be best for the running of his ship, for himself, for Talmage? He felt as if he were in deep waters. It occurred to him that Talmage was in far deeper.

"What's done cannot be undone," he said, coming to a conclusion. "The question is, what are we to do now?"

Talmage shifted uncomfortably in his chair.

"I will offer you a choice," Charles said. "You may stay as you are, as a passenger on board, so long as there are no further incidents. You will have the freedom of the ship and no regular responsibilities until we come upon Admiral Nelson. But I warn you, if there is a further altercation with Mr. Winchester, or anyone else, I will have you put under confinement." He waited for the lieutenant to indicate his understanding.

Talmage nodded cautiously.

"Or, at your request, I will enter you as second lieutenant. You would perform your duties under the direction of Mr. Winchester, with Mr. Beechum as third. You would still be free to request a transfer if that becomes available, or you may continue on board until we return to the fleet at Gibraltar."

At that moment Penny reentered, ushering in Attwater with a tray of three steaming mugs of hot cocoa. As they were being placed before the men, Charles said, "I will expect your answer in the morning."

Penny sat down with a sympathetic glance at Talmage and then a more cursory one at Charles as Attwater set a small plate of sweet candies on the table.

"What's this?" Charles asked. He had no sweets of any kind that he knew of.

"I bought them in Chester. That's the last," she said, studying Talmage's face intently.

Charles blew across the top of his chocolate and sipped, eyeing his wife over the brim. "We will have to discuss this hoarding of supplies," he said.

Penny's face pinkened, but she kept her gaze intently on Talmage.

The lieutenant cleared his throat, perhaps feeling uneasy under such close scrutiny. "Sir," he said, rising to his feet, "I will not apologize for my behavior. I believe myself to have been justified. I will accept the second's position until a suitable transfer is available." He placed his untasted cocoa on the table.

Charles rose. "I will inform Mr. Winchester of your status. You may report to him in the morning."

Talmage nodded stiffly, then turned to Penny. Holding his hat in front of his chest with both hands, he said, "I apologize if anything in my behavior has caused you distress, Mrs. Edgemont. Please be assured that your efforts on my behalf are appreciated."

"Thou art most welcome, Jacob Talmage," she answered softly. "I have great faith that thou will do the correct thing in this time of trial."

Talmage bowed to her and cast a cold glance at Charles. "If that is all," he said.

"A moment," Charles said, and went to collect the surrendered sword. "You will require this. Keep it in its scabbard."

The lieutenant slid the blade into its holder without speaking, nodded to Penny again, and made for the door.

Charles followed. In the open entryway, he dismissed Cooley's additional marines. With the door firmly closed, he turned to his wife. "I think I have never met a more irksome person."

Penny remained silent.

After supper, Charles sent for Winchester. "Would you like a sweet?" he said as his first lieutenant entered. "It's the last one. It turns out that we have hot chocolate also." Penny stuck out her tongue at him, crinkling her nose prettily.

Winchester accepted the candy, declined the chocolate, took off his hat, and expressed his greeting to Penny.

"Stephen," Charles spoke directly, "I've offered the second's position to Talmage, and he's accepted it. He's to report to you in the morning."

Winchester's jaw tightened, but he did not object. "How shall I deal with him?" he said.

"In the normal way," Charles answered. "Deal with him as civilly as possible under the circumstances. If there are difficulties, I expect you to come to me. There will be no duels; that's a direct order."

Winchester considered this and then nodded.

"And you need to inform Beechum that he is now third," Charles added.

After Winchester had left, and after Attwater had finished clearing away the dishes, Charles felt the tension of the day drain away. As he observed his wife passing near his chair, he caught her by the arm and pulled her down into his lap. "Do you know what the penalty for hoarding sweets is, my sweet? It's very, very serious."

"I was hoping it were so," she said.

A SENSE OF routine settled in as *Louisa* and her shadow, *Pylades,* ran easily across the southern Ionian Sea under cloudless skies, pyramids of weathered canvas on their masts. The brilliant blue water slipped beneath the dark hulls, sharp white waves curling back from their bows. The whisper of the wind through the stays, the gurgle of the passing seas, and the soft creaking of the ships' timbers as they pitched gently over the rippling surface were the only accompaniments of their passage.

Charles ordered practice with the guns most mornings, running them in and out, in and out, the topmen exercising aloft. He also ordered Sergeant Cooley to establish a regular course of instruction in the use of small arms—pistols, muskets, cutlasses, boarding axes, and boarding pikes. In the event of taking an enemy ship of war by main force, or repelling the same, hand-to-hand fighting might be necessary.

Relations with Talmage remained distant and strictly formal, although Charles noticed that the lieutenant took the opportunity to speak with Penny, with whom he had sometimes lengthy conversations, whenever the opportunity arose. Charles wondered what they spoke about, but did not object.

Two days of favorable westerly winds across an unvarying empty sea saw them to the tip of Crete, with Cape Kiros jutting out fine on the port bow. A scattered flock of local fishing boats dotted the water under the cape. Charles thought to stop and ask for news of the French, but decided against it, since he already knew they had passed a week before, and the fishermen would have little knowledge of where they had gone. He decided to continue along the southern coast of the island in hopes of discovering some ship from farther east that might have more recent information.

The sheer cliffs of Crete's southern coast glided past on the port beam as the day wore on, broken occasionally by small river inlets and tiny fishing villages clinging to the shore with their clusters of whitewashed, flat-roofed houses. Shortly before dusk, the sails of a ship, almost certainly a warship but of an unusual and outdated sail arrangement, was sighted rounding the headland of Cape Lithinon. The strange sail quickly altered her course to intercept them.

"Hoist the colors, Mr. Sykes," Charles ordered. Talmage had the watch. To him, Charles said, "We will clear for action, if you please, and then beat to quarters."

She proved to be a very large fifty-gun, single-decked warship flying the red flag of Turkey. Her design was of a type not seen in England for almost a hundred years, with doubled fore- and aftercastles and a lateen rig on her mizzenmast. The Turkish frigate—if she was, strictly speaking, a frigate—stood directly toward *Louisa*'s bow and, from about two cable lengths' distance, signaled her demand that the English ships heave to by the rather direct expedient of firing a gun. The Turk had her ship's barge, with twenty men at the oars, in the water before *Louisa* had gotten all of her way off.

"Call Sergeant Cooley to assemble his marines in smart order by the entryport," Charles said to Talmage. "I wish to greet these gentlemen with full honors."

Three men climbed the side steps onto *Louisa*'s deck. As the first appeared above the ship's side, the boatswain blew a shrill call on his whistle, and the marines snapped to present arms. The three were clearly officers, with red and blue jackets piped in yellow, over baggy blue pantaloons. Each had an impressively thick mustache and a heavy, almost semicircular sword at his side.

"You papers," the youngest of them demanded in passable English, holding out his hand.

Charles removed his commission from the Admiralty from the inside pocket of his jacket and handed it over. The officer passed the paper, unopened, to his superior, who unfolded the document, held it in front of him, and perused it at some length. Charles doubted he could read a word, as he held it upside down. After an appropriate time, the paper was refolded and returned with a nod from the superior, indicating his satisfaction.

"What are you business in Turkish national waters?" the younger officer asked.

"We are searching for a large French fleet known to have passed near here one week ago," Charles said. "I would be most obliged if you could give me some indication of their whereabouts."

This was translated, and some discussion passed back and forth before the English speaker turned again to Charles. "How large are these French?" he asked.

"I have reports of thirteen sail of the line, a number of smaller warships, and several hundred transports from Toulon and Genoa."

"And they are directed to where?"

"East of here," Charles answered curtly. Clearly, this was all new information to his interrogators.

Translation followed, and again there was discussion, a great deal of discussion. Finally, the junior officer turned back. "There is no French in the waters of the Empire of Turkey," he said with some dignity. "I am sorry."

"Have you seen any other British warships?" Charles asked.

"There is no English, excepting you, in the waters of the Empire of Turkey," the officer answered.

"I see," Charles said. "Thank you for informing me. May I ask from which port you have sailed?"

The Turkish officer looked doubtful but answered, "*Sultan Balikesir* is based in Izmir, your Smyrna, I believe. We have been cruising in the south of what you call the Aegean Sea."

"And you have seen no French warships?"

"Of course, none."

"Thank you," Charles said.

With that, the Turks seemed rather agitated to depart. Bows were made and hats touched. The marines snapped to attention, and the visitors climbed down over the side as quickly as their not wanting to show they were in a hurry would allow.

"You may dismiss your men, Sergeant Cooley," Charles said. He walked to the quarterdeck, where he told Eliot to resume their course eastward. Looking over the rail, he noticed that the Turkish ship was just hoisting in her barge but had already begun to fall off the wind to go back the way she had come.

As soon as Beechum assured Charles that his cabin had been

restored, he went below. "Do you know where Smyrna is?" he said to Penny, opening his bookcase and removing an atlas. They found it on the western coast of Turkey, about halfway up the Aegean to the Dardanelles. He studied the page, with its small-scale map of the eastern Mediterranean, for some time. The only new information he had was that the French (and hence Nelson) had probably not gone into the Aegean. There were only five hundred more miles until the Mediterranean ended, he reasoned. His admiral had to be somewhere.

Charles arrived on the quarterdeck at dawn the next morning, the early sun lighting the now lower slopes of the Cretan shore. Cape Goúdhoura showed on the bow, the empty sea beyond. Already the air felt dry and unusually warm.

"A good day to you, Mr. Eliot," he said, approaching the master.

"Aye," Eliot responded conversationally. "It'll be a warm one."

"The wind has shifted to the north," Charles observed.

"It's the Meltemi," Eliot said, lifting his chin as if to smell the air. Seeing Charles's puzzled expression, he explained, "It's a local breeze what comes down the sea between Greece and Turkey. Makes for hot days. They're be no rain for a time, that's a fact."

Charles had come to the sailing master for a purpose. "As we clear that headland," he said, pointing to the cape, "we'll make to the northeast. I'd like to have a look at the island of Rhodes."

"Is that where you think the Frenchies have gone?"

"I don't know where the French have gone," Charles answered. "If we can be comfortable that it's not Rhodes, then we'll try Cyprus, then down along the Levant, and to Egypt."

"And if we find nothing?"

Charles rubbed his chin thoughtfully. "If we haven't found anything after we've looked into Alexandria, then we have to assume that they've vanished into the air. We return to Gibraltar; we did our best." For all his calm, Charles did not wish to return to Admiral Jervis to explain why he'd been sailing fruitlessly the length of the Mediterranean for two full months, searching for Nelson's squadron, which, for all he knew, had long since returned to port.

The ship's bell rang eight times for the end of the morning watch and the beginning of the forenoon. Lieutenant Talmage replaced Beechum as officer of the watch. Charles had been watching Talmage closely. He would have to consult Winchester for a more detailed assessment, but from what he had observed, Talmage was carrying out his duties as second in a serious and capable manner, more capably than he had the more difficult responsibilities of first. Charles knew he would have to write a full report on the incident; it had been a violation of the Articles of War. How serious a violation depended on how the act was interpreted. Talmage had, after all, bared his sword against another officer. He had already drafted a description of Talmage's outburst and the events leading up to it, but he had left incomplete his evaluation of the lieutenant's subsequent performance and his own recommendations for disciplinary action. He found himself inclined to be forgiving, but he knew that no matter how carefully he worded his statement, it would be a black mark against Talmage's record, probably black enough to see him discharged from the navy. Talmage himself would be well aware of this by now.

As the morning wore on, the easternmost tip of Crete receded ever farther behind. The island of Kasos rose on the horizon, the first of two they would pass before reaching Rhodes. Already the warmth of the day was such that Charles began to feel uncomfortable in his heavy uniform coat. He focused on *Pylades*, sailing along happily to leeward. Even without his glass, he could see her commander's familiar stocky form pacing back and forth on her tiny quarterdeck. If he used his telescope, he could make out Bevan's expression and a soup stain on his waistcoat. In time he saw Molly appear, and the two moved to stand together on the nearside rail, her arm linked in his. It had been four days since Molly went over. Charles wondered how they were getting on.

"Good morning, my love," Penny said from close behind him. Charles started in surprise.

"A Penny for thy thoughts," she said, smiling broadly at her joke, one they both too frequently employed.

"I was thinking about you and how as lovely as any rose you are," he said, which was his firm answer every time she asked. He reached into his coat, came out with a small pocket telescope, and snapped it open. "Look," he said, handing her the glass and pointing toward the brig.

Penny lifted it to her eye. Molly evidently noticed her, because she raised her free arm and waved. Penny lowered the glass and waved back.

Charles thought it was like two neighbors back home, exchanging greetings across a field.

"Is that where thy thoughts are?" she asked.

"I wonder how they are together," Charles said. "If anything has changed. They look happy enough."

"I am uncomfortable not being able to speak with her," she said. "Can we have Molly back, if just for a visit?"

"How about we invite them both to supper?"

"I would like that. Canst thou make such a signal?"

"Indirectly," Charles said. He turned to Sykes. "Signal *Pass within hail,* if you please."

Pylades trimmed her sails and put down her helm. The brig fell marginally off the wind, the gap between the ships slowly narrowing. At about five fathoms, Charles shouted almost conversationally, "Captain and Mrs. Edgemont would be most welcome of both your company to supper this evening."

"Just a moment," Bevan answered. "I'll have to consult my social secretary." Charles saw Molly beam and nod vigorously. "You are in luck," Bevan came back. "We've had a recent cancellation. About seven, then?"

"How art thou, Molly?" Penny called.

"Ain't I fine," she answered. "I can't wait to talk with you."

At noon, with Kasos looming ever larger off the port bow, Charles and Penny went down to their dinner, Charles gratefully pulling off his jacket.

"I need to bathe," Penny said unexpectedly. "I have not been able to do so these past two weeks."

"You bathe every day," he said. "I've seen you."

"No," she said rather strongly, "I wash with a sponge from a bucket of cold seawater."

"I could have the cook heat the water," he offered helpfully.

"Then I would wash from a bucket of warm seawater. I cannot clean my hair at all in salted water. I wish to have a proper bath in a tub of hot fresh water. I long for such a thing."

"I see," Charles said, slicing another piece of meat and putting it into his mouth before he had to expand on this line of discussion.

"I must also wash my clothing. I have nothing newly cleaned since Naples."

This was easier. "I'll have the cook boil them for you."

"In fresh water," she added firmly.

This presented a problem. *Louisa* was capable of carrying a three-month supply of fresh water in casks in her hold. Every drop had to be rigorously rationed and accounted for, and there was absolutely none for baths or laundry tubs. How could he explain to his seamen that they were limited to a gallon a day, on pain of punishment, while his wife consumed unending quantities for her personal hygiene?

"I'll have to consider this," he said, having no immediate notion of a solution.

"Please, wilt thou consider it quickly."

At the appointed hour in the evening, with Kaşos declining stern-ward and the island of Korpathos rising, *Louisa* hove to while *Pylades* sent her boat across. Bevan climbed the side while Molly was swung aboard. *Pylades*'s cutter returned, and both ships resumed their course. Penny immediately latched onto her companion, and the two women started below, their heads close together.

As soon as they were alone, Charles looked meaningfully at Bevan. "Yes?" he said.

Bevan removed his hat and wiped a handkerchief across the sweat on his forehead. Even in the relative cool of the evening, the heat remained oppressive. "We've had a pleasant enough time," he said, as if having a hard time finding a place to start. "I've never known a woman with so much to say."

"Yes, yes," Charles said impatiently. "What do you talk about?"

"Oh, everything: the weather, England, Wales, ships, babies, sheep. Her father was a shepherd, did you know that?"

Charles searched his memory. "Yes, I knew that," he said. "Babies? What does she say about babies?" They were getting closer to his central interest.

"She wants them; I want them." Bevan hesitated. "Charlie, I'm happy when I'm with her. More happy than I thought I had any right to be. I don't care about her background."

"And this means?" Charles prompted, trying to edge the conversation along.

"I never in my life thought I'd say this, but I want to wed her. I've asked."

Charles grinned his biggest grin. "She won't come across otherwise, is that it?"

"She won't budge, Charlie. She's as obstinate as a wall on the topic. But it's what I want also. I'm set on this."

Charles slapped his friend on the back. "I've always said no good comes from having women on board."

"You've never said any such thing," Bevan answered.

"Not yet, maybe," Charles admitted. A practical concern occurred to him. "How are you going to get it done?" The nearest proper church official he could think of was Nelson's chaplain on board *Vanguard,* wherever she was.

"You can do the ceremony," Bevan said. "You're a ship's captain, the closest thing to God's direct representative in these waters."

"Christ," Charles said, "I don't know."

"You can do it," Bevan repeated.

"When?" Charles asked.

For the first time, Bevan looked doubtful. "She said something about having to do her laundry first."

LOUISA AND *PYLADES* skirted around the southeastern coast of Rhodes to the port of Lindos the next morning under the same lazy blue skies, over the same gleaming deep blue sea. Little shipping was to be seen beyond a few dhows, feluccas, and a solitary xcbcc in the old port. The ancient walled city, with its fortifications in some disrepair, stood behind in the shimmering heat. There was certainly no sign of French or British warships and no indication of the excitement that might have been aroused had any passed this way. Charles sent Winchester in the cutter to the harbor. He returned to report that no one, including the Turkish harbormaster, had any knowledge nor had heard any rumors of any European warships anywhere.

Two days carried them farther to Cyprus and nearly to the easternmost limit of the Mediterranean. The midday sun was such as to soften the pitch between the seams of the decking, and the dry heat sufficient to shrink the deck boards themselves. On the advice of the surgeon, Charles increased the ration of water to the crew and ordered that they stay below as much as possible and wear shirts and hats when abovedeck to prevent stroke. He also had a large canvas awning raised over the after half of the ship to provide shade. In the first light of dawn, the two ships weathered the ten-mile promontory of Cape Gata on the southern underbelly of the island and into Akrotiri Bay. The two warships, the Union flag of Great Britain at their mastheads, dropped their anchors in the just-waking harbor of Limassol.

Charles immediately dispatched Sykes in the gig to *Pylades* with a detailed message for Bevan, and had both *Louisa's* launch and cutter hoisted out. He was determined to accomplish several important and overdue tasks before the heat of the day overwhelmed them. The launch he sent under the boatswain with a dozen hands and four marines, with as many of the ship's empty water casks as they could carry. This would mean several trips back and forth, heavy work at the oars, and hoisting the filled casks back on board, but Charles could then increase the water ration yet again.

Into the cutter went Penny, with all of her laundry in a large canvas sack, Attwater, Black the purser, a half-dozen marines, acting Lieutenant Beechum, and Charles himself. They were met at a quay on the seawall by a deputy to the port governor, dressed in slippers with long pointed toes curled upward, baggy pantaloons, an equally baggy cloak, and a large yellow turban wrapped loosely around his head. He'd had the sense to bring someone who could translate into English, and a small army of attendants.

Greetings were exchanged on behalf of His Most Sublime Excellency, whom Charles took to be the governor of the island, and His Most Gracious Majesty, King George III. Charles offered a golden sovereign as a gesture of his esteem. Business proceeded thereafter on an amicable basis.

"How may our small, inadequate city be of assistance to your gracious sir?" the interpreter asked.

Charles ticked off his requests on his fingers. "I would like to replenish my ships' supplies of water. We will pay four pence a barrel. Two of our boats with casks are already at the water jetty."

"Most certainly, it is arranged," said the interpreter, after interpreting.

"I wish to send my purser and some others into the market to purchase lemons, limes, onions, sheep, goats, and whatever else is available. I will agree to an honest price in gold and silver coins, of course."

"Of course," the translator said with a small bow. "The market is open to you. I will send an assistant to see that you are treated fairly."

"Thank you," Charles said, bowing in return and suspecting that the role of the assistant would be to ensure that they were overcharged and that the port administrator got his fair percentage. "Third, and this is in the nature of a personal request, my wife and her companion are traveling with us. They have requested the services of a laundry. I am sure you understand that this is a significant matter, and I would be most grateful, as would King George himself, if this could be done as quickly as possible, say, before noon."

The translator spoke to his superior, who immediately clapped his hands. A second assistant came running. "This man will escort you to the most prosperous" (—Charles was sure he meant to say something like "proficient," but perhaps not—) "laundry in Limassol. A small gratuity only would be appropriate."

Charles sent two sailors with the sacks of laundry and two marines as guards to follow the man. He gave orders that they wait until it was all dried and folded and handed a sailor several copper coins. That should be more than adequate.

"I have a final request of which I am sure, as a man of the world, you will understand the delicacy. My wife and her companion have been at sea for a considerable period without the opportunity to bathe their persons properly. I am told the Turkish have the finest baths in all the world. Would it be possible—"

The interpreter threw up his hands. "I am Greek, you understand," he said with some indignity. "But the Turks also have adequate such facilities." He signaled for yet another assistant to approach. "If you will give him two silver coins, he will make all the necessary arrangements."

Charles thought two shillings an exorbitant price for two baths but knew he was in no position to bargain. "Beechum," he said, fishing the coins from his purse, "take Mrs. Edgemont and Miss Bridges and two of the marines. Follow this gentleman. The women are going to a bathing house. Wait until they come back out. If Mrs. Edgemont is satisfied, give him these and return here."

"Yes, sir," Beechum said, spinning one coin nonchalantly in the air, a gesture that irritated Charles greatly. He took a moment to think about the principal reason why he had come to Cyprus. He didn't want to excite so much interest that he would have to pay for it. "Has there been any talk of French warships in these waters?" he asked in his most offhanded manner.

"No," the interpreter answered. "We have seen nothing of the French for many years. I have heard that they have captured Venice, and now we have seen not even them."

The deputy port administrator spoke, evidently asking after the subject of their conversation. An exchange followed, and the interpreter said, "He has heard of a French fleet, very large, far to the west some weeks ago, possibly near Crete. But they would never come here. No one comes here."

The party that had gone to the market returned late in the morning with a hired donkey cart piled with local fruits and vegetables, several dozen scrawny chickens tied up by their feet, and four goats tethered behind. By the time these items had been stowed securely in the cutter, the women's laundry appeared, neatly tied into bundles with twine. Finally, Beechum, the two marines, and pinkly fresh Penny and Molly emerged from an alleyway and came toward them.

"How was it?" Charles asked.

Penny blushed brightly. "It is a public bath for women only," she said. "I have never been the object of such intense curiosity about my person. You would think they had not seen an Englishwoman before. But we are clean, very clean." Charles thought she looked somehow pleased with the experience.

During the row back to his ship, he considered the information, or rather the lack of it, that he had obtained about the French. It was beginning to look as though he had taken up a fool's errand. He had come to the farthest extremity of the Mediterranean and found nothing. It would take only a few days to sail down the coast of the Levant, but he certainly would have heard of some rumor if the French had landed there. He could call on the British consul at Acre, on the unlikely chance that he might have some intelligence, and similarly the government's representative at Alexandria, so that he could at least say that he'd been thorough. The simple fact was that he would soon run out of places to search.

BETWEEN CYPRUS AND ACRE, Charles married Daniel Bevan and Molly Bridges in the relative cool of the evening of Monday, the ninth of July, 1798. The ceremony took place on *Pylades*'s quarterdeck. Molly came across in *Louisa*'s launch, along with Charles, Penny, Winchester, Beechum, and most of the ship's warrant officers who knew Bevan from when they had served together. The bride-to-be arrived in fine looks, shining eyes, and high spirits, almost bubbling with infectious excitement. Bevan wore a wide grin that he did not seem to be able to suppress.

Charles stood by the binnacle with a Bible and some hastily scribbled notes in hand, Bevan and Molly before him. As quiet fell over the assemblage, Charles read a few suitable passages from the book, made a personal observation about the joy and meaning of matrimony, and asked solemnly if each took the other with all the appropriate requirements that went with it. As the last "I do" was uttered, he closed the book. "I order you man and wife," he said. "Make the best of it."

Molly squealed in delight as Bevan lifted her off the deck and kissed her. *Pylades*'s crew tossed their hats and cheered, echoed by a loud "Huzzah" from *Louisa,* lying to a hundred yards off. Charles had asked Mr. Black to draw up a suitable certificate, which the couple now signed, then Charles himself as "Charles Edgemont, Captain RN, presiding"; Winchester and Eliot witnessed the document.

For the occasion, an extra ration of ship's spirits was served up to the crew. Charles and Penny took a glass of wine in Bevan's cabin with the other officers, then ordered that those from *Louisa* were to return and both ships resume their course. Before he could leave the room, Molly caught his arm. "Captain Edgemont," she said seriously, "in a million years I couldn't thank you and Missus Edgemont for all you've done for me." She kissed him on the cheek.

Charles flushed in embarrassment. "You've done it yourself," he said. "You've turned out to be full of surprises. I wish you nothing but happiness."

Bevan and Penny found them, and they all went up to the deck together. At the rail by the side steps, Charles waited while Penny was lifted down into the launch.

"Thank you, Charlie," Bevan said. "You're a true friend."

"If you want my opinion, Daniel," Charles said as he swung outboard and started down, "between you and Molly, you got by far the better of this bargain."

THE SWELTERING MIDDAY heat lay over the Bay of Haifa like a physical presence, leeching moisture, energy, and willpower from all who chose or were forced to endure it. Charles thought that this was what it must be like to live in a baker's oven. There was no place cool on *Louisa*. Even in the regions below the waterline, the airless, unventilated space was like a foul-smelling steambath.

"The bower's down, sir."

"Thank you, Mr. Beechum," Charles responded. The ship now lay at anchor in the outer harbor of the ancient Palestinian city of Acre, shimmering in the haze over the water, reflecting a million glances of dancing sunlight so brightly that he had to shield his eyes. It was not difficult to imagine this as the principal port for the crusader armies of centuries past. Richard I, the Lionheart, had sailed the same course from Cyprus to this very spot. Charles couldn't recall, exactly, but he hoped Richard hadn't done it in mid-July.

"Will that be all, sir?" Beechum asked, still standing in front of him.

"What?" Charles said, startled from his reverie. "I'm sorry. We will hoist out the gig at the beginning of the second dog watch, if you please. I will be calling on the British consul."

"Aye-aye, sir."

The second dog would begin in about four hours, Charles calculated, after the sun had lost some of its power; a cooling breeze should have started up off the sea. Any breeze, even a forge billows, would be welcome now.

Charles glanced out again at the stultified harbor with its Arab dhows, feluccas, xebecs, and other lateen-rigged craft. Nothing moved on the water's surface. How different from the brisk activity of an English harbor.

Bestby, one of two seamen he had posted as lookouts from underneath the canvas canopy, called to him: "Captain, sir."

"Yes?" Charles answered.

"There's a boat comin' out from the 'arbor, sir. I swear it's set a course for us."

"Where away?"

"There, sir. Fine on the beam. Just afore that green-'n'-red thing with the eyes painted on the bow."

Charles looked as directed and saw a small skiff with two men pulling on the oars, making toward them. He found his pocket glass and raised it to his eye. A single man sat in the back, wearing a full-length, not particularly clean gown and a checkered scarf wrapped loosely around his head. Charles's first thought was that the man might be some kind of local merchant coming to peddle his wares. But judging from the urgency with which the taximen strained at their oars, and the absence of any obvious merchandise in the craft, Charles decided not. As the boat neared, he trained his glass on the passenger. He looked more European than Arab, with a deeply tanned face and a weeks' old stubble of beard. To belay all doubt about his intention, the man raised an arm and waved. Charles had the impression that he had seen the man somewhere before, but couldn't think where.

"Boat ahoy, state your business," Beechum called down as the skiff glided under *Louisa*'s side.

"I have information of the utmost importance for your captain," the passenger called back in impeccable, American-accented English.

Charles immediately recognized the voice as that of the curious American he had encountered off Cádiz. "You are welcome to come aboard, Mr. Jones," he said to the man in the boat.

"Captain Edgemont, isn't it?" Jones said as he gained the deck. "I thought I recognized your ship." The two men shook hands. "What on earth are you doing in this godforsaken end of the Mediterranean?"

"I might ask the same of you, sir," Charles answered. "For myself, we are searching for a British squadron which I had hoped to find in these waters. A squadron, I might add, that I had thought to be dogging the French fleet you warned us of at Cádiz. I've had no luck, though. It seems I've been on a wild goose chase. But I am a poor host; may I offer you some refreshment in my cabin?"

Jones shook his head. "Another time, perhaps. I must return to the port before I am missed. There are French agents everywhere. I can answer both of your questions, though, at least to some degree."

"What do you know?" Charles said.

Jones took a breath. "The French force I informed you of landed at Alexandria in Egypt ten days past. They have already taken the city and occupy the surrounding countryside. I expect they will be in Cairo by now."

"How do you know this?" Charles asked, somewhat suspicious that anyone could have such recent intelligence.

"I watched as they landed with my own eyes, sir," the American answered, as if offended by his word being doubted. "I sailed from Egypt in a native dhow only five days ago to inform the British consul here. Unfortunately, he is not in residence at present."

"You mentioned knowing the whereabouts of my squadron," Charles prompted. This was his central concern. He could pass any information about the French to Nelson.

"Only this," Jones said, rubbing at a small scar on his chin. "A squadron of English seventy-fours were seen looking into Alexandria only two days before the French arrived. They were too early, and where they've gone since, I have no idea."

"I see," Charles said, disappointed to still not know where he could find Nelson.

"Possibly you do not," Jones said emphatically. "Your Admiral St. Vincent must be informed of the French landing as soon as possible. I cannot emphasize this strongly enough. Their presence so near to India cannot be allowed to stand. Those colonies are already in rebellion; even a small modern force acting in concert might tip the balance. It is vital to the war, to England, to the world, that this force be destroyed, or at the very least isolated. Do you understand?"

Charles nodded. "I understand full well, sir," he said. "What can you tell me about the disposition of the enemy, so that I may put it in my report?"

"Their warships were at anchor off Alexandria when I saw them last,"

Jones said. "They are a strong assemblage. Here, I've written it down for you." He fished in a pocket of his garment and came up with a scrap of paper.

Charles glanced at the hastily scribbled list and whistled under his breath.

L'Orient, 124
Le Franklin, 80
Le Guillaume Tell, 80
Le Tonnant, 80
L'Aquilon, 74
Le Conquérant, 74
Le Généreux, 74
Le Guerrier, 74
L'Heureux, 74
Le Mercure, 74
Le Spartiate, 74
Le Timoleon, 74
Le Peuple Souverain, 74
Artémise, Diane, Félicité, Justice—frigates

"You will have to return to Gibraltar, in any event," Jones continued. "I doubt the squadron you are seeking is sufficient to engage them."

SEVEN

"I DON'T KNOW, SIR, I'M SURE," SAID SAMUEL ELIOT, RUBBING at the back of his neck. "It's Egypt, that's a fact, but exactly where along the shore, I can't say. There ain't no landmarks that I know of."

Charles looked out at the line of surf, a featureless, dun-colored landscape beyond. A single miserable village of a dozen mudbrick huts with reed-thatched roofs lay huddled among a few scrawny palm trees set back from the shore, three weathered fishing boats pulled up on the beach in front.

"Don't look like much, does it?" Midshipman Sykes observed. Beechum, standing beside him, shook his head disparagingly.

Louisa and *Pylades* had departed Acre two days earlier, sailing to the southwest to pick up the Egyptian shore, with the intention of looking into Alexandria and see with their own eyes the French presence there before proceeding westward with their precious intelligence. The wind had turned variable, sometimes from the north, sometimes west of north. At present it blew fitfully along the coast from due west.

"Have we any charts?" Charles asked.

"Naught, sir," Eliot answered. "Nothing for this far into the Mediterranean. Nobody does. The navy don't have much call to come this way. I have some small maps with broad features; no use for taking bearings on anything."

"All right, in general terms, do you reckon that we are to the east of Alexandria?" Charles asked.

"Aye," Eliot offered readily, "I think that's safe. It's how far to the east, I don't know."

"We are agreed, then. Put her on the starboard tack, we'll make to the west. Mr. Sykes, please make the appropriate signal to *Pylades*. Mr. Beechum, make sure that the lookout in the masthead keeps a sharp eye."

"Aye-aye, sir."

"Yes, sir."

The boatswain blew on his call. The cry "All hands to tack ship" passed up and down the decks. The men trundled up from below, some to the ratlines and aloft, others to the braces. Charles listened as Eliot bellowed out the orders. The wheel spun, and the yards were hauled and lowered; the ship slowed as her head turned. The main and mizzen topsails flogged as they lost their bellies, snapping and shivering. The fore-topsail laid back against the mast, pushing her bow to swing through the eye of the wind. "Midships," Eliot commanded. "Meet her." The lines were hauled and the sails filled. Gracefully, *Louisa* laid over on her new course, her canvas braced up tight against the breeze.

On the starboard tack, the ship sailed away from the shore, some ten miles out, came about, and angled back in again, all the while progressing slowly westward. The day passed, and they tacked and tacked again. The lay of the land transformed to great inland saltwater lagoons filled with all manner of brilliantly colored birds, separated from the sea by thin ridges of palm-dotted sand. Increasingly widespread stands of marsh grasses grew about their rims. The coast itself began to tend northward, and the salt marshes became more extensive until they appeared as a great unbroken sea of reeds.

"What do you make of it?" Charles asked Eliot late in the afternoon.

"I'm thinking we'll soon come upon the first of the great mouths of the Nile," the master said. "We're in the ancient land of the pharaohs."

Before nightfall, they saw a town a few miles inland from the sea with what seemed a broad curving ribbon of gold meandering southward.

"That would be Damietta," Eliot said, "and that what has the sun reflecting off is the Damietta mouth of the Nile River. A hundred miles will find us off Alexandria."

"We will stand out and look in on the port of Alexandria tomorrow, Mr. Eliot," Charles said. He noticed his wife standing by the rail, looking out over the sight. He went and stood beside her, a fertile smell from the land reaching them, until the blood-orange sun settled on the horizon and, by degrees, slipped beneath it.

Half an hour before the first hint of dawn, *Louisa* cleared for action and stood southwest for the dark Egyptian shore. The men were called quietly to their battle stations, the gunports opened, and the cannon run out. As had become her custom, Penny dressed quickly and went below to the officers' wardroom, where Attwater would bring her breakfast. Slowly, imperceptibly, the sky to the east lightened. All lanterns, except the shaded light in the binnacle that lit the compass dial, had long since been extinguished, but Charles fancied he could make out the base of the mizzenmast where it rose through the deck, then the foot of the main course farther forward. He stared over the railing to starboard into the darkness and saw nothing. No, not nothing, a patch of light, or at least less dark, hovered in the distance. That would be *Pylades,* her white sails aloft above the sea.

"Deck!" the lookout from the tops called down. "There's a second sail off the port bow. I can't tell nothing else."

Charles's heart quickened. He moved quickly to the larboard rail and looked forward but could see nothing except black. "How far away?" he yelled upward.

"Can't tell, sir. Sorry. It's still too dark. I can only just see the shade of her canvas. I can't tell nothing else."

"Can you tell how many masts? Is she a warship?"

"Don't know, sir."

Beechum, standing nearby, offered in a timid voice, "I believe that's what he meant when he said he can't tell anything else, sir."

"Yes, thank you, Mr. Beechum," Charles said with a small laugh. "I believe you to be correct. Do you have the watch?"

"Yes, sir."

"Then we shall run down on her and see what we shall see. It'll be light enough soon."

The horizon slowly brightened, the Egyptian coast a low black line under a still-dark, star-speckled sky. Charles saw her sails, then the dark line of her hull underneath, under a mile distant.

"Deck there. She's a French corvette, I'm pretty sure."

Charles thought that looked about right. A corvette was a common type of ship with the French, larger than a brig but smaller than a frigate; probably eighteen or twenty guns; probably six-pounders, possibly eights. As he watched, she braced her yards around to wear away.

"She's seen us," Winchester said from behind him.

"Indeed she has, Stephen," Charles said, his eyes still on the corvette. The wind was light, what there was of it still from the west, the sea almost a flat calm.

"We'll never overhaul her in these airs."

"We'll get a bit of a breeze as the land heats up," Charles said. "But we don't want to catch her. We want to see where she goes."

Whatever was to occur, he considered, he had best settle in for a long stern chase. "House the guns and stand the men down from quarters. It would be a good time to send them to their breakfast."

Out of the corner of his eye, he noticed *Pylades* drawing ahead in determined pursuit of the corvette. "Mr. Sykes! Where is Mr. Sykes?"

Beechum answered, "Mr. Sykes is forward, sir. Shall I fetch him?"

"No," Charles said. "Signal to *Pylades,* please, *Maintain station to starboard.*"

As the light increased, more features of the land and sea became visible. Ahead was a low-lying peninsula projecting several miles into the sea. After a short time, Charles noticed the corvette sending men into her rigging.

"She's going to tack to weather the point," Winchester observed.

"And we shall do the same. See to it, if you please."

Winchester called out the orders. *Louisa*'s bow swung through the wind and settled on the starboard tack, directly taking up the corvette's wake. The land to port, closer now, appeared as sandhills with groves of date and palm trees. There was a town visible, the thin smoke of early-morning cooking fires filtering into the sky, and a broad river running placidly to the point.

Charles approached Eliot. "Do you make that to be Rosetta?" he said. He had a picture of the general lay of the coastline from the map in his atlas.

"Aye," Eliot answered. "That'll be the Rosetta mouth. Other side of the point will be Aboukir Bay, then Alexandria. We should be able to see the French there by noon."

Charles saw Penny approaching across the deck. "Good morning to thee, Samuel Eliot," she said cheerfully, coming to a halt beside him.

"Good morning, Mrs. Edgemont," Eliot answered, lifting his hat.

"What is that ship?" she asked Charles, pointing forward.

"She's French," Charles answered, "a small warship."

"Art thou attempting to catch it?"

"No," he said. "We are only following. I want to see where she goes."

"Thou wilt not shoot at it?"

"Not unless she shoots at us first." Charles guessed she was worried that he intended to attack the smaller ship. He might have, under different circumstances, but not today. He tried to reassure her. "I plan to follow this ship to see if she leads us to the French fleet at Alexandria. As soon as I can confirm that the fleet is there, we will turn away. I don't intend that we stand and fight anyone."

"Thou said that at Malta," she said doubtfully, then fell silent.

The corvette neared the end of the point, her tightly braced sails golden in the just-risen sun and slightly ethereal in the hazy air. A small white bow wave churned along her side. She was reaching on them, he knew, making slightly better speed into the gentle wind than the heavier *Louisa*. It didn't matter, Charles decided, so long as he could keep her in sight.

"Oh, look," Penny said. "They have flags. Aren't they pretty."

Charles noted the signal flags running up her halyards with a feeling of alarm.

"The corvette's telegraphing, sir," Beechum reported at the same time. "Can't see who to."

"Mr. Beechum," Charles said urgently, "take a long glass up to the masthead, to the crosstrees if you have to. Take Sykes with you to report back. I want to know what's on the other side of that point." Beechum left at a run without replying.

"Stephen, we will beat to quarters," Charles ordered. He looked up and saw Beechum climbing the ratlines. He also saw the lookout already in the mainmast top lean out over the side.

"There's a frigate making for the headlands on t'other side, sir," the lookout called down. "She's a thirty-two, I think. You might see her masts from the deck."

Charles looked across the narrowing peninsula. *Louisa* lay about a half mile from the shore and a farther mile to the end of the point. He saw nothing he could identify as a ship's masts.

"There," Winchester said, a telescope to his eye, "just behind the town." Charles had not even noticed that his first lieutenant had come onto the deck. The marine drummer reached the forward rail and started his long roll.

"What's happening?" Penny asked above the din.

Charles opened his glass and looked in the direction Winchester indicated. Almost immediately, he picked out the set of topgallant sails, coasting behind the palms toward the point. He lowered his glass and tried to gauge the distances. The French frigate was a good mile farther from the Rosetta Point, but had the wind behind her, while *Louisa* and *Pylades* were braced tight and struggling into it. He thought they would still reach the point first, but not by any comfortable margin. The Frenchman might lay off the wind and meet him broadside to broadside, or she might stand on if her captain thought Charles would bear away.

"Charlie," Penny repeated, "what's happening?"

What should he do? The corvette, he noted, had rounded the end of the land, making for the safety of her companion. The drummer ceased his drumming. Talmage had gone into the waist to command the gundeck. The gunports opened; the port side cannon rumbled loudly on their trucks.

"What are you doing?" she demanded, pulling on his arm.

"There are two French warships joining on the far side of that spit of land," Charles said. "I fear they mean to attack us."

"Why dost thou not turn away?"

"I will in a minute. I want to know if there are other ships in the bay first," he said. "I would be grateful if you would go below." He looked up to the mainmast crosstrees and saw Beechum with his glass trained out into the distance over the weather beam.

Ahead lay the point where the Rosetta branch of the Nile emptied into the sea. He looked at the sandy beach beneath the dunes. There were men there, some, he thought, on horseback. He took up his long glass and raised it to his eye. In the lens, he saw that the figures wore the dark blue uniforms and plumed vermilion shakos of the French army. Scanning along the beach, he found more infantry with their officers on horseback. That was enough. He now knew for a certainty where the expeditionary force from Toulon had gone. He saw Sykes starting down from Beechum's place on the crosstrees.

Louisa began to come abreast of the point, and Charles could see the slow, muddy mouth of the great river, nearly a mile across, and the sails of the corvette wearing around behind the frigate, both approaching from beyond a low sand island three quarters of a mile away.

"We will bear away, Mr. Eliot," he said. "Put her across the wind."

"Aye, sir," Eliot answered, and signaled to the helmsmen at the wheel. "Hands to the braces," he roared. Charles could feel on his cheek that the wind was light and fitful, still westerly but with increasing impetus off the land. *Louisa*'s bow slowly swung until it pointed directly away from the coast, and the two French ships, toward the vast empty sea.

"Mr. Beechum's respects, sir," Sykes reported breathlessly.

"Yes?" Charles said.

"He says he can't see very far into the bay. He says there's a power of mist in the air, sir."

"Very well," Charles said, "you may—"

Two closely spaced bangs of distant cannon fire sounded over the water. Charles turned in time to see a small cloud of gray-black smoke hovering on the leading French frigate's bow. He scanned the sea surface and saw two plumes of water spout up, one a hundred yards to port and only slightly astern, the other farther off.

"Mr. Sykes, signal *Pylades* to make all possible sail."

"Yes, sir."

"Now what is happening?" Penny asked, still standing beside him.

Charles had almost forgotten she was there. "That French ship has opened fire on us with her bow chasers," he said. "We are trying to run away."

"Are we faster than they?"

"I hope so," Charles said. "I would be more comfortable if you went below."

"It does not seem so dangerous," Penny answered. "I wish to stay. I will go if it becomes more menacing."

Charles didn't have time to argue with her. He turned to the sailing master. "Mr. Eliot, I want every fathom of speed we can manage. Send up the royals if you think it advisable."

"Aye, sir."

"Stephen," Charles said next, "pass the word for the carpenter to see if he can cut ports for stern chasers. We could move two of the quarterdeck nine-pounders aft."

Twin clouds of gun smoke ballooned again from the frigate. The booms of the cannon reached him a moment later. Charles saw one splash forty yards to port, even with the mainmast. He didn't see the fall of the second ball.

"Sir," Beechum said, arriving on the deck and touching his hat.

"Yes, what have you to report?"

The acting lieutenant took a moment to collect his breath. "I couldn't see anything for certain. The visibility is very poor. There was a moment I thought I saw the barest outline of something, but it could have been an illusion. I'm sorry, sir."

"Thank you anyway, Mr. Beechum," Charles said. "You've done well. You may speak to Mr. Winchester for your duties."

Charles looked aft again and did not like what he saw. Both enemy warships looked noticeably closer, perhaps only half a mile astern. *Pylades* lay a cable length to starboard, her bow even with *Louisa*'s mainmast.

Since Charles had hoped that the French would be satisfied with chasing him well away from the shore and then turning back, he became increasingly disappointed as the morning wore on. The wind freshened, and before long, the distance between *Louisa* and the leading frigate stabilized at just under a half mile, the corvette lagging somewhat behind. The frigate continued to methodically fire her bow chasers, although at very long range, and while several balls had passed through the rigging, no real damage had been done. He knew this was a situation that could change in the blink of an eye, however, if a lucky ball struck a mast section or cracked a yardarm. He had the guns housed and allowed the crew to stand down, but kept the gundeck cleared.

As vexing as it was to be under fire without being able to answer, this was not his biggest worry. Hour by hour, Bevan's brig slipped slowly behind. The two had been about even when they had turned away to run. Soon *Pylades*'s bow was level with *Louisa*'s mainmast, then the mizzen, later the rudderpost. Now, as Charles looked, she lay nearly a half a cable's length behind.

"Why does not Daniel Bevan keep up?" Penny asked anxiously.

"Because we are the faster ship on this point of the wind," Charles answered. "Bevan's doing all he can."

"Surely the French warship will overtake him," she said. "What will happen then?"

"It depends on whether he decides to surrender or fight. If he surrenders, he will be taken prisoner. If he fights, the two French warships are both larger, and one of them is much stronger."

Penny bit her lip. "I fear Daniel Bevan will resist," she said finally. "Thou canst not allow that to happen."

Charles knew that his duty, at whatever cost, was to carry his information about the location of the French fleet to Nelson or, failing that, to St. Vincent at Gibraltar. The fate of Bevan's brig was small beer in this calculation. At the very least he must communicate with the British consul at Syracuse, in Sicily, who was the closest British representative in that direction and could pass the intelligence forward. Charles could not, no matter his personal feelings, unnecessarily engage two enemy ships of war, even if he had better than half a chance of success, which he judged he did not. He also knew that as soon as Bevan decided his situation to be hopeless, he would throw tiny *Pylades* into the path of the French in hopes of delaying them long enough for Charles to escape. If *Louisa* had half a chance, *Pylades* had none. There had to be something he could do. He conceived of a plan—a plan that he knew to be flawed.

"Stephen," he called to Winchester.

"Sir?"

"Belay moving the nine-pounders aft. Get the men back to their battle quarters."

"Yes, sir."

"Mr. Sykes, signal to *Pylades,* if you please, *Set course for Syracuse.* You'll have to spell out 'Syracuse.' Tell me the moment he acknowledges."

"Aye-aye, sir."

"What art thou preparing to do?" Penny asked.

Charles looked at her for a long moment before he spoke. "I am going to try to slow the leading frigate," he said. "I plan to cut across her bows and fire at long range, then sail to the west. Maybe we will disable her. If we don't, and the larger one turns to follow us, Daniel can outsail the second." He knew that it was a compromise, to keep his ship and his wife out of harm's way for as long as possible. The chances of disabling the frigate at this range were less than small. If the frigate ignored him and continued after *Pylades,* Charles would be unable to come back against the wind in time to do anything. On the reverse of the coin, it was just possible that he would damage the frigate enough for Bevan to escape. In the back of his mind, he knew that part of his plan was guided by a caution against exposing his wife to danger. He didn't like it; he didn't know what else to do.

Penny's mouth set in a hard straight line. She stood rigidly erect, looking at the near French warship, then up at Charles. "Will that accomplish thy goal? Will it permit both Daniel Bevan's ship and thine to escape?"

"Maybe," he said, a trace of doubt in his voice. "I don't know. It depends on what the captain of the first one, the bigger one, does." Finally, he said, "Possibly not."

She was silent for a moment, then asked, "What would thou do if I were not present?"

"If you were not on board?" Charles did not have to think long. "In that event, I would attack her directly to be certain of stopping her, regardless of the consequences."

"Then do that," she said. "I expect thou to do nothing different on account of me."

"No," he said. "It is too dangerous."

"Too dangerous for whom?" she persisted. "Thou or Daniel Bevan?"

"For you," he said in frustration. "If we are defeated, you may be killed. If not killed, you will surely be captured. I do not know what would happen to you then, and I do not wish for either of us to find out."

"Would it be different for Daniel and Molly Bevan?" she said.

"No," Charles said reluctantly.

"Thy ship is larger than Daniel's," she said quietly. "Surely we have the better opportunity."

Midshipman Sykes interrupted: "*Pylades* has signaled *Interrogatory,* sir." Charles had expected some such response. Bevan was protesting his orders.

"Repeat the signal with an imperative," Charles said, "then ignore him."

The frigate fired her bow chasers again, one ball screaming loudly through the air close above their heads.

Turning back to his wife, Charles said, "What about your Quaker beliefs? Do you really want me to attack?"

"I abhor violence in every form," Penny said, her expression anguished. "But I cannot allow others to be sacrificed for my benefit." She hesitated, then added, "Perhaps thou can only damage it and sail away?"

Charles smiled thinly. "I would be pleased to do so, were it possible. Once we begin, it will not likely end until the thing is finished, one the victor and one defeated."

She nodded silently in what he took to be approval, or at least resignation.

"All right," Charles said. He glanced across at *Pylades,* even farther behind. He turned to Winchester. "We will soon present the armament on the starboard side."

"Yes, sir."

"Do not have the gunports opened until we begin to turn. I want the first broadside to be chain shot. Aim high for her rigging. The range will be about four hundred yards. Tell me when we're ready."

Winchester called down the orders to Talmage, who commanded the gundeck. The round shot in the guns would have to be drawn, then replaced with specially manufactured projectiles consisting of two half-balls connected by a yard of medium chain. Their purpose was to wreak havoc among an opponent's lines, cables, yards, and canvas aloft. Chain shot was notoriously inaccurate at long range. If he was lucky, very lucky, Charles thought, he might sufficiently damage the frigate's upper works to effectively disable her in a single salvo. If so, *Louisa* might turn again and resume flight before the corvette even came within range. Of course, it was also possible that daisies grew on the moon.

"Mr. Eliot," he continued, close to completing the necessary sequence of preparations, "we will come about on the starboard side in a moment. Send no one aloft until after we begin the turn." There was no point in giving away their intentions until the last possible instant.

Sykes approached from the forward quarterdeck rail. "Lieutenant Talmage reports that the guns are prepared, sir."

"Thank you," Charles said. He turned to Penny. Her gaze was directed over the stern at the following frigate. There were clouds of sail on the masts and white water curling back from the stem, the hard bulk of the hull in between. "It's time that you go below," he said. "We are about to begin."

She tore her eyes away only for a moment to glance at him. "I do not wish to," she said.

"Penny," he said patiently, "you must. I told you, it will be too dangerous."

"It will be dangerous for thou as well," she argued. "I want to see that Molly and Daniel are safe."

"No," Charles said. "Go down and assist the surgeon. I cannot engage an enemy warship with you on the deck; I fear too much for your safety."

Penny looked at him, undecided.

"You must go," he said firmly.

Reluctantly, she nodded, then turned and went toward the hatchway leading below. The moment she had disappeared, Charles said, "Mr. Eliot, put the helm over."

Louisa began her turn to put the wind behind her and the French frigate off her beam.

"You may fire when ready," Charles said to Winchester. As he watched, the starboard gunports flipped open, the gun crews straining on their lines to drag the cannon up hard against the bulwarks. The frigate did not anticipate *Louisa*'s turn but reacted quickly to it, veering belatedly, her port side gunports opening.

"Fire," Winchester shouted.

The deck erupted in a deafening blast, half hidden in billowing smoke as the guns lunged inward on their breechings. The gun crews were already at work sponging out as Charles looked for the trajectory of the shot descending toward the Frenchman. Even as he watched, he knew that his gunners' aim had been thrown off by the frigate's turn, most of the shot falling into the sea, although one or two ripped through the mizzen sails, causing the canvas to jerk and tear. No mast tilted; nor did he see any yardarm snap. *Louisa*'s guns were just being hauled back out when the frigate produced her own billowing gray broadside, the orange flash of the explosions stabbing through. A second later, round shot screamed across the deck and through the halyards and stays.

Louisa's cannon fired again, this time with solid shot. The salvo told against the Frenchman's hull, striking a gunport and pounding her bulwarks. The two ships angled closer as they exchanged broadsides. Four hundred yards became three; three hundred, two. Charles concentrated his fire against the Frenchman's gundeck, the frigate mainly toward *Louisa*'s masts. He thought to search for the corvette, but a quick look yielded nothing, and he decided she must be somewhere behind the frigate.

Another increasingly drawn-out broadside, as the faster gun crews fired early, the slower later; and another, with the carronades barking sharply in between. The distance closed to a hundred yards, musket range. So far all of *Louisa*'s masts still stood, although the sails were punctured in dozens of places, and strings of severed rigging swung like vines in the wind. The French frigate's hull had taken some damage, with gaps in her railing and her sides along the row of gunports pierced and scarred.

Charles was not pleased. His ship and crew were holding their own against the more powerful Frenchman, but he could not keep it up indefinitely. All he had wanted was to rob the frigate of her speed until he and Bevan could escape into the darkness of night. Now he had been forced into a grueling match, like two bare-knuckle fighters facing each other tied to a bench at half arm's length, until one beat the other insensible. Charles did not wish his ship to be pounded into the equivalent of insensible; nor did he need to subject his opponent to such treatment. He would like it better if he could get up off the bench and run, but he couldn't with the French ship intact.

Louisa's broadside thundered in a long ragged discharge, sending fresh clouds of dense smoke along her deck. Charles smiled as he saw the frigate's mizzen shiver and then twist sideways, straining the main topgallant backstay and pulling the mast section with it. The ship's crew gave a loud cheer. They'd wounded her, he should take the opportunity to run, he thought. But with a little more damage, he could take her. If he could bring down one more mast, she could not maneuver and would have to strike. To Winchester, he ordered, "Keep the men about their business."

"Silence on deck," Winchester shouted. "Attend to your guns."

The Frenchman fired her broadside together. Someone must be calling out the firing sequence, probably to make sure it was done correctly in the heat of battle. Two of her gunports, Charles noted, had remained empty. If he had wanted to carry her, it would be best to close now and board. No, that would be risky, she would have a far larger crew. If he could knock down one more mast, he could cross her bow and rake her. He thought about the options. Did he really want to be encumbered with the badly damaged prize? It would be better to run while he still had the masts to do it. He hesitated, trying to make up his mind. Where was the corvette? *Louisa*'s cannon fire was becoming almost continuous. He quickly looked around the surface of the sea and found the smaller French warship in an unexpected place, beating up to get windward of his stern. That was enough; it was time to break it off and flee. Only the corvette could follow, and he could deal with that.

The frigate fired again. A loud rending crack came from above, and *Louisa*'s foretopmast and main topgallant mast came crashing down. The main topgallant landed in a heap of rope, mast, and yard on the deck; the foretopmast fell over the starboard side of the bow and splashed into the water.

"Damnation," Charles swore, furious with himself. "Clear that wreckage forward," he yelled to Talmage in the waist. He had hesitated, greedy for a prize. The moment to escape had passed.

With the foremast acting as a sea anchor, *Louisa* slowed, her stern swinging to port. The Frenchman, with her mizzenmast dragging astern, could not maneuver. Of her own volition, *Louisa* drifted sideways across the enemy's stern.

"Belay that!" Charles screamed down at Talmage. "Leave the mast where it is. Rake her!"

Charles stared at the frigate's stern directly across from him. The maindeck twelve-pounders crashed out as one into the undefended after-structure of the frigate. Charles saw briefly that her name was *Félicité* before the thunderous barrage smashed gap after gap in the transom and exploded the stern windows. A second broadside widened the holes so he could see the men inside running from their guns, some trying to drag wounded shipmates below. After a third broadside, her mainmast, repeatedly struck between decks, broke and fell forward. The fourth sent ball after ball screaming the length of the deck, upending guns, smashing timbers, and killing almost every remaining living thing. He saw a man with both legs blown off attempting to crawl to a hatchway.

Something pulled violently on Charles's arm; a small fist beat frantically on his back. He turned to see his wife wide-eyed in horror. When the French ship had stopped firing, Penny must have come back on deck to see what was happening.

"Stop, you'll kill them all. They cannot even defend themselves," she screamed at him. Tears welled in her eyes and ran down her cheeks. "Look, look," she said, pointing into the void of the stern galley. "Look how many are dead."

Charles rubbed his palm across his eyes. He could see the length of her gundeck, a scene of hellish carnage, the deck awash with blood and deserted except for unmoving forms, and parts of forms, lying by overturned weapons. A revulsion came over him. He had not wanted to fight the frigate at all, and now he was shocked by what he'd done, saddened that his wife had seen it. He should have stopped it sooner. He temporized that the French ship had not struck her colors; of course, with two masts gone, she had no obvious flag to strike.

"Cease firing, Stephen," he said. "Send Talmage across to see if she will yield. Send him with enough marines to encourage her to do so."

Charles quickly looked to windward for the corvette. He found her lying to just out of cannon range, as if undecided what to do. Behind her, he saw Bevan's *Pylades* closing to attack. He sighed.

"We have to help them," Penny said, pulling on his arm to attract his attention. "There must be very many injured."

"We will," Charles said, trying to order his thoughts. "I am just now sending Lieutenant Talmage to ask if they will permit it. Mr. Sykes!" he yelled.

"Yes, sir?" the young midshipman answered, skidding to a halt in front of him.

"Signal to *Pylades,* please, *Maintain position.*"

"Yes, sir."

"Then run up a white flag on"—Charles looked upward and surveyed the damaged rigging"—the highest mast we have."

"A white flag, sir?"

"Yes, a white flag, a big one. Quickly, please."

"Why a white flag?" Winchester asked. "A truce?"

"A parlay," Charles answered. "I want to talk with the captain of that corvette before Daniel does something foolish, like sink her. Will you please hoist out the cutter with another flag and go over. Invite her captain on board with my compliments and my guarantee of his safety. I have a proposal to make."

"What can you possibly need to ask him?" Winchester said.

"I require his assistance," Charles answered. He had to force himself to concentrate. How many officers did he have left? "Mr. Beechum," he called, seeing the young lieutenant in the waist, supervising the clearing away of the remains of the topgallant mast.

"Sir?" Beechum yelled back.

"You will please see that the starboard guns remain manned and run out." This to emphasize the desirability of *Félicité*'s surrendering without further argument. He saw Talmage, Cooley, and the marines climbing down into the ship's cutter.

"Mr. Keswick!" Charles was beginning to feel that he was trying to deal with too many things at once. "Someone pass the word for the boatswain."

"The signal to *Pylades* has been acknowledged, sir," Sykes reported. "I've sent a white flag up the mizzenmast."

"Very good," Charles said. "Get you down to the surgeon with my compliments. Request a report on our dead and injured. Would you also ask when he will be free."

"Yes, sir," Sykes said, and departed at a run. Charles wished he had half as much energy. He felt drained, tired, disgusted with himself.

"Yes, sir?" Keswick said, arriving on the quarterdeck and touching his hat.

"How long before you will be able to report on our damage aloft?"

"Within the half hour, sir," the boatswain replied. "We're working on it now."

"Thank you, keep me informed. You may draft as many men as you see fit to effect the repairs." Charles paused as another thought came to him. "I believe you may also be able to go across to that French frigate to take off whatever spars and cordage may be of use."

"That'll be a help," Keswick said. "If I may ask, what are you planning to do with her?"

Charles considered. "We'll burn her, I think that's easiest," he said. "Feel free to take off whatever you need."

Penny overheard the exchange and reacted with alarm. "Burn that ship? Thou canst not burn the ship. What will happen to all of the people? To burn them would be inhuman."

Charles exhaled slowly. "We will take everyone off first," he said to reassure her, "the wounded as well as the healthy. It will be all right."

"Canst thou do that? Canst thou just burn a whole ship?" she asked, somewhat calmer. "It seems a terrible waste."

"I have captured her," Charles said patiently. "I can do as I think necessary. We have no time to make repairs and sail her to a prize court. I cannot allow the French to retain her; therefore, I shall sink her. But not until the crew are taken off."

"Where will thou put all the people?" she asked, looking around. "We are not so large a boat."

Charles saw that Talmage and the marines had reached *Félicité* and were climbing onto her abandoned deck. *Louisa*'s gig, with Winchester and his white flag aboard, had hoisted her fore and aft sails and was standing toward the corvette.

"Captain, sir," Sykes reported, "Mr. Lincoln's respects. He says we have three injured, only one seriously. That's a broken arm from when the foretopmast fell. He asks me to tell you that he will be at liberty in just a moment."

"Thank you," Charles said. He was only moderately surprised at how few casualties *Louisa* had sustained. It was well known that the French navy preferred directing their fire into an opponent's masts and rigging, in hopes of quickly impairing mobility, while British tactics normally concentrated on an enemy's hull to degrade fighting ability over the longer term. In such exchanges, the French frequently incurred the higher numbers of casualties. Charles knew that he had been lucky—his victory had, ironically, been the result of the frigate's success in bringing down *Louisa*'s foremast. He saw Talmage appear at *Félicité*'s shattered stern. Beside him stood a very young French officer, probably the equivalent of a British midshipman, his sword in Talmage's hand. Charles assumed that meant the higher ranking of the ship's officers had been killed or injured. Talmage waved across to signal that all was well and that the French had officially surrendered.

"Mr. Sykes," Charles said, "if you would assist Mr. Lincoln in assembling a party to go across and help tend to the French wounded."

"Yes, sir," Sykes answered, and left.

"Where will thou place those people?" Penny demanded, reclaiming his attention.

"In the last resort, on board *Louisa*," he answered. He looked over his shoulder and noted that Winchester had gone aboard the corvette, the gig bobbing in the sea alongside. "My hope is to persuade the other French ship to carry their countrymen away."

"I will go across with Matthew Lincoln to assist with the injured," she announced.

Charles opened his mouth to object, or at least to say that it wasn't necessary, then he shut it. He was uncomfortable with her being in the presence of so many injured men. It was a disgusting business. But it would do no harm; perhaps it would help her come to terms with what she had witnessed if she could do something useful. He felt a sadness again that she had been present to see it. "I am sure the surgeon and wounded will be grateful," he said.

He raised his glass and watched as Winchester climbed back down into the gig, followed closely by a French officer. The ship's boat pushed off, raised her sails, and started back. Lincoln arrived on deck with his case of instruments.

"I have hopes of transferring the French crew with their wounded into that corvette," Charles said. "I'll know for certain after I talk to her captain. In the meantime, do what you can."

"All right," Lincoln said. "I'll have them laid out on the deck."

"And Mrs. Edgemont will accompany you. She wishes to be of assistance."

Lincoln did not object. Instead, he said, "It would be useful to have someone who speaks French."

"I may be helpful," Penny said. "I have studied it."

"You have?" Charles said. "I had no idea."

"There are many things thou dost not know," she said mysteriously, then turned to follow the surgeon.

Keswick approached to report that the damage to *Louisa*'s upper works was extensive, especially to halyards and lines. He had no suitable spar to jury-rig the upper mast sections but hoped something might be found on the French ship. When pressed, he allowed that if they worked without a break, they might be fit enough to sail by morning, especially if they had some assistance from *Pylades*.

"I'll see if that can be arranged," Charles said.

The gig arrived alongside, and Charles went to the entryport to meet the corvette's commander as he came aboard. Winchester climbed up over the side first, followed by a scowling, hard-looking man of medium height and broad shoulders. The Frenchman surveyed the damage to *Louisa*'s masts with satisfaction but, aside from a quick glance, avoided looking at the savaged frigate lying forlornly in the water off the opposite beam. Charles struggled to summon some remnant of his energy. He had to concentrate.

"May I have the honor to present Capitaine de Frégate Jean Louis Baptiste," Winchester said formally. "Captain Edgemont."

Charles stepped forward and extended his hand. The Frenchman ignored it. "Ask if he would like some refreshment," he said.

The corvette's captain replied in a tone that could only be interpreted as disdainful. "The captain says he does not drink with the English," Winchester translated judiciously. Charles, who spoke a little of the language, had distinctly made out the words *"merde"* and *"cochon."*

"Fine," Charles said with a tight-lipped smile. "Please inform Captain Whoreson Sodomite that I will permit him to take the crew off the frigate, if he wishes it, before I burn her."

Winchester suppressed a grin and translated an expurgated version. The French captain responded more briefly. "He asks what we will do if he refuses."

Charles stared at the French captain. He found the man's manner irritating in the extreme. *Two can play at this game,* he thought. "Tell him it is a matter of indifference to me. With the crew aboard or not, I'm still burning her."

"You wouldn't," Winchester said.

"Just translate," Charles answered, then did his best to chuckle menacingly. "Add that I am only making the offer because my officers have requested it. You might hint that I would just as soon watch them burn." He would not give the Frenchman the satisfaction of any concessions.

Winchester did as he was asked. The Frenchman gave a lengthy and heated reply. "He says how does he know you won't attack him? He wants us to move out of cannon range first."

"Tell him he has my word of honor as a British naval officer. If that is not satisfactory, then there is no arrangement. You may also tell him that if there is no arrangement, we will attack the corvette the moment he is back on board. The decision is his."

Charles watched the French captain's face darken as Winchester translated. Capitaine Baptiste asked a question in which Charles heard the word *"honneur"* mentioned twice, which Winchester answered. Then the captain gave a lengthy speech. Charles could guess what it was about from the few words he'd understood and the way the man gestured with his hands.

"He says he'll do it," Winchester said. "He has three conditions—"

Charles shook his head dismissively. "I'm not offering any conditions," he said. "This is what I will allow. He will take one of my officers on board his ship; Beechum, I should think. Beechum will remain on the side rail by the entryport, where I can see him at all times. The corvette is to approach with her gunports closed and guns unmanned. *Pylades* will follow directly behind him. The corvette will proceed to tie up with the frigate and take off her crew and the wounded, nothing more. He will leave Beechum on the frigate and return to Egypt. If, at any time during the approach, Beechum signals that something is amiss, we will engage and, if successful, will burn both his ship and the frigate. Make sure he understands this."

Winchester launched into a lengthy monologue while Charles watched. The French captain was not pleased by what he heard. Charles began to feel sympathy for him. It must be difficult to take orders from an enemy, but he didn't know what else the man could do.

Winchester and the Frenchman talked back and forth before Winchester said, "It's no good. He's afraid it's a trap."

Charles made a show of stifling a yawn. In a barely interested voice, he said, "Argue with him. Tell him Bevan's an experienced commander who has outfought larger ships than his. Tell him that although *Louisa* is damaged, she can still sail well enough to cut off his retreat. When you're finished, look at me as though you want me to change my mind." He fished in his pocket and came up with a piece of paper.

Winchester spoke in imploring tones. At the mention of Bevan's ship, the French captain's eyes narrowed, but he gave nothing away. Finally, Winchester turned back to Charles with a pleading expression.

Charles smiled broadly at the Frenchman. He bent to take up a length of smoking slow match kept by the guns in case the flintlocks failed, and blew on the tip until it burned cherry red. Then he lit the paper. He held the burning scrap up where they could all see it. When it threatened to burn his fingers, he dropped it over the side. *"Bonne chance, Monsieur Capitaine,"* he said, extending his hand once more. *"Au revoir."*

Capitaine Baptiste did not shake the offered hand, but he did not turn to leave, either. Instead, he spoke to Winchester with harsh, angry words, a torrent of words, gesturing and pointing several times at Charles in disgust. After two or three minutes, he stopped. Winchester bowed with his hand over his heart and spoke a single sentence in which Charles heard the word *"honneur."*

"He'll do it," Winchester said.

"That's all he said?" Charles asked.

"Well, no," Winchester answered, "he said he thinks you're a madman. He asked if I would guarantee on my sacred honor that you would keep your word. Really, he thinks you're crazy."

Beechum was called and his duties explained to him. As Capitaine Baptiste and the young acting lieutenant went over the side into the gig to make the trip back to the corvette, Charles said, "That man is one tough son of a bitch. Bevan got off easy."

It wasn't until sometime later that he realized he'd burnt the list of French warships that Jones had given him in Acre.

EIGHT

"YOU JUST CAN'T MANAGE TO STAY OUT OF TROUBLE, CAN you?" Daniel Bevan said, climbing up through *Louisa*'s entryport. "And yes, before you ask, *Pylades*'s boatswain and his crew will be over presently to show you how to put your ship back into order. It's shocking the state you allow her to fall into."

Charles, who had been determined to maintain a firm scowl, broke into a grin. "And you have a quaint notion that orders are something akin to polite suggestions."

The French corvette, having taken off *Félicité*'s crew without incident, lay just visible hull down on the southern horizon. Mrs. Daniel Bevan swung up from the cutter alongside to be set gently on the deck.

"What orders?" Bevan said, the very portrait of innocence.

"To go to Syracuse. I signaled you to sail for Syracuse. Twice," Charles said as sternly as he could.

"Oh, that," Bevan answered. "I appreciated your concern, but there's nothing particularly interesting in Syracuse."

Penny came forward from Charles's cabin. She had returned from the frigate with Lincoln and most of the others of *Louisa*'s crew as soon as the wounded had been taken off. Charles had noted an unhappy expression on her face and bloodstains on her dress when she came aboard, but he hadn't had an opportunity to talk with her. She appeared now in fresh clothing and a smile on seeing Molly. The two women embraced and went aft.

"The information we have on the destination of the French fleet must be conveyed to the consul in Syracuse," Charles continued. "My instructions were for you to do that."

Bevan turned serious. "I know," he said. "I also know why you turned *Louisa* to engage the French frigate. As noble as that was, I couldn't let you face the both of them alone."

"Next time . . ." Charles began.

Bevan looked at *Félicité* wallowing in the water nearby. She lay deserted and empty except for *Louisa*'s boats occasionally plying back and forth with any useful items that could be taken off. "Yes, next time," he said. "What do you plan to do with her?"

"Set fire to her, sink her. I can't tow her all the way to Syracuse," Charles said. "We're taking everything useful off. Attwater's over there now, looking through the captain's stores. God knows what he'll bring back."

"Goose liver," Bevan said confidently. "French captains are crazy for goose liver, I'm told. They call it patty. Revolting stuff."

"I was planning on going over myself," Charles said, "to see if I can find the ship's papers: orders, signal books, charts, the log, that sort of thing. I know Jervis would appreciate having them. Perhaps you would be so good as to join me."

"Be my pleasure," Bevan answered. "Nothing I'd like better than crawling around in the dark, airless hold of a ship that carries a lot of garlic."

The two men went across in *Pylades*'s gig, which still lay alongside. Climbing up *Félicité*'s side ladder, Charles surveyed the eerily empty deck, with its battered sides and broken gun carriages. The dead— including, he had been informed, her captain and all of her three lieutenants—had been put overboard. There were bloodstains on the deck boards and all manner of splintered wood, pieces of clothing, broken lines, and cables scattered at random. As the ship had been cleared for action, he could see the length of the gundeck from the bow all the way to the broken stern under the quarterdeck. Where the French captain's cabin would have been was now open space lined by overturned guns.

"His things will have been taken below," Bevan said. "We'll have to find them."

Charles nodded. It was not pleasant walking through the shattered hulk of another captain's ship. He found it unnerving, a little like standing on a fresh grave. For a moment he had a picture in his mind of a French captain passing through *Louisa*'s battered remains. It made him shiver. They went down the after ladderway to the lower deck, still lit by isolated lanterns hung from the beams. If it were his ship, Charles reasoned, they would have brought the captain's furnishings somewhere convenient, thinking that everything would have to go back up again when the battle was over. He soon spotted a hasty pile of furniture off to the side. Bevan found two sea chests and dragged them into the middle of the room while Charles forced the locks on a desk with his pocketknife. Inside, he found what he was looking for: the captain's log, the muster book, some volumes of naval instructions and regulations, and a collection of envelopes and loose papers. Since he could read little of it, he put them in a pile on top of the chests. He would send someone to collect them later.

"Attwater should be around here somewhere," he said. "The gig was still alongside."

"The captain's pantry would be aft, wouldn't it?" Bevan said. "Attwater," he shouted. The sound reverberated in the hollow space.

"Maybe he went down into the hold," Charles said. "He could have been looking for anything." He took a lantern from overhead, and they started down the ladderway into the cavernous space below.

"Attwater!" Charles shouted.

" 'Ere, sir. Forward," Attwater's reedy voice reached them. Charles looked and saw a faint circle of light near the bow.

"Christ," Charles muttered. "Come aft to the hatchway."

"Wouldn't it be best if you didn't come forward, sir. You'll see."

Charles muttered some more but started forward along the narrow walkway between the stowed water casks and barrels of the ship's stores, holding the lantern in front with Bevan close behind. The space was close and humid and stank like a cesspool.

"What have you found that is so important you couldn't come to the ladderway?" he asked as he neared the light.

" 'Ere, sir," Attwater said. He was sitting cross-legged on the deck, holding a bundle of loose clothing against his chest. Then Charles saw that it wasn't a bundle of clothing. Two large brown eyes stared at him from beneath a disheveled mop of curly dark hair.

"Oh my God," Bevan breathed.

There, in Attwater's lap, sat a very frightened child, a girl, Charles guessed, of about four years old, clutching at his servant's coat lapels.

Charles knelt and stroked the child's hair. "There, there," he said softly. "It will be all right. No one will hurt you." To Attwater, he said, "Where did you find her?"

"Down 'ere in the 'old. I thought I saw something from the 'atchway and came down to look. I caught up with 'er up 'ere. I wasn't never so surprised. Do you think she's a stowaway?"

"No," Charles said, "I think it's more likely she's someone's child, an officer's, probably. She was placed down here for safety during the battle." He ran the back of his fingers gently across the girl's cheek. "Hello, my little one," he said, smiling reassuringly. "*Jeth* Charles. *Et vous?*" The girl hid her face against Attwater's chest.

"Christ, Charlie," Bevan said, "you call that French?"

"Can you do better?"

When Bevan refrained from answering, Charles tried again. "Charles," he said, poking his chest. "Daniel." He pointed upward at Bevan. "Attwater." Finally, he touched her hand. "*Vous?*"

"Claudette." It came in a whisper so tiny he had to bend close to catch it.

"Well, Claudette," Charles said, "we can't leave you here." To Attwater, he said, "Can you carry her?"

"She don't weigh next to nothing," he answered.

"Let's go, then." Charles stood. He and Bevan helped Attwater to his feet, still clutching the bundle. As they were making their way forward, Bevan asked, "What are you going to do with her?"

"Haven't a notion," Charles said. "I'm going to give her to Penny. She'll know."

Claudette was handed down into *Pylades's* cutter, which excited much conversation among the boat's crew, and back up onto *Louisa*. Winchester stared in surprise as Charles led the little girl, her grip firmly around his finger, toward his cabin. "What's this?" the lieutenant asked.

"Claudette," Charles answered. "She's come to visit us." He bent in front of the child and pointed to Winchester. "Stephen," he said.

"Stepen," she repeated.

He touched his own chest again. "Charles."

"Charle," Claudette said with the very smallest of smiles, softening the C and rolling the R so that it came out as "Sharrle."

The marine sentry at the door to Charles's cabin snapped to attention with wide eyes. "Claudette, this is Private Thomas," Charles said. "Private Thomas, Claudette." The marine took the liberty of chucking the girl under her chin, for which he received a cautious upturning of the corners of her mouth.

Charles entered first. He found Penny and Molly seated together on the bench under the stern windows.

"Charlie," Penny said, rising, "I have something to tell thee."

"In a minute," he answered. Opening the door wider, he said, "May I introduce Mademoiselle Claudette. She has come to stay with us for a time." To be complete, he added, "She's French."

The girl clung shyly to Charles's leg, but her eyes widened at the sight of the two women. Penny and Molly crossed the cabin quickly, Penny dropping to her knees, taking the child into her arms, and holding her against her chest.

"Where did you find her?" she asked.

"In the hold of *Félicité*," Charles said. "Attwater spotted her."

"Where are her parents?" Penny stroked the child's hair and picked her up as she rose to her feet.

"Her father, probably," Charles said. "Killed, taken off with the injured. I don't know."

"Poor little girl," Penny cooed, hugging her closer. "You must be starving." Then she said something in French to which Claudette nodded. To Charles, Penny said, "Get her some food. Something soft and hot; none of your salted meat."

"The galley should be relit by now," Charles said. "Attwater, see what you can arrange. Bring some ship's biscuit in the meantime."

"And some boiling water, please," Penny said. To Molly: "Would thou bring the remainder of our chocolate?" To Charles: "Have we any milk?"

"Goat's milk," Charles answered. "Someone will have to convince the goat to give it up."

"See to it," she said. "Have it heated. Not too hot. And find the rest of her clothing, it must still be on board the French ship. Get me some fresh water so that we can bathe her, and see that it is heated also."

Charles nodded and, with Bevan, left the cabin to find one of his lieutenants. Beechum was closest.

"Send Sykes and a half-dozen seamen across to the frigate," Charles said, pulling on his ear. "Have them search her from stem to stern, especially the hold. I want to be certain there is no one of any age, size, or description left on board." He also told Beechum of the chests and papers on the lower deck and requested that they be brought back to his cabin.

"Yes, sir," Beechum answered, touching his hat. "Will there be anything else?"

"Oh, yes, have someone milk the goat. Have it heated, not too hot, and sent to my cabin."

"Yes, sir," the lieutenant said, and left.

Charles remembered that Penny had said she had something to tell him. It would have to wait, he decided. She had something else to occupy her now. Anyway, how important could it be? He went forward to find Keswick and see how the repairs to *Louisa's* rigging were progressing.

Daniel and Molly Bevan were asked to stay to supper, during which most of the attention was devoted to the very young Claudette, who ate happily and smiled suspiciously when addressed. Once, when Charles helped her slice her food, she nodded seriously to him and said, "*Merci,* Monsieur Sharrle," which sent an arrow through his heart.

Toward the end of the meal, he studied his wife, seated on the other side of the girl. She seemed both pleased and content, and had a rosy sort of glow about her. "I am sorry," he said, "you told me earlier that there was something you wanted to tell me. What was it?"

Penny met his eyes, then looked back down at her plate. "I will speak with thee later," she said. Charles noticed Molly glance quickly across the table at Penny, who furtively glanced back with a small shake of her head. Daniel Bevan contentedly chewed on his roast chicken, picking a bone clean and dropping it on his plate. Charles stared intently across the table at Molly until he caught her eye. Molly turned pink.

"Ain't we had nice weather today," she observed a little too loudly. "Wasn't I worried when I saw you fighting that other ship. Wasn't I worried, Daniel?" she said, elbowing him in the ribs.

"What?" Bevan said.

"Wasn't I worried."

"About what?"

Charles studied Penny, whose rosy glow seemed to have heightened. He knew what it was she had to tell him.

"Are you?" he said. "We?"

She nodded once, then looked at him, a hopeful, serious, apprehensive look.

Charles smiled his largest smile.

Penny smiled back, her eyes glistening.

"What?" Bevan said, laying down his knife and fork and wiping his mouth with his napkin.

Molly jabbed him in the ribs again, then raised her hand to his ear and whispered into it.

"You mean there will be more of them?" he said in apparent dismay. He took his wife's elbow firmly in his two hands.

Charles rose from his chair and knelt beside Penny. He lay one hand on her belly and kissed her cheek. He said into her ear, "A child couldn't have a better mother."

"*Qu'est-ce que c'est?*" Claudette said, her big eyes following the activity in the room.

Penny turned and spoke to her in French that Charles followed well enough to understand his wife was explaining that she was about to become a mother. Then the child asked something that he did not follow, to which Penny gave a long, serious answer, then kissed her on the forehead and smoothed her hair.

"What was that?" Charles asked.

"She told me that she has never had a mother, only an aunt, and that she lived with her father, only she doesn't know where he is now."

"Oh," Charles said.

"And she said that so long as I was going to be a mother, would I mind being her mother also."

"What did you tell her?"

"I told her that I would be especially pleased, but I would have to speak with thee first."

"Of course we will," Charles said. "Ask if I may be her father also, at least until her real father is found."

Penny smiled and pecked his cheek. She spoke to the girl, who nodded solemnly, meeting Charles's eyes with her own.

"Ask her," Charles said carefully, "her father's name, so that I will know him if I meet him."

Penny asked.

"Paul," Claudette answered promptly. "Capitaine Paul."

Charles kept his expression neutral. His heart went out to the little girl. "Well," he said, in his first official act as at least a temporary father, *"mangez votre legumes."*

Bevan and Molly excused themselves soon afterward, and Charles walked with them to the entryport. "I ain't never seen Penny so happy," Molly said. "I'll draw you a picture of her and the baby, and send it with the post. Ain't you the lucky one."

"I am," Charles said, "and so is Daniel."

As Molly was secured in her chair to be lowered over the side, Charles overheard her say to Bevan, "What she's with child already. Ain't you got a lot of work to do."

"It's back to the office, then," Bevan said, touching his hat and descending over the side.

Near the entrance to his cabin, Charles saw the two sea chests and a canvas satchel containing *Félicité*'s books and papers. He left the chests to deal with in the morning but took the satchel inside with him. Rummaging through the bag, he soon found a thin ledger with page after page listing names, birth dates, birthplaces, ratings, and other entries relating to the bureaucratic record keeping of the French navy. He opened it to the first page and found what he was looking for: *Paul André le Baux, Capitaine de Frégate.*

After the name were entries showing that the man had been thirty-five years old, born in Arles, and served as the frigate's captain for the past three years. Charles wondered what kind of man he had been, why he had a child but no wife, why he had found it necessary to bring his daughter to live on board with him. Charles thought the captain must have cared a great deal for her.

Little doubt remained that Claudette was Captain le Baux's daughter. The entry *Claudette Marie le Baux* had been penned later, wedged in beneath the line for her father and above that of the first lieutenant. She had been born on 12 Vendemiaire, 1794, by the French revolutionary calendar, in the village of Maussane in Provence. With her father dead and her mother unknown, Charles knew there would be no finding her relatives with the war in progress, and little hope afterward, whenever that would be.

IN THE MORNING Charles inspected the jury-rigged fore and main topmasts and the repaired stays and halyards. Satisfied, he sent Beechum across with two seamen to set fire to *Félicité,* stay until it had taken hold, then return to *Louisa.* With the party back on board, he watched the darkening smoke rising from the frigate's hatchways with mixed emotions. It saddened him to watch a once-living, vibrant ship consumed to ashes like some cast-off scow.

"Syracuse," he said to Winchester. "Signal *Pylades* to keep station." His intentions were to call at the Sicilian port and inform the British consul of the French presence in Egypt, then continue on directly to Gibraltar to report to Admiral St. Vincent what he had learned and of his failure to find Nelson's squadron. From Gibraltar he could also arrange safe transportation for Penny, Molly, and now Claudette, back to England.

It took twelve days before sighting Syracuse. They sailed against largely contrary winds, tacking to the northwest toward the familiar south coast of Crete, then to the southeast, then to the northwest again, an irregular course that resembled the teeth of a saw. So it went, day by day.

Penny, Charles noted, took to instructing Claudette in English for several hours each morning and afternoon. The results of this the child would demonstrate for him by approaching on the quarterdeck and saying something like " 'Ow art thou today, Sharrle Edgemont?"

Charles would reply that he was fine and that it was a beautiful day, and Claudette would toddle in her clean, pressed dress and white apron and cap back to Penny to ask what he had said. She acquired a facility with the language remarkably quickly, although with a strong Provençal accent. She proved a serious, inquisitive child, except when he would sit her in his lap and tickle. There she would shriek with delight and beg him to stop, then dare him with an impudent look to begin again. This game, he discovered, could continue indefinitely.

ON THE TENTH day, after supper, Penny asked Charles to remain at the table as the dishes were cleared away. She went to a chest that she had traveled with and produced a ledger book.

"What's this?" Charles asked.

"We must discuss issues regarding thy estates in Cheshire."

Charles sighed loudly in hopes of conveying that he would rather not.

"Would thou discuss this another time?" she said with a certain stiffness. "When?"

Charles sighed again, this time hoping to indicate a grudging indulgence. Ignoring his sighs, she opened the book on the table in a businesslike manner and licked her finger, then leafed through the pages until she found the one she wanted. "This page is a summary of income from rents and sales for the three months I have been resident there, and this the costs and expenditures," she announced.

"Ah," Charles said, rapidly scanning the surprisingly detailed column of figures. At the bottom he noted an entry for excess of income over expenditures. The sum was thirty-seven pounds, twelve shillings, and eight pence. "These are John's accounts?" he asked. Somehow Charles imagined his brother keeping more casual figures.

"No," she said. "These are my accounts. Thy brother, dear human being though he may be, does not keep adequate accounts."

Charles wasn't sure he understood. "Who is managing my land?" he asked.

"I see to the Tattenall estate," she said. "Thy brother is attending the part attached to his properties. I will wish to speak with thee about this arrangement also in time."

"I see," said Charles doubtfully. He was pretty sure he had left his brother in charge of the whole thing. "Just one more question, and we'll get on to the accounts. How did you come to be in control of the Tatte-nall lands? Did John agree with this?"

"Thy brother has agreed . . . in truth, reluctantly," she said. "We dis-agreed about some improvements I proposed but he did not wish to make. I conversed with him directly, as any Christian would. In time we came to a loving agreement."

Charles felt that he would have liked to witness these conversations. Still, this arrangement raised other questions. "How can you manage an estate? You're a woman. A woman can't even open her own bank account." He thought he had a very good point.

"A woman can, if she is persistent," Penny said. "I went to the bank in Chester, where they agreed, if I would bring a letter of thy approval on my return." She pulled out a blank piece of paper and wrote a note on it: *Letter from C.E. to Chester Bank, 1.) estate account.* She looked at him with a fixed expression. "I have learned that thou has an account at this bank also."

"I do," Charles answered reluctantly. He had left all these arrange-ments happily in his brother's hands precisely so that he could avoid con-versations such as this.

"How much does it contain?" she asked.

"Ah . . ." Charles said.

Penny's eyes seemed to pierce his skin. "Oh, come," she said. "I am thy wife, thy helpmate, thy life's partner. Thou must confide in me if I am to be useful to thee. Especially if I am to manage thy properties."

Charles knew this was the time for him to stand firm, to maintain his place as head of the household and master of his domain. This was his Rubicon; if he crossed now, there would be no going back.

Penny's attention remained fixed, her mouth a determined line. "Charles Edgemont," she said firmly.

"About six hundred pounds," he said finally. This was safe; he was certain the sum was more like seven hundred and fifty.

"It is necessary to mention in thy letter that I may draw on these funds," she said, and added to her note: *2.) C.E. account.* She then returned to her ledger and opened it to another page without waiting for Charles to reply. "These are thy crofts and their tenants," she said, showing him a list of entries several pages long. "This shows their production, averaged over several years, their estimated expenses to others for milling, carting, marketing, and so on, their customary rents, and their adjusted rents as I have proposed."

Charles groaned inwardly. "I see," he said.

"Now," she said, licking her finger and turning to yet another page, "this is thy—our estimated income from thy lands for one full year. This number is the same for the rents as they have traditionally been."

Charles followed the finger to her lips and watched as her pink tongue wetted it prettily. Now he followed his finger across the page and saw a very comfortable number.

"And this is the sum after I have adjusted the rents and made several other improvements."

He looked at a number about one quarter larger. "You increased the rents?" he asked.

Penny smiled at him. "Thou are not attending," she said patiently. "I have reduced the rents by a percentage, but to achieve the increase, certain investments are required. These will be incurred as costs in the short term, but will yield permanent gain. Thou will then be able to afford other improvements."

Charles remembered the letters he had received from her and had avoided answering. He didn't want to disappoint her, but he didn't want to throw all his money away, either. "This is where your school and mill come in, isn't it?" he said.

She patted his hand consolingly. "I have conceived of three projects as a beginning," she said, "a school, a market, and a mill." Step by step, she took him through each, their expense, their potential for profit and benefit, both for him and for others in the community. A school would require a building, a schoolmaster and a schoolmistress (one for boys and one for girls, to avoid distractions), and certain other expenses such as a well and firewood. Fees might be requested for the children from wealthier families, but she acknowledged that the school would cost him a certain amount from year to year. The benefit would be an increase in literacy and the advancement of the village as a whole.

"It is thy moral and Christian duty to see to the improvement of those less fortunate than thyself," she insisted.

Charles scratched his chin and pulled on his ear. "Humm," he said. "Ah." He had a sense that she was set on this, there was a certain inevitability about it. He knew he was one of the wealthier landowners around Tattenall, and it was appropriate that he patronize something. Still, he had concerns about the expense; perhaps she would compromise. He could think of one area right away.

"Is it really necessary to have two schools?" he said reasonably. "I mean, one for girls? What benefit comes from educating girls; for what, to become women?"

"Are girls less worthy of education?" Penny answered almost calmly. "I have been educated. Would thou not wish to see Claudette learn her letters and sums? If our child is female, dost thou wish her ignorant?" Her brow creased. "Are girls less worthy than boys?"

"No, no. I wasn't referring to our own children, or Claudette," he said. "I meant for the crofters' children, the farmers, shepherds, and—"

"Surely thou art not serious." Her lips tightened.

Or perhaps she would not compromise, he thought. Charles had known her long enough to understand that he needed to be subtle. "A school for girls, ordinary girls. It takes one a moment to appreciate what a good idea that is." Then, in an attempt to find calmer seas, "So, you also wish to build a market? I thought Tattenall already had a market."

"Yes, in the village square, exposed to the weather," she said suspiciously, but turned her ledger to a new page. "It is open two days each week. There is a need for a covered market, open every day except First Day." She went on with some evident knowledge about the general benefits to the region from stimulating economic activity, benefits that would, of necessity, accrue to him as well. A license would have to be obtained, and there would be costs for acquiring a suitable plot of land and erecting a structure, but these would be repaid over time through small fees.

Charles did not immediately object to this, although the initial costs were substantial. At least the likely benefits seemed somewhat more tangible. "All right," he said, "I will consider it. Your third project is a mill?" He was beginning to conceive a strategy to graciously allow her the school or the market, but not both. "I am opposed to these projects on the basis of their expense," he would say firmly. "In consideration of my affection for you, I will allow one of the first two. I will not approve a mill." It would be as simple as that. Having decided, he leaned back in his chair with his arms crossed and waited for her to finish.

Penny nibbled on her lower lip in concentration as she leafed through her ledger book in search of the correct page. Charles found this distracting; he had nibbled on that same lower lip very agreeably himself. Having found her place, she ran her palm along the crease of the binding. "This is the most important," she said, and smiled at him uncertainly. "It is the most dear, but it is the foundation—the anchor, in thy terms—for everything that follows." She went into a long explanation of the benefits to his crofters, to the community, and to his purse. It would provide employment; reduce the costs to his tenants for milling their grist and cartage back and forth; and draw more farmers and their families from the lands around Tattenall to the village and its market, creating more opportunities for future projects.

At ease now that he had made up his mind, Charles watched her as she spoke, the way her finger moved on the page, the rise and fall of her chest as she breathed. He idly wondered if it was true that a woman's breasts became larger when she was pregnant. Penny's seemed fuller, pressing more tightly against the front of her dress when she inhaled. This interested him far more than the numbers.

She was saying she had already picked out a place for a millpond, conveniently close to the village center; her father, who owned and managed his own mill, had agreed to oversee its construction and operation. "It is an opportunity that if thou dost not seize, someone else surely will," she said, laying her hand on his and looking up into his eyes. Seeing the direction of his gaze, she said, "Charles Edgemont, thou art incorrigible. Pay attention."

Charles was momentarily tempted to acquiesce to anything she wanted. She had clearly put a lot of thought and effort into her plans, and at least some of it seemed plausible. She looked so desirable; she was soon to be the mother of their child. He truly did not want to disappoint her, but everyone knew that no woman, schooled or unschooled, could carry out such a complex scheme. Particularly not a woman in a maternal state. It was in opposition to the female nature. He realized now that he couldn't just say he forbade it. He thought he saw a safe way out.

"How much would it cost?" he asked innocently.

She showed him the figures in her book, and in truth, it took him aback. She described the labor costs and the material costs and the anticipated income and how it might pay for itself in seven years but not more than ten. Charles knew what his answer would be, and his attention soon drifted back to the more fulsome subject of her bosom.

"But sweetheart, love of my life," he said when she had finished, "I haven't that much money."

"I never believed that thou had so much as thou hast, my love," she said evenly. "I have included payments against borrowing in my calculations. The income from thy tenants is more than sufficient."

"Sweetness," he reasoned, "do you think it wise—prudent, I mean— to borrow so much when we are anticipating so blessed an event?" He patted her hand consolingly.

Penny slid her hand out from under his and tapped her fingernails on the tabletop. "I believe it to be prudent to build a mill in Tattenall, dear heart," she said. "It will be a blessing for a great many people. In a short time, it will enrich thy purse, if thou thinks that important."

Charles felt that he wasn't making the kind of progress he had hoped for. He scratched his nose to give him a moment to think. For one thing, he was running out of endearments. "Sunshine of my garden—" he began.

"Charles Edgemont," she said firmly, "tell me honestly. Dost thou think me incapable of such a venture? Dost thou think me incapable because of my sex?"

"Oh, no, no, no," he said immediately. "Of course not; certainly not. You are the most capable girl I have ever known. But with a baby . . . everyone knows that girls become, well . . . emotional when they have babies." He thought to try a little humor. "And remember—ha, ha— that girls' emotions are barely comprehensible to begin with—ha, ha. You wouldn't believe the things girls get exercised about."

In some corner of his mind, Charles understood that this had not helped. Perhaps she had not taken his joke the way he'd intended. He reached for her hand to show his affection. She yanked it away.

"It's not you personally," he said in an overly hurried attempt to make amends. "It's your nature, don't you see? It's the feminine nature, you know, the things that girls—women, I mean—excel at. Things like having babies and managing household servants. Men aren't good at that. I mean, I could never do those things. It's the humors, you see. Women have different humors than men. Ours are more . . . masculine."

Charles thought that his cabin had grown awfully close and uncomfortably warm. There must be something he could say that would make her see the soundness of his point. At the moment she was looking at him as if he had just suggested roasting Claudette for their supper. Maybe if he offered his compromise. Maybe if he improved on it.

"All right," Charles said, "a school. Women can run schools, I grant you that. Even a market, although that's more complex. It's business, you see. You do see, don't you? But a mill is too complicated, too . . . too . . . mechanical for girls'—women's minds to grasp. You see," he said finally, "I am doing you a favor, really."

A silence filled the small cabin, a silence so preternaturally profound that the wash of the water along *Louisa's* sides and the gurgle of her wake seemed deafening. Penny sat rigidly erect, her face pale, her bloodless lips set in a line as straight as any ramrod. Charles perceived that she was having trouble controlling her breathing, which he found interesting in itself. When she finally spoke, it came as a relief.

"Art thou finished?" she asked.

"Yes," Charles said.

"Quite finished? Thou art sure that thou dost not wish to compare feminine humors to those of milch cows or brood mares?"

"Yes, no," Charles said.

"I apprehend that thou dost not wish the mill," she said.

"No, I don't want the mill," he answered. "I'm sorry."

"Good. At least we are clear." She thumbed through her ledger until she came to a page she had shown him earlier. It displayed the traditional income from his estates and the amount that could be expected after her improvements. "The mill is necessary for everything that follows. I will make it simple for thee," she said with only modest sarcasm. "Dost thou comprehend this number?" She pressed her finger down on the page under the smaller sum, so hard that its nail left an impression on the paper.

"Yes," Charles said.

The finger moved to the second figure. "Dost thou comprehend this number?"

"Of course."

"Follow me closely," Penny said. "Which is greater?"

"The second," Charles said, "any fool can see that."

"Possibly not," she said. "Of these two numbers, one greater and one lesser, which dost thou prefer?"

Charles sighed a sigh that he hoped would convey sweet reasonableness while maintaining his opposition. "The larger," he answered, "but is a mill really required?"

Penny allowed him a small smile. "As thou were so intently studying the bodice of my dress," she said, "I explained that the increase was not possible without the mill. Perhaps thou wert not attending."

Charles leaned back in his chair and steepled his fingers. Her calculations did not include all of his sources of income: his salary as a naval officer, or the proceeds from his half-ownership of the estate still managed by his brother, whatever that would be. Of course, those monies went automatically into his bank account, which he had agreed to give her access to. But there must be a way around that. Perhaps he could write to the bank; maybe they could help him. And he would receive a certain amount of head-and-gun money from the Admiralty for the frigate *Félicité*. He regretted burning her now; he would have made more if he had towed the prize back to Gibraltar. Of course, that would have added weeks to the journey.

He picked up the ledger book and leafed through the pages. One thing was clear: She had put an impressive amount of thought and effort into her plans. Perhaps she could accomplish such a thing. The worse that could happen would be that he would lose his money. He decided there were more important things than money.

"You're set on this?" he said.

"I am," she answered. "It is for thy benefit as well."

"And you believe that you will have the ability—the time—to attend to all of this with the coming child?"

"I will not be alone," she said. "I have assistance from Molly and thy sister, and my father. I am well supported."

"All right," Charles said with all the grace he could muster, "you may do it."

Almost before he had finished the sentence, she had a fresh paper in front of him.

"What's this?" he said, looking at the printed page. All of the blank spaces had been filled in with various sums and numbers, except for a space at the bottom for his signature.

She pushed an ink bottle and quill in front of him. "This is thy application to borrow monies for our projects," she said. "After thou hast completed the necessary letters and forms, we shall discuss thy views on women, the limits of their abilities, and especially an exact description of the nature of feminine humors."

"I trust that this will be a loving discussion, involving a good deal of Christian charity," he said.

LOUISA AND HER shadow, *Pylades,* continued their struggle eastward against obstinate headwinds across the empty Mediterranean Sea. Charles felt an increasing anxiety to be rid of the responsibility for carrying the intelligence on the French invasion of Egypt and the battle fleet from Toulon. After passing his report to the British consul at Syracuse, he could then make for Gibraltar, report to Jervis, and secure transport for his wife, their expected child, and adopted daughter home to England. He would rest easier when that was done.

Louisa's crew got ample work aloft, tacking the ship and tacking again, so Charles exercised the gun crews with powder taken off *Félicité,* and at small arms for boarding and repelling boarders.

On the tenth day since leaving Egypt, a Tuesday, the twenty-fourth of July, just after four bells in the forenoon watch, the lookout in the maintops called down to the deck, "Land ho, fine on the starboard bow, five leagues near enough."

Charles turned to Eliot, standing with him on the quarterdeck, with an inquisitive look.

"Unless I miss my guess, sir," Eliot responded with a touch of pride, "that would be Cape Murro. Syracuse will be just up the coast a touch, t'other side of the headland."

"I find myself impressed," Charles said. "A very good landfall, Mr. Eliot. It's been over eight hundred miles as the crow flies since we left the Rosetta mouth. I measured it from my atlas."

"Aye, it's closer to twelve hundred if you measured our wake, what with all the back and forth. It were a healthy distance."

Soon the point of land, the smallest speck of dark, could be seen from *Louisa*'s deck as she rose on the crest of a wave. The speck slowly became a low hump, with its features visible and the shore falling away on either side. Charles went below to his cabin to collect the report he had written for the British consul in the city.

"What is all the commotion, Charlie?" Penny asked, emerging from his sleeping cabin.

"We have arrived at Syracuse. We'll be in the port in a couple of hours."

"I have just put Claudette down for a rest," Penny said. "I will come upside as soon as she is asleep."

"Topside," Charles said. "You'll never be a seaman."

Penny stuck her tongue out at him. With a chuckle, he departed the cabin to go upside. On the ladderway to the quarterdeck, he heard a loud cry from the tops: "Deck there! There's warships in the harbor. Can't tell how many, but it's a quantity."

"Can you tell if they are English or French?" Charles shouted up.

"No, sir. It's too far. Should be able to tell soon, though."

"Mr. Beechum," Charles called as he came upon the quarterdeck.

"Yes, sir," Beechum said, touching his hat as he hurried past with a long glass under his arm, and started up the mizzenmast shrouds.

Penny soon arrived. "Canst thou not be more quiet?"

"In a minute," Charles said. His head tilted back, he yelled upward, "Beechum, what do you see?"

"They're English, sir," the young man's voice came down. "More than a dozen ships of the line."

"What does that mean?" Penny asked.

"It means," Charles answered, "that we have found Admiral Nelson and his squadron at last."

NINE

LOUISA ROUNDED THE POINT MARKING THE SOUTHERN LIMIT of the great port of Syracuse, the ancient city of peeling white and yellow buildings with their red-tiled roofs rising along a finger of land on the harbor's northern side. Charles came onto the quarterdeck in his best uniform coat and hat, the hat being somewhat the worse for wear, as it also served for daily use. He stood for a moment by the rail and surveyed the double line of English warships riding at anchor in the bright afternoon sun. All were familiar to him as ships attached to the Mediterranean Fleet. He saw *Orion, Culloden,* and *Goliath,* which had been present at the Battle of Cape St. Vincent, and Nelson's blue rear admiral's flag flying from *Vanguard*'s mizzenmast. He counted thirteen ships of the line, all seventy-fours, *Leander,* fifty, and a solitary brig.

"Mr. Talmage," Charles said, moving toward the lieutenant, "a word with you, please." It was an unpleasant business, but with any luck, it would be soon finished.

"Sir," Talmage responded curtly.

Charles leaned forward and spoke in a low voice. "In a few moments, I will be going across to report to Admiral Nelson. I take it that you still wish me to request a transfer on your behalf."

"That would be my preference," Talmage replied.

Charles nodded. "You should know that I have a report prepared on your service as first lieutenant and on your altercation with Lieutenant

Winchester, as I am required to do. I have written that your deportment and abilities as second have been satisfactory." He had decided that some positive recommendation would be helpful in encouraging the admiral to agree to a trade.

Talmage nodded stiffly but said nothing.

"All right," Charles said. "I will put it to Admiral Nelson in as favorable a light as I can. You do understand that I don't know if he will approve it or not, or what his reaction to the incident will be. But I will request it."

"I am aware of the possible outcomes."

At that moment Charles heard the cable run out through the hawse, followed by a loud splash from forward. He glanced to see the topmen already aloft, beginning to furl the sails. "The bower's down, sir," Winchester called from across the deck.

"Very good," Charles said. "Begin the salute and have my gig hoisted out, if you please."

Winchester called down to Beechum on the gundeck, and the first cannon bellowed out its powder charge, the first of thirteen guns, the salute due to the flag of a rear admiral.

"Begging your pardon, sir," Sykes reported smartly. "*Vanguard* has signaled *Captain report on board.*"

"Thank you, Mr. Sykes."

"WHERE IN THE devil's name have you been, Captain Edgemont?" Admiral Sir Horatio Nelson demanded hotly, almost before Charles had stepped onto the flagship's deck. "Do you realize I have been scouring the Mediterranean these past two months without a frigate to be had? Where the hell are the rest of my frigates? Where is Captain Pigott?"

"Sir," Charles said, standing rigidly erect and touching his hat, "*Pylades* and I have been searching for you. *Emerald* and *Terpsichore* returned to Gibraltar from the rendezvous, *Emerald* in particular for repairs to damage sustained during the storm. *Terpsichore* was ordered back by Captain Pigott."

Nelson was a slight, almost frail man of less than middle height with a lined face and prematurely gray hair. The right sleeve of his uniform coat lay pinned empty across his chest, a token of an assault on Tenerife the year before, and Charles knew that he had lost the sight in one eye as a result of action in Corsica some years before that. But he still possessed something irresistible in his manner, an alertness, enthusiasm, intelligence, the undivided attention he paid to those addressing him. "Well, I devoutly wish you had found me earlier," he said, still aroused. "We've been the length of the Mediterranean looking for the French, who, you may know, have escaped from Toulon. I've had reports that they are here, others that they've gone there, but I've found nothing at all. It's the most vexing experience of my life. A frigate or two would have made a world of difference."

"Sir," Charles said, "the French are in Egypt, off Alexandria."

"Egypt? They can't be in Egypt. I looked into Alexandria not a month past."

"You were two days ahead of them," Charles said. "Just ten days ago, I saw elements of the French army at Rosetta and encountered a frigate and a corvette off the mouth of the river. I am informed there are thirteen ships of the line: the first-rate *L'Orient,* three eighty-gun ships, nine seventy-fours, and three frigates. I have it all in a report I had intended to pass to the British consul." He reached into his coat pocket and handed the paper over. Since he had inadvertently destroyed Jones's list, he had reconstructed the composition of the fleet from memory.

The admiral took the document, unfolded it, and read with raised eyebrows. Then he placed it in his pocket. "Did you look into Alexandria? Did you see the whereabouts of the transports?"

"No, sir," Charles said. "I was unable to do so. I saw that they have landed their army, though. We were pursued from Rosetta, and I thought it best to take such intelligence as we had and return."

Nelson's good eye looked out over the side at *Louisa* and the makeshift repairs to her masts. "Quite rightly," he said with a smile. "This was the result of one of the frigates?"

"Actually, there had been four," Charles said. "Now there are three. We were fortunate enough to carry the fourth, and then burned her. I allowed the crew to be taken off by one of her sister ships."

"Upon my word," Nelson said, breaking into a grin, "I thought you had mettle when I first spotted you from *San Josef*'s deck; what was it, a year back? I do enjoy being proved prescient." He paused as if remembering something. "Did you know I met your wife at Naples? She was looking for you. A Quakeress, I believe, a bit queer on warfare, but quite enchanting all the same."

"Mrs. Edgemont is on board *Louisa* at this moment, sir," Charles said. "She also speaks highly of you. I was hoping to carry on to Gibraltar so that she can be seen safely home."

"That will not be possible," Nelson said flatly. "*Louisa* is the only frigate I have now. Still, I will be sending dispatches to Lord St. Vincent. I'm sure something can be arranged. Possibly I'll send *Pylades* back. What state is your ship in?"

"Aside from our mast sections, we require renewal of our water, victuals, and firewood before any prolonged cruise. I believe *Pylades* to be in a similar situation." Charles hesitated, thinking of Talmage's transfer and Beechum's advancement. "I have another pair of issues that require your attention." He reached into a different pocket and produced the report he'd prepared on Lieutenant Talmage.

"Trouble?" Nelson asked.

"Of a sort, sir," Charles answered, and briefly explained the problems that had arisen with respect to his former first lieutenant, including the provisional advancement of Beechum. "I am in hopes of sending Mr. Talmage to another ship in the squadron in exchange for a replacement. I believe such an arrangement would be best for all concerned, sir."

"I never agreed with placing Talmage as a first on a fighting ship," Nelson said with a frown. "I suppose it had to be done on account of his family and his seniority, but he's a touchy sort of fellow. Allow me to read this, and I will consider it." He pocketed Charles's report with barely a glance. "Now, sir, I have much to do in light of your intelligence about the French. If you would be so good as to attend on me after supper with Lieutenants Talmage and Beechum, I will have your orders and the answers to your other concerns. The squadron will sail for Alexandria in the morning. Please convey to Mrs. Edgemont my fondest remembrance and that I am sorry I will not be able to greet her. I expect you at the top of the first watch, sir."

Charles had himself rowed back to *Louisa*. He went first in search of Talmage. He found the lieutenant on the quarterdeck.

"What do you think he'll do?" Talmage asked after Charles had given him the gist of it. It was the first hint of uncertainty that Charles had noted in Talmage's otherwise unbending demeanor.

"I don't know," Charles answered. "He didn't confide in me. He asked for your presence on board the flagship. Read into it what you will."

Talmage nodded. "I see," he said.

From Nelson's expression, Charles did have a suspicion of what his admiral might do, but wasn't sure he agreed with it. Quarreling with a fellow officer, no matter how carefully Charles had phrased it in his report, wasn't something any admiral would smile upon. He turned as he caught sight of his youngest lieutenant. "Mr. Beechum," he called, "a moment, if you please."

"Sir?"

"Your presence is requested aboard the flagship this evening for an interview with Admiral Nelson."

"Just me, sir?" Beechum said with alarm.

"Alas, I am afraid not. Mr. Talmage and I will be there. I have informed the admiral of your acting status as lieutenant and asked him to confirm it. He said he will consider doing so. I recommend that you present yourself as shipshape as you can and bring your logbook and certificates."

Beechum puffed out his cheeks in concentration, then seemed to be in a great agitation to depart. "I should go wash and shave myself, sir."

Charles gave the briefest glance at the young man's smooth cheeks. Eliot, standing just behind, broke into a loud guffaw. "I should think the washing would answer both tricks," he chortled.

Soon afterward, Charles went down to his cabin, where he found his wife at the table with Claudette, in the midst of an English lesson.

" 'Ow art thou, Sharrle Edgemont?" Claudette asked prettily. " 'Ow go thy . . ." She turned to Penny. *"Bateau?"* she asked.

"Boat," Penny said.

" 'Ow go thy boat today?"

"Why, I'm as fit as can be," Charles said, wiggling his fingers as if to tickle her. "And the boat goes very well, considering she's at anchor." As the girl clasped her arms to protect her middle, he ruffled her hair and pushed her cap down over her eyes. When she moved to reset her cap, he tickled her ribs.

To Penny, he gave a buss on the cheek. "Admiral Nelson conveys his deepest appreciation of you."

"Didst thou speak with him about Jacob Talmage?" she said.

"I did. I passed him my report on the incident, and he agreed to read it. He has requested that Talmage present himself after dinner. I expect he will make some kind of decision then."

"What dost thou think he will decide?"

Charles hesitated. "I am in hopes that he will arrange for a transfer, but he may decide to convene a court-martial."

"Is that serious?" she asked.

"It could be," he answered easily. "If found guilty, Talmage would be dismissed from the service or, in theory, executed." Charles would not mind terribly if Talmage were booted from the navy.

"Executed, surely that cannot be," she said.

Charles began to say "I don't think it will come to that," when he came up short, the true enormity of Talmage's offense dawning on him for the first time. He had assumed that, at worst, the lieutenant would be found guilty of quarreling with a fellow officer, the penalty for which would be his automatic dismissal. But if the act was interpreted as drawing his sword against a superior officer, the required punishment was death. The Articles of War were firm. His mind raced to recall exactly what he had written in his report. My God, he realized, if Winchester was considered Talmage's superior at the time of the incident, they would hang Talmage. "I am afraid that is a possibility," he said.

"Thou must protect him from this," Penny said.

"Probably Nelson will just arrange the transfer and let it go at that," Charles answered, his mind far less confident of that outcome than his words expressed.

Apparently satisfied, Penny changed the subject. "Did he speak of how Molly, Claudette, and I shall return to England?"

Charles dropped into a chair, preoccupied with the repercussions Talmage faced. "I mentioned the necessity of it, and my preference for going on to Gibraltar," he said absently. "But he won't send me. I'll have my orders this evening. It's likely you will have to return to Gibraltar with Daniel on *Pylades*."

———

"THE ADMIRAL REQUESTS your presence in his cabin, sirs," *Vanguard*'s flag lieutenant said. While waiting, Charles and Talmage had sat tensely silent, as Beechum chattered nervously about what obscure elements of seamanship Nelson might or might not quiz him on.

"Please be seated, gentlemen," Admiral Sir Horatio Nelson said. To Charles, he looked more careworn than usual and remained standing at the head of his bare dining table in the large cabin. Charles and Talmage found places on either side, and Beechum seated himself at its foot. "We have several issues to consider, and they must be dealt with expeditiously."

Charles sat uneasily, his hands folded on the tabletop to keep his fingers still. He noted that no refreshment had been offered, which was unusual, and that there had been three marine sentries posted outside the cabin door instead of the customary one. He glanced across at Talmage, whose face was rigidly expressionless. Beechum, he observed, had beads of sweat on his forehead, in spite of a cooling breeze through the open gunports and windows.

"We will take up Acting Lieutenant Beechum's case first, as that's the easiest," the admiral said seriously. "Is that agreeable to you, Mr. Beechum?"

"Y-yes, sir," Beechum stammered.

"It is my unvarying practice in these instances," Nelson continued, "to query such a candidate as yourself on all manner of naval lore so that I may be assured that he is fit, even for a temporary posting." Charles thought he saw the hint of a smile showing at the corners of the admiral's mouth. "I trust you have prepared thoroughly," Nelson said.

Beechum seemed to be having trouble swallowing something risen in his throat. "Yes, sir," he croaked.

"Acting Lieutenant Beechum," Nelson intoned gravely, "you are standing on your quarterdeck facing the bow. The lookout shouts down that an enemy is approaching from starboard. Which side is that, sir?"

"From the right side, sir?"

"That is correct. Very good. And if the wind is blowing in over the railing to your left, which direction is to windward?"

"To the larboard, or port side, sir," Beechum answered more firmly, but clearly mystified at the line of questioning.

With a wink to Charles, Nelson said, "I do profess myself impressed with this young man's firm grasp of the fundamentals of seamanship. Mr. Beechum, I am pleased to approve your status as acting lieutenant to *Louisa* until such time as I can convene a proper board of examination to make it permanent."

"I . . . I . . . thank you, sir," Beechum managed, a puzzled look still on his face. Then he smiled.

"Always remember to do your duty to the best of your ability and to see that your deportment is a credit to your ship, your king, and the Royal Navy."

"Yes, sir. Of course, sir."

Nelson shifted his gaze. "Captain Edgemont, I have already sent orders to *Pylades* to convey my reports on the location of the French, and my intention to engage, to Lord St. Vincent at Gibraltar. I have also ordered that Commander Bevan provide accommodation to the charming Mrs. Edgemont. I trust this is acceptable to you."

"Yes, sir," Charles said. It was the only thing he could say.

"As for *Louisa,* I have determined that suitable mast sections are available from *Leander*. They will be delivered to you at first light. The squadron will set sail for Alexandria at four bells in the forenoon watch. Your orders are to complete the repairs to your ship and resupply as expeditiously as possible. Then you will immediately take up our wake, sir. We are no flying squadron; I am confident you will catch us up well before we reach Egypt."

Charles was not entirely displeased by this. He would part from Penny sooner than he liked, but then he would be a participant in the coming battle against the French. "Yes, sir," he said again.

"So far, so good," Nelson said reflectively. "Now we come to the troublesome problem of Lieutenant Talmage." He glanced down at Charles's report, which lay on the polished table before him, then he stared directly at Talmage with a frown. "I must say, sir, that I am deeply disappointed in your behavior. In his report, Captain Edgemont tends to be forgiving. Reading it, I find that I am not. There will be no transfer to another ship, Mr. Talmage, not while I am in command. Drawing your sword in the presence of a superior officer is a most serious breach of discipline, expressly prohibited by the king and by act of Parliament. What have you to say for yourself?"

"Sir," Talmage said immediately, casting a scowl at Charles, "I am the senior officer to Lieutenant Winchester, whom Captain Edgemont unfairly placed above me. This was a direct insult to my reputation and my honor, as Mr. Winchester well knew. No gentleman could allow such an affront to go unchallenged."

Charles saw that Talmage was about to sink himself. "Admiral Nelson, sir," he interjected.

"In a moment, Captain," Nelson said. "I can well appreciate your objection to this line of defense." Turning back to Talmage, he continued, "It does not answer that you are the longer-serving officer. I'll grant that it's unusual, but Captain Edgemont is well within his rights to appoint his lieutenants as he sees fit, particularly if his first's abilities are found wanting, as he has clearly stated. However that may be, there is not a shred of doubt that Lieutenant Winchester was officially your superior on the date the altercation took place."

"Sir," Charles said again.

Nelson ignored him. "Mr. Talmage," he said harshly, "I find that your deportment has been contrary to every tenet of good discipline in His Majesty's Navy. I am ordering you placed under arrest for breach of the twenty-second article of the Articles of War, for drawing your sword against a superior officer. A court-martial will be assembled to determine your guilt and pronounce punishment immediately after we have dealt with the French force at Alexandria. Mr. Beechum, if you would be so good as to instruct the marine guard outside the door to enter."

"Beechum, wait," Charles said quickly. To Nelson, he pleaded, "Sir, may I speak?"

The admiral looked at him with raised eyebrows. "What is it?"

"Sir," Charles said, trying to collect his thoughts, "I do not believe arresting Lieutenant Talmage to be warranted. The incident in question occurred several weeks ago, and there has been no repeat of it. Since he agreed to assume the position of second, his deportment has been more than satisfactory. I believe the rift between Talmage and Winchester to also have been healed, sir."

"I do not—" Talmage began loudly.

"For Christ's sake, shut up," Charles snapped. He hurried on: "Admiral Nelson, sir, this is no rogue officer. The issue is that he felt himself unfairly treated by me, and he quarreled with my first as a result of that frustration. Since then we have come to an agreement, and the issue has been resolved."

Nelson eyed Charles steadily. "But he quarreled, as you say, with a naked blade in his hand, did he not?"

Charles's heart sank. This was the single unavoidable damning fact. "Yes, sir," he said. "But its point rested mostly on the deck. I believe that the lesser charge of quarreling with a fellow officer under the twenty-first article to be more appropriate in this case."

The admiral stared at him, either undecided or disbelieving; Charles couldn't tell which. "Furthermore, I have the utmost confidence in Mr. Talmage's conduct," Charles added hopefully, "and I will personally vouch for his appearance at trial."

Nelson hesitated. He cleared his throat, paused a moment longer, then said, "All right, if that is your wish, Captain. Mr. Talmage, are you agreeable to remaining on board *Louisa,* and do you give me your guarantee of future obedience to orders?"

"Yes, sir," Talmage said, stone-faced.

"Then I will amend the charges against you to include violation of both the twenty-first and twenty-second articles," Nelson said. "I will leave it to the court to determine which applies."

The sky had turned moonless black when they emerged onto *Vanguard*'s deck. In tense silence, Charles, Talmage, and Beechum climbed down the side steps to their boat waiting below.

"Mr. Talmage," Charles said after they had settled themselves and the boat had shoved off.

"Sir," Talmage answered.

Charles detected resentment in the lieutenant's voice. "May I take it that you are agreeable to remaining on board *Louisa*?" he said.

"It seems that I have little option."

"I am sorry. I'd hoped it wouldn't come to this."

"It is your doing that brought me to this pass," Talmage choked. "I have been sorely treated, and now my career is in ruins."

"Goddammit, man," Charles growled, "it's that kind of prickly arrogance that has brought you to where you are. You know that if you go before a court-martial, they will hang you, don't you? No jury of navy captains is going to overlook the fact that you drew your sword. Make no mistake, Jacob, they will hang you by the neck until dead. Is that what you want?"

Charles could hear Talmage's labored breathing in the darkness beside him. "No," Talmage managed.

"Then I strongly suggest that we look for some way to repair your reputation before any court can be convened."

Charles allowed Talmage and Beechum to mount *Louisa*'s side by themselves. To Williams, the coxswain, he said, "Take me across to *Pylades*.

"You've orders for Gibraltar?" Charles asked Bevan as soon as he had climbed to the brig's deck.

"Aye," Bevan answered. "The moment we've replenished our water and such. I'm instructed to provide accommodation for Mrs. Edgemont. I'm sorry, Charlie."

"It's probably for the best," Charles said. "When do you think you'll up anchor?"

"Sooner rather than later," Bevan answered vaguely. "What are you thinking?"

"Could you delay for a day or so? I was hoping you could help with our repairs."

"I believe that can be arranged," Bevan said.

AT TWO BELLS in the morning watch, Charles stood on his quarterdeck as a ship's cutter, tied up alongside *Leander* the past half hour, spread its oars to begin the pull across the low gray chop of Syracuse harbor. He could see the line from the boat's stern and the two long spars being towed through the water behind.

A swarm of activity showed itself on board the men-of-war of the British squadron as anchors were hove short, men swarming aloft to loosen the gaskets on the yardarms prior to dropping their sails, and a multitude of ship's boats on last-minute errands plying back and forth between the heavy two-deckers like so many water bugs.

As *Leander*'s cutter neared, Charles observed the somewhat unusual sight of an officer—the lieutenant commanding the work party, he presumed—standing in the bow, sawing back and forth with his arm as if playing an imaginary fiddle.

"Boat ahoy, what is your business?" Charles heard Beechum, standing officer of the watch, call down.

"His Majesty's lieutenant Jack Aubrey of *Leander,* youngster. I've two mast sticks for you. Permission to come aboard?"

"Come aboard, Mr. Aubrey," Charles shouted. "It's all right, Mr. Beechum, he's expected."

That the lieutenant was a man of robust proportions Charles could tell while he was still in the boat alongside. On deck he saw him to be tall, taller than Charles, with a ruddy, good-natured face and long blond hair tied in an old-fashioned queue behind.

"You would be Captain Edgemont, sir?" Aubrey asked.

"I am he," Charles answered.

"I'm honored, sir," the lieutenant said, extending a very large hand and a rather infectious smile. "We was at Cape St. Vincent together a year and more back."

Charles shook the hand, which gripped his almost painfully. "What ship were you on?" he asked.

"Third on *Colossus,* I was. We lost some yards on the foremast straightaway." Aubrey laughed, a hearty, uninhibited laugh that seemed to come up from his belly. "Almost the first whiff of gunsmoke, and we was out of the battle." He took a moment to compose himself. "And you were second on little *Argonaut,* I recall. I winced when I saw her poor battered state. That must have been the devil's own trial."

"I wouldn't want to repeat it," Charles said.

"No, I imagine not. Still, it got you your step," Aubrey said happily. Then he seemed to remember his business. "I've brought your spars for you. If you will just sign for them." He removed a piece of ham and then produced a wrinkled paper and the stub of a pencil from a jacket pocket. Charles scratched his signature.

The lieutenant tipped his hat. "Good day to you, sir. The admiral has us off for Egypt. You've just been there, I hear tell. I don't suppose you'll be coming along?"

"We'll catch up as soon as your sticks are in place," Charles said with a small laugh. "Don't worry, I won't leave you to fight them all by yourself."

"How many do you reckon they are?" Aubrey asked, turning serious.

"Thirteen big ones, including *L'Orient*," Charles answered. "Enough to make a fair fight."

The lieutenant whistled his appreciation. "We've nothing approaching that size. Still, Nelson has never been known to be shy." Then, with a nod and a smile, Jack Aubrey hoisted his bulk outboard and descended the side steps with surprising agility.

"Mr. Keswick," Charles called for the boatswain. "Your mast sections are alongside. See to hoisting them aboard, if you please."

As the morning progressed, Charles watched while Keswick, his mates, and a handful of the crew began disassembling the jury-rigged mast sections to send them down to the deck. The work went methodically. Charles was in no hurry to see it done quickly, had no urgency about sending the ship's boats into the port for resupply, and felt no anxiety to set sail in pursuit of Nelson's squadron. There would be plenty of time for that. *Louisa* could sail rings around the lumbering battleships in all but the heaviest weather. He knew that he would have to send his wife over to *Pylades* and away too soon. He would not see her again for . . . who knew how long, months, years even. In all likelihood, by the time he was able to return home, their child would have been born, perhaps even would be toddling around and speaking its first words.

Eight bells marked the beginning of the forenoon watch, and the arrival of a bleary-eyed Talmage onto the deck to replace Beechum. He nodded stiffly and touched his hat as he passed, but said nothing. He looked as if he hadn't slept at all during the night. Possibly he had come to realize the full ramifications of his actions and spent the hours worrying about them. On returning from the flagship the evening before, Charles had described to Penny Nelson's decisions and what they meant. She'd been clearly upset. "What canst thou do to prevent this?" she'd said. Charles had no answer. He'd racked his brain on the subject. Something would have to be done to improve Talmage's standing if he was to receive any sympathy from a court-martial. It would help if it were something truly heroic and spectacular. But what? All Charles could think was that the coming battle with the French might offer an opportunity, but as the small *Louisa* would most likely be ordered to stand off while the line of battleships pounded away at one another, he had no inspiration.

In time, Charles watched as flags ran up *Vanguard*'s halyards, signaling for the squadron to prepare to make sail. At precisely four bells, the flags came down, the signal to execute. Charles watched as, one by one, the hulking warships dropped their sails and pulled their anchors. Braced up in the light airs, their heads swung as they wore around to stand for the harbor mouth and the open sea beyond. He ticked them off as they made way, adding clouds of canvas as they went—*Vanguard, Alexander, Theseus, Orion, Defense, Bellerophon, Minotaur, Audacious, Goliath, Swiftsure, Zealous, Majestic, Culloden, Leander, Mutine*—until the harbor seemed strangely bare. Thirteen seventy-four-gun ships of the line, a fifty, and a brig, tiny by comparison, on their way to meet a French fleet of similar numbers but greater force, off a distant harbor nearly a thousand miles to the east.

Nodding again to Talmage, he went forward to speak with Keswick about their progress with the rigging. The fore topmast section, he saw, was already being hoisted skyward to be set in its place. *Pylades*'s boatswain and his mates were preparing the mainmast to receive its spars. Charles thought it was all going quickly, too quickly where time with his wife was concerned, but about what he would have hoped for with respect to following after Nelson. He was satisfied that his ship would be ready for sea by the following morning.

As the receding specks of the squadron's sails dropped one by one over the eastern horizon, Charles went down to his cabin for the noon meal with his wife. Penny had been occupied the entire morning, packing and repacking her and Claudette's things in preparation for the journey back to England. He realized that it would be their last dinner together until he, too, was able to return home.

Charles entered his cabin to find a shambles, with opened sea chests dragged onto the floor and untidy piles of clothing and other belongings spilling over the chairs and table. Penny stood in the center, her hair tied up above her head and covered with a cloth cap. Even so, flimsy wisps had escaped in disordered strings around her face. Her expression was one of intense distress.

"How goes it?" he asked brightly. "Where is Attwater? Can't he help with all this?"

Penny glanced up at him, her lips quivering, and promptly burst into tears. "No, he cannot help," she exclaimed. "I have sent him away. No one can help."

Charles had never seen her in such a state. For an instant he thought something had gone terribly wrong, or that some tragedy had occurred. "Where is Claudette?" he asked, not seeing the child.

Penny crossed the room and threw herself into his arms. Charles could feel her heart beating against his chest. "Claudette is asleep," she managed. "I put her down for a rest."

"Then what's the matter?" he said, holding her tightly. "Why can't anyone help?"

With an effort, she composed herself. She took a deep breath and pulled away, wiping at the tears on her cheeks with the backs of her hands. "I do not want to go," she said. "I do not wish to leave thee."

Charles used his thumb to wipe away a little moisture that she had missed. "You must," he said softly. "You know that. You must return home for our child, for Claudette. Who will manage our estates?" He struggled awkwardly to find words to comfort her. "It will be all right, you'll see. We will be parted for only a time. I'll be back myself before your new mill is built."

She smiled a crooked smile. "Thou dost not approve of my mill."

"Yes, I do," he answered. "It just took me a little time to get used to the idea, is all."

"Oh, Charlie," she said, "I don't know what has come over me. I am not usually so . . ." Another thought came to her. "Why art thou here?"

"This is my cabin. I live here," Charles answered. "I came for my dinner."

"Oh. No wonder Timothy Attwater was so adamant. I will call him."

"No," Charles said. "I'll find him and make amends. You clear off the table. Afterward, you must allow him to pack for you. It can't matter that much where all this stuff goes."

Over their dinner, she asked if he had as yet devised a plan to rescue Jacob Talmage.

"I have not," Charles answered. "But I am still thinking on it. Don't worry yourself; I will come up with something." He wished he had even an inkling of what that something would be.

In the early afternoon, Bevan and Molly came to call. Charles saw the boat rowing across, sent word for Penny, and went to the side to greet them. Molly, he noted, had brought the flat wooden case that contained her sketches and supplies.

"Since it's our last day together, we've come to make you sit for your portrait," Bevan said cheerfully as he climbed aboard. "I'm to hold you in a headlock if necessary."

Penny arrived, holding Claudette by the hand, as Molly lighted on the deck. " 'Ow art thou, Capitaine Beban?" Claudette said dutifully. " 'Allo Aunt Molli. 'Ow goes thy boat?" She smiled brightly. " 'Ast thou wet thy swab yet today? Avast there, ye lubber."

Penny sighed, as fully recovered from her outburst as if it had never occurred. "Timothy Attwater has been assisting with our practices," she said.

After Claudette had been chucked under the chin, kissed, and tickled, Bevan straightened. "What are your plans, Charlie? We have some decisions to make."

Charles thought for a moment. He knew what he should say but wasn't sure he wanted to. There was no point in postponing the inevitable. "We'll be as good as new by tomorrow morning. Would it be agreeable if I brought Penny and Claudette across at the top of the forenoon watch?"

This was agreed to. Molly then put herself forward. "Good, ain't you able to sit for me today," she said.

Bevan excused himself to return and attend to responsibilities on his own ship. Charles offered to send Molly back when she was ready. Penny soon went below to resume her packing.

Molly wasted no time. "I want to set you by the rail on the quarter-deck," she said. "That's how I see you in my mind." Charles positioned himself, stiff and self-conscious, by the weather rail, the port of Syracuse behind him as, he imagined, a suitable backdrop. Molly had asked Midshipman Sykes to fetch her a chair, and the boy had run down to the officers' wardroom below Charles's cabin and back up again. Molly now settled herself with her case squarely in her lap and appraised him.

"You ain't a statue, Captain Edgemont, and you ain't no admiral, neither," she said critically. "Stand the way you normally stand."

"You mean like this?" Charles said, assuming a casual but vigilant attitude, one knee slightly bent and his left hand resting easily on the hilt of his sword. Four fingers of his right hand he tucked inside his jacket. He imagined the effect rather pleasing.

"You never in all your life stood like that," she said crossly.

"How, then?" Charles said.

"If you had been on deck all day and you were going to be there all night, how would you stand?"

Charles leaned back against the rail with his elbows resting on top in order to think.

"That's almost it, sir," Molly said. "Just turn to the left. This picture's for Penny, so we want to hide your sword a little. Just a little more. There, now don't you move." She opened her case, removed a pencil, and sharpened it carefully on a rather vicious-looking knife with a long thin blade honed along both edges. Charles imagined that, given her past, she probably knew very well how to use it. Satisfied, Molly replaced the knife in the box and extracted a sheet of paper.

"Shouldn't I smile?" he asked.

"You can if you want to," she said, staring at him intently, "but you'll find that your cheeks begin to ache after a time." Her pencil began to move across the page. "Ain't you handsome," she said, more to herself, Charles thought, than to him. She worked with intense focus, the pencil sliding in quick slashes and stabs with lightning jolts, dashes, and squiggles in between. He could not see the surface of the paper, only the top of her rapidly moving hand and the blunt end of the pencil as it danced like a mast truck in a storm.

"How are you enjoying married life?" he asked, as much to distract himself from the pain he was beginning to feel in his elbows as to engage her in conversation.

"Won't it take longer if we talk," she said, barely glancing up at him. "I want to do one of your face next. I can talk then. It's the attitude of the body and the hands that I have trouble with."

Charles became acutely aware of his hands and fingers and how they were arranged.

After a short time, her pencil strokes became finer and more delicately placed. She glanced up frequently, her tongue poking between her lips in concentration. "There," she said. "Won't be a second. There." Molly looked at him for a long minute, up and down, her eyes resting on his hands. She stared at her paper, made a small mark on it, opened her case, and slipped it inside.

"Can't I see it?" Charles said.

"No," Molly said firmly. "It ain't finished yet. Nobody likes it before it's finished. Now we need another chair. Penny asked special for one just of your face."

"Mr. Sykes," Charles called.

While they waited for the midshipman to return with a chair from Charles's cabin, Molly spoke. "You asked about me and Daniel. I'm honest, sir, I ain't never been more blessed. With my past, I had no right to ever hope for such a thing. Even if I hadn't never been a whore, my pa was a sheep herd, bless his heart. My Daniel is a gentleman. I am very pleased in my life, Captain Edgemont. I don't know if it's fair to Daniel, I'm no lady, and maybe it's not. Sometimes it seems like a dream to me, and I'll wake up back like it was. But don't I hope not."

Charles's chair arrived, and he sat. Without any instructions to him, she sharpened two pencils with her blade, placed a fresh sheet on top of her case, and began to draw as she talked.

"I don't know if it is an even bargain for Daniel, and I worry about that. But he wasn't born so high, you know. His pa was a fisherman in Wales, like my pa kept sheep. He was a pressed man and served as a common sailorman, 'before the mast,' he said. He worked his way up to where he is now. He worked fearless hard, and there's a price to be paid for it."

Charles had first met Bevan when they had both just made lieutenant on *Argonaut*. They had quickly become friends. Now that he thought of it, Bevan had never volunteered much information about his upbringing, and Charles couldn't remember asking. "I didn't know," Charles said. "I guess I'd just assumed—"

"There's a lot about Daniel that people don't know," she said, concentrating on her drawing. "Don't he talk funny a lot, but he's close with his feelings. In the early days, when I first met him in Portsmouth, when you was repairing your ship, mostly what we did was talk. We did the other thing, too, but we talked and talked, all night sometimes. It was then I knew I cared special for him, hard as I was against men. Of course, I didn't think it was possible. It wouldn't have been if it weren't for your Mrs. Edgemont."

"Penny," Charles said. "You can call her Penny with me."

Molly flashed a smile. "Your Penny," she said, "now, she's highborn. I know her pa's a miller, but she was made to be a lady. She wouldn't be half angry to hear me talking like this, but it's the truth. Do you know why my Daniel is so taken with you?" Molly said.

"No, why?"

"Because he says you can speak what's on your mind. Not that I agree, I think you're shy, but compared to Daniel, you're a circus performer. I saw a circus once when I was little. It was amazing how some people can do those things with everybody watching."

She made some small strokes on her paper and studied it without enthusiasm, then darkened some of the lines. She began to nibble on her lower lip in contemplation.

"I'll tell you this," she said, looking up at him. "Daniel don't like being no ship's captain. For me, I don't care what he does. I'd work my fingers till they're stubs. I just want him to be as happy as I am in his life. Your life ain't nothing if you ain't happy in it."

As she talked, Charles listened with a different understanding of her, and of his friend Daniel Bevan. She went on with an unself-conscious optimism about herself, her husband, and their future. She spoke of a time when Bevan could be home for good. He'd told her that he had enough money set aside to purchase a small piece of land, not as grand as Charles's, but with several farms where they could put down roots, raise children and perhaps sheep. "Wouldn't I love to have a few sheep of my own," she said, opening her case a crack and slipping the pencils inside. "Here, you can see this one. Faces are easy."

Charles looked at the sketch and saw pretty much the same face he saw in his mirror, only better. She'd done something around his eyes and the corners of his mouth that made him look . . . what . . . thoughtful, considerate, something like that.

"Penny will like that one," Molly said happily. "Ain't I pleased you could sit for me. If it's all right, I'll go speak with her now. She must be beside herself, what with leaving and all."

THE MORNING ARRIVED overcast and squally, low roiling clouds bringing scattered spitting showers, the wind shifting to out of the west. The turn in the weather had slowed the work on *Louisa*'s masts, as a strong shower had passed through during the night. Still, at seven bells in the morning watch, all that remained was to run the halyards and bend on the canvas for the forward two topgallant yards. Those of *Pylades*'s crew who were helping had returned. Charles would be ready to make sail within a scant few hours. *Louisa*'s cutter lay idle in the water alongside, his wife's luggage at that moment being passed down.

"It's time," he said to Penny, standing beside him, her head lowered, her face hidden by the edge of her bonnet.

"I am reluctant to leave," she spoke hoarsely. "Oh, I cannot cry two times in two days."

"It's all right," Charles said, something catching in his own throat.

Penny looked up at him, her expression fixed, with renewed dampness around her eyes. "Thou wilt return to our home when thou canst?"

"Of course," he said, not trusting himself to say more.

A tear started down her cheek. Charles smoothed it away, and despite his crew gathered around, even watching from the rigging, he held her tightly against him. He felt her chest heave, and then she pulled herself away.

"I am recovered," she said in a whisper. "I do love thee. I always shall." Without waiting for a reply, she turned to slip into the chair, taking Claudette from Attwater and clasping the girl in her lap.

Charles watched as the cutter put out its oars and rowed across to *Pylades*. It felt as if his heart had been wrenched from his chest. He did not notice that those of his officers on the quarterdeck had moved unobtrusively to the opposite rail. He raised his pocket glass as Penny and

Claudette were hoisted aboard the brig and watched as Molly and Bevan greeted them.

Almost immediately, *Pylades* upped her anchor. Her head soon fell off, and billows of canvas appeared on her twin masts as she made for the harbor entrance, gathering speed as they filled.

Through the lens, he saw Penny come to the rail. She looked so close that he could almost speak to her. She lifted an arm and waved. Charles lowered his glass and waved in return. After a few moments, she stepped back to rejoin Molly, and the women made their way below.

Charles remained alone by the rail, watching the brig as she made her steady way toward the horizon. As her hull dipped gradually beneath the waves, he noted a speck, the merest dot on the horizon, in the distance beyond. The appearance of other traffic in these waters was nothing to remark upon. Still, it made him uneasy, a reminder of the ever present dangers in wartime seas.

"How long till the masts are complete?" he almost snapped at Winchester, who was standing at the base of the mizzen, observing the work aloft.

"We're close, sir," the lieutenant answered equably. "Not more than an hour and a half, two at most."

"We will weigh the moment they are prepared," he said unnecessarily.

"Sir," Talmage's voice came from behind him.

"What?" Charles said.

"I do believe that *Pylades* has altered her course."

TEN

CHARLES TURNED TOWARD THE TAFFRAIL AND SEARCHED the horizon. He immediately picked out the two tiny slivers of lighter gray that would be *Pylades*'s topgallants. Instead of being in a line, as they had been when she sailed away from the harbor, he could distinctly see both masts, which indicated that she was broadside on and, from the curve of her sails, pushing southward. That was unusual, he thought. Given the direction of the wind, it would have been more normal for Bevan to stand farther out, far enough so that he would have been well beyond sight before coming about so he could make Cape Murro on a single tack. An uncomfortable feeling started in the pit of his stomach.

He turned his gaze northward along the line separating gray sea from gray sky and too soon found the second set of sails he had noticed before. They were slightly larger now, ship-rigged, he could tell, with three masts, also standing to the south. His discomfort became a feeling of dread.

"Sir," Beechum said, close beside him. Charles saw that the young man had a long glass up to his eye. "Sir, I think *Pylades* is signaling."

Charles fished for his pocket telescope. "What's she saying?"

"I can't make it out. I can't see but the first flag or two. She's too low down, sir."

Charles snapped his small lens open. With the overcast, visibility was not good, but he thought he caught a flash of color on Bevan's mizzen halyards. "Mr. Beechum," he said as calmly as he could manage, "please take your glass up to the tops and report back to me *Pylades*'s signals." Charles had to catch Beechum by the arm before he bolted. "And," he continued, "I want to know what you can make of that second ship just to the north."

"Aye-aye, sir," the young acting lieutenant said and was into the mizzenmast ratlines before Charles had attracted Winchester's attention.

"Sir?" Winchester said, coming aft from where he had been watching the progress of the work aloft.

"Stephen, I have a great fear that a French warship has taken up Bevan's wake outside of the mouth of the harbor," Charles said. "The wind's dead foul for returning to port. I think Bevan's decided to run southward. *Pylades* is not a fast sailer."

Winchester quickly scanned the horizon and soon found the distant sets of sails. "Dammit," he said.

"Captain, sir!" Beechum's cry carried down from the platform at the tops. "*Pylades* is signaling *Enemy in sight to the north*. The second ship is a frigate. She hasn't shown her colors yet, but she appears to be in pursuit."

"Thank you. Please keep me informed," Charles shouted back up. He turned again to Winchester. "Speak with Keswick, if you will. I want our sails bent on as quick as humanly possible. Draft as many men as you need, the entire company if necessary. And tell Keswick he can cut every corner in the book so long as the canvas will carry us to that warship."

"Yes, sir," Winchester said, and hurried forward.

Charles looked again over the rail. At this distance, it was hard to be sure, but he thought the frigate had closed on Bevan's brig. If they weren't already, he guessed they would soon be within cannon range. What would Bevan do if the frigate fired on him? Charles could feel his heart pounding in his breast. He hoped his friend would strike as soon as he was overhauled, but knew he wouldn't. He heard a faint hollow boom as it reached him across the water.

"Captain, sir," Beechum shouted down from his place aloft, "the frigate's raised her colors and opened fire with bow chasers. She's French."

Charles did not answer. Instead, he called for his signals midship man. "Mr. Sykes, signal to *Pylades* to strike."

"Sir?"

"Goddammit, signal to *Pylades* to strike her colors, to surrender to that frigate."

"But I can't, sir," Sykes said, his voice quavering. "There's nothing like that in the book."

"Hell's fire and damnation. Fuck. Dammit!" Charles swore. Then he looked at the frightened boy. He knew Sykes to be correct; there was no such signal. The British navy had apparently never considered ordering anyone to surrender to an enemy. He also realized that he would have to gain control of himself if he was going to be able to do anything to rescue Bevan's boat. He took a deep breath. "Thank you, Mr. Sykes. I am sure you are correct," he said more calmly. "I apologize for my language."

"That's all right, sir. I understand," Sykes answered.

"Thank you again. If you would go forward and convey my respects to Lieutenant Winchester. Ask if I might speak with him when he is free." That was a much better tone, he thought.

"Yes, sir," Sykes said, and departed.

Charles looked around the nearly empty quarterdeck. His eye soon rested on Talmage, staring over the far rail. "Mr. Talmage, a word, if you please," he said.

"Yes?" Talmage said, crossing toward him. A pair of reports of cannon fire sounded, distant and menacing.

"I would appreciate your thoughts," Charles said.

Talmage glanced over his shoulder at the distant sails. "I think *Pylades* will soon be overhauled, sir."

"And then?" Charles said.

"I hope she strikes. Otherwise the frigate will employ her broadside. The brig hasn't a chance." Talmage seemed genuinely concerned about this outcome. "Either way, she will be taken," he added. He didn't look pleased about this result, either.

"What do you think our response should be?"

"We should run them down as soon as we can make sail," Talmage replied firmly.

"I agree," Charles said. "Should we rely on our armament or come aboard her and attempt to take her by main force?"

Talmage paused in contemplation. "I believe we should board

directly and try her that way. There will be the frigate and the brig, though. Have we enough men to carry both?"

"I don't know, but I'm bound to try," Charles answered. "Are you with me?"

Talmage smiled grimly. "I'm with you, if only for Mrs. Edgemont's sake."

Charles looked at the prickly lieutenant. "That's good enough," he said. "If you would please find the armorer and have him bring his wheel onto the deck. We will sharpen all of the cutlasses, axes, and boarding pikes."

"Yes, sir," Talmage said. Without further comment, he went forward.

A distant roll of cannon fire, more intense and drawn-out, reached Charles. He saw Winchester hurrying aftward. A glance into the masts told him that the fore and main topsails were nearly in place.

"Captain," Beechum shouted down. "The frigate has fired her broadside. *Pylades* has lost her foremast from the tops up and all her mizzen. I think the Frenchman is about to go alongside."

"Thank you, Mr. Beechum," Charles called back.

"Fifteen minutes, Charlie," Winchester said, coming to a halt. "We'll be able to make sail in fifteen minutes, not more."

"Thank God," Charles said. "Send two men with axes to the hawse; we'll cut the anchor cable the instant we're ready."

It seemed an eternity before he heard the ax blades begin to chop into the cable . . . five, six, seven strokes. He heard the heavy line fall into the water and felt his ship, freed from the restraint, fall off with the current. "Sheet home!" he heard Winchester order as *Louisa* turned and made for the harbor mouth. He felt vastly relieved to be under way. It occurred to him that he had never been involved in boarding an enemy ship before.

As soon as he saw that Mr. O'Malley had set up his grinding wheel in the waist, Charles went down and had his sword honed to an edge that he could cut his finger on. Talmage, he noticed, stood waiting his turn.

"You do know that this may be your one chance to redeem yourself before a court-martial," Charles said in a low voice.

Talmage nodded and scowled. "I've thought of that, but it doesn't matter. I would do the same in any event."

"I know that you would, Mr. Talmage. I want you to know that I appreciate it."

"Thank you, sir."

Sykes appeared with his midshipman's dirk, making his way through the crowd of sailors gathered around the wheel with their own weapons. "Sir," he said, "I've heard that a French thirty-six carries a crew of three hundred or more. Won't that make a difference?" Every man on board knew that *Louisa*'s complement, marines included, barely exceeded two hundred.

Charles frowned at the boy, then looked around at the body of men watching him closely. He shook his head. "Not with these men it won't," he said loudly enough for everyone to hear. "Perhaps we'll only take half across to make it more sporting."

There was laughter at this, and a cheer went up, deafening in the middle of a hundred men or more. Charles slid his sword back into its scabbard and raised his hat in acknowledgment. The crowd parted as he passed through to make his way to the quarterdeck.

"Stephen," he said, "I'll take the deck. Make sure all of the officers have their weapons prepared, and then ask them to attend to me here."

Looking forward, he could easily see the rectangles of the Frenchman's sails on the horizon. If the frigate hadn't noticed *Louisa*'s approach yet, she soon would. What would her captain do? He thought it likely that she had come from Toulon on her way to Malta or Egypt, had run into *Pylades* by chance, and had snatched her as an easy prize.

If he were the French captain, Charles thought, he probably wouldn't be too worried by *Louisa*'s appearance. The Frenchman would have the superior broadside. He might see it as an opportunity to take a second prize. Probably he would keep the captured brig close, thinking that the Englishman would be more intent on retaking one of his countrymen than a prolonged engagement with a superior ship. If he dropped his anchor and put on a spring, he could turn his guns in any direction he chose, and wouldn't have to worry about handling his sails or being out-maneuvered. The smaller enemy would have to come to him. Charles doubted that the captain would expect the English ship to bear straight down on him and board, although that would become clear soon enough. He guessed that *Louisa* would be within long range of the

Frenchman's guns within the half hour. As he watched, her topgallant sails vanished from their masts. That confirmed his speculations.

"Sir," Beechum yelled, "the frigate's let go her anchor and is taking her sails in. *Pylades* appears to be tied alongside just behind her."

Charles smiled a smile he did not feel. "Thank you, Mr. Beechum," he called. "You may come down now."

As they finished with the armorer, *Louisa*'s officers began to report back to the quarterdeck one by one: Winchester, Talmage, Beechum, even Sykes. They waited only for Sergeant Cooley; Charles had passed the word for him, but he was still attending to the preparations of his marines. Of those present, Charles realized, not one of them had ever boarded an enemy ship. He didn't think Cooley had, either, although he wasn't sure.

"Sir," Cooley said, resplendent in his red uniform coat and a shining saber. To the others, he touched his hat and said, "Gentlemen."

"Sergeant Cooley," Charles said, "have you ever gone aboard an enemy ship and carried her?"

"No, sir," Cooley answered comfortably. "I've heared tell about it often enough, though."

"Please share with us what you've heard."

"It's not complicated," the marine said. "Gain control of her quarterdeck, if you want to get it over with in a hurry. Chase the rest of the crew belowdecks. Armed or not, they can't do nothing from down there. All you have to do is guard the hatches."

"That's it?" Charles said, expecting some closely held secret to be revealed.

"I said it wasn't complicated, sir."

"All right, thank you," Charles said. He turned so that he faced them all. "This is what I am thinking; please feel free to add your own thoughts." He looked around hopefully and received equally hopeful stares in response. "We will run directly up to the frigate without turning to fire off our guns. It'll be a long run, and she'll have her broadsides trained on us. We'll just have to take what she sends our way." He half expected an objection but received none.

"In deference to Mr. Cooley, we will try to run our bow aboard her quarterdeck and board from there. We will fire our main armament as we make contact, grapeshot on ball. Gun captains only at the cannon. Everyone else forward, the captains to follow as soon as they've pulled the lanyards. I hope to catch the majority of her men on deck readying to repel us, and so we might expect to do the most damage. Our purpose is no less than to carry both the frigate and *Pylades,* and to do it as quickly as can be done. It all hangs on the first rush." A silence followed as Charles studied their faces, looking for doubt or hesitation. He found none. "Questions?" he said. "Objections?"

An expectant silence came from his audience.

"We are agreed, then," Charles said. "Mr. Beechum, you will command the forecastle guns. They will be the most critical. Have both carronades charged with a double load of grapeshot. I rely on you to aim them where they will do the most good. Fire ahead of the boarding party. Is that understood?"

"What am I to do after, sir?"

"When the guns are emptied, you may come across and do as much mischief as you can."

"Aye-aye, sir," Beechum answered. "I understand, sir."

"Mr. Cooley," Charles continued, "as we close within musket range, line your men along the forward rail and keep up a steady rate of fire on her decks. After we make contact, you may board and support Lieutenant Winchester as he directs."

"Yes, sir," Cooley said.

"Stephen," Charles said, "you will lead the assault on the frigate. Get your men across, and take control of her quarterdeck by whatever means you think desirable. If she doesn't strike then, work your way forward and press the remainder of the men below. You will have every able-bodied man available except the foremast topmen and a half dozen to be left on board with Mr. Sykes. Mr. Sykes, you will have command of the ship. Is that agreeable?"

Winchester nodded with a sober "Yes, sir." Midshipman Sykes assumed his own serious expression and said the same.

A rippling explosion came from across the water, and Charles looked up in time to see the smoke blowing clear of the distant Frenchman's decks. Shot churned the water forward and along both sides of *Louisa's* stem. One ball crashed into the head at the bow of the ship. He took his watch from his pocket and looked at it.

"Lieutenant Talmage," Charles said carefully, "I am in hopes that you will lead the retaking of *Pylades*. You will have the foretopmen under your command. It will mean forcing your way across the French quarterdeck to get there. I will accompany you."

"It will be my honor, sir," Talmage replied.

"Are there any questions?" Charles asked. "None? Collect your men and make sure they know what they are about. I suggest you keep as many as possible belowdecks until needed."

The quarterdeck soon cleared except for Samuel Eliot, two quartermasters at the wheel, Midshipman Sykes, and Charles. He turned his mind to Penny and what she must be enduring.

"Begging your pardon, sir," the master said, approaching him.

"Yes, Mr. Eliot?" He noticed the sword hanging from Eliot's hip, which he seldom wore.

"I couldn't help overhearing your plan to go aboard *Pylades*," the master said. "I would like to accompany you, if I may, out of consideration for Mrs. Edgemont, sir."

"Thank you," Charles said. "That would be welcome."

"My two mates, Mr. Cleaves and Mr. Withers, are of a similar sentiment," Eliot added.

Charles nodded his agreement, thinking that if he wasn't careful, the entire crew would rush straight across the frigate's deck to save Penny, leaving the French to do as they pleased.

He saw Attwater making his way up to the quarterdeck just as the Frenchman's broadside roared out, closer now. Round shot screamed through the lower rigging and close alongside, punching holes through the sails and striking a port side carronade on the forecastle. *They're not firing at our masts this time,* he thought. Charles looked again at his watch: two and a half minutes from one firing of the frigate's cannon to the next. He noticed almost as if it were an abstraction that his hands were shaking violently. He dropped the watch back into his pocket and clenched them behind his back. The French warship loomed larger in his vision, a cable or a cable and a half's length forward of the bow.

"Here's your pistols, sir," Attwater said, holding one out in each hand. "They're charged and primed."

Charles had forgotten to ask for the weapons but took them without speaking and stuck them into his belt. His mind turned again to Penny. Was she safe? Was she alarmed by the cannon fire? Did she know that it signaled his approach? Had the French mistreated her? Would they when he came aboard? What about little Claudette, and Molly, and Bevan? Charles felt his heart hammering in his chest, his breath rapid and shallow. God, he hoped nothing had happened to them.

A cable's length, less now. The passage of time seemed to have slowed to a crawl. He saw a line of redcoats starting toward the forward rail with their muskets held in front. He noted the heads of his crew just inside the hatchways to the deck below. The marines reached their place and raised their weapons to their shoulders as the French frigate clouded itself in smoke at a hundred yards. Shot ripped along the decks, one into the rail by the marines, throwing several backward onto the deck like broken furniture. Two balls screeched past Charles, taking his breath away completely. He forced himself to gasp in a lungful of air.

The marines' volley popped along the forward rail, an insubstantial sound compared to the frigate's broadside. *Louisa* angled to port at the last minute, her bowsprit aiming at the Frenchman's mizzen shrouds. Charles could see the mass of packed men on her deck waiting for the impact, and the rush of his own crew pouring up out of the hatchways and running forward. He started down from his quarterdeck toward the bow, followed closely by Eliot and his mates.

A grinding crash sounded as *Louisa*'s bow came harshly aboard the frigate, sending a shock through the ship that almost caused Charles to fall. The maindeck cannon exploded inward, unattended now by any crew. He heard the deep bark of the forecastle carronades a heartbeat after. He did not pause to observe their effect.

"HUZZAH!" An insanely loud shout went up as *Louisa*'s crew rushed over the bow and along the bowsprit onto the French deck; the clash of steel, screams, cries, and the bangs of pistols and muskets accompanied the seething mass of struggling men. Charles saw the marines stand back from the rail, fix their bayonets, and start across behind Sergeant Cooley, whose sword was drawn and held before him.

"There you are," Talmage said as Charles approached. Twenty young, fit foremast topmen clustered around him, armed with cutlasses and pikes. "As soon as the marines are across, we'll go."

"Remember to look out for Mrs. Edgemont and Mrs. Bevan," Charles said.

"They all know about the women," Talmage said. "I think they're as anxious about them as you are."

Beechum arrived, slightly breathless, from the forecastle. "I'll come with you sirs, if I may."

"Of course," Charles said.

"Remember, lads," Talmage declared, drawing his sword, "straight along the deck and over the rail as fast as we can. No dawdling to kill Frenchies just for the fun of it." He grinned wildly, his teeth showing white, and started forward.

Charles followed, sliding out his own blade and feeling its weight surprisingly light in his hand. The men came next, Beechum bringing up the rear. They were at the forecastle, then the beak and over, dropping onto the French deck. All around was a wild tumult of struggling, cursing, brawling men hacking and stabbing with their weapons at the chaotic mass around them. Almost at once Charles was confronted by a young officer, his sword slashing down. Charles raised his own in time to block the strike, and steel clashed loudly against steel with a force that sent a shock through his shoulder. The man raised his weapon to strike again, then, with a shocked look, slipped toward the deck as Talmage yanked his blade back from the man's belly. Frantic confusion followed as more men poured across, several slipping on fallen bodies and the blood-soaked deck. The odors of spent powder, sweat, fear, and death filled the air. Pistols banged, swords rang on steel, wild screams, grunts, cheers, and curses overwhelmed every other sensation.

"This way," Talmage shouted and threw himself against a wall of men, lunging and jabbing with his hanger. Charles focused on the urgency of getting to Penny and pressed forward, slashing desperately to break through the enemy in front. He barely dodged a boarding pike thrust viciously at his middle; it sliced along his ribs and caught momentarily in his coat. As the man pulled back to free his weapon, Charles swung his sword wildly at the face, opening a spurting gash from ear to shoulder. The French seaman fell backward and disappeared beneath him. Charles found himself pushed forward from behind, chest to chest with a Frenchman whose breath stank and whose eyes were wide with panic or bloodlust. With hardly room to move his arms, Charles heaved the man back a crack, pulled one of his pistols from his belt, cocked, and fired, the muzzle hard against his opponent's abdomen. The mortally wounded man had no space to fall.

From somewhere came two loud explosions that tore through the massed French with terrible effect. The wall of humanity before him wavered and, step by step, gave way. Charles found space to raise his sword and swung it in a wide arc before him.

"Lunge, sir, don't slash," a voice close beside him said.

"What?" Charles glanced to see Talmage.

"Stick 'em, don't hack 'em," the lieutenant said, intense concentration on his face as he jabbed his blade forward. "Parry and lunge, it's more efficient."

Charles lunged at a man with a thick black mustache over white teeth and an ax held high, stabbing the blade into his throat. The man toppled backward. Through the gap, Charles glimpsed the far rail of the frigate's deck, no more than ten feet distant.

"Here!" he yelled, desperate to get across. "To me! This way!"

The men following pushed forward, by sheer weight forcing the thinning line of defenders back and apart. Charles heard another pair of piercing explosions behind him and turned in time to see a cloud of spent powder drifting from *Louisa*'s forecastle. He decided that Sykes must be directing the few men left on board in the reloading of the carronades to fire them into the frigate's defenders.

Charles had little time to admire Sykes's initiative. He ran for the railing and looked over. Six feet below lay *Pylades*, tied up alongside, bow to stern, her foremast shrouds opposite him. Without hesitation, he mounted the rail cap, balanced himself, and jumped, landing with a harsh jolt against the cables. The impact knocked the sword from his hand and took the air out of him. He scrabbled frantically for purchase, to keep from sliding down over the side into the narrow line of sea between the two hulls. A foot found a ratline and then his fingers. He hung, secure for the moment, to catch his breath.

Scarcely had he inhaled than he saw a man running toward him with a pike held out, intent on stabbing him with its iron point. Charles pivoted sideways toward the far edge of the shrouds and jumped, landing heavily on the deck. The Frenchman hesitated a fraction, then lunged wildly, swinging his weapon sideways. Charles stepped inside the arc of the sweep and took the blow on his ribs, pinning the shank against his side, then clutching it with his hands. As he wrestled for control, he glimpsed Beechum and Eliot climbing down the shrouds, then several of his crew leaping from the frigate's rail to the deck. One, whom Charles recognized as the foretopman Baker, cleaved his cutlass down on the Frenchman's skull with horrible effect.

Charles threw the pike down and knelt to retrieve his sword while a bloodied Talmage and a half-dozen more men made their way across. Charles counted fourteen seamen, Beechum, Eliot, and Talmage, who had suffered a gash to the side of his forehead and had blood running over one eye and down his face.

"Are you fit?" Charles asked.

"A scratch," Talmage replied, wiping an already saturated sleeve across the eye to clear his vision.

Charles paused for a moment and bent from the waist with his hands on his knees to collect his last reserves. His breathing came in ragged gasps, and he became aware for the first time of a burning pain along his left side. As he straightened, his sword arm hung limp, almost too much used to raise the heavy blade. It seemed the fingers of his right hand could neither tighten around the grip to wield it nor open to let it drop. He dimly heard the noise of the battle still raging on the frigate as he looked aft along the brig's deck. Clustered around the main hatchway, he saw a dozen or more French seamen with swords and axes. Beyond them he made out a smaller group near the wheel including two women, a child, a pair of French soldiers with muskets, and an English officer lying on his back on the deck. Irritated by the hurt along his side, Charles searched with his fingers along his wet and sticky waist until they bumped against the butt of a pistol. It was enough. He couldn't remember what had happened to the other of the pair he had brought with him.

"Let's go," he rasped to the men around him, and started toward the French at the hatch. He saw that they were standing on top of the grating that confined *Pylades*'s crew below. Charles launched himself toward the first person in his way, a middle-aged seaman with a kerchief around his head and an ax in his hands. Charles thrust at the man's middle to force him to lower the ax handle for protection, then drove his sword deep into his chest, where it wedged firmly between the ribs and stuck fast. Charles heaved to withdraw the blade, succeeding only in wrenching the dying seaman's body off the grating and partway across the deck. Disgusted with himself at losing his sword, he released his grip and looked for Penny.

He found her immediately, standing in front of the wheel next to Molly and holding Claudette tightly in her arms. He saw Bevan next, lying on the deck a few yards away, his thigh heavily wrapped and two soldiers standing over him with their muskets. His and Bevan's eyes met, and despite Charles's shake of his head, his friend reached out to grab the legs of the nearest soldier. Charles moved forward, scratching for his pistol. The first soldier struggled to free himself from Bevan's grip, lowering his musket for balance. The second reversed his weapon so that its bayonet poised in the air, pointing downward. He moved to thrust it into the struggling Welshman.

Before he could act, Charles saw Molly dart forward with a shrill scream, pulling the knife she had used to sharpen her pencils out from inside her sleeve. She stabbed her blade up into the soft underarm of the soldier moving to strike her husband. The other soldier wrenched one boot free from Bevan's grasp and stumbled sideways, clutching tightly to his musket, one of his fingers within the guard for its trigger. The pan flashed, and a ball of gray-black smoke exploded from the barrel. Molly jerked backward as if she had been kicked by a horse and fell to the deck. She lay unmoving, her arms spread, her legs casually crossed, the hem of her dress around her white-stockinged calves.

From twenty feet away, Charles cocked his pistol and raised it. The soldier with his still-smoking musket stared at him wide-eyed, resigned.

Charles's finger tightened on the trigger, but he couldn't fire on the defenseless man. "Surrender, you son of a bitch," he snarled. "Surrender or I'll blow your fucking head off."

"*Rendez-vous, s'il vous plaît,*" Penny said, moving forward and taking the heavy weapon from the soldier's hands. "*Merci, monsieur,*" she said, then slid the thing over the rail, where it fell into the sea with a splash. Still holding Claudette, she returned and dropped to her knees beside Molly. She took one look at the wound over her companion's heart and gave a small cry. Penny pushed the little girl's face against her breast so that she would not see and held her tightly. After a moment she closed Molly's eyes one at a time with her fingers, then straightened her skirt.

Charles looked forward to see that the Frenchmen around the hatch had surrendered; his men were herding them toward the rail. He didn't see Talmage anywhere, although he did hear the report of a pistol from somewhere forward. *Someone else can deal with it,* he thought. *Pylades's* crew members were pouring up and across the deck, onto the frigate to participate in what, to Charles's ears, sounded like the tail end of the struggle for control. He felt a weariness come over him. With a final effort, he crossed the deck to where Bevan lay and lowered himself to sit cross-legged beside him.

"I'm sorry," Charles said. "There was nothing I could do. I would have tried anything in my power to save her."

Bevan pushed himself to a sitting position, his injured leg held stiffly out in front. "It's nothing to do with you, Charlie," he choked. "She decided it herself. She must have known what the result could be." He looked across at Molly's form at rest, and added, "I wish to God she hadn't."

Charles felt Penny kneel beside him. She set Claudette on the deck. There was worry on the little girl's face, so he grinned and reached out his arm to wiggle his fingers. Claudette smiled uncertainly but clasped her sides to protect her middle. Charles stroked her hair instead.

"Charlie, what hast thou done to thyself?" Penny said, pulling back the left side of his coat.

He looked down to see a ragged tear in his shirt, a large area soaked with blood that had run down as far as his knee. The entirety of his struggle to cross the French frigate's deck and along the *Pylades* began to run together in his mind. He couldn't remember when he had received the injury.

"Sorry," he said stupidly as she stripped off the coat, then began to undo the buttons of his shirt.

"I am not pleased with thee," she said through clenched teeth. "Thy warfare has taken my friend."

Talmage appeared from the direction of the hatchway, walking with some difficulty and still wiping at the blood seeping down the side of his face. Charles noted a second stain of red on Talmage's shirt, partly hidden by his coat. He patted the boards beside him. "Sit," he said. The lieutenant sank down, dropping his sword loudly on the deck.

"Ouch!" Charles said as his wife's fingers probed the gash along his ribs. Another seaman arrived from the frigate.

"Lieutenant Winchester's respects, sir," he said, touching his knuckles to his forehead. "He asks if you require any assistance."

Charles opened his mouth, but Penny spoke first. "I require thee to bring me a pail of clear, fresh water," she said. "Stephen Winchester may inquire later, when I have more time."

The messenger looked to Charles, who nodded and said, "Get the water, please." As soon as the man turned away, she raised the hem of her dress and tore off a strip from one of her petticoats.

"Hold this here," she said, pressing the cloth against his side. She spoke tersely, tight-lipped and strained. Charles saw tears running down her cheeks. She turned to examine Talmage, now lying full-length on the deck. "Oh, dear God, no," she exclaimed.

"What?" Charles said, turning to look more carefully at his lieutenant. He saw that Talmage's face and lips had gone a ghostly white, and a growing pool of red was spreading beneath him. "Jacob," he said. "Jacob!"

Talmage's eyes flickered open. His mouth moved as if to speak, but only a trickle of red liquid bubbled out. The eyes rolled up in their sockets and went dim.

The water arrived, followed closely by *Pylades*'s surgeon with his case of unguents and dressings. "Please, help this man," Penny pleaded. She was holding Talmage's hand, rubbing furiously at his wrist.

The surgeon knelt down to examine Talmage. After the briefest look, he straightened. "He's gone, missus. I couldn't have helped him anyway. He's been shot through the lung."

She lay Talmage's hand gently on the deck. "I'm so sorry," she whispered. In a firmer voice to the surgeon, she said, "Please, wilt thou attend to my husband."

A heavy bandage was being wound around Charles's ribs when Winchester came across himself. He looked at Molly and Talmage, and the two men sitting on the deck, then removed his hat out of respect. His own uniform coat and breeches were flecked with drying blood, but he had no obvious injury.

"The frigate is carried?" Charles asked.

"The last surrendered a quarter of an hour ago. We've just finished disarming them."

"The butcher's bill?"

"Don't know yet. Not too bad, I think. There are a lot of cuts and scrapes; Lincoln and his mate are looking after them now. How are things here?"

"Things here? How are *things here*?" Penny interrupted, her voice rising. She set Claudette on the deck next to Charles and stared ashen-faced at the hapless Winchester.

"*Things here* are terrible," she said, rising to her feet and advancing on him. "Terrible, terrible, bloody, bloody, horrible. Thou, Stephen Winchester, are whole. Molly has died, her life stolen away. Poor Jacob Talmage has passed, drowned in his own blood. Those men"—she pointed toward the bodies of some Frenchmen by the hatchway—"those men are dead or soon to die."

Winchester took a step backward. Penny followed him closely, enraged, her voice risen to a scream. "Men speak of a butcher's bill as if it were sheep flesh. By this thou means the human beings killed and grievously injured. But even that is not the true bill. Each of them is a son and a brother, a father, a husband. They are gone. The many who nurtured and loved them remain. They are the ones who must pay thy precious butcher's bill for all these dead, for this war, for all wars."

Winchester's backside bumped against the brig's wheel, and he could retreat no farther. "I am most sincerely sorry if I sounded callous or uncaring," he said. "I assure you that I did not mean to be. I beg your forgiveness."

Penny's bloodstained hands covered her face, and her shoulders heaved.

Charles pushed himself painfully to his feet. Holding the child by her hand, he moved to stand behind his wife and put his arm around her shoulders. "Penny," he said.

"Don't thou touch me," she choked. "I have agreed to abide thy profession. Here, see the fruits of it. In truth, thou hast a very sad career." She turned away from him, picked up Claudette, who had started crying, and walked to the taffrail. There she sank to the deck with the child in her arms and sobbed.

Charles followed and carefully lowered himself beside her but did not speak. Penny turned her face against his shoulder, her tears running down his arm. "Molly was so brave. She tried too hard to become something better than fate made her. No person should have to struggle that hard in all their life. Jacob Talmage once confided to me that all he wanted was to please thee, which he could never do. Now both are gone."

Charles could not hold her because she was on his left side. The pain around his ribs had grown into a fiery ball as severe as any he had ever experienced. The slightest movement brought stabs of almost unendurable agony. Instead, he contented himself with patting her knee with his right hand and stroking Claudette's back. After a time, when Penny had calmed, he said, "You should speak with Daniel."

"Yes," Penny said, rubbing her palm across her eyes, "he will be heartbroken." She rose, picking up the child. "Thou should come also."

"I can't," Charles said. "I don't believe I can stand."

She called two crewmen, who lifted Charles under his arms until he came to his feet. Even so, the movement left him breathless. From an upright position, he saw that *Pylades*'s decks had been cleared of the dead and wounded. Bevan, he learned, had been taken below, the surviving French returned to their frigate under guard. Molly, Talmage, and the other English dead had been carried below to be sewn into hammocks with round shot at their feet. Charles's sword was found, wiped clean, and returned to him.

"I will see thee back to thy cabin and into thy bed," Penny said.

Penny, Claudette, and Charles walked to the side, where he stared at the rail of the French frigate, six feet above. A ladder had been rigged for the crew to pass back and forth, but he knew that he could not climb it. Penny summoned a seaman, who went across to arrange for assistance. Soon a handful of men rove one whip to hoist them on board the ship and then another to get him over to *Louisa*'s decks. Charles saw topmen aloft working to disentangle his ship's bowsprit from the Frenchman's mizzen rigging. Neither ship looked to be so badly damaged that she would be unable to make sail before long.

In his cabin, Charles stood while Attwater helped him into a fresh shirt, then he sank cautiously and gratefully into a chair at the table. The pain along his side was just manageable so long as he made no attempt to change his position and was careful not to breathe too deeply. Penny busied herself tending to Claudette. When the child was settled, she spoke with Attwater about having hot soup prepared for Charles, and making sure her husband stayed in his chair and did not exert himself.

Charles was not worried about exerting himself. He didn't think he would be capable of rising if he wanted to.

"Thou art comfortable?" Penny said when they were alone.

"I don't know if I would say 'comfortable,' " Charles answered. "I do know that I'm not moving."

She sat in the chair on his right side and took his hand in hers. "I am sorry that I spoke harshly with thee before," she said. "It was shameful of me. I want thee to know that I appreciate thou rescuing us. I only wish it were not necessary."

"You'd better apologize to Stephen," Charles said with a chuckle that he instantly suppressed. "I think you frightened him more than the French ever would."

"I was angered," she said. "Stephen Winchester was not responsible. I shall speak with him and ask his forgiveness."

"I'm sorry about Molly," Charles said. "For all the world, I would have prevented it were it in my power. I admired her also."

"And Jacob Talmage?" she said.

"And Talmage," Charles answered.

She rose from her chair. "If thou can manage, I will visit with Daniel Bevan to see if I can comfort him. I will put thee to bed on my return."

"What about Claudette?" Charles said, eyeing the girl dubiously, thinking he might be called on to tickle her.

"Timothy Attwater will attend to her when he returns. Please be sure that she has something to eat."

"On your way, would you ask Winchester to call on me at his earliest convenience?" Charles said. "Tell him I would appreciate a report on the condition of our little flotilla."

"YOU'RE NOT SERIOUS," Charles said.

"I'm decided, Charlie," Bevan answered. "I've given it a lot of thought. I don't like being a ship's commander. I'm resigning my commission; in fact, I have already written the letter to send on to Gibraltar."

Charles and Bevan sat at the table in Charles's cabin, Bevan's crutch leaning against its edge. Penny had withdrawn to put Claudette down for the night. Charles listened to his friend's words, but he couldn't believe what he was hearing. It was heresy of the highest order. Commanding one's own ship and making post were the whole point.

"Daniel," he said, "I know you're upset. Losing Molly is a blow to us all. But don't throw away your whole career because of it."

"It's not because of Molly," Bevan said patiently. "At least not in the way you think. I've never liked being a ship's commander. I told you this before, when we were at the rendezvous waiting for Nelson. Don't you remember?"

Charles nodded. "I remember. You were daft then, and you're daft now."

"No, I'm not, Charlie. I'm not good at it. I worry about every little detail, so much that I can't sleep. Molly and I had talked about this. I was going to quit anyway and find a place where we could be together."

"Jesus, Daniel," Charles said. "What will you do? Where are you going to go?"

"There's not much point in buying a farm now," Bevan said. "However, I recall that I slept quite well as the first lieutenant on *Louisa*."

Charles stared uncomprehending at his friend. "What do you mean?"

"I mean that you should send Winchester to Gibraltar with *Pylades* and the prize. You could even give him leave so that he can see Penny safely home and visit with his own wife and child. I've already spoken with him. He's agreeable if you are."

"Then who would be my first?"

Bevan smiled. "You could enter me as a volunteer for the time being," he said.

Penny came out from the sleeping cabin. "Shhh," she said. "Speak softly, Claudette is asleep."

"Did you know that Daniel has decided to resign his commission?" Charles said.

"Yes, I know," she said. "What a very good idea. Others should follow his example."

"PLEASE CONVEY MY fondest congratulations to Ellie," Charles said, standing on the recently tidied quarterdeck of the former Republican national frigate *Embuscade*. The afternoon before, the French wounded had been carried below, where they were looked after by *Pylades*'s surgeon and confined along with the rest of the crew. The Union flag of Great Britain had been hoisted above the French tricolor on the mizzen, signifying that she was a captured prize.

After Charles's discussions with Bevan, he had agreed to send the crippled *Pylades* and the frigate to Gibraltar under Winchester's command, carrying Penny and Nelson's dispatches with them. There was no time for him to see to the repair of the brig's masts if he was to overhaul his admiral before the squadron reached Egypt. The solution he had settled on was to transfer most of *Pylades*'s crew to *Embuscade* and have the frigate tow the brig. He took off a few of Bevan's former crew to bring *Louisa* up to her complement. In exchange, he sent Sergeant Cooley and all but a corporal and a half dozen of his marines over to keep order among the French prisoners.

With nothing else to say, he reluctantly moved to stand in front of Penny. Finding the right words was difficult. "I'm going to miss you," he offered. He knew from her expression that she was unhappy. He also knew that it wasn't only because they were about to separate. After Bevan had left, they'd spoken of little else the night before.

"I still do not wish thee to go on to Egypt," she said. "I wish thee to return home to heal thy injury."

"I appreciate your concern," he answered. "Under other circumstances, I would consider it. Please understand that I must do this. There is no one who can take my place."

"I understand perfectly," Penny said, unsmiling. "But I do not agree."

"Then those are the terms on which we must part," Charles said stiffly. "Please hold up Claudette so that I may say good-bye to her."

Penny bent, hoisted the child into her arms, and straightened. "*Au revoir,* my little one," Charles said. He carefully leaned forward from the waist and kissed the child on her cheek. "Be a good girl for Mama."

"Gud-bye, Sharrle," Claudette said with a small tear in the corner of her eye. She held out her arms to embrace him. Charles leaned a little farther forward, which brought a pain from his wounded side. He held the pose for only a minute, with the child's arms around his neck, before, with a sharp intake of breath, he pulled away.

"I must return to my ship and you to England," Charles said to Penny, unhappy at the tension between them. Not knowing what to do or say, he nodded to her, then turned toward the chair in which he would be swayed over the rail and back down into *Louisa*'s cutter, waiting alongside.

Penny placed Claudette back on the deck and came after him. He stopped. "Charles Edgemont," she whispered, taking his arm, "go and do what thou must do. Take my tenderness and caring with thee. Know that my heart goest where thou goest. I will look for thy return when thou art free to do so."

Charles put his arm around her and held her close. "Never doubt that I love you more than anything on earth," he said. He stepped to the chair, sat carefully, and signaled that he be hoisted away.

ELEVEN

"EVERY STITCH OF CANVAS SHE'LL CARRY, DANIEL," Charles said as soon as he was set down on *Louisa's* deck. "East-by-southeast."

"East-by-southeast, if you please, Mr. Eliot," Bevan said, leaning on his crutch.

"Aye, Mr. Bevan," Eliot answered with a broad smile. "And, may I say, it's good to have you back. It's like old times, to my way of thinking."

"The pleasure is all mine," Bevan said. "Besides which, someone has to see to it that you tend to your duties."

Charles did not find himself in the mood for lighthearted banter. He'd slept little the night before due to the pain along his ribs, which now throbbed as if someone were trying to drive a spike into his side with a mallet. He looked forward and saw Keswick blow on his call, signaling the topmen aloft to let fall the canvas. The waisters soon came pounding up the ladderways to take their places on the halyards and clew lines. Amid the immaculately organized confusion, the sails billowed down like descending curtains, to be tautened and braced around to catch the breeze. Almost immediately, he felt the deck begin to move beneath his feet. With a strong, steady westerly wind on her starboard quarter, *Louisa* would fly.

Feeling satisfied but drained, he walked to the port side rail and looked outward. He saw *Embuscade* already sliding rearward, a half cable's length away. He picked out Penny behind the railing and raised his hat to wave it. Penny waved back, then bent to lift Claudette so that she could see. "Write to me," Charles started to shout, but filling his lungs for the effort brought a jolt of pain. "Write," he muttered to himself as the frigate, the almost mastless *Pylades* in tow, drifted farther and farther astern. As the figures on *Embuscade*'s quarterdeck grew indistinguishable, he replaced his hat. A kind of emptiness came over him.

"I'm going below, Daniel," he said. "Call me for any reason you think necessary."

"All right, Charlie," Bevan said, then tilted his head skyward to study the set of the sails above.

Comfortable at least that his ship was in good hands, Charles descended the ladderway, placing his feet one at a time on the steps and holding tightly to the rail with his right hand. He acknowledged the sentry at the door and passed into his cabin. "Attwater," he called wearily.

"Yes, sir?" his steward answered, emerging from the small room to the side where his bed hung.

"Help me with my coat, will you? I can't seem to manage."

With Attwater's assistance, Charles pulled his right arm out of its sleeve but had to have the garment lowered to slide below his left arm, which hung more or less uselessly by his side. He found he could move the limb if he had to, but doing so brought a sharp protest from his damaged muscles. Without prompting, Attwater unbuckled the belt that held Charles's sword and hung it from its peg on the bulkhead.

"It ain't the same without Mrs. Edgemont not being here, ain't it, sir," his steward said.

"No," Charles said, guessing that was the answer Attwater wanted.

"Can't I get you a mug of coffee?" Attwater asked, clearly trying to be cheerful.

"Thank you, no. I only want to rest." Charles pushed a chair back from the table with his foot and lowered himself carefully into it.

"I'll just fetch you a bowl of nice 'ot soup, then. Don't you need something in you."

"It's not necessary," Charles said. "I'm not hungry. I'll just sit here for a bit."

"I'll get the soup anyway, and some biscuit," Attwater insisted. "If you don't mind my saying so, you've lost a mess of blood, and ain't you as pale as a sheet. I won't be a minute."

Charles was too tired to argue. "Fine," he said.

With his servant departed, he took a look around the cabin. The room seemed oppressively empty and quiet with Penny and Claudette and all their things gone. He half expected to see his wife emerge from the sleeping cabin or to hear the child's excited giggles. He raised his right hand off the table and wiggled his fingers as if to tickle, but no sounds came.

When Attwater returned, Charles obediently ate his soup and drank a tankard of small beer. "Didn't Mrs. Edgemont not order me to see that you don't get your nourishment and your rest," the steward told him at least a half-dozen times. From the way that Attwater went on, Charles decided Penny must have put the fear of God into him on the subject. The thought improved his spirits. Afterward, he allowed himself to be helped into his bed and was asleep before Attwater had his shoes off.

LOUISA DID FLY over the seemingly vast, unbounded sea. With an unvarying westerly wind, she made twelve and even thirteen knots, by the casting of the log, hour by hour and day by day. They shortened sail only at night after the third day, for fear they might run upon the stern of one of the lumbering seventy-fours in the darkness, or else pass them completely by.

Charles and Bevan soon resumed their long-established and easy relationship. Sometimes, Charles thought, it was as if Bevan had never been gone. If anything, he seemed to be enjoying himself as he hobbled across the deck on his crutch and one good leg to bellow out orders or point to some deficiency of workmanship. Then he would hobble back to rest on a chair lashed to a ringbolt near the wheel and offer good-humored comments about whatever entered his mind. Except, Charles knew, when his memories of Molly intruded. Then he would stare silently out at the sea until a new object for his attention presented itself.

As they ran, they made repairs to damage inflicted during the boarding of *Embuscade* and the final touches to the rigging. By the fourth day, thanks to Bevan's efforts, *Louisa* was as trim and shipshape as she had ever been. Charles found that he took no small pleasure in looking at her when everything was proper and in its place. She was a beautiful, living presence, with a spirit of her own. Gradually, his strength began to return, so he spent longer hours on deck, although he could still not do anything strenuous involving his left side or arm. Getting up from a chair or sitting down was also an adventure best engaged in cautiously. To lower himself into bed, he welcomed assistance.

He and Bevan took to having their suppers together most evenings, which helped assuage the emptiness left by Penny's departure. One evening when the two men were alone in the cabin, Charles asked his friend how he was getting along.

"You mean my leg?" Bevan said. "It gets a little better day by day."

"No," Charles said. "I mean without Molly. How are you getting along with Molly gone?"

"Oh, yes," Bevan answered, looking out through the stern windows. "I miss her, of course. I miss her badly. But you know, your life is what it is. You decide for yourself whether it makes you happy or sad. She always said, 'Your life ain't nothing if you ain't happy in it.' I'm not happy that she's gone. I'm blessed that I knew her."

On their fifth day, shortly after noon, a cry came down from the lookout in the fore crosstrees: "Deck there. I see sails two points to starboard off the for'ard bow."

"Ask him how many," Charles said to Bevan. To Eliot he said, "Two points to starboard, if you please."

Bevan bellowed up into the tops. The lookout answered hesitantly, "I can just see their t'gallants, zur. I see two . . . might be three . . . I see more, could be any number."

"That'll be Nelson, unless I miss my guess," Charles said. "Mr. Sykes, would you see to the hoisting of the recognition signal, please."

Within the hour, the lookout had counted fifteen sail, thirteen of them ships of the line. The recognition signal had been answered and another set of flags, relayed by the rearmost seventy-four, ordered them to close on the flagship. Charles could just see the distant white rectangles each time *Louisa*'s stern rose on the crest of a wave. By the end of the afternoon watch, the ponderous warships were visible from their hulls up, mountains of canvas on their masts, the fleet spread over the now-crowded horizon.

As they passed *Majestic* to port, Charles saw the figure of Captain Westcott on her quarterdeck and raised his hat. Westcott waved his own in return. *Vanguard* was visible several ships ahead.

Charles nodded to Beechum in the waist, and the first gun of the salute to the rear admiral's flag boomed out. On the count of five, the second cannon fired its powder charge and lurched inward. Then the third. On the thirteenth gun of the salute, signal bunting soared up the flagship's halyards. Charles knew what it said; he'd expected it.

"Captain to report on board," Bevan observed.

"Yes," Charles said. "Prepare to heave to and have the gig hoisted out." He tested his left arm tentatively. It was growing stronger daily, but he didn't want to stress it. "I think I'd best be lowered down in a sling."

"A sorry lot we are," Bevan said, thumping his crutch on the deck. "Two old cripples." Charles smiled.

Vanguard took in most of her sails, came to, and laid her fore topsail against its mast. Charles's gig skipped across the water to come to a halt under the two-decker's tall side, where they found a chair swung down from the main yardarm. "Must have seen you needed assistance getting down to yer boat," Williams observed.

"I expect you're right," Charles said, seating himself. "Please wait alongside. I don't think I'll be long."

"Captain Edgemont," Admiral Nelson greeted him as he was set down on the deck. "I see that you are impaired, sir. I trust it is not serious."

"More painful than serious, sir," Charles said, touching his hat. "We were obliged to board a French frigate upon leaving Syracuse harbor. I've prepared a report on the incident." He removed an envelope from his coat pocket and held it out.

"My word," Nelson said. "I'll read it later, if you agree." He took the paper and waved it in front of him. "Does this require any action on my part?"

"No, sir," Charles said. "I've sent the prize on to Gibraltar with *Pylades.*"

Nelson pocketed the document. "I shall certainly read it as soon as I am able," he said. "But for now we've only the moment. I make it that we are two days out from Alexandria. I thought it important to acquaint you with my thinking for the coming battle."

"Yes, sir," Charles said.

"I intend to keep my fleet in tight order and fall upon the French the moment we sight them. It doesn't matter what time of day or under what conditions. I'll not give them additional time to prepare." The admiral seemed genuinely excited by the prospect.

"Yes, sir. I see."

"How we engage will of course depend upon their disposition. I've no doubt they will be well aligned. My preference is to break their line and double the near part so as to destroy them piecemeal, but we shall have to see what they offer. I also have no doubt," Nelson continued, his good eye shining, "that our little band of brothers—as I have termed the captains of this squadron, including yourself, sir—will be more than adequate for any eventuality."

"Yes, sir," Charles said. "Of course."

"I haven't had time to put your orders in writing," the admiral hurried on. "I'll give them to you direct. *Louisa* will take station well forward of the squadron. I should think five or six leagues so that you are just within signaling range. Once you sight their battle fleet, you will note how they have arranged themselves in such detail as you are able, then return to *Vanguard* to report. Is that clear, Captain?"

"I understand, sir," Charles answered. It seemed straightforward enough.

"Good, good," Nelson said. "I will not detain you further." He looked at Charles again with concern. "You're sure that you are fit?"

"I'm as fit as I need to be, sir," Charles answered firmly.

"I have every confidence in your abilities," Nelson said, taking Charles by the arm and walking with him to the chair. As Charles settled himself in before being lifted off, the admiral added, "Oh, yes, one last thing. How has Lieutenant Talmage acquitted himself? Appropriately, I trust. Or do I need to intervene?"

Charles met Nelson's eye. "Mr. Talmage died of injuries he received during the taking of the frigate, sir. He acquitted himself with both honor and valor."

Nelson had no visible reaction to this.

With Charles back on board, *Louisa* soon passed easily through the heavy, slow-moving line of battleships with their twin parallel rows of gunports. Many of them were left open for ventilation, the hollow circles of their cannon mouths visible behind. The men at the railings or in the rigging waved their greetings as she slid effortlessly onward. *Louisa*'s crew happily returned the sentiment. Charles raised his hat to acknowledge the similar gestures of the warships' officers. Toward the end of the afternoon watch, they came to their assigned position, with the topsails of the leading ships of the squadron just visible from the masthead. Charles ordered the courses taken in so as not to outpace the squadron completely. He began to turn his mind toward the orders he had received and what he might expect when they reached Alexandria.

"Mr. Eliot," he said, approaching the sailing master.

"Yes, sir?"

"Do we still have the charts from that Frenchman we took off Rosetta? You know, the one we burned."

"Aye, from *Félicité*. I have them below."

"Were there any for Alexandria, showing the port and the roads?"

Eliot rubbed his chin in contemplation. "There's the one with the port and the coast a fair distance in each direction. As far as Rosetta itself, if I recall. It's possibly the only such chart in the entire British navy."

"Might I borrow it for a time?" Charles asked.

The master nodded. "I'll just send one of my mates to get it for you." After a moment, Jonathan Cleaves, the first master's mate, returned with the neatly rolled tube of paper, bound with a piece of string.

Charles took the document and went below to his cabin, where he opened it on his dining table. After laying his sword along the top edge, he weighted the lower corners with books to keep it from rolling back up. He struggled out of his coat (managing unassisted) and sat down to see what he had.

It was a gratifyingly detailed chart of the Egyptian coast, from the Rosetta mouth of the Nile to beyond Alexandria, with its inner and outer harbors clearly drawn. Features of the land—including villages, roads, hills, and even stands of date and palm trees—were sketched in. Most gratifying of all, the waters had been sounded, and the chart showed the depths of the seabed and the shoals and reefs that would hazard navigation.

Charles studied the chart closely, particularly the port and its approaches. The harbor itself, he quickly decided, would not do as a haven for the larger of the French warships. It was small and shallow, with a narrow mouth. While it could be defended easily by fortifications on the two moles that projected inward like crab claws on either side of the entrance, the restricted passage meant that the entire place could be bottled up effectively by only one or two British warships on blockade outside.

If the French fleet could not seek protection in the port, Charles thought, they would most likely anchor in a defensive arrangement in the open waters somewhere outside. For divining what sort of arrangement, the chart proved singularly unhelpful. The seas were still relatively shallow at six and seven fathoms close in, but they deepened fairly quickly by a mile out. There was no indication of any shoal or reef that might present a natural defensive feature. What formation would be most advantageous for the large ships of the line? Presumably their frigates, the three that remained, and the belligerent Capitaine Baptiste with his corvette, would be arrayed far in front to warn of any approaching enemy. Charles stared at the paper, attempting to imagine himself as the French admiral, waiting for some spark of insight that would reveal the single obvious solution that the enemy would employ. By nightfall, when Attwater insisted that he go to his bed, Charles was still waiting for that spark. Well, he resigned himself, he'd know soon enough. By noon the day after tomorrow, Alexandria and whatever awaited there would be in full view.

POMPEY'S PILLAR SHOWED first, the ancient Roman monument rising like a large finger over the dun-colored shore. The landmark promised that the ancient Greek, then Roman, and now French city of Alexandria lay just over the low sand hills along the coast. Charles heard the ship's bell ring five times; it was two and a half hours into the forenoon watch. Scattered fluffy clouds dotted the sky but provided no relief from the glaring midmorning sun. He glanced up at the foretops where the lookout was stationed, resisting the urge to call up and ask what the man saw. He was uneasy that there had been no reports of outlying frigates. He would have expected to have sighted at least one, even at a distance. He glanced at Bevan, staring over the rail at the shoals and dunes that lay off the shallow Maraboo Bay, sliding by to starboard. Bevan met Charles's eyes and shrugged. Whatever awaited, it wouldn't be long coming.

At eight bells, ten o'clock in the morning, the lookout in the foremast shouted down, "I can see into the harbor. There's a mass of shipping inside."

Charles picked up a speaking trumpet, and without thinking of the rapidly healing injury to his rib cage, shouted back, "Do you see anything outside the harbor mouth?"

"Naught, sir. It's as bare as a—there's nothing at all outside, sir."

"Are there any warships inside?"

There was a hesitation. "Don't think so. Not any big'uns, anyway. It's hard to tell at this distance."

"Dammit," Charles muttered. Where the hell was the French fleet? He didn't think Nelson would be pleased. After all, it was Charles who had insisted they were at the port.

"Mr. Beechum!" he shouted. It came out louder than he'd intended.

"Yes, sir?" said the startled acting lieutenant, three feet to his left.

"Please take your glass up to the fore masthead and report back to me what, if anything, you can see of the French battle fleet."

"Yes, sir," Beechum said. He hurried to collect his telescope and started forward.

Now what? Charles thought. If the French weren't here, where were they? More troubling, he would have to signal something to his admiral, and soon. He stood, consciously attempting to appear unconcerned, and waited for Beechum to return. After what seemed an inexpressibly long time, the lieutenant came hurrying aftward along the waist.

"Sir," he reported breathlessly, "the harbor is chock-full of transports and merchantmen. There might be a few corvettes in among the lot, but there's no large battleships, not a one."

"And outside?" Charles said, disappointment growing in his stomach.

"I couldn't see a hint of anything as far as the horizon," Beechum answered. "I looked carefully. I'm sorry, sir."

"I see. Thank you for your effort," Charles said. "Mr. Sykes, if you would signal to *Vanguard* that no enemy warships are present."

"Aye-aye, sir," Sykes said.

Charles leaned against the rail and drummed his fingers in an unending tattoo. He had a gnawing feeling that he was missing something. What? He tried to picture the chart still unrolled on the table in his cabin. If they weren't here, where? Probably they would be someplace close by; they would be required to protect—what was that general's name?—Bonaparte's lines of communications. With a start, he remembered something and stopped tapping. He wished he had the chart in front of him, but he could see it well enough in his mind.

"The flagship has signaled the recall, sir," Sykes said, standing by his elbow and jolting him out of his reverie.

Charles ignored him. "Mr. Beechum," he said, "do you remember when we first saw that frigate on the far side of the Rosetta point a few weeks back? The one that chased us."

"Sir?" Beechum said. "Yes, sir. I climbed to the tops with my glass and picked her out."

"Think carefully now," Charles continued. "Do you remember looking into the bay beyond the Frenchman? Aboukir Bay, its name is."

"Yes, sir," Beechum said, clearly lost at the line of questioning. "There was a strong haze in the air. I couldn't see anything."

"But you thought you might have," Charles pressed. "Just for a moment, you said, you thought there might be something there."

Beechum's face wrinkled in concentration. "Well," he said doubtfully, "there *might* have been a ship in the far end of the bay. But it was very indistinct. When I looked again, it was gone."

"Thank you," Charles said. "Please see to it that there is a sharp lookout posted in the foremast crosstrees. Make sure he has a long glass, and send someone up to relay his messages."

"Sir," Sykes said, thankful to finally get his captain's attention, "what about the admiral's signal?"

"What signal?" Charles said firmly, turning to the boy.

"The admiral's signal to—"

"No, Mr. Sykes," Charles said. "I mean, *what* signal? If Nelson has telegraphed an order, we must have missed it. Do you understand? He's at a very great distance. Signals get missed all the time."

"Ah," Sykes said, the glow of understanding spreading across his face.

"You mean like at home, when you are called to supper but you're busy with something else."

"Exactly," Charles said. To Bevan, who had overheard the conversation with obvious interest, Charles said, "We will continue eastward along the coast. Proceed at the same reduced pace so as not to outrun the squadron. It is my intention to look into Aboukir Bay. Hopefully, Admiral Nelson will follow."

"That's where you think the French are?" Bevan asked, eyeing Charles with a kind of dubious curiosity.

The longer Charles thought about it, the more firmly convinced he became that it was the logical place for the enemy fleet to anchor. For one, it was relatively close to Alexandria, a scant twenty miles or so along the coast, and so could be communicated with by either sea or road. Second, the bay would offer better protection from the elements than the open waters in front of the harbor. And third, it might provide any number of defensive advantages if they were beset by a superior force—anchoring as deeply as possible to prevent the enemy from doubling their line, for example.

"I think it to be a distinct possibility," Charles said. "If I were the French admiral, that's what I might do."

"And Nelson's signals recalling you?" Bevan said. "You're supposed to do as he says, you know."

"I am aware of that, thank you," Charles said uncomfortably. "However, I am doing what I believe Nelson would wish me to, had he but known of the circumstances." He paused, then said seriously, "These are my direct orders, Daniel. We will continue eastward until we know for certain whether the French are at Aboukir Bay. I will put this in writing, if you wish, in the event there is an inquiry."

"That will not be necessary," Bevan said.

Before noon, the town of Alexandria came into full view off the starboard bow, a rather unspectacular, low-lying place, its skyline broken by a few minarets and Pompey's Pillar in the background. Aside from the towering monument, it didn't look at all like the kind of place Alexander the Great would have built as one of the finest cities of his empire. Charles saw that the port was indeed crowded with small shipping, and French tricolor flags flew from the forts on either side of its entrance.

"Sir," Sykes reported, "*Vanguard* has signaled again. It's the third time, this one with an imperative. You're to report on board without delay."

Charles scratched at the stubble on his cheek. How long would Nelson continue to follow if he received no answers to his signals? There was a very real possibility that he would anchor off the port so as to blockade the shipping there and detach a single ship to run *Louisa* down. Charles took a deep breath. It was one thing to ignore his admiral's signals, and quite another to send his own false ones. In for a Penny, he decided, which led him to another thought that he quickly banished from his mind. "Very well," he said, "you may reply to the flagship, *Enemy in sight to the east.*"

"Have we really seen them?" Sykes replied excitedly. "I hadn't heard."

"Not yet," Charles replied. "Make the signal, please."

"I sincerely hope they're there," Bevan said after the midshipman had left.

"Not nearly as much as I do," Charles said. "It will be very inconvenient if they're not."

Louisa sailed steadily eastward, Alexandria slipping farther and farther sternward. The coast became a series of small palm-dotted sand ridges and outcroppings. He saw ample signs of the French army along the dirt tracks: once a battery of artillery caissons moving in a dusty column, and another time a collection of what he took to be engineers building an emplacement atop one of the ridges. On a point of land well forward, he could make out the form of an old fort with a settlement nestled not far from its walls. That would be the village of Aboukir, he decided, or Le Village du Bequier, as the chart called it. Through his pocket glass, Charles looked briefly at the collection of whitewashed mud and reed huts amid a grove of palms. Beyond the point, he knew, lay the Bay of Aboukir. They were close enough that the lookout in the foremast should be able to see into the bay soon.

Charles heard the ship's bell and counted five strokes. It was half past two in the afternoon, Tuesday, the first of August. A day that might be celebrated for all history as a great naval victory, he reflected. But for which side? Or perhaps the French fleet had gone somewhere else, to Corfu or back to Toulon, in which case it would be nothing out of the ordinary. No, not nothing, he decided grimly. It could signify the end of his naval career. If the French were not in the bay, he knew full well he could be court-martialed for disobeying Nelson's signals under any of a number of rules and regulations, or even the Articles of War. As for sending his own misleading signals . . .

"Mr. Sykes," Charles said, "is the squadron still following?"

"Yes, sir," the midshipman answered promptly. "They've flown the interrogatory with respect to our last signal several times, but I thought it best not to bother you."

"Thank you," Charles said. "That was considerate." Unusual, but still considerate, he thought.

Charles felt that he could wait no longer. The lookout would surely be able to see a sufficient distance into the bay by now. The man's continued silence did not bode well. He probably found the waters empty and had nothing to report. A desperate anxiety began to creep over Charles. He opened his mouth to instruct Sykes to climb to the crosstrees and inquire directly what the lookout did or did not see, but he did not get the words out before an excited shout came down from aloft.

"Deck there! I see masts, a whole line o' masts t'other side o' that spit for'ard."

A sense of intense relief swept over Charles. He snatched up his trumpet. "How many do you see?"

"Can't tell yet. More than a dozen, anyway," the lookout answered.

"Mr. Beechum!" Charles shouted.

"Yes, sir," Beechum answered, grabbing his telescope. "I'm on my way, sir."

"Bring a pencil and paper," Charles said. "I want you to sketch their formation."

"Mr. Sykes, you may signal to *Vanguard, Enemy fleet at anchor, east-by-southeast.* Fly an imperative with it. Nelson will know what it means."

"Aye-aye, sir," Sykes answered. He left at a run.

Charles had to stop to think what he should do next. "Daniel," he said after a moment. "We will give that fort on the point a wide berth in case it is manned. I want to be able to look into the bay with my own eyes so that we may see how the French have arranged themselves. Afterward, we will come about and report back to the flagship."

Bevan nodded, then said, "My God, Charlie, but you're lucky."

"A little luck can be a good thing," Charles said seriously, then broke into a wide grin.

Louisa sailed placidly past the crumbling castle a mile and a half distant. Charles noted the French flag waving from the castle's battlements, and the black tubes that were probably a hastily positioned battery of six-pounder field artillery. He also carefully noted the shoals at the base of the point, which he knew extended to a small barren island two miles to the east, marking the seaward edge of the bay. The wind held steady from west of north. As they passed the castle, he saw, in all their majesty, the French battle fleet behind the island, arrayed in a long shallow V as close as they dared to the shore.

He stared at them in awe. They were a thing of terrible beauty, riding placidly at anchor in a line stretching south nearly two miles long. His attention was quickly drawn to the flagship *L'Orient* at the center, far larger than the others with three full decks of guns, 124 in all. Charles felt a lump rise in his throat. She was big, he thought, too big for the British seventy-fours.

Charles remembered Nelson's orders. He was to note the manner in which the French fleet had arranged itself in as much detail as he could, then report back to *Vanguard*. He also remembered Nelson saying that he intended to attack without hesitation, and his preference for doubling their line so as to engage one section at a time with overwhelming force. From what Charles observed at the northern tip of the line, looking along its length, that didn't seem possible. Perhaps the view along their front would reveal some opportunity. It would delay his return to the flagship, but he thought it worth the time.

"Daniel," he said. "We will proceed beyond that small island up ahead and then turn into the bay for a better viewpoint. It would be advisable to place someone reliable in the forechains to take soundings as we go. It wouldn't do to run aground now."

"No, it wouldn't," Bevan said, his eyes fixed on the French fleet. He turned to issue the necessary orders.

"Mr. Sykes," Charles called. "Would you be so good as to run down to my cabin and bring me the chart off my dining table." From his memory, the bay was shallow, rarely over seven or eight fathoms, and shoaling to one or two a mile or more from shore. *Louisa* needed a minimum of three in order not to run aground, four to be safe. The heavier seventy-fours required the entire four fathoms.

Soon Sykes returned, and the chart was laid out on the binnacle. Charles moved to study it again as *Louisa* wore around the western end of the island. Aboukir Bay was thirty miles from west to east, about four miles deep, and relatively open to the sea on its northern side. The western end, just behind where the French had positioned themselves, was a treacherous warren of shoals and shallows, undetectable on the water's surface. Out of curiosity, he took a pencil from his pocket and, using the soundings on the map as a guide, sketched where the four-fathom line ran. The outside of that would be safe for navigation; the landward side would not.

As they cleared the island, the entire front of the French fleet showed itself spread across the bay. From three miles away, Charles raised his pocket glass. The warships rode at single anchors by the bow, and there was a full cable's length between them. That was interesting, he thought. They'd left themselves plenty of room to swing with the changing wind and current, although they had springs on the cables to keep their starboard broadsides facing outward. He surveyed the length of the line with his glass, lingering again on the massive flagship. It was a strong defensive formation, he decided grudgingly. Probably too strong, with the three-decked first rate anchoring the center, for any frontal attack by Nelson's squadron. Charles searched for some weakness but found none other than that they were more widely spaced than would be usual for a battle in the open sea. Of course, this was necessary if they were to swing.

He also noticed three frigates and a familiar corvette, similarly moored behind the line of battleships. It seemed curious that they would be kept confined like that, instead of at sea scouting for an enemy, but it was not especially remarkable.

"I think that is enough, Daniel," Charles said. "Wear ship. We shall return to *Vanguard*."

Charles breathed a little easier. He'd found the French and would soon be able to report on their alignment to his admiral. He could congratulate himself that he'd done his duty, even if he had stretched the truth a little to accomplish it. Nobody would be upset about that now.

He stared idly at the French line as the wheel came over and the sails braced around, putting the wind first on *Louisa*'s stern and then on her port beam as she turned. It was a little unnerving that he'd sailed baldly in front of an entire enemy fleet. He wondered if any of them guessed that Nelson's squadron was at that moment running down on them from the west.

As they passed the island on the opposite beam, Charles returned to the chart. He thought to mark on it the exact location of the French formation to pass to Nelson. He looked up at the land to pick out some feature he could line up with the warships, found a suitable low hill, then bent over the chart to mark where they lay. He jerked up his head to stare at the French warships again. "My God," he uttered.

"What's that, sir?" asked Eliot, standing by his shoulder.

"They've left room to swing," Charles said, more to himself than to the sailing master. "They've left room to swing," he repeated.

Eliot eyed him, uncomprehending. "Aye," he said. "It's either that or put down two anchors. Twin anchors is a bother getting up."

"Don't you see?" Charles said, excitement growing in his voice. "The French have anchored themselves too far from the shallows. They've left room for a seventy-four to sail in behind them. They can be doubled."

Before Eliot could respond to this, Beechum's voice carried down from the foremast tops. Charles had forgotten that he was still up there. "Captain, sir," he shouted, "*Goliath* is signaling. You should be able to see her from the deck."

Charles turned to look forward. He saw two sets of sail from the topsails up, bearing down on him. They couldn't be over five or six miles distant. He could see the signal flags.

"She wants to know how many French warships there are, sir," Sykes reported.

"Answer that there are thirteen. Give a bearing," Charles said hurriedly. The appearance of the two British ships of the line was troublesome. Where was the rest of the squadron?

"Beechum, what are those two sail?" he shouted up.

"*Goliath* and *Zealous*, sir," Beechum replied.

"Where are *Vanguard* and the rest of them?"

The answer came back promptly: "About a mile behind, maybe

more, in a bunch like. One or two are trailing." After a pause, Beechum added, "*Vanguard* is signaling for us to return, sir."

"Thank you, Mr. Beechum," Charles shouted back up. "You may come down now." *Oh, hell,* Charles thought. As Nelson had promised, his fleet was coming pell-mell at the French so as to give them no time to prepare. There was no way Charles could report to Nelson in time for the admiral to use the information *Louisa* had gleaned to shape the battle. By the time Charles reached the flagship, any number of the squadron would already be engaged. There was also no signal available to the British navy that would allow him to say the French line could be doubled, that they'd left room to swing on the landward side. He thought it unlikely that the English captains would see the opportunity on their own.

He took a deep breath. There was only one way he could think of to communicate unmistakably what he knew. "Daniel, put the ship on the reverse tack and clear for action," he said. "After that, we will beat to quarters."

TWELVE

"WE'LL LAY TO AND WAIT UNTIL THEY CATCH US UP," Charles said. *Louisa* took in most of her sails, laid one on the mast, and slowed to a near standstill in the bright afternoon sunshine off the eastern tip of the small sand island at the edge of Aboukir Bay. The two leading British seventy-fours appeared hull up to the west, the masts of the rest of the squadron visible behind them. Charles turned his attention to the French line. Signal flags had soared upward on the nearest warships, indicating that they had sighted at least part of the squadron. *L'Orient* soon answered with her own bunting. Charles felt a sense of foreboding whenever he looked at the huge flagship. "Mr. Sykes," he said, "please inform me when the leading British vessels have closed to within a quarter of a mile."

Charles began to think about the preparations he must make if *Louisa* were to lead *Goliath, Zealous,* and others of the squadron into the narrow channel behind the French, and have any chance of survival.

"The ship is cleared for action, Charlie," Bevan said. Just then the drummer began his roll to send the men to their battle stations.

Charles waited for the noise to end. "See that the guns are charged and the crew at their stations, if you will," he said to Bevan. "Do not open the gunports and do not run them out."

"May I ask why not?" Bevan said.

There were several reasons that Charles could think of. It was ludicrous to consider placing the tiny *Louisa* alongside an enemy ship of the line and opening fire on her. He doubted his twelve-pounder guns would even penetrate her planking. A single French seventy-four, however, could deliver such a weight of twenty-four- and thirty-six-pound cannonballs that his frigate would be crippled and might well sink in a single broadside. He had thought to leave the guns unmanned, but that might unsettle the crew, who took courage from their weapons. In any event, it gave them something to focus their attention on other than the large enemy line of battleships that would be passing within speaking distance along their port side. Another reason—this one admittedly more hope than certainty—was the centuries-old tradition among European navies that heavily armed ships of the line did not fire on smaller vessels such as frigates, corvettes, or brigs. It was not considered a fair contest and thus it would be dishonorable for a captain to do so. Unless, of course, such frigate fired, threatened to fire, or in some other way angered them first.

"I do not wish to provoke them," Charles answered.

Bevan assumed a look of disbelief. "I understand, Charlie, that you are planning to sail blithely along behind the French line in order to demonstrate for the squadron that they might safely do the same. This is not a provocation?"

Charles answered hesitantly, "Daniel, I don't know of any other way to inform the squadron that the French have left room behind them. It is our duty to do this. If we are fired upon, sunk even, in the course of doing what we have to, then so be it." He met Bevan's eyes firmly. "If you have a better plan, I would like to hear it."

Instead, Bevan had a question: "Do you intend sailing their entire length?"

Charles hadn't yet gotten around to what he would do after they were behind the line. "What do you suggest?" he said.

"Two ships, Charlie," Bevan said. "I suggest that we pass behind the first two ships only. That's enough to show there is room, and it is remotely possible that their captains will allow us to pass, from either surprise or disbelief. Then we cut between the second and third and, with the wind behind us, run like all hell for the open bay."

Charles considered this thinking very sound. With a smile, he said, "All right, two ships only. It's a pity, though; if we tried the entire line, we could have taken wagers on how many we might pass."

"My money is on none," Bevan said.

"Sir," Sykes interrupted. He had been waiting and finally sensed a pause. "You asked me to tell you. *Goliath* and *Zealous* are within two cable lengths. *Goliath* has signaled *Take station to leeward. Vanguard* has also signaled the recall again."

Charles looked over the starboard rail to see the two leading British warships bearing down on him and racing toward the French. It was probably a point of honor with their captains as to who got there first. *Goliath*'s captain was ordering *Louisa* to get out of his way. It crossed Charles's mind that Admiral Nelson would be growing quite vexed at him for responding to so few of his signals. *Louisa*'s bell sounded eight times, ending the afternoon watch. It was late in the day to begin a major battle.

"Mr. Sykes, if you would be so kind, please signal for *Goliath* and *Zealous* to form line astern," Charles said in an elaborately calm voice that he hoped masked a growing anxiety. He strongly suspected Bevan to be correct: The first French warship they came to would perceive exactly what he was doing and blow them to kingdom come. He turned to Bevan. "We will begin," he said. "I suggest we show as much canvas as possible."

"Aye-aye," Bevan said, and issued the orders. *Louisa*'s sails soon filled, and she began to gain way.

Charles looked over the stern and saw that the two warships had taken up his wake. To his surprise, he noticed that both had run up *Acknowledge* flags on their halyards in response to his signal for them to follow. Both of their captains were vastly senior, and he knew he had no business issuing them orders of any kind.

Louisa rounded the island and braced up toward the end of the French line. On the far side of the island, he saw *Audacious, Orion,* and *Theseus* already beginning to make the turn, the remainder of the squadron not far behind. He looked ahead at the endmost French seventy-four. Even at two miles, she looked large and menacing. Charles thought of another detail that he should attend to.

"Mr. Beechum," he said. "Where the hell is Beechum?"

"Here, sir," the young man said, mounting the ladderway from the waist. "I've just been attending to the guns forward."

"I apologize for my language. Please see that the boats are hoisted out. We will tow them along our starboard side." If they were fired upon, it wouldn't do to have the ship's boats destroyed as well.

"Yes, sir." Beechum touched his hat and went back into the waist.

"Mr. Sykes," Charles called.

"Sir," Sykes said, "*Vanguard* is still signaling for our return. Don't you think we should answer?"

Nelson would not know what Charles was doing or why. He was probably furious by now. *Well,* Charles thought, *that can't be helped.* It would all be clear within the hour. "Ignore any signals from *Vanguard,*" he said. "If you would, please run up the Union flag on the mizzen."

The French battleships looked larger now, impossibly large, still a mile away. The closest ship's masts seemed to soar into the sky, a tiny wash of white surf around the dark hull where the current pushed against it. With his pocket glass, Charles could see a great deal of activity on her. The gunports swung open, and the black cannon poked out. Her officers stood in a group on her quarterdeck, looking in his direction, he was sure. There was a lump in his throat that made it difficult to swallow. He clasped his hands behind his back to keep them from fidgeting. It would be only about fifteen minutes until his precious little ship would pass just beyond the Frenchman's bowsprit before turning to run at point-blank range along her far side. What would those French officers decide then?

Charles glanced aftward and saw that *Goliath* and *Zealous* were still dueling to see which would have the honor of being the first to engage. *Goliath* seemed to have a small lead. He noted with relief that both were closely following his course. He suspected they may have divined his intention to lead them behind the French, but he couldn't be sure.

The arching bowsprit of the French ship of the line pointed like a giant spear into the clear blue sky as *Louisa* sailed across her bow. Charles could see the scrollwork at her beak and the rather admirable figurehead of a woman showing alabaster skin and gilded hair, with both breasts exposed. A single seaman stood just above and waved tentatively as they passed. Charles raised his hat and nodded in return.

"Put down the helm," he said almost calmly to Eliot. Then, "Brace her around." Bevan stood tensely beside him.

As *Louisa* turned under the bow of the warship, Charles noted with intense relief that her gunports were closed and no cannon awaited them. It took an almost desperate effort for him to remain standing motionless, as if he hadn't a care in the world, while the towering oak side slid silently by not twenty yards away. A figure in an officer's hat and epaulettes appeared at the railing when they were opposite the ship's quarterdeck. Again Charles raised his hat, a polite greeting in passing. In response, the man produced a pistol, extended his arm, and fired. The ball gouged the deck near his feet with a sharp *thunk*.

"Don't answer," Charles said to anyone who might be listening on his own quarterdeck. "They have a lot bigger they could throw at us."

The warship's stern showed just ahead. Charles took a deep breath. Open water appeared beyond, and a full cable's length before the next battleship. As they passed the rudder, he looked up at the ship's ornately carved stern gallery; her name was *Guerrier*, carved in gold letters. He thought to turn and run now, before he reached the second in the French line. He looked behind to see if *Goliath* or *Zealous* had made it around, but saw nothing, his view of them blocked by the mass of the *Guerrier*. All right, he decided, they might as well do it properly. One more ship and they would turn to escape. Their luck had held this far, it might well serve a little further.

In the gap between the first and second French ships, he saw that more of Nelson's squadron had rounded the island and were making for the head of the French line. He quickly identified *Vanguard, Minotaur,* and *Defense,* with several more close behind. The second enemy warship loomed just ahead.

"What do you think, Daniel?" Charles said.

Bevan was standing by the wheel, his eyes fixed on the nearing seventy-four. "It surely focuses your attention," he answered, flashing a grin. "If we get away with this, I'll buy you the best bottle of wine I can find."

"Ha," Charles answered, more relaxed now that they had passed at least one French warship without incident. "If we get past this next one, you'll owe me the vineyard." At that moment he heard the crash of a ship's broadside from close behind. He turned and saw *Goliath* just emerging from across the bow of *Guerrier,* the British ship's side swathed in smoke. *Guerrier's* foremast tilted and fell.

Charles looked forward. *Louisa's* bowsprit was just coming level with the second ship in the line. He was committed now. Her dark sides reminded him of the walls of a fort. His heart stopped as her gunports flipped abruptly upward, the hard stubs of her armament thrusting out.

"Bear away, bear away!" he shouted at Eliot. To Bevan, still looking aft, he said, "Clear the decks. Get everyone below."

"What?" Bevan said, turning back. His face paled when he saw the twin rows of cannon waiting and ready.

"Clear the goddamn decks," Charles repeated. "Hurry, we are about to be fired upon." "Fired upon," he realized full well, was a grim understatement.

"Sir, we can't turn away," Eliot protested. "It's too shallow; we'll run aground."

The master had not had time to grasp the significance of their situation, Charles thought. It was likely *Louisa* was going to find the seabed, and soon, no matter whether they bore away or not. It was preferable to do it in shallower water. "Do as you're ordered," Charles snapped. "Put the wheel over and lash it in place. Then get below."

"Aren't we going to return their fire?" Bevan asked.

Louisa's momentum carried her inextricably forward. Her bow already ranged along the warship's side. It would be another fifty yards before her rudder even began to bite. The Frenchman would wait until every gun bore before delivering her deadly broadside. Charles guessed that would not be long in coming.

"You can't be serious," Charles said. "We are about to be destroyed. Firing off our popguns won't change that in the slightest. We must save as many of the crew as possible. Send them belowdecks and go there yourself."

Bevan turned and began bellowing orders for everyone to abandon their guns and clear the decks. Some reluctantly, some eagerly, the crew began to make for the ladderways and below. *Louisa* continued forward, all her canvas still aloft, her head only just beginning to turn toward the too distant shore. At twenty-five yards, she came within full view of the French ship of the line's guns.

The deck had largely cleared. Charles noticed that Bevan stood unmoving beside him. "Get yourself below, Daniel," he ordered.

"I don't think so," Bevan answered. "It's stuffy down there."

"For Christ's sake," Charles had begun when he clearly heard someone on the battleship shout, "*Tirez!*" Her cannon immediately exploded in the loudest sound Charles had ever heard in his life. The deck beneath him jumped so violently that he lost his footing and fell to his knees. All around, his ship erupted into shattered pieces of railing and smashed gun carriages, the cannon themselves hurling backward and across the deck like so many broken straws. The wheel and the binnacle vanished abruptly. All three masts collapsed in a rain of falling lines, cables, blocks, torn canvas, and shattered spars. Then there was an unnatural silence, filled by a ringing in his ears.

Charles staggered to his feet. He saw Bevan on his hands and knees, reaching for his crutch. "Are you injured?" he said.

"Possibly not," Bevan answered shakily. He turned himself to a sitting position and began to run his hands over his arms and chest. "No," he concluded.

Charles looked around at the shattered remains of his command. Much of the railing was gone; cordage, splintered wood, dismounted cannon, and other useless debris lay strewn over the deeply gouged deck. The mizzenmast, with all its canvas, lay over the starboard side, the mainmast similarly to port, and the foremast tilted down into the sea at the bow. Only the bowsprit seemed to remain whole. The French ship, he noted, lay fifty yards to larboard. She had withdrawn her guns but hadn't closed her ports.

Charles helped Bevan to his feet. "Call the hands," he said. "We'd best see what sort of state we're in." He guessed from the sluggish way she rolled under his feet that his ship was taking on water.

Bevan picked his way around the obstacles on the littered deck toward the main hatchway. Already some of the men were beginning to emerge. Charles thought to cross to the starboard side and see if any of the ship's boats had survived. When he managed to get there, climbing over and through a labyrinth of tangled cables and lines, he saw that the cutter and gig seemed undamaged, but the launch had been cut in two by a ball that must have passed through both of *Louisa*'s sides.

Beechum found him still looking over the side near a wide gap in the railing. "Are you all right, sir?" he asked.

"I'm whole," Charles answered. "Do you know how the men fared?"

"We lost a number, sir," the young man said. "Some balls just went straight across belowdecks. I don't know how many; not too bad, I think."

Charles saw that Bevan had already begun organizing work parties to cut the masts free and clear the wreckage. "Would you please speak with the surgeon and the carpenter. Tell them I will expect their reports at their earliest convenience. After that, you may look to Mr. Bevan for your duties as he directs."

"Yes, sir," Beechum said, and began making his way back through the tangled rigging.

Charles saw that they had drifted farther from the warship that had fired into them, now something like a half cable's length away. He also noticed that *Louisa* seemed to be making no further progress through the water. The crash of broadsides caused him to look at the battle beginning along the French line. *Goliath,* he saw, had already passed *Guerrier* on the near side. She clouded herself in gun smoke with a tremendous roar as she reached the second in line, the Frenchman responding half a heartbeat later. *Zealous* was stationary beside *Guerrier,* firing methodically into her. Poor *Guerrier's* remaining masts quickly went by the board as *Audacious, Theseus,* and *Orion* each crossed her bow, loosing their guns with deadly raking fire at point-blank range. *It must be all hell on her decks,* Charles thought. He saw *Vanguard,* closely followed by most of the remainder of the squadron, start along the French line on the seaward side. He felt some sympathy for the badly mauled *Guerrier.* She had, after all, allowed *Louisa* to sail past her unmolested.

Davey Howell, the ship's carpenter, moved toward Charles, pushing his way through the clusters of seamen hacking with axes at the shrouds to free the broken masts.

"How much water is in the well?" Charles asked without preamble.

"About six feet, sir," Howell answered. He looked both harried and genuinely unhappy.

"Are the pumps holding, or are we losing ground?" Now that he thought of it, Charles couldn't remember hearing the normally unmistakable sound of the chain pumps as they clanked away. They were certainly quiet at the moment.

Howell rubbed a hand across his forehead. "It don't matter about the pumps," he said. "They were smashed. You might say we are holding our own. We're resting on the bottom. We're sunk, sir. As far as we can sink, that is."

"We're sunk?" Charles said stupidly.

"Aye," Howell said with some distress. "There are holes beneath the waterline you could crawl through. Ol' *Louisa* will never swim again."

Charles looked over the side. He could see that his ship was low in the water, but now he knew she would get no lower. His *Louisa* had been transformed in the blink of an eye from a graceful, swift sailing vessel to a battered, mastless island. He looked around in dismay, not wanting to believe that she had been destroyed. "Thank you, Mr. Howell," he said after a moment. "I am sure you have done all that is possible."

The surgeon found him soon afterward. Lincoln reported a dozen and a half killed outright, and a score and two injured, mostly with lacerations from flying splinters. All considered, the crew had gotten off lightly, for which Charles was grateful.

He found himself with little requiring his immediate attention. There wasn't that much he could do, commanding a ship that couldn't sail. The decks were soon freed of the fallen masts, which drifted lazily in the sea alongside. The tangles of rope, broken timbers, and dismounted guns were rapidly being cleared away. The sun sat low on the horizon, a large red-orange ball that tinted the sails of the British warships a pinkish color.

The thundering clash of cannon along the lower end of the line had become more or less continuous. Charles saw that the squadron had worked its way up to the fifth French ship. *Guerrier*, brutally battered by several of the British warships and still being systematically pummeled by *Zealous*, valiantly refused to yield. Only a few of her cannon seemed to be still functioning. The second warship, the one that had loosed her broadside on *Louisa*, had hauled her colors as soon as ships her own size had begun to fire on her. He thought there was no justice in this. The gallant *Guerrier* was being subjected to the most brutal kind of torture, while the honorless second French seventy-four had surrendered before receiving serious damage. *Goliath* and *Theseus* were anchored next to the third and were pounding away furiously at her. *Orion,* he noted, was moving up the inside, searching for the next unengaged ship in the line. He could tell from their masts that others of the British had taken positions on the far side. He could not identify them through the cloud of smoke that shrouded the third, fourth, and fifth. Only two ships beyond, Charles counted, lay the huge *L'Orient,* waiting for the battle to reach her. It wouldn't be long; he could make out several British seventy-fours crossing the bay to attack. He didn't relish the odds of whichever drew the flagship.

He regretted not being able to participate in the battle, even in some small way. The decks were very nearly cleared, and the few guns that were still serviceable had been put back in place. He decided to see about supper for the crew, assuming they still had a galley stove. He saw Beechum hurrying toward the quarterdeck, gesturing frantically at him.

"Sir," the young lieutenant shouted, pointing with his arm over the bow quarter. "Look there!"

Charles immediately saw that the French corvette previously anchored farther up the bay had slipped her cable and was bearing down on them. "Christ," he swore. Capitaine Baptiste would see this as an opportunity for his own personal revenge. *Louisa* could offer little more than target practice. Supposing she had all of her guns, they could not be transited far enough around to even frighten the corvette. "Goddammit all to hell," he swore again.

"May I be of assistance, sir?" he heard a distant voice call from across the water.

Charles turned to look over the larboard railing, had there been one, and saw the seventy-four-gun *Orion* just passing his beam fifty yards away. The tall, erect figure of her captain, Sir James Saumarez, stood on the quarterdeck with a speaking trumpet in his hand. Charles had no trumpet, so he cupped his hands to his mouth. "That corvette forward," he bellowed out. "I would be grateful, sir."

"Consider it my pleasure," Saumarez answered, and lifted his hat in salute.

Charles lifted his own hat and bowed.

Orion shifted a point to starboard and soon turned hard to port, presenting her broadside to the much smaller Frenchman, then hesitated, offering an opportunity for her to strike. Incredibly, the corvette brought her own guns to bear on the seventy-four and fired, covering herself in smoke. *Orion* immediately replied in a roar. The frail French ship, as *Louisa* had before her, dissolved under the onslaught, her masts falling as one. She immediately began to sink in deeper water than *Louisa* had managed to find. *Orion* sailed on to anchor beside the fifth ship in the French line, with whom she began to exchange broadsides.

Charles found himself appalled at Baptiste's decision and its consequences for the crew. Charles had never considered exchanging broadsides with one of the enemy line of battleships. It was an act akin to suicide. He decided that he should do something to assist the corvette's crew.

"Mr. Beechum," he called to the lieutenant, who was standing in the waist.

"Sir?"

"The cutter and the gig are still alongside. Please organize a party to go over to the corvette and take off any survivors you may find. Sykes may command the gig. You'd better see that at least some of the boat crews are armed."

"Yes, sir," Beechum answered.

The sky grew rapidly darker, although a dull band of orange lingered on the western horizon. Charles found Bevan, who informed him that the galley had been relit and supper would be available before long. Charles turned his attention once again to the battle raging a hundred yards to port. It became harder to identify individual ships in the dimming, smoke-filled air. He could see the crackling flashes of exploding cannon and clearly hear their nearly incessant thunder. He determined that the first five of the French line had surrendered, or at least ceased firing. The most intense part of the action had shifted up to the center, including *L'Orient*. From what Charles could tell, she was giving a good account of herself. One British ship that had attacked her was already drifting mastless into the bay.

He knew that the 124-gun French flagship would be a costly objective for the relatively small seventy-fours to overcome. Any number could be battered until useless under her heavy cannon. If too many of the squadron were disabled, the tide of the battle might well turn, the still-untouched half of the French fleet at the rear of the line descending to take up the offensive against the few remaining British. None of the squadron that had followed him to the inside of the French had as yet moved that far up. He wondered if there was something, some weakness that could be exploited, that might distract the flagship, force her to divide her energies or in some way impair her abilities. He soon decided it was a fanciful notion.

"The boats are returning, Charlie," Bevan announced on the darkened quarterdeck. "They'll be alongside in a minute. Where do you want to put the prisoners?"

Charles thought for a moment. "We'll put them in the after part of the mess deck," he said. "Lincoln can deal with any wounded there, and they'll be relatively easy to guard." An idea crept into his head: an insubstantial, unformed idea. "I want to be present when they come aboard," he said.

Charles made his way into the waist, to where the entryport had been before the bulwarks were blown away. *Louisa*'s six remaining marines and a number of the crew were already assembled to make sure there would be no difficulties with the French survivors. Charles heard the rhythmic dipping of the boats' oars before he saw them in the reflected starlight. First the cutter and then the gig tossed their oars and came against the side with muffled thumps. Soon a score of men from the corvette stood dripping on the deck.

"Is this all there are?" Charles asked Beechum as he clambered aboard. Sykes followed a moment afterward.

"Yes, sir," Beechum said in a shaken voice. "She sank in waters deep enough to cover her. We found these clinging to bits of flotsam. There's sharks about, lots of them. We lost one man just as we reached for him. It was gruesome."

"I see," Charles said. He found the whole idea of sharks unsettling. "Did you have any other trouble?"

"No, sir," Beechum said. "None of their battleships paid any attention to us. The Frenchies here came willing enough."

Charles's unformed idea began to grow. "No one paid any attention to you?" he said.

"We passed within a stone's throw of one of them," Beechum related. "It was light enough that they must have seen what we was up to. No one even challenged us."

Suddenly, Charles knew what he could do. "Of course, it's darker now," he said, more to himself than his lieutenant.

"I beg your pardon, sir?" Beechum said, not seeing the connection.

"That's all right," Charles replied, his mind moving too fast to explain. "Find the boatswain. Tell him I require a rope ladder about twelve feet long, twenty feet of small line, and a stock of combustibles."

"Combustibles, sir?"

"Yes, anything that will burn: paint, pitch, paper, kindling, bits of wood, things like that." He turned to Sykes. "Run to the gunner. Bring me a small keg of gunpowder."

Charles went back to the quarterdeck to inform Bevan of his intention.

"You're going to do what?" his friend demanded.

Charles tested his injured side and flexed his arm. He thought he could manage. "I am going to see if I can't set a fire in the French flagship," he answered. "If you would, please find a half-dozen topmen and Williams, my coxswain. Have them armed with pistols and report to me here."

"You're going to go? Yourself? You're sure? You can't even dress yourself," Bevan said. Apparently, he thought this ill advised.

"Yes," Charles said. "You can't go, and I'm not sending Beechum. I want no argument about it, Daniel. You will be in command until I return. Every man with me must be a volunteer and know what we're about. My intention is to board *L'Orient* through her stern windows and start a fire. At the very least, she'll have to take some of the men away from her guns to deal with it."

Charles went down to his cabin, or what had once been his cabin. He found his steward standing amid a shambles of broken beams, smashed windows, and several holes in the starboard hull that he could see through. His desk had been put back in its place, although there were no chairs and no table.

"Oh, there you are, sir," Attwater said. "I was just coming to see if you wanted your supper." He looked around him. "I'm afraid it ain't much. Most of your furnishings got damaged."

"It doesn't matter," Charles said. "I don't want to eat now. I've come for my pistols." He unbuckled the belt holding his sword and placed the weapon on his desk. The thing would only hamper him.

"Your pistols, what do you need them for?" Attwater said, eyeing him suspiciously.

Charles knew he was going to get an argument, and he could guess why. "Just get them," he said.

Attwater stood firm in the middle of the room, actually folding his arms across his chest like a disapproving father. "You're figuring to go on board one of those Frenchie ships, ain't you?" he said. "Well, you can't. Mrs. Edgemont, didn't she not speak to me very strict about this. You're not to endanger yourself till you're better 'ealed, and not even then."

Charles sighed. "I will fix things with Penny," he said firmly. "Get me my pistols, or I'll get them myself."

When Charles emerged on deck, his pistols tucked in the band of his breeches, he saw the dim light of a lantern at the entryport where a group of his crew were passing objects down into the cutter below. He recognized several of them as he approached. "Hello, Saunders," he said to the nearest. "You're coming along?"

The captain of the foretop grinned, his white teeth reflecting the lantern light. "Aye, zur, we wouldn't miss it for all the world. There's eight of us—Dickie Johnson, Mick Connley, and the rest of the foretop. We all volunteered when we heared you wuz going across. Dickie, he's especially partial to fires. He was a sheriff's quotaman, do you know. Done at the assizes for arson."

Charles thought them a good selection. They were all young, muscular men and adept at climbing. He did wonder about Johnson's fondness for fire. At least he would be useful. "That's very commendable of you," he said.

"It ain't nothing, zur. It's our duty, you might say," Saunders explained. "Don't you remember? We promised Missus Edgemont to look out for you."

"Yes, I remember," Charles said. "I appreciate it." He began to wonder who was the real captain of his ship, he or his wife.

Soon the materials were stored in the cutter, and the men went down into her. Charles stood by Bevan for a moment at the side ladder. "You don't have to do this, Charlie," the lieutenant said. "You've done enough already."

"Yes, I do. It's my responsibility; I have to do something."

"Do you have everything you need?" Bevan said in a resigned tone.

"I think so, Daniel." With a quick handshake, Charles started down over the side.

"Good luck, Charlie. I'll see that there's a light by the bow so you can find your way back."

The effort of climbing down the battens brought a protest from Charles's injured side, a painful but manageable annoyance. Hands reached for him as he stepped on the cutter's gunwale, and after a moment he was seated in the stern sheets. "We're making for their flagship," he said to Williams, but loud enough for everyone to hear. "She's bow on to us, so I want to give her a wide berth, then swing around and come up under her stern. We'll go aboard from there."

"Aye-aye, sir," the coxswain said, then, "Let go all. Smartly now, but dip yer blades quiet."

The cutter shoved off *Louisa*'s side, then started forward at a rapid clip with eight men pulling at the oars. The pounding explosions of the heavy guns reverberated incessantly across the ink-black waters of the bay. Charles saw the outlines of the French line of battleships by the light of the muzzle flashes, which also reflected off the low chop like transient dancing flames. As his eyes adjusted to the darkness, he could see obstacles on the sea surface: timbers, broken mast sections and yards, barrels, a hatch cover, and the bobbing lumps of human bodies, many bodies. Once he saw an agitation in the water to his left and heard a thrashing sound. The form of the dead seaman that had been floating there vanished. There was a flash of a dorsal fin, then nothing. Charles took a deep breath.

L'Orient was easy to make out, the largest silhouette in the line, as she roared back at two English seventy-fours on her far side. In the flickering light, he could see that her masts all stood, and from what he could hear, her rate of fire seemed undiminished. The cutter moved even with her stern, a hundred yards to port.

"Just a little more, Williams," Charles said, "then we'll angle back toward her counter."

After a few moments, the coxswain pushed on the tiller. "Larboard side, lift yer oars," he said. The cutter turned in the water, then started toward the towering black form that was the French flagship's stern.

Charles strained his eyes to see if anyone on the ship's decks might be on watch for approaching boats on her unengaged side. He could make out nothing against the dark sky, but he doubted anyone was there. The battle had been in progress for several hours, and there would be more pressing needs for idle hands.

"Make for her rudder," Charles said in a subdued voice, as if someone on the warship might hear them over the crashing carronade. The cutter slipped quickly and relatively silently toward the deep shadow under *L'Orient*'s stern galleries.

"Boat your oars," he ordered even more softly when they were twenty yards off, and allowed the craft to glide the remainder of the way under its own momentum. "Fend off," he said, and they came to a stop beside the foot-thick trailing fin of the flagship's rudder.

Charles looked up at the railing of the lowermost of the three galleries—narrow balconies that projected out from the stern—ten feet above. The uppermost, just below the poop deck, was for the captain's use. The middle extended off the admiral of the fleet's cabin. The one just above would adjoin the wardroom and served the lieutenants and other officers. Charles's great hope was that the wardroom would be empty while the battle was in progress.

"Who's the best climber?" he asked.

"Connley, zur," Saunders answered. Charles thought this likely. Connley was a short, wiry man with thick forearms, one with a tattoo of a mermaid sitting on an anchor.

"Do you think we can get a line on that railing for him to shinny up?" Charles had to repeat the sentence as a broadside from *L'Orient*'s three decks of guns obliterated all other sound.

"Begging yer pardon, we'll just hoist him up like," Saunders said.

"Can you do that?"

"Oh, yes, zur. Dickey, come here." Two men bent down side by side over the thwarts. The nimble Connley hopped on their backs, and the men straightened. Connley climbed up on their shoulders, then stood, reaching above him. "I got it," Charles heard him say, and he disappeared up into the night.

There was a thunderous crash of cannon fire from a British warship fifty yards away. Then *L'Orient*'s own broadside exploded outward in a deafening roar. The heavy, acrid smell of burnt gunpowder stuck in his throat. In the relative silence that followed, Charles spoke upward: "Connley, what do you see?"

A head appeared over the railing. "Nothing, sir. There's nobody here."

"Pass the line up," Charles ordered. "Tie off the ladder on it."

Saunders stood in the bow of the cutter and tossed the looped line to Connley. The rope ladder was hitched to the line's end. The line and then the dangling ladder snaked upward. After a moment, Connley reported that it was secured.

"I'll go first," Charles said. "Jones and Williams, you are to remain with the cutter. The rest of you men bring up those tubs of paint and the other things when you come." He stood, grabbed the inch-thick hemp strands that formed the sides of the ladder, and placed his foot on a rung. Pulling himself up from rung to rung was more difficult than he had expected. After the third or fourth, the muscles on his left side protested loudly. By the time he managed to breathlessly hook his right arm over the top of the railing, they were screaming at him. "Give me a hand, will you, Connley?" he said. The seaman obliged by pulling him bodily over and onto the gallery.

"Are you all right, sir?" Connley asked.

"Thank you, I'll be fine," Charles answered between gasps for air. He could barely move the arm on his injured side.

Saunders soon clambered up with an armful of kindling. Charles got to his feet and began to examine the gallery windows running the full width of the stern. The officers' wardroom behind them was darkened, the lamps that would have illuminated it extinguished in case one of them should be damaged and start a fire. By testing the windows, he soon found one that was unlatched.

"Do we have a lantern?" he asked Saunders.

"There's one in the cutter, zur."

"Send the line down for it," Charles said. "Then have the paint and powder and the rest of it placed outside this window." As Saunders left, Charles pushed the window open and climbed through. No challenge came from inside, but he could hear the rumbling of the gun carriages and the loud cries of the crews working them from beyond a bulkhead forward.

A form came in through the window to stand beside him. Saunders held out the lantern. "Here, zur. I thought it best not to light it outside."

"Thank you," Charles said, "you may do so now."

The light revealed a long table set athwartships, with chairs lining either side. He could feel his heart racing. Only a few undisturbed minutes, he thought, and he would have done what he came to do. "Johnson"—he beckoned to a figure by the window—"come in here and start passing the kindling and the rest of the combustibles through."

The flagship fired its tremendous broadside. The noise in the enclosed room seemed overwhelming. Charles felt the deck reverberate from the recoil of the cannon as they were brought up by their breech-ings. "Lay the starters and the kindling under the table. We'll set the fire there," he said, anxious to get the thing done quickly. "Pour the paint and pitch over that and then sprinkle the gunpowder on top." As Saunders and Johnson worked, Charles moved along the line of windows, unlatching and opening each with his one arm, for air to feed the fire.

"We're done, zur," Saunders reported.

"Light it," Charles said.

Johnson opened the lantern and stuck a long sliver of wood inside. As soon as it caught, he knelt and put the flame to the tinder under the kindling and blew gently on it. A small, gratifying trail of smoke started upward.

"Quickly," Charles said, "slide those chairs closer. Put a few on top of the table." A wavering orange tongue appeared among the shavings and quickly grew. As soon as it touched the corns of powder, the flame sparked and popped, spreading rapidly over the pile in a blaze of light.

"That should serve," Johnson said with an almost ecstatic smile.

"Back to the boat, all of you," Charles ordered. "You can admire your work from afar." He waited for an instant, staring at the growing flame already licking at the underside of the table. Saunders and Johnson had gone. He had turned toward the window and bent to pass through when a door opened at the room's far side. A startled man stood framed in the entryway.

"Feu," he shouted. *"Le feu!"* Then he saw Charles and screamed, *"Les Anglais!"*

Charles jerked one of the pistols from his belt, pulled the hammer back, pointed it at the figure, and fired. The ball struck the jamb beside him. The man jumped back, slamming the door shut. Charles scrambled through the window, where he saw four of his men. "Give me your pistols," he said quickly. "Then get down into the cutter."

"But zur—" Saunders began.

"Do as you're told," Charles ordered. The men surrendered their weapons. Charles laid the pistols on the windowsill. "When these are empty, I'll jump from the railing. Be ready to pull me out." The men went to the ladder and down.

Charles cocked his collection of weapons and knelt behind the sill. The fire continued to grow, having engulfed the table and some of the chairs. It gave off a foul-smelling black smoke as the paint and pitch took hold. The door flew open again, with three soldiers and their muskets in its frame. Charles snatched up one of his guns and squeezed the trigger. The middle soldier staggered back with his hand to his breast. The others shouldered their weapons. Clouds of gray smoke mushroomed from both, and Charles felt one ball pass close beside his ear. He picked up another pistol and fired without aiming, then another. That was enough, he decided. Even now the flames were licking the deck beams above. He threw the remaining pistols into the fire—where they would go off on their own—stepped back, and forced himself over the gallery railing with a gasp of pain. As the water closed over him, he remembered about the sharks.

"It's all right, zur, we got you," Saunders's voice said as four hands grabbed him, hauling his body out of the water and over the side. Charles lay in the bottom of the boat, spitting out seawater and taking deep gulps of air.

"Away, all. Put your fucking backs to it," Williams said loudly. The cutter started from the hulking flagship, rapidly picking up speed. Looking upward, Charles could see the bright orange glow from her lower stern windows, and a dimmer glow from the deck above.

"AHOY, WHAT BOAT?" Bevan's voice carried across the water.

"Louisa," the coxswain answered. "We've your captain for you."

"Thank God," Bevan said.

Standing naked on *Louisa's* quarterdeck, Charles watched almost unbelieving as *L'Orient's* stern slowly blossomed into flame. He rubbed his hair with the towel Attwater had brought him before accepting a dry pair of breeches. The fire illuminated the other warships around the French flagship. *Swiftsure* had taken a position off her stern quarter and trained her guns so as to discourage anyone from fighting the conflagration. *Alexander, Orion,* and a number of others also fired into her from different angles like a pack of dogs harrying a bear. *L'Orient's* mainmast shivered, then toppled sideways into the sea. The blaze swelled to an inferno, consuming the afterdecks, its tongues reaching high into the sky through an acrid yellow cloud.

"Sweet Jesus," Bevan muttered from beside him.

Charles stared in silent awe. The flames had reached the waist. The mizzenmast became a tall fiery spire. There would be no diverting men to extinguish the blaze. It was beyond that now. He could feel the heat against his skin. The figures of men, hundreds of men, began pouring over the doomed flagship's side into the water. The other warships closest to *L'Orient,* English and French together, began to cut their anchor cables to gain some distance.

"She's going to blow up," Bevan said. "It'll reach the magazine soon."

"Yes," Charles said.

A blinding flash lit the sky and everything under it. A huge orange-yellow ball of flame rose up out of *L'Orient's* bowels into the heavens, followed immediately by a thunderous explosion that pushed the air against him with physical force. The noise echoed into infinity, then ceased. Near-total silence followed. There was no cannon fire, no shouts or screams, no sound of any kind. After a moment, a rain of burning wood, fittings, canvas, and flesh began to descend, hitting the water with a splash or a hiss. Some fell on *Louisa's* scarred deck. As his eyes readjusted to the darkness, Charles saw that the three-decked French flagship, with her crew of one thousand, had vanished as if she had never been. *My God, what have I done?* he thought.

"Get fresh boat crews for the cutter and gig, Daniel," he said. "We must save as many of her men as we can."

As Bevan moved away, Charles stood staring mutely at where

L'Orient had been. What did it mean? Not the battle, the contest between nations and their fleets and armies, he thought. What did *it* mean: the deaths, the spilled blood, the loss of human futures? Penny had said they were all somebody's brother, husband, son, father. How do you balance those lives against victory? Penny knew. It was an easy equation for her. But what was the calculus? How did you decide that this many was enough, that many too much? Charles was sure that he didn't know. He looked up and saw a blood-red moon rising over the sand dunes to the east.

IN THE FIRST rays of the morning sun, Charles sat alone in a chair brought up for him from the wardroom and placed on *Louisa*'s unmoving deck. He had spent the long night watching the progress of the battle, or at least the changing patterns of the sparkling cannon flashes. After *L'Orient* had exploded, there was a lull of ten or fifteen minutes before the gunfire resumed. Slowly, methodically, the British had worked their way up the line, he knew; but exactly how far, at what cost, and with what results he could not tell in the smoke-filled darkness.

Beechum had the morning watch. There was little for him to do besides greeting the two ship's boats as they returned with sailors pulled from the sea, providing an escort to take them below, and arranging for fresh crews. From what Beechum reported after each new batch, Charles surmised that there had been few survivors from the French flagship.

As the light strengthened, he saw a thick haze of cannon smoke clinging to the sea surface. Battered, mastless ships lay still in the water from one side of the bay almost to the other. Two French warships were hard aground well to the south of him. One or two toward the rear of the once powerful line still held out, firing their cannon in a desultory way against an ever increasing number of British. In the far distance, toward the southern limit of the bay, he thought he could see three warships yet to be engaged. But the battle had been concluded in an overwhelming victory for Admiral Nelson, with his squadron of undersized seventy-fours against a superior enemy force with every defensive advantage. Charles could not think of any naval battle in the last century in which one side had so completely vanquished the other.

"Sir," Beechum said from close behind him.

"Yes?" Charles said. "Good morning, Mr. Beechum."

"Good morning, sir. The cutter's just returned. They've got two this time. The gig's still searching."

"Thank you," Charles said. The cutter and gig had been out for over an hour on this last search, and two souls were all they'd found.

"Sir," Beechum continued, "Williams, he says he doesn't think there are any more—living, that is. He says there are sharks everywhere, thousands of them. Anyone still in the water is—"

"Thank you," Charles interrupted. He didn't want the young man to have to complete the sentence. "You may recall the boats and stand their crews down for now. Thank you for everything you've done."

"Yes, sir." Beechum wearily touched his hat and went forward. Within two minutes, he was back. "Sir, there's a boat approaching to larboard. She's from *Orion,* I think."

Charles looked out and saw a ship's launch coming toward them. He pushed himself to his feet, which transformed the dull ache in his side to a sharp stab of pain. "We shall go to the side and greet them."

A young lieutenant in his mid-twenties climbed smartly up *Louisa's* broken side. "Captain Saumarez's warmest respects, sir," he said, coming to a halt and saluting smartly. "I am to inquire as to the status of your frigate and whether you require any immediate assistance."

"Your name, lieutenant?" Charles said.

"John Chatterton, sir."

"Mr. Chatterton, His Majesty's frigate *Louisa* has sunk to what passes for the bottom of the sea in these parts. I am informed by my carpenter that she is irreparable. If you would be so kind as to return Captain Saumarez's respects, you may inform him that we are in no immediate peril. We will, however, require to be taken off to another vessel at some point."

The lieutenant smiled. "My captain guessed as much," he said. "He has authorized me to inform you that *Orion* will be free before noon. Our ship's boats will be available to transfer you and your crew at that time."

"Please convey my sincerest thanks," Charles said. "That will be more than satisfactory."

As soon as Chatterton had descended over the side, Charles turned to Beechum. "You had better send someone to see that Mr. Bevan is awakened. Tell the cook that I want an especially good breakfast prepared for the crew. There's no need for him to worry about rations. Afterward, everyone will need to collect their belongings. The injured will require assistance. The whole lot—baggage, crew, prisoners, and wounded—need to be sent up on deck as the time nears."

"I got it, sir," Beechum said.

"Oh, yes, one more thing, Isaac," Charles said. "Find Seaman Dickie Johnson. I would like a word with him."

At seven bells (had *Louisa* still had a bell) in the forenoon watch, Charles saw two cutters and a launch cast off from *Orion* and start across. *Louisa* had been emptied of everything useful and easily portable. There was surprisingly little of it, and most had already been stowed in their own cutter tethered alongside. Soon the wounded were lowered carefully into *Orion*'s boats. Then the French mixed in with a number of the crew. When all four craft were full, they pushed off for Saumarez's seventy-four, then to return for the remainder.

Charles saw Daniel Bevan and asked his friend to accompany him below. The two men went to the main hatchway and started down, Bevan leaning on his crutch and favoring his injured leg, Charles carefully protecting his aching side. The lower deck stood empty and forlorn, the mess tables with their benches bare and unused. *This is her heart,* Charles thought, *the center of my precious, once-lovely ship.* Now the space was deathly silent, except for the foot traffic above. There was no wash along her side; not a timber creaked in the gentle sea.

"We'll go forward," Charles said.

"Where?" Bevan asked.

"To the galley."

"Why?"

"Don't ask. It breaks my heart."

As they passed through the low doorway into the ship's galley, Charles saw Dickie Johnson sitting on an overturned keg by the stove. Against the wood box lay a carefully arranged pile of tinder and kindling. Johnson rose and touched his forehead.

"Not long now, Dickie," Charles said. He found another barrel and sat on it. Bevan remained standing.

"You're going to burn her?" Bevan said.

Charles breathed out. "I can't let them plunder her," he said. "I'll not allow some French officer to walk through her, deciding what to take away."

Soon they heard the boats returning, and the shuffle of feet and muffled chatter as most of the rest of the crew went over the side. *She is officially dead now,* Charles thought. His *Louisa* was empty and lifeless.

"Captain, sir," Sykes said as he entered the room. "Everyone's off. There's only the gig's crew, and they're waiting for you alongside."

"Thank you," Charles said. He turned to Johnson. "Do your duty."

AFTERWORD

H ISTORY RECORDS THAT ON WEDNESDAY, THE FIRST OF August, 1798, Rear Admiral Sir Horatio Nelson and his thirteen ships of the line discovered a French fleet of similar numbers and superior firepower anchored in a defensive line deep in an obscure bay on a far distant Egyptian coast. Nelson fell upon them immediately in the late afternoon, without waiting for all of his squadron to maneuver into a coordinated formation for attack. The battle that followed, fought throughout the evening and all during the night, in uncharted and shallow waters, resulted in the almost complete annihilation of the French, arguably the most decisive victory ever in the history of war at sea. Eleven of the French warships were sunk, burned, or captured; only two enemy sail of the line and two frigates escaped the bay. Of the flagship *L'Orient*'s crew of a thousand, sixty survived. Charles Edgemont was never to mention to anyone, or to write in any report, that he had started the fire that resulted in her destruction. Even today, its cause remains a mystery.

News of the triumph at Aboukir Bay, two thousand miles from Gibraltar, did not reach Admiral St. Vincent for almost two months, on the twenty-sixth of September; it did not reach London until early October. In addition to the virtual destruction of the French Mediterranean fleet at the Battle of the Nile (as it came to be known), a veteran army of fifty thousand, commanded by a previously little-remarked-upon Gen-

(2 7 4)

eral Napoleon Bonaparte, found itself stranded conquerors in a hostile land, presumably with any hopes of threatening English wealth in India diminished. A year later, Bonaparte was to abandon his army and return secretly to France. This expeditionary force, steadily decimated by insurgency and disease, capitulated two years later.

ON FRIDAY, THE third of August, Captain Edgemont was ordered to appear on board the flagship *Vanguard*.

"You may not stay long," *Vanguard*'s flag lieutenant informed him. "The admiral has sustained an injury and is in dire need of rest."

"Thank you," the captain replied. The marine sentry opened the door to Nelson's cabin and allowed him to pass through. Edgemont was distressed to see Admiral Nelson, always frail, slumped in a chair looking pale and weak, with a dressing on his forehead.

"You do not attend well to orders," the admiral said immediately.

"I do apologize, sir," Edgemont said. "I was attempting what I thought you would have desired, had you but known the circumstances."

Nelson seemed to have difficulty focusing his attention. "I suppose," he said vaguely. "Well, all's well that ends well. I'll not submit charges on it."

"Thank you, sir."

"Your frigate, what was her name?"

"*Louisa*, sir."

"*Louisa*, yes, that's right. I regret she was lost. Her crew and warrants will be distributed around the fleet, of course, to make up for our losses. You and your officers are to be returned to England. I will be sending *Orion* and some others with our prizes to Gibraltar as soon as they are fit enough to sail."

"Yes, sir," Edgemont said.

Admiral Horatio Nelson seemed to sink into lethargy. "It's all right," he said distractedly. "I've already sent *Leander* with my dispatches. I met your wife, you know. At Naples, I think."

Charles Edgemont grew increasingly concerned at his admiral's mental lapses. Clearly, he had suffered a serious head wound and would require convalescence to repair his constitution. "If you will pardon my saying, sir," he ventured carefully, "as the French naval forces are no longer a threat, you might consider taking some of the squadron to Naples for repair. Sir William and Lady Hamilton would be delighted to learn of your success. I am sure that your own person would benefit from a period of rest. I know Lady Hamilton in particular speaks highly of you and would cherish your company."

It was a suggestion that he would long regret. Nelson did take three of his most seriously damaged seventy-fours, *Vanguard, Culloden,* and *Alexander,* to Naples, arriving on September 22, 1798. There, Lady Emma Hamilton proved too willing to succor the admiral, the "Hero of the Nile," as he was to be known, and he was too willing to be succored in the most intimate and personal of ways. The resulting public scandal did much to injure Nelson's otherwise soaring reputation.

ON TUESDAY, THE fifth of March, 1799, the Admiralty in London approved the purchase into the service of the thirty-six-gun former French national frigate *Embuscade,* captured off the port of Syracuse the year before. The sums due from the prize court, together with the head-and-gun money for the taking and burning of *Félicité* earlier that same year, were divided among the officers and crew of *Louisa,* one quarter of which went to her captain through his prize agent and ultimately into his account at the Bank of Chester. Coincidentally, the sums deposited almost exactly equaled the amount withdrawn by a surprised and pleased Mrs. Charles Edgemont for the construction of a thoroughly modern water mill in the village of Tattenall, Cheshire.

PHOTO: © PETER WORRALL

JAY WORRALL is the author of *Sails on the Horizon*. Born into a military family and raised as a Quaker, Worrall grew up on a number of continents around the world, in Africa and Europe as well as the United States. During the Vietnam War he worked with refugees in the Central Highlands of that country and afterward taught English in Japan. Later, he worked in developing innovative and humane prison programs, policies, and administrations. He has also been a carpenter. Married and the very proud father of five sons, he currently lives and writes in Pennsylvania.